Tony: A New England Boyhood

Charles Reis Felix

Tony: A New England Boyhood

University of Massachusetts Dartmouth
Center for Portuguese Studies and Culture
North Dartmouth, Massachusetts
2008

PORTUGUESE IN THE AMERICAS SERIES 10
General Editor: Frank F. Sousa
Editorial Manager: Gina M. Reis
Graphic Designer: Spencer Ladd
Typesetter: Inês Sena

Grateful acknowledgement is made to the following for permission to use previously published material:

"My Blue Heaven," Donaldson Publishing Co./George Whiting Publishing. All rights reserved. Used by permission.

"A Beautiful Lady in Blue," words and music by Sam Lewis and J. Fred Coots © 1935 (renewed) Chappell & Co., Inc. Lyrics reprinted by permission of Alfred Publishing Co., Inc. All rights reserved.

"Dinner for One Please, James," words and music by Michael Carr © 1935 (renewed) Peter Maurice Music Co. Ltd. (PRS). All rights administered in the US and Canada by Chappell & Co (ASCAP). Lyrics reprinted by permission of Alfred Publishing Co., Inc. All rights reserved.

"Pennies from Heaven," words by John Burke, music by Arthur Johnston © 1936 (renewed) Chappell & Co. Lyrics reprinted by permission of Alfred Publishing Co., Inc. All rights reserved.

Library of Congress Cataloging-in-Publication Data
Felix, Charles Reis.
  Tony : A New England Boyhood / by Charles Reis Felix.
    p. cm. -- (Portuguese in the Americas series ; 10)
  ISBN 1-933227-24-9 (alk. paper)
    1. Portuguese Americans--Fiction. 2. New Bedford (Mass.)--Fiction. 3. Nineteen thir-
ties--Fiction. I. Title.
  PS3606.E388T66 2008
  813'.6--dc22
                                2008004514

For Barbara, Matthew, and Mona

CONTENTS

Acknowledgments

A writer can write books but they don't always get published. That was ix
my fate late in life. One day I sent a manuscript to an outstanding
critic, Professor George Monteiro, who then brought me to the attention of Professor Frank Sousa of the University of Massachusetts
Dartmouth. Frank is a scholar, a spokesman, a fund raiser, and a pub-
lisher. His tireless energy and vision created a structure that made it
possible for my books to be published. Without him, there would be
no *Tony: A New England Boyhood* to read.

C.R.F.

Prologue

Tony had no brothers or sisters and no father. His father died of pneumonia when Tony was three. His father had been the wage earner and when his pay envelope from the mill vanished, the outlook was grim for the two of them, Tony and his mother. They were saved by her needle and thread and her foot-pedaling Singer sewing machine, which she had bought in the early days of her marriage.

She was a wonderful sewer. She could make anything. Either by hand or by machine. She had always sewn for her Portuguese neighbors and acquaintances to make a little extra for the family, but now it wasn't extra money. It was the only money.

As word of her skill and economic situation spread, her clientele increased in numbers. The Portuguese ladies brought her the cloth and she made dresses for them and their daughters and shirts for their husbands and sons. But she never made as much money as Tony's father had made in the mill. This may have been partly due to the peculiar form of capitalism she practiced, a Portuguese variation build upon good manners and diffidence. It was unseemly to set prices. She accepted whatever the customer wanted to give her. It was a relationship based on good faith.

And so she and Tony lived with a roof over their heads but not with the table groaning under the weight of viands. It was also a difficult time for many others in Gaw. Mr. Hoover had promised each family two cars for their garage, but with the inevitable overlooked detail every great promiser and planner falls victim to, that somber statesman had forgotten that their tenement had no garage.

CHAPTER I

The Gang

There was a gang on his street, just as there was on every street. Some streets were just one nationality, but his street was mixed. In the gang there were fellows of all nationalities—Polish, French Canadian, Portuguese, and English. In other words, to put it in everyday language, the gang was made up of Polocks, Frogs, Portagees, and a couple of Jickies.

The gang mostly liked to sit around the corner talking, but sometimes they played games. Once when he was just a kid, before he had actually become a member of the gang, he participated in one of their games.

He was just a small kid, standing by his fence, watching the boys of all sizes run back and forth in some exciting game. He desperately wanted to play with them, but of course when you're a little kid you don't just go over and invite yourself in.

Finally one of the boys, one of the bigger boys, noticed him standing there watching, and he said, "Hey, kid, you wanna play?"

He nodded happily. He could hardly believe his luck, to be invited in.

"C'mon, you guys, follow me," this same boy said. He was obviously one of the leaders. He had kind of a long pointed nose. "We're gonna play Fireman, Fireman, Save My Child. You know how to play that, kid?"

He shook his head sadly. He was afraid they would kick him out now. But Long Nose reassured him.

"Well, don't worry, I'll teach you."

He strode mightily to keep up with Long Nose. He was walking with Long Nose at the place of honor, in front of the whole pack. He felt very warm toward this boy, who was being so nice to him and who of all the boys had been the only one to notice him. Everyone seemed in good spirits. In fact, some of the fellows were even laughing. It made him feel good, like he was going to have a lot of fun. He walked alongside his friend and protector, feeling great.

They took him around to the alley behind the Blue Gable Grocery Store. There was a big fence at the end of the alley.

"Okay now, you get up against that fence," Long Nose instructed him. "Turn your back to us and put your head on your arm, like this—" and he demonstrated. "And keep your eyes closed."

"Like this?"

"Yuh, that's right. Just like that. Okay, now when I give you the signal, you start singing this song:

> *Fireman, fireman, save my child,*
> *My little red house is on fire.*
> *Fireman, fireman, save my child,*
> *My little red house is on fire.*

"And make it sound as sad as you can. You got that?"

He turned around to face Long Nose. "Yes, I've got that. But what's the signal?" He wanted to do this just perfect. He wanted to do it so good that they would always let him play with them. That's why he had listened so very carefully to everything Long Nose said.

"The signal will be when I yell, 'Fire!'" Long Nose said. "Okay. Now turn around and wait for the signal."

He did so. He heard the scuffle of feet behind him and muffled voices. He was curious and turned his head a little and started to peek.

"Keep those eyes closed, kid!"

Long Nose's peremptory command snapped him back to the proper position.

"Okay. Fire! Fire! Call the firemen, kid!" It was Long Nose spreading the alarm.

He immediately started his little chant, putting as much feeling into it as he could.

> *Fireman, fireman, save my child,*
> *My little red house is on fire.*
> *Fireman, fireman—*

A gentle pressure against his short pants and then something wet running down his bare legs made him stop, puzzled. He turned around.

Three boys were standing directly in front of him, shoulder to shoulder, like a trio singing "Sweet Adeline," except that they were pissing on him. Aghast, he scrambled out of the way. Long Nose the Conductor had retired to the wings where he was doubled over with laughter.

"We put your fire out, didn't we, kid?" one of the pissers chortled, and with that the whole gang, laughing like crazy, ran away, leaving him there all by himself. What hurt more than getting wet was knowing that they hadn't taken him in, that they had been nice to him just to fool him.

That was his introduction to the gang. They pissed on him. No more fitting act could have been conceived and executed. It was at once a perfect forecast of things to come and a recapitulation of their entire relationship.

He started in school, and gradually he became a quasi full-fledged member of the gang. Long Nose was a pen name for that well-known creator of original games, Rudy Lenkowski, and his acquaintanceship with Rudy grew by leaps and bounds. He learned what it is to live in dread of a voice that others obey. He felt apprehension at every good-natured syllable, for that voice could change with terrible suddenness and in a moment bring catastrophe down upon him.

During a lull in things, that hateful voice would rise in high-pitched anticipation—"Let's take Pneeku's pants off!" Willing hands seized him, carried him bodily off the electric-lighted street into the nearest darkened yard, and slung him to earth. Treacherous hands, his friends of a moment before, laughed and plucked at his belt, all the while he was fighting and kicking viciously. But they ground their knees into his arms and legs and sat on him and he could not even wiggle. Being held down, immovable, while his pants were being yanked off to the accompaniment of jeers and catcalls was humiliating, but it was nothing to what he felt when the essence of his masculinity was left exposed and unprotected. Terror that they might do something to him down *there* surged through him, and in panic he fought to free himself, groaning with the effort. But it was no use. He remained stretched out and helpless. They waited until one of the guys had had time to go over to a telephone pole and throw his pants high up on one of the iron foot-bars. Then they let him go.

All this resulted from a single suggestion from a familiar voice. Yet,

3

could it have happened if the impulse had not already been in the gang? Did not Rudy provide only the impetus and the leadership? Was he not merely the catalyst, the agent, the integrator, the connector, the one who pressed the terminals together and joined the gang and their victim? Was he not in the end just an idea man who offered up to the gang possibilities that would permit them to work out their dislike of a certain Portuguese boy? Look at the time they went up to the Bostwick to play Workups. There was an idea there, provided by Rudy, yes, but there was also cohesion among the gang. They stuck together against him.

In those days Bostwick Field was covered with rocks and boulders. Especially in the outfield it was bad. You had to watch your step running after a fly ball or you'd break an ankle. Sprained ankles were common. This was before the time of the WPA. Later the WPA picked up all the rocks and boulders, graded the field, built a backstop, planted some grass, and, all in all, made a dandy diamond out of it. But on this pre-WPA afternoon the fellows picked out four good-sized rocks and set them up in place for home plate and first, second, and third bases.

Workups was played with three men at bat and everybody else out in the field. It was a case of every man for himself. The first batter tried to get on base, and then move along when the second and third batters hit. If he could cross the plate after their clouts, he was ready to hit again and the process repeated itself. When a batter made an out, except for a caught fly, he went to right field and everybody moved up one position, the catcher becoming the new batter. In the case of the caught fly, the lucky fielder exchanged positions with the batter, but no one else moved up. As long as the batter did not make an out, he remained a batter.

The position you got at the start of the game was crucial. It determined how quickly you were going to get up to bat. The gang decided the positions in this manner: they yelled up for them. The biggest and oldest boys, the boys with the most prestige, yelled for catch, pitch, and the plum—at bat. The boys next in size and prestige yelled for the infield. Naturally he was a candidate for the outfield. He could have yelled, "Second base!" but of course when he went out there he would have been shoved on his ass and threatened with something more, and that would have ended his claim. By wasting all that time, he would also have lost dibs on every other position—except right field. The

4

thing to do was to yell quickly for a position you thought you could hold against your own competition.

"Left field! Left field!" he yelled. He was the first to call it.

"I'm playing left field," Johnny Lenkowski said matter-of-factly. Johnny was a few months younger than he was, which meant that Johnny wasn't supposed to have any priority at all on a position, not against him.

"I called it first!" he exclaimed heatedly. His sense of justice was outraged.

"You play right field, Pneeku," Rudy said.

"Yuh, you're right field, Pneeku," said Jimmy Hedgeley, "or you don't play." Jimmy owned the bat.

Put on that basis, he was right field. And oh, what a long time he was out there. He shagged all kinds of balls—hits, foul balls, wild throws by the infielders, pick-off plays by the catcher, everything. The trouble was that the three best hitters were up and the guys in the field were having a heck of a time getting any of them out. Once they had Ray Archambault out at first base by three steps, but Ray was ready to fight about it, so no one wanted to press the issue. You had to get Ray out with minutes to spare, or he'd never admit it.

Rudy Lenkowski got so tired of running around the bases that now he walked or just trotted, and they still couldn't get him out. But finally Ray Archambault knocked a fly ball to center field that Frankie Machado caught. It was an important breakthrough. For even though there was no general moving up on that play, now they had a weak hitter to work on, Frankie, and they quickly got him out. They began to move around.

But it was slow going. Meanwhile the afternoon sun broiled them. They stripped to the waist and the spit disappeared from their parched mouths. The heat was so unremitting that the guys started getting silly. They lay down on the field and tried to bean the hitter and threw the ball yards over the first baseman's head, anything for a laugh. He hated to see them get that way, but what could you do? After a while they sobered up and they began to play rather grimly. Now it was no more good-fun wisecracks as at the beginning. Now it was talking little, swearing viciously at one another, snarling. The tone of the game became very unpleasant.

They didn't hustle. They walked slowly after balls. But somehow he kept moving around, to shortstop, to third base, to second base, to first

5

base. He didn't have any luck in getting fly balls hit in his direction. He had to work his way around. But he was getting closer and closer.

Finally he stood on the rubber, just as calm as Carl Hubbell, and he was pitching them in, laying that ball in there right over the heart of the plate. And then he was—catcher. There were men on second and third and Johnny Lenkowski was up. Johnny popped the first one foul out-of-reach, ticked the next one, let two go by, and then swung at the next pitch. He missed it cleanly. He had struck out.

At last, at last! All afternoon he had waited for this, from when the sun was straight up in the sky to now, when it was on his back. He was up! He grabbed the bat and stood poised at the plate. He was waiting for that pitch. He was going to smash it. There was new strength in his arms and new spring in his legs. They were going to have to hustle to get him out.

"Let's see the ball," Rudy Lenkowski said to Kenny Farnsworth, the pitcher. Kenny threw it to him.

Rudy turned around to face the fellows. "Hey, you guys, Pneeku's up. Let's quit!"

Jimmy Hedgeley took it up. "Yuh, let's go home."

"Everybody come in!" Ray Archambault said, laughing.

And they all walked in from their positions. He was left in the batter's box, facing an empty field.

The unwritten law was that nobody quits until the guy who started in right field gets his bats. It was treachery, smirking, hateful treachery. Once more Rudy had spoken and the gang had listened.

Rudy was always by his side, an incubus devoted to making life miserable for him. Rudy had a sense of timing about each situation; he knew when an outrage would fit in perfectly. At the proper moment he'd pull the gang to instant action like a master puppeteer. And when he was not active along these lines, he was inventing games. He did not think up Fireman, Fireman, Save My Child. The origins of that game were sunk deep in the folklore of that time and place. But Morning Bath was one of his, a Lenkowski original, so to speak.

For weeks after this game Rudy's playing companion was greeted by the gang with, "Have you had your morning bath yet, Pneeku?" amid gales of laughter.

The rules for Morning Bath are simple. Any two can play. It works best on a bright, clear Saturday morning, and the initiator of the first and last move should live on the first floor of a tenement house, as Rudy did. Low altitude increases accuracy.

At any rate those were the conditions under which he played Morning Bath. He was walking along the street when he heard someone calling him.

He looked around.

"Over here, Pneeku!"

It was Rudy Lenkowski. Rudy was inside his house, by the window that faced the street. The window was wide open and Rudy was leaning out, motioning with his hand for him to come over.

"C'mere, Pneeku."

"What for?" He had the alertness of the deer, but not the sure knowledge of the fox. That takes longer to learn.

"I've got something to show you."

He hesitated.

"Oh, come on," Rudy said cajolingly.

He crossed the street and entered Rudy's yard. He went over by the window. Still alert but curious, he said, "What is it?"

"This," Rudy said simply, and like Blackstone the Magician suddenly there was a big pan in his hands and—

Slosh!

It caught him full in the face, soaked his shirt, and ran down his pants. Good clean cold water.

That was Morning Bath.

He preferred it to Grab the Golden Stick, a delightful title with its wee hint of a magic fairy world. Grab the Golden Stick, which was another Lenkowski original, was played at night in the dark. Rudy explained the rules, and sides were picked. There was a stick involved. It was a picket that hung loosely on Old Lady Charbonneau's fence. They just kind of leaned on the picket and it came off. They hammered down the nails with a stone and now they had all the equipment they needed.

When you had the stick, the other side chased you and tried to wrest it from you. You ran about dodging them. But if you felt yourself getting winded or if you were being surrounded, you ran toward one of your own teammates and thrust the stick at him with the cry. "Grab the golden stick!" He took it and ran off, the enemy now pursuing him.

Jimmy Hedgeley had the stick. He ran far down the street. Guys from both sides chased after him, some to get him, others to help him.

But most of the guys stayed behind to rest for they knew that soon the action would return to where they were and they would be fresh for it. Rudy Lenkowski was one of the guys chasing Jimmy, and though they could not see what happened, it was too far away, apparently Rudy had succeeded in getting the stick away from Jimmy, for now Rudy was running back, pursued by Jimmy and a couple of others. They were catching up to Rudy. Rudy was winded. "Pneeku! Grab the golden stick!" he gasped, extending it to him as he ran by.

He grabbed it—right on the end—and took off like Red Grange. But strangely, nobody chased him. Everybody was laying around, sitting on the curb or leaning against the fence, laughing.

"Look at your hand," Jimmy Hedgeley said, grinning at him.

He looked.

Rudy had stuck the end of the stick in some dog droppings. It was brown and it stunk horribly and it was all over his hand. Not on his shoe, the usual place for it, and goodness knows it would have been bad enough there, but all over his hand—on his skin.

That was Grab the Golden Stick.

They all laughed, and none laughed harder than Ray Archambault. Ray was a great appreciator of other people's jokes. When Rudy made a funny crack about a guy, Ray would repeat it for the next two weeks.

Ray had an astonishing head. For one thing, it was very small. And secondly, even more unusual, it was perfectly round. It sat on his shoulders like a smooth round marble—magnified, of course. A prominent nose would have broken the perfect circularity of this rather remarkable head. As if understanding what was at stake, the nose was a mere button. There were other miniatures. The ears, the teeth were small. The eyes were tiny and when he laughed and his face screwed up, they disappeared. Even the hair cooperated. If it had been fluffy or wavy or curly, the pure lines of cranial roundness would have been blurred and the effect attenuated. But the hair was completely without a wave or curl of any kind. It grew long and was combed, not to the side, but straight back, sloping with his head, slicked down to a shiny radiance with Vaseline. The simple truth was that the hair complemented and accented the stark, abstract perfection of his head.

Ray was known informally as Ouch-my-balls, a nickname that would make anyone testy. It was prosonomasia in painfully poor taste, but they never said it if girls were passing by. It started this way. A Frenchman once came up to them on the corner and asked if they knew where the Archambaults lived. But this Frenchman did not pronounce the name the English way, *Arch-am-balts*. He pronounced it in real French and to their ears it came out something like *Owsh-eem-bowls*. After they had pointed out the house and the man left, Frankie Machado mimicked him. "Say dere, boys, can you tell me w'ere dis familee lives, dey got t'ree kids and da fadder works fa a blacksmit', dey call demselves da Ouch-ee-balls?" It was picked up. It became Ouch-mine-balls, and soon after was changed to Ouch-my-balls, possibly due to the pedagogical influence, for grammar was stressed in the schools of that time.

They never called him that to his face. They might say, "Where's Ouch-my-balls?" when he wasn't around. But when he finally did show up, nobody said, "Hello, Ouch-my-balls." If they had, retribution would have been swift and terrible, for Ray was the best fighter in the gang. He was undisputed champ. He wasn't as big as some of the guys, but he was tougher. He couldn't be hurt. When he tackled somebody in football or accidentally crashed into a guy in baseball, he was not the one who limped away. Others might be bigger, but his body was lean and hard.

There are those who contend that the Slavs are Asiatic, and not truly European. This may be so. Certainly Rudy Lenkowski's persecution of his young friend was Oriental in its orientation, being imaginative, ingenious, subtle, and devious. Ray was clearly a Westerner in his approach to things. He was crude and direct. He did not devise elaborate games. He simply punched a chap on the arm.

His fist was a second tongue to him, a genuine aid in interpersonal communication. He used his hard right hand to facilitate and enhance his discourse—to secure attention, to emphasize meaning, to punctuate thought. The word was always on the tip of his knuckles, and he used this language in many situations.

As a greeting:

"Hello, Pneeku, where you been?"

Sock!

In parting:

"See you later, Pneeku."

Sock!

As a reminder:

"What time is it, Pneeku?"

"I don't know."

Sock!

"Next time, know."

In an experimental mood:

Sock!

"It hurts, doesn't it, with the knuckles that way?"

And for no reason at all:

"Here's one I owe you, Pneeku."

Sock!

After socking him, Ray'd laugh to himself, *hee-hee-hee*, not *ha-ha* like most people laugh, and he'd open his mouth in a big grin, showing all his little teeth. The only response of the assaultee was a pretty feeble one. "What's the big idea?" he'd exclaim indignantly. What else could he say? What could he do?

Ray was worse at certain times. He'd be walking down the street going to the store for Ma, and Ray would see him coming, and when he got close, Ray would suddenly break away from the gang and dash across the street after him. If Ray caught him, he'd punch him once or twice. On the way back, he'd be carrying the quart bottle of milk, and Ray might make a false motion as if to run across the street again, and he'd break into a sprint with no one chasing him, and the whole gang would hoot and holler. In time he learned that when Ray was like that, where he'd actually chase you, the best route to a store was by the backway, cutting through his back yard, hopping the fence, going through Szulik's yard and coming out on Locke Street. There was a little variety store one block down on Locke Street. And he'd come back the same way. Thus, Ray and the gang wouldn't even see him.

But his arms were a mess. From shoulders to elbows, his arms were in various stages of discoloration. The background was of murky yellow—these were old bruises healing up. Imprinted over these yellows were rich blues and interesting purples—all the colors, old and new blending skillfully in a balanced composition. A colorist would have clapped his hands in admiration, reproduced it on canvas, called it *Spring*, and won first prize at Provincetown.

Ma was horrified when she saw his arms. "That's how you get cancer!" she warned. "Too many black-and-blue marks! You don't give the

10

blood a chance to recover. Do you want to die before you are twenty, huh?" she demanded. "You must take better care of yourself, son, or some terrible sickness will suddenly come one day when you are least expecting it, and then it will be too late."

Her words frightened him, and he thought, Good God, suppose he actually did get cancer from this? That goddamn Ray!

"What kind of games do those boys play anyway?" Ma asked, shaking her head despairingly. "You shouldn't play with them. They're too rough, too rough."

But he paid Ray back.

Before the mirror on his dresser, he waited calmly. He was stripped to the waist. He flexed his arms and looked admiringly at the reflection of his biceps in the mirror. He pulled on the ropes. And then the bell sounded. He sprang out of his corner like a tiger. The grinning Ray was in front of him—but he wouldn't be grinning for long. Pow! Right on the nose. They moved around one another. There was a flurry of punches from Ray, but he blocked most of them, and when Ray tried to clinch, he pushed him away. He jabbed two or three times, but missed. That little round head, it was an elusive target, but then he feinted with his left, dug his right into Ray's midriff, and Ray dropped his guard. Smack! A left hook. Pow! A right cross. Another right. A left. Another right. He was panting with exertion and Ray had two black eyes. He knocked Ray against the ropes and when Ray bounced back, he doubled him up with a right to the breadbasket. Smack! Pow! Right on the old button. Ray was reeling, unable to protect himself, but he showed him no mercy. He almost tore his head off with a left uppercut. And now to finish him off with a haymaker, everything he had was behind this punch—boom! Ray was down, flat on his back, out cold.

He was breathing heavily, but he didn't stop to rest. He turned to Rudy Lenkowski.

"All right, Rudy, you're next. Get in here."

But even before the words were out of his mouth, Rudy was running away, while the gang hooted after him.

And now he turned his attention to the gang. His eyes coldly passed from one boy to another. They all dropped their eyes before his gaze.

"All right," he said, "the next guy who gives me any shit on this corner is going to get laid out. Everybody understand that?"

They all slunk away.

Disconsolate, he sat down on the edge of his bed, still panting from his battle with Ray. It was all a dream, a miserable dream. Ray was bigger and stronger than he was. In a real fight he wouldn't have a chance against him. It would be like Kid Barboza, the Gaw featherweight, taking on Jack Sharkey, the heavyweight champ. Ray was only one grade ahead of him in school, but that was because he was dumb and had stayed back twice. Actually Ray was three years older than he was. And Rudy Lenkowski—Rudy was also three years older than he was, and much taller and heavier. Both of them were too big for him. He wouldn't stand a chance against either one. It would be suicide to try it. It was preposterous to even think about it.

So there he was. That was the truth of it. Rudy and Ray had him on the run, and there wasn't a thing he could do about it. But, oh my, it was really something when you stopped to consider it. Rudy and Ray and the rest of the guys were always picking on him. And yet, take a guy like Jimmy Hedgeley, a dirty, odious, cowardly boy, a liar, a cheater, a hogger, a boy who had not one single solitary admirable quality. You would have thought he'd be the one they'd pick on. But nobody, absolutely nobody, abused Jimmy. They treated him fine. There were no punches, no names, no dirty tricks for Jimmy. It was fantastic.

There was an imaginary line, like the equator, going around Jimmy's neck. Below that line soap never sudsed. This lower half of his two-toned neck did not have the dusty smudges mothers call dirt. It had real black caked dirt. Jimmy passed close to Ma once and later she wrinkled up her nose in memory. "I never saw a neck like that," she averred. "Is his mother trying to save on water? You could plant potatoes in that neck."

Yes, his neck did have visual impact, as the men in advertising say. But his friends did not stare. His neck was always like that; they would have stared if it had been clean. Besides, when you were in his presence a bit of dirt suddenly became a thing of small importance, for there was something rather overpowering about Jimmy. It was a smell. It was a smell that assaulted the nostrils like a palpable force. It was a smell that he carried with him even on a windy day. It was the smell of old urine. He stunk with it. The crotch of his pants was stiff from a thousand drippings. Clearly, what with his disposition to leakage, his mother did not wash his pants often enough. Also, he still did it in his sleep. His mother had told Kenny Farnsworth's mother that. Just imagine what the gang would have done with information like that if it had been a certain somebody who wet the bed at night and not Jimmy.

Jimmy was a walking refrigerator. He carried his own food supply. He not only carried it, he manufactured it himself. When he was hungry and wanted a little in-between snack, he would reach up into his nose, bring down a curling wet black string, roll it up into a ball, examine it thoughtfully, and then pop it into his mouth like it was a delicious raisin. It was disgusting to watch. Jimmy was a real snot-eater, but did the gang ever call him that? No.

And he was a big baby. In baseball he closed his eyes on grounders and stepped out of the way of line drives. He was afraid of being hurt. One time at the Bostwick, in running across the first-base bag, which was actually a rock, he tripped over it and fell down. You would have thought he was being killed, the way he screamed. He lay on the ground and just screamed. They were worried about him; they thought he might have broken a bone, an ankle maybe. But when they asked him where it hurt, all he did was shriek and kick and he couldn't talk. It was like he was out of his mind. Well, come to find out, when the fit left him, the only thing wrong with him was that his knee was a little skinned. But that was Jimmy, no control over himself.

So there it was. This boy, with so many things wrong with him, wasn't picked on, and he was. It didn't make sense. Jimmy was his age and he couldn't fight at all, why should everyone treat him so nice? Because he had something to offer, that was why.

His father had the best job on the street and consequently his family had the most money. His father was an overseer in one of the mills, and of course while that wasn't such a terrific job any more, because the mills were running so slow and there were just a few workers under him, not like the old days, still it was a darn good job compared to what everybody else had.

Jimmy was the only kid on the street who had a bike. And so everyone would beg him for a ride around the block. He'd sit there on his bike, happy, taking his time about picking a guy, while they all clamored around him. Well, almost all, because there was one boy who wouldn't ask that bastard for anything. It would just give him the

13

chance to refuse anyhow.

Jimmy's family was the only family on the street to have a charge account at the Blue Gable Grocery Store. He'd walk in there, go behind the counter like he owned the joint, take a Milky Way out of the box, flash it to Annette the bookkeeper and say, "Charge it!" And his mother let him do that. And then he'd come out and eat it in front of the gang, cramming it into his mouth with big bites, while three or four guys went crazy watching him

"Gimme a bite, Jimmy, gimme a bite!"

"Aw, save me some, Jimmy."

"Dibs on the wrapper!"

He would stop short of the last bite, and he'd give that to one guy. That's why they were all so nice to him. They wanted to be that one guy.

Johnny Lenkowski was the biggest beggar of them all. When Jimmy was eating an apple, Johnny would cry, "Cores! Cores!" The first guy to call was supposed to get it. Jimmy would eat the apple right down to where most people eat it, and then he'd hand over what was left to Johnny, who would nibble away on it until he was holding nothing but the stem. He would eat the whole thing up, of course spitting out the seeds.

And Jimmy eating a Fudgsicle was something to see. Fudgsicles were very popular and Jimmy got a lot of them. In fact, Jimmy liked anything that was chocolate-flavored. When he came around with a cone of ice cream, it was always chocolate. But he would eat this Fudgsicle in rather a disgusting way, slobbering all over it. You licked a Fudgsicle, you didn't bite it. Jimmy would race the sun in its melting of the Fudgsicle. He would stick his tongue way out and try to keep up, slurping noisily, while a rivulet of brown dripped on his hand and a lesser amount ran down his chin. Meantime Johnny Lenkowski led the chorus. "Gimme a lick, Jimmy, gimme a lick!" As the Fudgsicle disappeared, their cries got more desperate. Jimmy would relent and give two or three of his favorites a lick. Johnny Lenkowski would get the stick.

Think of begging for food like that. And then to lick it with Jimmy's spit all over it. It was disgusting. He himself had never tasted a Fudgsicle in his life, but he'd be darned if he'd beg for it. He wouldn't have taken a lick even if it had been offered. He wasn't that hungry. Him take something with that guy's spit all over it? That would be the day. He didn't like chocolate anyway.

Jimmy was the only guy on the street who could step off the curb and say casually, "Guess I'll go down to LaBonte's for a milk shake." He wasn't just talking. You could go down to the Avenue and pass by LaBonte's, and you'd see him inside drinking it at the fountain. Sometimes, and to them this was incredible, he'd have a milk shake as part of his meal. His big sister would come by and say, "Jimmy, Mom won't be home for lunch. There's twenty cents on the table. Take it and get yourself a hamburger and milk shake." Think of having a wonderful meal like that. It made everybody's mouth water, for a hamburger and milk shake weren't food—they were treats. Their mothers were always home. And even if they weren't, they sure wouldn't leave twenty cents for a hamburger and milk shake.

So because Jimmy had something the gang wanted, candy, fruit, Fudgsicles, things to eat, they let him alone. They never took his pants off. Come to think of it, maybe that was just as well, for his underclothes must have been really something. When those yellowed shorts got out in the open air, the closest guys would have needed gas masks.

Jimmy, like himself, couldn't lick either Rudy or Ray and so win the respect only fists can bring you. Food was Jimmy's protection and insurance. But what of the other fellows who were in circumstances similar to Jimmy's and his, of the same age, of the same size and strength, approximately? How did they manage? Johnny Lenkowski? Well, of course, Rudy was there to see that no harm came to him.

Kenny Farnsworth? Kenny was a goof with only one accomplishment to his name. He had a space between his two front teeth and he was able to eject spit through this space in a fine, accurate stream. He was proud of this ability. He'd spray his spit out on your shoes and watch you jump back. That gave him a big laugh. But Kenny had an older brother, Ed, who had a car. Ed was much too old for the gang, but every summer, during the months of July and August, Ed would take the guys out to White's Pond in Lemenville. He'd do this four or five times during those hot months, and each time it would be a big occasion for the gang. They'd talk about it for days before and for days afterward.

White's Pond, from what the guys told him about it, was a beautiful place. It had clean, calm, warm water, perfect for swimming. It got deeper quite gradually, and so was very safe. It had a smooth sandy bottom; your foot did not suddenly step down on a sharp rock like it did in the ocean.

15

And the water was so clear. You could float down to the bottom and open your eyes and see things far away, they said that was the most fun. If you tried that in the ocean, the salt water hurt your eyes and besides, it was always so dark underwater you couldn't see a thing anyhow.

They practically had the whole pond to themselves. White's Pond was way out in the country, with no streetcar or bus service and much too far to walk. You had to have a car to get out there, and since not too many people had cars, it was never crowded.

But here was where Kenny had everybody by the short hair. Five guys could go, beside Kenny and Ed. One sat up front with Kenny and Ed, and four sat in the back. Five could go, but there were fifteen who wanted to go. And Kenny got to pick the five out. It gave him considerable leverage with the gang. Before each trip, there was always a good deal of politicking going on, a lot of hanging around Kenny, sucking around it was called, to ingratiate themselves into Kenny's good graces.

He always held himself aloof from Kenny at these times. He knew he didn't have a chance to get picked, so why demean yourself by suck-ing around? And he was right, he was never picked. He was always left standing on the corner along with the other rejects, while Rudy and Ray and Jimmy happily rolled down the windows, waved their swim-ming trunks in farewell, sang and yelled, and they stared after them until the car, a square '28 Buick, could no longer be seen. The remaining guys were dispirited, without pep, not willing to go up to the Bostwick to play baseball, and they gradually disappeared off the corner, until he was left alone with maybe just one other guy, and the long afternoon ticked off its seconds slowly and suddenly the whole street seemed intolerably quiet and still and life was unbearably lonely and desolate.

So, Jimmy had his Fudgsicles, Johnny had Rudy, and Kenny had White's Pond. There was one other guy their age—Frankie Machado. Frankie had something every bit as good as a pond. In fact, better. He had a big brother of the type a guy dreams about. This big brother, like Ed Farnsworth, was too old for the gang, but there the resemblance ended. This big brother had no car and gave the gang no rides. He offered nothing in the way of a swell time. He was not even civil to them. When he went by the corner, he acknowledged Rudy Lenkowski's fearful, "Hi, Tiger," with a surly nod of the head. He despised unnecessary words. He was a silent menace, and he was known as Tiger.

"Chasing Shadows" was a popular song of the previous year, and people still sang and whistled it quite a bit. Rudy Lenkowski made up a joke about this song.

Rudy waited until Frankie Machado came walking up to the corner, and then he said, "Say, Frankie, did you hear that Portagee song on the *Hit Parade* last week? It's a big hit."

"No, I didn't," Frankie said. Frankie was surprised and interested. The true son of Portugal can always be identified by his pride in all Portuguese accomplishments. "What was the name of it?"

"'Chasing Ma-chado,'" Rudy said.

In English the *chado* of Machado is pronounced like *shadow*. It was a pretty good joke. Or at least everybody thought so, because they all laughed, including Frankie. Ray Archambault, who didn't have the wit to make up jokes, laughed the hardest. "'Chasing Ma-chado,' the Portagee song," he laughed, "that's a good one. I'll have to remember that one. There's a guy I know at school, Manny Machado. I'll spring it on him."

Just about then who should come out of his house and start walking down the street toward the Avenue, but Tiger. This was just after supper.

He was in his usual white T-shirt, his powerful arms bulging with muscle. He did not walk heavily. He did not walk casually. He walked tensely, tightly, like he was holding himself together only by great effort. Deep inside him there burned irrational and primal fires, those hidden flames which could at any moment ignite him into an explosion. Dark, seething, his black hair wild on his head, his eyes inflamed with inarticulate rage, he was being consumed by an anger baseless, mad, and suicidal.

Ray, who had more guts than brains, hailed Tiger cheerfully when the latter was a few feet from the corner.

"Hey, Tiger," Ray said, "I hear there's a Portagee song written about you."

Tiger's eyes were wide and fixed on Ray, as if he couldn't believe that he was being addressed.

Stupid Ray, who didn't know when to quit, continued. "Yuh," Ray laughed, "it's called 'Chasing Ma-chado'!"

Tiger didn't like the joke.

"Whattaya, a fuckin' funny guy?" he snarled alliteratively, hinting

17

that within that rude breast there beat the heart of a natural poet.

Tiger clenched his fists and Ray blanched. It was a moment of inexpressible joy for one of the spectators. He had visions of Ray finally being laid out, kissed by that hammer fist. But Ray was not in Tiger's league—too small. Tiger looked at him carefully in warning and then he walked on. He left behind a stunned Ray and a hushed gang.

No wonder Rudy and Ray were always so nice to Frankie Machado. Ray knew that if he ever dared mark up Frankie on the arm, Tiger would lay him out cold. Ray knew that, Frankie knew that, the gang knew that, Tiger knew that, and so Frankie walked around a free man. Tiger was a definite big stick that enabled Frankie to talk softly. Frankie had the best kind of big brother there is, a brother who is a presence and a legend.

But what about a guy who has no big brother? What is he supposed to do? Yes, that was the question, and the only answer seemed to be— just take it.

The hostility expressed toward him was sometimes physical as when Ray, amidst general laughter, used him for a punching bag. But other times it was psychological—humiliating, but leaving no bruises. Such was his nickname, Pneeku. The gang knew he didn't like it, so they called him that. He had not heard his real name from them for over three years.

Yes, once he had a name but that was a long time ago. It was a bad day, that day. Ma had just cut his hair, and he ambled out to the corner. He was completely unaware that his haircut was any different from anyone else's. But it must have been round in the back, because the moment Jimmy Hedgeley saw it, he shrieked, "Look at his hair! Look at the back of his head!" Jimmy got his haircuts in a barbershop.

Ray spun him around roughly. "Lemeesee."

"Aw, lay off," he growled. He didn't like hands on him.

"Your mother put a bowl on your head for sure," Rudy Lenkowski said.

"She did not!" he said. And she hadn't.

"Aw, come on, tell us the truth. She did, didn't she?" Rudy coaxed him mockingly.

"Yuh, it sure looks like a bowl to me," Jimmy Hedgeley said.

"It looks more like a *penico* to me," Frankie Machado joined in. This was the fateful line. On this line his destiny paused and waited.

"What's a *penico*?" Rudy asked curiously.

"That's the Portagee word for a pisspot," Frankie said.

Every Portuguese family had a *penico* in their home. It was what little kids used because the toilet was too big to sit on. The guys all laughed as they pictured one turned upside down on his head.

"Is that what your mother used—a *penico*?" Rudy asked. Rudy pronounced it *pee-nee-ku*, which was pretty close.

He made no answer.

"And in this corner, ladies and gentlemen," Rudy announced like he was at Madison Square Garden, "at nineteen and three-quarter pounds, wearing red trunks, we have Kid Shit, the Local Stink—otherwise known as Pneeku!"

"Yay, Pneeku!" Jimmy Hedgeley cheered.

"Yuh, Pneeku, take a bow," Ray said, and he socked him one.

So a nickname is born, unanticipated, irrevocable. The teachers at school had always told him that when children call you a name, just ignore it, don't show that it angers you, and soon they will stop it. He tried that. He acted like he didn't mind the name at all. It might have worked too. The guys didn't seem too excited about it after that first day, but that dimwit Ray, with the perseverance of the true moron, kept it up, *Pneeku, Pneeku, Pneeku*, and finally the others took it up and it stuck.

In translation, he was being called a pisspot. He found it deeply humiliating. They yelled it up and down the street and sometimes some Portuguese people would be passing by and they would laugh when they heard it. Everybody called him that. He had to take it even from guys he could lick, because he knew that if he warned them, Ray would take them under his protection and encourage them at it and dare him to do anything.

One night, not too long after the gang started calling him Pneeku, he went out on the corner to be met by Ray.

"Shake hands."

"I don't want to shake hands."

"I tole you to shake hands!" Ray cocked his fist.

He stuck out his hand.

Ray took it a certain way, by the bone, and squeezed till he dropped to his knees in pain.

"Ow! Let go, Ray!"

Ray grinned down at him.

19

"Aw, c'mon, Ray, let go," he implored.

"Whatsamatta?" Ray asked. "Don't you like to be friendly with a guy?" Ray was proud of how strong he was.

"Yes, I like to be friendly," he groaned.

"All right then. Next time I ask you to shake hands, shake hands. Understand?"

"Yuh, I understand," he said angrily.

Ray increased the pressure and the pain. "Don't say it like that. Say it nice."

"Yes, I understand."

"That's better."

Ray let him up.

Then the guys started having fun shoving him around. He'd go near one guy and the guy would shove him, "G'wan, I don't wantcha near me."

It was all a game, of course, but it began to get him down, because some of the shoves really jarred him.

They began to make jokes about his nickname when they shoved him. "Get away from me, Pneeku, you stink."

And the next guy would shove him and say, "Yuh, Pneeku, your mother should've emptied you out."

Finally Frankie Machado, a guy about his own size, shoved him and he turned on Frankie with his fists primed, his eyes blazing. "You son of a bitch, who do you think you're shoving?"

He was ready to fight and Frankie was supposed to be tough, so there was no telling who would have got the worst of it. But they didn't get to find out, because Ray got him from behind. Ray whipped an arm around his neck, applying a devastating strangle hold, and dragged him backwards a step or two.

"Don't you know I don't like no bad language used on this corner?" Ray said.

While Ray held him, helpless, gasping for breath, his mouth wide open, somebody, he couldn't tell who, took off his shoes and slung them in the middle of the street.

Ray let him go. He waited until an approaching car had passed and then he retrieved his shoes. Luckily, the car had not run over either shoe. He sat on the curbstone, slowly putting his shoes on and tying the laces.

A great sadness and resignation filled him. All he could hear was their laughter and *Pneeku, Pneeku, Pneeku, Pneeku.* He could not deny the terrible knowledge that was in him. They were his enemies. They were, had always been, and would always be. Nothing he could do would change that. But the very certainty of it was something of a release. With optimism gone, hope gone, he felt calm and strengthened.

He got to his feet.

Somebody said, "Pneeku."

"Listen," he said seriously, "a joke is a joke. But this one's gone far enough. I don't want to be called that any more."

They laughed so hard they almost fell over.

Something inside him went over the edge. His heart started pounding violently, always the precursor of madness for him, and the dizziness began in his head. He could not feel his feet touching the ground.

He walked away from the corner, his eyes on the ground, looking for something. He found it. It was a stone, scarred and balanced.

He returned to the corner.

He faced them.

"I'd like to see somebody call me Pneeku now."

They all scattered.

All but Ray. Ray stood his ground. "What're you going to do, Pneeku?" he sneered.

"You call me that once more. You'll find out."

"Pneeku," Ray snarled, contemptuously and menacingly.

He slung the stone with every ounce of strength he had right at Ray's head. It missed.

There was an instant when they stood facing each other, and then Ray sprang at him. He wheeled around to run. But Jimmy Hedgeley and Rudy Lenkowski had circled behind him, and now they grabbed him before he could get started.

The gang formed a circle around him and Ray.

"Let him go," Ray said quietly, ominously.

They took their hands off him.

He faced Ray. He did not cower. He expected to be socked, and he was, but he never felt it. He never saw it either. It was a right, he was told later, and he got it on the side of the head. It was really nothing. There was no pain, just sudden blackness, and a dizzy, swirling head when he came to on

21

the sidewalk. Oddly enough, this gave him more prestige with the gang than anything he had done previously. For none of them had ever been knocked out, and so they were very curious as to what it felt like. They were still asking him days later, "How did it feel? Did you see lights?"

It even brought him closer to Ray for a time, for he was the walking, tangible proof of Ray's power. Whenever strangers from other streets happened by, he was pointed out to them with the comment, "That's the guy who got knocked out by Ray Archambault." Ray recognized the value of advertising, and as it has been said, where would Cadillac be without double-page color spreads of a virile, white-haired man in tails opening the door for a young girl in furs, while the footman admires the fender, so in the same sense where would Ray have been without him? Just another Frenchman named Archambault. Instead, he became fairly well-known. In appreciation of this and wonder at his own strength, Ray took it easy on him for a while.

The blow had caught him mostly on the side of the head, but enough of Ray's fist had made contact with his left cheekbone to discolor that area. He discovered this the next morning when he looked in the mirror. That the area was sore and tender he had known before looking in the mirror.

Ma noticed it immediately and she said suspiciously, "What's that? What's the matter with your face?"

"Oh, I bumped a guy going for a ball," he said casually.

"Sports! Sports!" Ma cried disgustedly, "They go crazy for sports in this country and someday you will kill yourself at it."

But of course the really significant thing about that punch was not that he was knocked out but that he had committed himself. He had shown that the nickname got under his skin. Now they would never give it up. And they never did. He remained Pneeku to them for good.

Oh, sometimes he used to dream. Suppose Rudy Lenkowski and Ray Archambault died, or, if he was feeling humane, suppose they lived on some other street? Things would be different then, yes, and he'd have wonderful dreams about how nice things'd be, but after a while he'd think—You're just dreaming. It wouldn't be like that at all. For one thing, there were other big guys around who were playing second fiddle to Rudy and Ray now, but should the opportunity arise, they would quickly take over and they were no better than Rudy or Ray.

Besides, you couldn't blame it all on two guys. The gang was the gang. Even without Rudy and Ray, even without any other big guys, the gang wasn't quite right. There was something wrong there. A lot of times Rudy and Ray didn't show up at all, and he still didn't have a good time with the fellows.

The gang was lazy. They didn't like to do things. They didn't like to go places. Try to get a couple of guys to go with you to Bellehaven Park to watch the mill teams in the Textile League in a good sharp game of ball. Nope. Nobody would budge from the corner. "Too far to walk," they'd say. Or try to get them during the summer vacation to go up to the Bostwick, which was much closer than Bellehaven Park, to play some baseball themselves. Nope. "Too hot," they'd say. And in the fall, how about a nice little game of touch football in the street? Then they couldn't say it was too far to walk or too hot. Nope. "Don't feel like it," they'd say. So you couldn't win. You couldn't persuade them either. Why, never mind a game, sometimes he tried to get just one guy to go up to the Bostwick to bat out some flies to him, and he couldn't even raise one guy.

What would they rather do? They'd rather sit on that corner and watch the cars go by and talk, talk, talk, and so often the talk was mean talk, directed at someone, insulting and meant to hurt. They'd get started on one guy and they wouldn't let up on him all night long. What fun was there in that? He didn't want to be persecuted, and he didn't want to participate in the persecution of someone else. There was no fun in that.

Their idea of fun was to wait until they saw a girl walking along all by herself. They'd let her pass the corner and get halfway down the block and then one guy, just one guy, would yell:

"Hey, good-lookin'!"

It never failed that the girl would turn around to see what was wanted, because he would yell it like he really had something to tell her. And since she was the only girl there, she knew it had to be her he was calling.

When she turned around to look, that was their cue. The whole gang would bellow out as one voice—"Not you, horseface!"

Well, it was kind of funny in a way, because you could almost see the girl jump she was so startled, but he always felt sorry for her, a hapless figure standing there all by herself while fifteen guys hooted and howled at her. It must have made her feel pretty lousy, especially if she

23

wasn't good-looking. A pretty girl could just laugh it off.

They had a lot of little jokes like that. For instance, if you were going home, after you had gone about thirty yards, one of the guys might call you back with a serious voice, and you'd think it was something important and you'd come back, and he'd say to you, "How far would you be if I hadn't called you?" Oh, well. You learned after a while.

But there were other jokes, they would probably be called practical jokes, that were a bit harder to take. A guy would be talking to you nicely, but it was all a trick, because he was only doing that to hold your attention while his partner sneaked up behind you. This joke had variations. The partner could suddenly thrust his arm between your legs and the guy talking to you would grab it, and they would hoist you up into the air. That wasn't so bad. But the partner might get down behind you on all fours and the guy in front give you a sudden, hard shove and over you would go, head over heels, spinning through the air. What a sensation when you were not expecting it.

They didn't like to get away from that corner so they played games right there. They liked to play baseball. You'd come walking up and the first guy to see you would go up to you and with a quick deft movement rip open your fly.

"Home run!" he'd shout triumphantly—if he got all the buttons. One button was a single, two a double, and so on.

So all night long you had to stand guard over your flyhole, covering it with your hands at any suspicious move, while they tore at one another's pants. You had to be alert and even then they got you, usually it was some guy who was being very friendly toward you in order to lull you into relaxing. Then suddenly—the quick treacherous movement and the cry—"I got a home run on Pneeku!"

Another game they like to play was Flinching. In this game the player made a pass at your private parts. If you pulled back, even slightly, he called, "Flinching! You flinched!" and he got to give you one punch on your arm—and he put plenty behind it. If he touched you in making his pass, you got to give him the punch. If you didn't flinch and he didn't touch you, there were no penalties either way. And this game would go on the whole night long, with alternating activity and lulls, but with the threat of attack always there. Everybody tried to catch you by surprise, when your reflexes would naturally cause you to jump back. That was the whole point—to get you by surprise—and quiet intervals helped set you up. If there was unceasing activity you would be expecting a pass, and you most likely could control yourself not to move. But after a period of quiet you relaxed and forgot and it was then that you were most vulnerable to sudden attack.

He detested these two games, Flyhole Baseball and Flinching. His stratagems in them were always defensive; he never attacked. He kept telling the guys, "I don't want to play. Leave me out of it." But they refused to listen. They permitted none to dissociate from the game. Observers were not allowed; all must be participants.

He spent long hours with the gang on the corner, but his position was always a somewhat tentative one. He was cast in the role of Benes attending a conference with Hitler and Chamberlain. He was always uneasy. What with the jokes and the games the gang played—and they had an endless supply of both—and added to that the compelling inventiveness of Rudy Lenkowski and the direct action of Ray Archambault, he could not fall asleep at the switch, as the saying goes. He had to be alert, apprehensive, watchful, and wary. He had to be ready to dodge or run at any moment. It was permanent war.

One night they would muss each other's hair, that was the game, and the next night, for no reason, he would hear the bloodcurdling cry, "Let's get Pneeku!" and off he would run like a rabbit. No wonder he got to be such a good runner. His survival depended on it.

About the only time that he could really feel safe was when the gang's attention was centered on cars. The gang loved cars. They discussed and argued why they would rather own one make of car instead of another. They were thrilled by the latest innovations in the automotive world.

It is said that Columbus as a boy liked to go down to the harbor in Genoa and watch the ships sail in and out. So did the gang like to go down to the corner and watch the cars roll by. Their street was a quiet one, but Beel Boulevard intersected their street at the corner. Beel Boulevard was a through street that ran north and south and it had lots of traffic. Beel Boulevard, or the Boulevard as everyone called it, was actually not very wide. When cars were parked on both sides of the Boulevard, the cars in motion were pressed into the narrowest of channels and the drivers had many thrilling tight squeaks.

Saturday afternoon was the gang's favorite time for watching cars, because it was then that traffic was heaviest. They sat on the dirt along-

25

side the cement sidewalk, with their backs up against the billboard that covered the wooden wall of the vacant store on the corner. This billboard had featured for many months a lady, now somewhat tattered, with a penciled mustache and smoking a Lucky, while all over the man's white pants—they were taking a break in their tennis match—were certain penciled invitations and other messages, many in rhyme, of interest only to the specialist in children's literature.

The gang made comments about the various cars as they went by, the age of one, the color of another, the beautiful lines of a third. But they didn't use the word *beautiful*. Instead they called the car *neat*. If the lines were exceptionally pleasing, then they called the car *real neat*.

They were proud of their ability to identify cars by the make and year. They often matched knowledge as a car approached.

"Lookit the side horn on this yellow car."

"The Olds?"

"The Olds? That's a Hudson, a 1931 Hudson."

"That was an Olds."

"You're fullashit, that was a '31 Hudson."

"How much yawanna bet that was no Hudson?"

"That was a '31 Hudson, I'm tellinya."

"Put up or shut up!"

"Awright, I'll betcha! How much yawanna bet?"

"I'll betcha a quarter!"

"Okay! Shake on it."

"Okay! You just lost yourself a quarter, buddy."

"That was a '31 Hudson, for chrissakes."

"The hell it was."

"Why don't you go take a shit for yourself?"

"Why don't pigs fly?"

"Because pork is too high. Ha!"

None of them had a nickel to their name, but they made bets like that all afternoon long. A bet wasn't binding till you shook hands, and they were shaking hands all over the place. But by that time the car in question was a mile away, so then how were they going to settle the dispute? It was all kind of silly. No bet was ever paid off, but they kept right at it. Unfortunately for him, he was the only guy in the gang who had no interest in cars, so he was kind of cut off from the bets and all the excitement of this car business. He couldn't tell the difference between a Ford and a Chevy, and when you couldn't do that, you were in a bad way.

Sometimes, for variety's sake, they played a game based on the number plate of each passing car. The idea was to look at the first number on the number plate. When you spotted a 1, then you could start looking for a first number of 2, then a first number of 3, then a 4, and so on. When you spotted the number you were looking for, you yelled it out, so that everybody else would know exactly where you were. "I got a 7 on that coupe!" It was slowgoing though. Jimmy Hedgeley claimed to get up to 29 one Saturday, but he was such a liar you couldn't be sure. Still Jimmy got credit for holding the record.

He had found the all-night game of Flyhole Baseball stupid and irritating. He found this all-afternoon game of Number Plates stupid and boring.

There were times when hanging around the corner didn't seem like much fun. Those dumb games, plus Ray, plus the name Pneeku, plus having everybody against you—sometimes he couldn't stand it any longer. When he felt like that, he went home. He went home and he stayed home, for two, three, four, as many as five days. He read books in his room during this time. But a boy cannot live by books alone, and loneliness crept up on him and then overwhelmed him. He returned to the corner, and the cycle began again.

The corner was the gang's window on the world. Here was activity and movement. Here he spent his days. The enuretic Jimmy Hedgeley continued to drink milk shakes. The guys continued to make his blood boil with the cry of "Pneeku!" Ray Archambault continued to map out his arm with islands of purple. And he continued to flee and to return.

He sat among them on the corner. He sat on the dirt with his back up against the billboard. He sat on the curbstone. And while he sat, he was waiting, waiting, waiting, waiting for something fine and wonderful to happen. He sat on the fire hydrant amidst all the noise and stared down the street in timeless expectancy.

CHAPTER 2

LOMMY

Just before the Easter vacation in the sixth grade, he brought home a green slip of paper from school. It was an announcement that swimming lessons would be held at the YMCA during the vacation week. There would be five lessons, one each morning, Monday through Friday, and each lesson would last forty minutes. And—this was the most important bit of information—the lessons were being offered free.

"This is a good thing," Ma approved. "I think you should go, son. You might fall off a boat someday."

"I don't go on boats," he said.

"You will be glad you went," she insisted. "How do you know what you will be doing ten years from now? You might be on a boat, and when you are down in the water it will be too late to learn then."

Actually, he agreed with her. How to swim was a good thing to know. It was just that he felt a bit nervous about going to the Y. He had never been there, and he wouldn't know anybody.

But Ma signed the paper and he returned it to school. Two days later he received his assignment—the 10:30 class.

He got up early Monday morning. He was very nervous. He had never done anything like this before. It took nerve to go all the way downtown to a fancy place like the YMCA and walk in alone.

It was only eight o'clock, and he knew there was lots of time, but still he was worried he might be late. Ma was making his breakfast.

"Hurry up, Ma, will you?" he said irritably.

"I only have two hands, boy," she chided him. "Sit down and stop fussing around."

"I don't even know where the place is," he grouched, as if that was her fault.

"Well, don't worry about that, son. You'll find it all right," she assured him.

"Yuh, and suppose I'm late for my lesson while I'm looking!" he exclaimed.

"It's downtown, that I know for sure," Ma said, "for I have heard people speak of it." She deliberated a moment. "I think it's near the City Hall," she said. "You know behind the City Hall there's three or four big buildings in a row. I think it's one of them, yes. The first is the Registry of Deeds, I saw the sign in the window. And the second one is, I think, the Courthouse, for I have seen many policemen going up and down the steps. And the third, I think, is the YMCA, yes. It seems to me that that's the YMCA. Yes, I'm almost sure of it. You go there first, boy, and if that's the YMCA—good, enter. But if it is not, then walk two blocks down, to where all the big stores are, and enter one of them, and ask for directions. They will be glad to tell you."

Why the heck walk all the way down to a store? he thought. Why not just ask the first person you meet on the street? But he said nothing, and just ate.

"The Woolworth's would be a good one," Ma said. "I have been in the Five and Ten here in the North End and I have seen people come in not to buy only to ask directions. So it is nothing out of the ordinary. People do that all the time, you don't have to feel embarrassed about it."

The Five and Ten! he thought. Swell. To go in there and bother some busy salesgirl. She'd be sure to appreciate it. Or maybe Ma wanted him to go up to the floorwalker, one of those snooty guys with a flower in his buttonhole who walked up and down looking for kids who might be stealing. Catch him asking that guy anything!

"Maybe the Five and Ten downtown is different from the one in the North End," he said straight-faced.

"Aaaa," she said, disagreeing. "How can it be different?" she asked.

"Maybe it's more high-class," he said.

"The prices are the same, how can it be more high-class?" she demanded.

"I don't know," he laughed.

"Ah," she nodded, "You're playing with me. That means you won't go in there at all. I know you!"

"Now, Ma, don't get so excited. I'll find that darn YMCA all right, don't worry."

"Yes, but how? You don't know where it is!"

"I know where it is—it's right next to the Courthouse, where all the policemen go!"

"Yes, but suppose it's not there?"

"Then I'll go in the Courthouse and ask the Judge. He'll be glad to tell me."

"Now you're playing with me again," she said.

"If you don't hear from me, I'll be at the House of Correction for one-to-three years!"

She laughed and shook her head.

He felt better with his breakfast down.

"Ma, where's my bathing suit?"

She rummaged about in a box in the closet, talking to herself, and then she brought it out. It was a dark blue one-piece suit, dramatically styled, with a round hole cut out of the side above each hip—the holes kind of gave your body a sensation of nudity. The suit was made of wool and it sure itched till it got wet. Then you didn't notice it. It was a little big for him because it had been given to them. Ma had fooled around with the straps, sewing them this way and that way, trying to make them tighter. But they still kept falling off his shoulders. It was a nuisance.

He went over to the towel drawer and took the towel on top. Ma was right on his heels. "Don't take that one," she said, and she snatched it out of his hands.

"Why not?" he asked.

"You have eyes and you ask why not? Look at it. It's not a towel, it's a rag. You didn't see the holes? You didn't see the threads hanging? And so thin—like a handkerchief!"

"It's good enough for me," he said.

"It's good enough for you, but it's not good enough for me. Do you think I want you wiping yourself in public with it, where other people can see you? With certainty they would say, 'From where did this urchin come from?'"

She fished around in the drawer. "I know there's a good one in here somewhere. . . ," she muttered.

"Aw, Ma," he said.

"Here it is! Here, take this one."

It was so nice, he was reluctant to take it. He did not like the idea of being responsible for the best towel in the house.

"Suppose somebody steals it?" he said.

"If somebody steals it, they must need it worse than you," she said. "Besides, how do you know there's going to be crooks there? Hide it under your clothes, it'll be safe there. And if not—too bad. It won't kill us."

"Okay," he said, giving in.

He laid the towel out on the table, smoothing away all the wrinkles, and then he placed the bathing suit, neatly folded, on the towel end nearest him. Next he carefully brought over each side of the towel to meet in the middle and cover the suit, and then he started rolling. He ended up with a tight, compact bundle.

"Ah, what a special job," Ma teased him. "There is nobody who can roll towels like you."

"I have to carry it a long way, Ma," he defended himself. "I don't want it coming apart."

He was ready to go.

"Well, I'll see you later, Ma."

"Okay, boy."

"So long."

"So long, boy."

She called after him as he ran down the stairs.

"Hey, one thing!"

"What?" he shouted up.

"Be careful! If the water is deep—stay by the man!"

"Okay!"

Now that he was walking and not just sitting around in the house, he did not feel so nervous. He was excited more than nervous. He walked at a good clip and arrived downtown in about an hour. He went to the street behind the City Hall where all the big buildings were, as Ma had suggested. He walked up and down that street a couple of times, staring at each building in turn. The buildings were all alike, rectangular stone structures, massive, old, encrusted with pigeon droppings, cold with the dirty-gray stone coldness of dehumanized official government. It was clear there were forms and folders inside those buildings.

They were ugly; it radiated out from them. He did not think this, he felt it. But in fairness to American practice, he did not know that in this country great ugliness in public architecture is purposely perpetrated in the belief that ugliness encourages sobriety of spirit, and thus the continuing probity of city and county officials is assured. What man could be lighthearted enough to steal in the presence of buildings so like depressing gray prisons?

It must be dark in there, he thought. He could see the high yellow ceilings. He could see the lights hanging from them on chains. The lights were turned on, and here it was only morning. He watched the people entering and leaving the buildings. They were all grownups; none of them were kids. That settled it. The YMCA wasn't here. So without asking anybody he just left. He walked away, toward the fresh air and a more joyful environment.

He walked aimlessly for a while. He had just about made up his mind that he was going to have to start asking, when he turned a corner and in that moment saw the answer to his problem. Up ahead of him were three boys, each with a towel under his arm. They were going to the YMCA, he knew they were! He didn't have to know where anything was, all he had to do was follow along behind them. They would take him there. But suppose they had already been to the Y and were walking *home*? But no, their hair was dry, they hadn't been in the water yet. They hadn't come from a swimming lesson, they were headed for one! And they knew where they were going, he could tell that. They weren't asking anybody and they weren't looking at the buildings or street signs. They were just walking along, talking, laughing, having a good time.

He walked along nonchalantly, but secretly keeping a sharp eye on the three boys. What a good joke, he thought. Nobody would guess from watching him that he didn't know the way. It was a good thing people couldn't read your mind, he laughed to himself. He was fooling everybody.

The boys turned up a quiet side street and something told him they were getting close. He hurried to catch up, taking rapid giant strides. He wanted to get right behind them, so he could go in with them. There's safety in numbers. They could lead the way and he could watch and see what they did.

He was right. They turned into a building and did so before he was able to catch up. He walked the last few feet so fast he was practically running. The building was not exactly what he had expected. He had expected something modern, something kind of square and made of red brick. Instead there was before him a big wooden house, with a roomy porch; it looked like it had been some rich person's mansion years before. It was very homey looking.

Over the door was a sign—*Young Men's Christian Association.* He wondered if that included him, or if it meant only Protestants. Would they let him join—if he had the money? He was Catholic, and he didn't know if Catholics were classified as Christians. He had never got that straight. Somehow he got the impression that when they said something like "a fine Christian gentleman," they meant a Protestant.

He opened the door and entered just in time to catch sight of the three boys. There was a corridor to the left and one straight ahead. They had gone down the one straight ahead and luckily he saw them disappearing around the corner.

He glanced around. Just in front of him, a little to the left, were some stairs. They were just about the nicest stairs he had ever seen. They weren't like the ones home. They had a banister and they were wide. Not only that, but instead of marching up in a straight line, they circled around and around, like in a story book, and tempted you to climb them to see what was up there. The banister was polished and made of some warm rich-looking deep-brown wood.

Close by the foot of the stairs was a cubicle, seemingly carved out of the solid wall. There was a combination desk-counter that stretched the length of the cubicle and sitting cozily behind it was an old man with white hair. He was neat and clean; his hair was neatly parted. He was smoking a pipe and he was wearing a gray sweater that buttoned down the front. On the wall over his head a large clock ticked comfortably.

He guessed that the old man was the one who looked at your YMCA card when you came in, and he prepared himself to state his business— I'm here for the swimming lessons—but the old man asked him nothing.

As he strolled down the wide corridor, he looked into the open room on his right. It was a big room, something like a gigantic parlor. There was a wonderful, stalwart pool table, as good as was in any pool hall, and three fellows were having a game. They were older fellows. There was a Ping-Pong table and two guys about his own age were playing. There was a soft sofa with a magazine rack handy and kids were sitting reading. On the top shelf of the rack he caught sight of *The American Boy*, his favorite magazine! He went to the library every month to read it.

The beautiful banister and its hint of history and romance, the clock ticking, the old man and his pipe smell, the balls clicking on the green sward of the pool table, the chirpy bounce of the Ping-Pong ball, the boys playing and reading quietly, nobody quarreling, it all gave him a wonderful feeling of peace and contentment. There was an unhurried, pleasant atmosphere here that appealed mightily to him. There was fun and good feeling in this place. Boy, he thought, wouldn't it be wonderful to belong to the Y! Think how it would be. You could come down here any time and there would most likely always be somebody around you could have a game with. Or, if there was no one around, you could shoot pool by yourself. Or you could read magazines. You'd have a place to go, you wouldn't have to hang around the gang so much.

35

And then he came to the end of the corridor and went around the corner. There before him were some stairs and much muffled noise coming from down below. He went down the stairs, opened a door, and found himself in a noisy locker room. Guys were slamming lockers shut and yelling back and forth. He didn't want to barge in on any group, so he found a bench that had only one other guy on it. The lockers were metal and painted dark green. He opened one of them self-consciously, thinking it might be full of somebody's clothes, and he would be accused of being a crook. But it was empty. He started undressing. He hung his jacket, shirt, and pants on the hooks inside the locker. He unrolled his towel on the bench and took out the bathing suit. Then he folded the towel, Ma's best towel, and slyly put it inside his pants. It was out of sight there and, he hoped, safe.

He took his shoes and stockings off, stripped off his underwear, got into his bathing suit, and he was ready to go. He closed the locker quietly.

"Hey, kid, you don't wear a bathing suit!"

It was the guy on the bench with him. He had been dressing all this time. He was from the previous class. He was bent over, tying his shoes, and was looking at him sideways.

"You don't?"

The guy sat up and shook his head. "No. You just wear your birthday suit." He laughed at his own joke.

He stood there, perplexed. Was the guy kidding him? So many help-ful guys were just trying to have a little fun at your expense. He'd turn up naked at the pool while everybody else was there with a suit on— that would be great. He could just see everybody staring at him. He decided the guy was lying. It was too much to believe, that a high-class place like the YMCA would want you to go bareass. That was the kind of thing you did when you went swimming in the woods where there was nobody around.

The guy, damn him, could read his mind. "You don't believe me, huh?" he laughed good-naturedly.

Just then three guys walked by, the same three guys he had followed, and they were bareass.

Shamefacedly, he opened his locker and started taking the suit off.

"I told you!" the guy laughed, vindicated.

Stripped to the buff, and with as much casualness as he could muster, he strolled out past the lockers. He saw an open archway and the green water of the pool beyond.

He went to the edge of the pool. It was early yet. Kids were playing around in the water, having some fun before the lesson began. He watched them closely, to make sure they were standing in low water. Assured of this, he went over by the iron ladder to let himself down into the pool.

But he had no sooner taken hold of the top rung of the ladder, still a long way from the water, when the instructor walked over to him. He was a young guy, in his twenties. He had on an old baseball cap, a gray sweatshirt with a whistle hanging over the front of it—the whistle was attached to a cord that went around his neck—and red trunks.

He noticed that below the trunks was a pair of real good-looking legs, slim and smooth-muscled. He noticed that the legs and also the face were deeply tanned, like it was in late August. Now where would a guy get such a beautiful tan at this time of year?

"Have you had your shower yet?" the instructor asked him in a nice way.

"No," he answered, shaking his head.

"Well, go in the shower room and wet yourself down. We always take a shower before getting in the pool."

"Oh, okay," he said apologetically. "I'll remember that." He climbed off the ladder and walked away, blushing, sure that some of the kids must have heard. Why was it he always did the wrong thing? Why couldn't he watch better and see what the other kids were doing?

The experience of having the instructor single him out for attention excited him. A nervous exhilaration took hold of him. He had the impulse to speak, to talk to somebody, to make friends with somebody, to yell and get in the spirit of the thing. When he got to the shower room, this curious elation was very strong in him. One other boy was in there. So, without any premeditation, without the customary reserve with strangers that always stilled his tongue, he blurted out to the boy, "Why do they want you to take a shower before you get in the pool?" He did not ask the question as much as he bubbled it out like some silly girl would have. He was, of course, not primarily after the information, although in truth the requirement that you go out and wet yourself down as a preparation for jumping into some water seemed rather odd to him. But primarily he just wanted to talk and be friendly with somebody.

37

The boy, a tall boy with light-brown hair and blue eyes, turned to him and his manner had a more chilling effect on his interlocutor than the cold water which cascaded off the latter's back, the warm water being all gone. It was clear he resented having been addressed. He was not an old kid, say like somebody who went to high school, but even at his age he managed to get something disdainful and superior into the curl of his mouth. And then he spoke. He spoke with a reluctance, as if the prospect of being drawn into a conversation with this presumptuous boor was most distasteful to him. He spoke with a languor, as if the very act of speaking required excessive effort, inspiring the instant image of some sick woman reclining on a couch. He spoke with an indolence, as if to one of his humble subjects, a careless indolence that was somehow peculiarly insulting in its rhythms and rich with insinuations.

"So you'll be clean, I guess," he said, and that was actually all he said, which only goes to show it's not what you say, it's how you say it. He didn't say, "So you'll be clean, I guess, stupid," but he may as well have. He didn't say, "So you'll be clean, I guess, you with your filthy body," but he may as well have. And he didn't say, "Don't bother me," but he may as well have.

Chagrin and humiliation flashed through the former friendly conversation-starter, who suddenly felt disagreeable.

"Well, if they want you to get clean, why don't they put some soap in here?" he countered in an argumentative way.

The boy did not choose to hear this comment.

"You can't get clean just with water," he continued, stressing his point.

But the boy did not choose to hear this either. Apparently he had already spoken on the subject and he did not intend to take it up again. This left the fault-finding soap-lacking debater in the awkward position of talking out loud to himself.

Then just as if he were all alone in the shower room, the boy calmly turned off his shower and walked past his erstwhile companion without so much as a glance his way. He walked out with complete dignity and assurance, his head held high, his carriage erect, his pride not intimidated by his body, which was rather unprepossessing, at least as seen from behind, with his narrow shoulders, his long skinny legs, and his white bony ass. Yes, his body was unprepossessing, but it had to be admitted—in the expression used to describe certain formidable matrons—he carried himself well.

A guy his own age lording it over him like that. Who the hell did he think he was? What had he ever done that he could walk around like Lord Knuck-a-Nuck? The son of a bitch. Well, that was the last question he was going to ask anybody around this place, and that was for darn sure. He had never met anybody like that before. He was like something out of the movies, the rich and haughty Count who sneers at the hero. A guy like that in the North End, boy, would the kids ever gang up on him! That's why it was just about one-hundred-per-cent certain that he was from the West End, where the wealthy people lived. But he still couldn't help wondering—how did a person get to feel so repulsively superior?

But he turned off the shower and went out to the pool, and the bad taste left in his mouth by Lord Knuck-a-Nuck was soon forgotten in the excitement of the swimming lesson. After taking roll, the instructor extended his two arms before him, keeping them straight and parallel to the floor, and then he moved them like a piece of machinery, alternately, in rhythm, in quick arcs, up, down, up, down, up, down. He was demonstrating the kick for the Australian crawl. Then he had the kids get in the water. He had them line up on both sides of the pool, at the shallow end, of course. There was a gutter cut into the wall of the pool. They got face down in the water, hanging onto the gutter with their hands, and extended their bodies at full length. Upon his signal they practiced the kick.

After a couple of minutes he stopped them. "Okay! Stand up! Rest!" He waited a moment for them to catch their breath. "That wasn't bad for the first time," he said pleasantly. "Some of you fellows are going to have to put more oomph into it though. You couldn't swim your way out of a paper bag kicking like that. Don't be afraid of hurting the water. The water's tough, no one's ever hurt it yet, believe me. So this time, really hit that water hard. Okay, everybody down! Let's go! Get down in that water!

"Ready—begin! Start kicking! . . . One, kick—two, kick—one, kick—two, kick—one, kick—two, kick. . . . Kick—kick—kick—kick. . . . Come on! Let's see that water splash!"

The boys liked a command like that. They giggled as they acted like so many whales. They sent the spray flying in all directions. What a racket they made! *Whoomph! Whoomph! Ploosh!*

"You on the end there, keep that fanny down!"

Even as he kicked, he couldn't help laughing. He had never heard it called that before. He liked the instructor. He smiled when he said things. And he made jokes. Even if that crack about the fanny had been directed at him, he still would have laughed. This was fun. He found himself thinking he was really glad he had come. He had thought it was going to be lonely by himself but he was having fun.

"One—two—one—two—one—two—kick—kick—kick."

The instructor walked back and forth up above watching them. He listened attentively to the instructor's voice, because that way he could fix his whereabouts, and when the instructor was directly overhead, he tried to do it extra good. Whew, but your legs got tired.

"Okay, everybody up! Rest!"

The next thing they did was take turns going across the width of the pool—underwater without moving their arms or legs. They just counted to three, took a deep breath, submerged, pushed hard against the side of the pool with their doubled-up legs, and with that single act of propulsion, they were on their own. They cut the green water like silent submarines, floating in a private world of aloneness, until forced up into the air of humankind by the need to breathe. The idea was to see how far you could get. And after several tries he could almost make it all the way across.

Then, standing in the water, they bent over and practiced the crawl stroke. The instructor showed them how to move their arms, how to

39

get the rhythm of the stroke. Then he showed them the proper way to breathe while doing this Australian crawl. In between strokes you turn your head sideways, getting your mouth up out of the water of course, and you take a quick breath, and then you put your head back in the water—face down. It was very realistic because they actually swept the water back with each stroke and they actually put their face in the water after taking a breath, and he was doing it real good, but of course he knew darn well it was going to be a lot tougher to do when he was horizontal in the water and not standing with his feet on the bottom of the pool.

Towards the end of the lesson the instructor let them fool around for a few minutes in some free play, and then he said, "All right, everybody in for a shower. Let's go!"

There was such a press of fellows and, as he knew, only three showers, so he kind of hung back and let the rest of the guys take their shower first. This patience stemming from a disinclination to be a member of a crowd got him a shower all for himself, but it also got him some of the coldest water seen south of the North Pole. It had one-half degree to spare on the liquid side of ice. The water had been cold when he took his shower before the lesson, but this—wow! The man who fired the boilers must have gone home. No wonder the kids yelled so much when they were in here. But with manly resolve, he quit testing it with his outstretched toes and jumped under. He caught it full in the face. He gasped with the shock, and in a moment he was shrieking and hollering. He stayed under a good while, jumping up and down and swinging his arms energetically every second of it. When he finally turned the shower off and walked out to his locker, he felt like a million bucks. He hummed happily as he vigorously dried himself.

A fully clothed colored boy stopped by his locker and asked timidly, "Is this where you dress for swimming?"

"Yes, it is," he informed the newcomer grandly, "only you don't dress up for it, you undress," and he laughed heartily at his own joke while the colored boy grinned rather sickly.

When he got out on the street, he still felt very much invigorated from the shower. How nice it was to feel so good, he was thinking, and the air was so crisp, he felt really alive and alert.

"Hey, wait up!"

He turned around.

It was a guy who had just come out of the Y, and he had a towel under his arm. The guy must have been in his class, but he didn't remember seeing him in there.

"You live in the North End?" the guy said when he caught up.

"Yuh."

"I thought I seen you before," the guy bobbed his head up and down affirmatively, pleased that his hunch had been right.

He was a guy about his own height, but heavier. He was roly-poly in figure. He had dark-brown hair, brown eyes, and a somewhat large nose. His face was wreathed in a big friendly smile. The first impression was that while this was not a particularly handsome face, it was an infinitely good-natured one.

"Do you mind if I walk home with you?" the guy asked.

"No, I don't mind," he answered quickly. Gee, this fellow was sure polite, asking permission like that. Actually he was glad of the company. It was a long way home.

They fell in step together.

"What's your name?" his new acquaintance asked.

"Tony."

"What's your last name?"

"Alfama."

"Tony Alfama, huh?"

"Yuh."

"Well, my name is Lommy. Pleased to meet you, Tony."

"Yuh, same here, Lommy," he said. He felt a little bit embarrassed at all these introductions. It sounded so formal.

"Of course that's not my real name," Lommy said. "My real name is Hector L'Hommedieu. Some name, huh? 'Course nobody calls me Hector except my mother and my father and the teachers. Everybody calls me Lommy. They couldn't call me Hec—it would sound too much like *heck*, and that'd be a heck of a nickname."

They both laughed wildly at Lommy's joke.

"So I gotta go through life with a pansy name like Hector," Lommy continued.

"I don't think Hector's a pansy name," he said seriously.

"You don't?" Lommy said, surprised. Lommy searched his face to see if he was kidding, but he wasn't kidding.

41

"No, I don't," he said. "Clarence is a pansy name, and Horace, but Hector—that's not so bad. Look at my real name—Antonio. Hector's no worse than that."

"You know," Lommy said wonderingly, "you're the first guy that's ever had a good word to say about my name. Thanks, I appreciate it." There was real gratitude in his voice.

"Well, I'm not trying to butter you up, Lommy," he quickly disclaimed. "I'm just telling you how I really feel about it." He was just a little bit embarrassed, but pleased. If he could make a guy feel good, why the hell not? And then he thought of something that really fit in here. "Say, did you ever hear about the Trojan War?"

"Is that the one where they had that big horse and all the guys hid inside it?"

"Yuh, that's the one. Well, did you know that the bravest fighter on the whole Trojan side was a guy by the name of Hector?"

"No kidding?" There was even more wonder in Lommy's voice now, and yes, perhaps even a wee bit of pride.

"Yuh, Hector his name was. And all the Greeks were scared shitless of him."

"Say," Lommy said, suddenly worried, "which ones were the Trojans? Were they inside the horse or out?"

"They were outside."

"Then they took the horse into their city?"

"That's right."

"They were kind of stupid, weren't they?"

"Well, yuh, I guess they were."

"How come you know about this guy Hector?" Lommy asked, curious.

"Oh, I read a book once about the Trojan War," he said deprecatingly.

"I'll bet you're smart in school," Lommy said suddenly.

"Oh, I do pretty good," he said modestly.

"You get any D's?"

"No."

"You get any C's?"

"No."

"Whew"—Lommy pursed his lips and mock whistled. "I'd like to borrow your report card sometime. My old lady'd fall over in a faint. Hey, let me ask you this—do you get any B's?"

"Oh, sure. I get lots of B's. I usually get about half B's and half A's."

"Jeez, what a brain," Lommy said wonderingly. He was not trying to be funny. He was honest in his admiration. "I had a feeling you were smart," he said almost to himself, and then aloud he said, "I'll bet everybody wants to sit next to you in class."

They both laughed heartily at this.

By this time they were near the City Hall and he just marveled at how fast time passes when you have somebody to talk to. He was glad Lommy had hailed him.

"Say, Lommy, are you in that ten-thirty class?" he asked.

"Sure! Didn't you see me in there?"

"Well . . . no, I didn't."

"Well, I was there, and I saw you. I think you were too busy concentrating on the exercises that's all."

"Yuh, maybe that was it."

"What do you think of the Y? Pretty good, huh?"

"Yuh, darn good."

"What do you think of their basketball court? Big, huh?"

"I didn't see that."

"It's right upstairs—you know when you come in, those stairs there, well, just go up them."

"I went straight down to the pool when I came in," he apologized.

"You didn't see anything but the pool then?"

"No."

"Well, look," Lommy said, "next time I'll take you around—if you wanna see the place," he added.

"Yuh, I do! Gee, that'll be swell."

"I got there early today," Lommy explained, "and I met this guy and he took me around. He showed me the whole place. There's not a room there that we didn't go in. You ever seen a game of handball?"

"Well, I've seen the firemen play outside behind the station."

"Shit, they play with a tennis ball. I mean real handball—with gloves."

"Well, no, I guess I haven't."

"We watched a game. It's really interesting. They wear gloves, see, one on each hand, because that ball's so hard it'll wreck their hands. And you can hit the ball with either hand. The ball is a little black rubber ball. It's . . . oh, I'd say . . . halfway between a golf ball and a tennis

43

ball in size. And boy, does it ever come at you fast! These two old guys were having a game. One of them was a skinny guy with *white* hair and he was pretty good. He could beat either you or me, you know. But the guy he was playing against, *he* was really good. This guy was a bald-headed guy with a potbelly, and he was skunking the skinny guy. When he hit that ball, boy—*zoom!* You couldn't even see it. I think it was because he had all that gut behind it. You take a skinny guy he just hasn't got the power. Right?"

"Probably."

"The guy I was with, he lives in some ritzy house out in the West End, but he's a good guy though, his name's Fred, and he was telling me that this game we were watching wasn't real handball."

"I thought you said it was."

"Wait now, let me finish. It was real handball but it's not what you'd call one-hundred-per-cent real handball. They were using a single wall, see. But in real real handball you play in a room with four walls, and you can hit the ball to any wall."

"Well, nobody can watch it then, huh?"

"Why not?"

"Well, if you had four walls to play against, where would the people sit?"

"H'm, I guess you're right. Nobody can watch it then."

"What about the referee? Where would he be?"

"He'd have to duck I guess."

"Well, that wouldn't work. You told me yourself that ball comes awfully fast—it'd hit him."

"I wish I had thought of that. I would have asked Fred. But let me tell you about the next place we went."

"Yuh, go ahead."

"Well, we walked in this little room," Lommy went on. "It's just about big enough to have two mats on the floor. They call it the weight room. They got this bar in there and it's got these iron wheels on it. They're all sizes, the only thing is when the guy puts a wheel on one end, he puts one the same size on the other end, naturally, otherwise it wouldn't balance. Well, this bar is laying there right in the middle of the mat, and, we were lucky, there's a guy in there warming up, he's a real weight lifter, see, and he's gonna lift it. Christ, you should've seen this guy. I never saw such muscles"—Lommy struck his forehead with the palm of his hand in disbelief. "His head was the same size as anybody else's, but his body was so gigantic that by comparison his head looked like a little pea head. He had developed every part of his body except his head, 'cause there's no muscles in the head, so it was really out of proportion with the rest of him. And his arms! You would have sworn he had thick ropes wound all over them, but they weren't ropes, they were muscles. And you should see in the back here—" Lommy twisted his torso and showed him the spot "—you and me have little itty-bitty muscles there, right by the bone—on him they stuck out so far it looked like he had a pair of angel wings. What a brute he was!"

"I'll bet he lifted that bar easy."

"Well . . . no. There was a lot of weight on that thing, you know. Probably two hundred pounds. But it's interesting how he does it. He uses psychology. When he warms up, you know what he does? He turns his back on the bar. He acts like it don't even exist. He just fools around, bends over, touches his toes, does stuff like that, and then—all of a sudden he turns around fast and he walks over to that bar and he kicks it with his foot. He fixes his legs just right, and he stands there, staring at the bar. He stays there a long time, not moving, just staring at the bar, see. It's like he's in a trance. Me and Fred didn't say a word, we didn't wanna disturb him. Then he's ready! He bends over quick! He grabs that goddamn bar! He throws one leg back! He hoists the goddamn thing! About up to here—halfway up. And then he starts to tremble and shake. He looks like he's having a chill. He's trying to move that bar—" Lommy groaned as thrust his arms out and struggled valiantly with the bar "—trying to lift it over his head—" Lommy groaned some more "—but he can't budge it another inch. He's there straining away—" Lommy's arms shook, his eyes popped, he groaned with agonizing effort "—you should see the veins standing out on his arms—" Lommy gasped. Then he stated coldly, "But the bar don't move. Oh ho, I thought, trouble. Then—*boom!* He drops it. That was that."

"Did he ever lift it?"

"I don't know. He didn't try it again while we were there. I think he was just waiting for us to beat it."

"Gee, I'd like to try weight lifting. I don't mean with big weights like that. I mean with little weights—at least to start with. They say you really get muscles from it."

45

"Oh, yuh, it builds you up. It'll make anybody strong."

"I'd like to have so much muscle on me punches wouldn't hurt. Then I'd go up to a certain guy I know and I'd say, 'Okay, you bastard, where do you want the body sent?'"

Lommy laughed.

"Gee, it'd be nice to be a member of the Y, huh, Lommy? You could go down there, have a nice workout with the weights, hop in the pool for a swim, and then go upstairs for some Ping-Pong and pool. How much is it anyway to be a member, do you know?"

"Six bucks a year."

"Whew! That's a lot."

"Yuh, it is."

"It'd sure be nice to be a member though, huh, Lommy?"

"Yuh, it would. It'd be nice if we both could join. We could go down there together and have a lot of fun. Right?"

"Right. Say, is that guy Fred a member?"

"No. But he could be if he wanted to—he's got the dough. His father's a member. His father keeps taking him down there so he'll get to like the place. His father wants him to join."

"Wow. Why doesn't he join then?"

"Aw, he don't like sports."

"Jeez."

"He's only taking swimming lessons because his mother made him."

"Jeez."

"Let me tell you about the next place Fred and me went. It's the last room of all."

"Okay. Say, one thing, is that guy Fred a tall skinny guy?"

"No, he's about your size. Why?"

"Oh, nothing. I was just wondering."

"Well, Fred and me we goes in this room—it's called the gymnastics room. They got a chin-the-bar there. And they got a rope hanging down from the ceiling. You climb that, see. It's a real thick rope. It's not like a clothesline rope. And I'll tell you another thing they got in there. They got these pulleys on the wall. You pull them out. Well, you don't pull the pulleys out, you pull the rope out. See, it's kind of a rope deal, there's a handle on the end, on the end of the rope, that's what you grab, and then there's a pulley in the middle, and on the other end of the rope there's some weights. But the weights are fixed, you can't pull them away from the wall. They just go up and down when you pull on the rope. You go in and out with the rope, what you're doing is lifting up those weights, see, and that makes your arms strong. It's a lot harder than it looks. Me and Fred tried it. Here, hold my towel," Lommy said suddenly. "You grab a rope in each hand, like this, and there's different exercises you can do. You can go over your head, like this . . . or sideways . . . or through your legs . . . ," he said, demonstrating each one. "Oh, but the best part! Let me tell you about this. In this room there was a guy in the corner, he was twirling these Indian clubs, you know what they are? They're like big bowling pins. He had one in each hand and he was awfully good at it, he was doing all kind of fancy tricks with them. You'd swear he was bound to hit them together, but they never touched. But that wasn't the thing. This guy was really something. He was wearing trunks, see, that was all he had on. Now I've seen guys with hair all over their chest. And I've seen guys with hair all over their arms. And I've seen guys with hair all over their legs. But this was the first time I ever saw a guy with hair all over his back. Well, actually he had hair all over his chest, his arms, his legs *and* his back. And I mean *hair*, you could comb it with a comb. Real black curly hair. From the front he looked like a human being, because of his face, you know, but when he turned around all you saw was this hair from his head to his feet. When I first looked over there he was standing sideways and I though it was a bear twirling those clubs. He didn't have a square inch of skin showing. I'll tell you what he reminded me of—did you ever see this picture where the guy drinks a bottle of this stuff and he turns into a werewolf and then he goes out and drinks a girl's blood?"

"Was that *The Werewolf of Hartley Street*?"

"Yuh, that's the one. You see it?"

"No. I looked at the pictures outside."

"Aw, you shoulda seen it. It was a real neat picture. This guy drinks this stuff, see, gurgle, gurgle, gurgle, and he turns into a werewolf right before your eyes. Hair sprouts all over him. His teeth change into fangs, and he starts to drool. He bends over like a dog and he goes through his window, looking for dames." Lommy grunted like an animal and ran down the street hunched over. He took several vicious swipes with his claws at enemies who happened to be in the vicinity.

47

He was very curious about this story, as he was about every story, so when Lommy circled back, still loping along and giving the eerie night call of the wolf, "Ahhhoooooo!" he immediately asked him, "How did it turn out?"

"Well," Lommy said, "he kills two or three girls. Two. He bends over them when they're sleeping and bites them in the neck and drinks their blood. He's engaged to this very beautiful girl—well, you see, in the daytime he's a very handsome guy, clean-shaven, you know. It's only at night when he drinks the stuff that he changes. So he's engaged to this very beautiful girl and he feels that old feeling starting to come inside him, he knows he's gonna try to drink her blood next, so he warns the professor, that's her father, about the werewolf. He tells the professor to get a pistol and keep it handy and he makes the girl promise she'll keep her bedroom window closed from now on. Well, the stupid girl, that same night she leaves her window wide open. All the kids in the show started yelling, 'Close it! Close it!' but she gets in bed. Well, the guy drinks the stuff and he turns into a werewolf and he comes looking for her. The wind's blowing the curtains and all of a sudden you see his head in the window, drooling, you know—all the dames in the show go, 'Eeeeee!' So he jumps in the room, he looks real crazy, you know, and he bends over her, she's sleeping, a real doll, you know, with long hair, these real nice lips—if it had been me I wouldna been drinking her blood, I woulda been doing something else. Anyway he's bending over her, and he's just about to bite her on the neck when the wind blows real hard into the room, the window was open, remember, and it knocks over a lamp. The professor, her old man, he's downstairs and he hears the lamp fall. He comes running up the stairs with this gun in his hand and he opens her door. The werewolf jumps him and they're fighting back and forth. The dame wakes up and she's real scared but then she sees on the werewolf's hand the ring she had given her boyfriend and so she knows who he really is, see, and she says, 'Don't shoot, father,' but it's too late. *Bang!* Right through the heart. The werewolf staggers over to the window—" clutching his chest Lommy staggered convincingly "—and he falls through. It's the second story, see, and there's a garden down below. They rush out there but—nobody. So they go to her boyfriend's rooming house and he's on the carpet—dead—but when they turn him over, it's the boyfriend, clean-shaven, see, not the werewolf. And that's how the picture ends. The professor's caught on and he says, 'It's all for the best.'"

"It sounds like a good picture."

"Well, it was."

"Real scary, huh?"

"Oh, yuh. See, it takes place in London. And you know how those London pictures are. There's that fog. And everything's dark, even inside the houses. Real creepy, you know. 'Oh, I say, old boy!'" Lommy cried out, trying out his English accent. "There was just one thing I didn't like about the picture."

"What's that?"

"Well, I didn't like them making the hero and the werewolf the same guy. After he kills the first girl, you know darn well he's gonna get it. So, I don't know, it kind of gives you a lousy feeling, waiting there for him to get knocked off."

"Yuh, that's a good point. Say, I was wondering, how did they make him look like a werewolf?"

"Well, he wasn't wearing a costume, that's for sure. Because with costumes you can always tell it's a fake, like on Halloween. And he had real hair coming out of his arms."

"Maybe he stripped down to his shorts and they sewed him inside some animal skins."

"I think it was some kind of a special outfit. I tell you, he was made up so good, you didn't think of what he was wearing. He really looked like a werewolf. It was real nifty."

"How did he get up in her room?"

"He climbed a vine," Lommy replied moodily.

They walked a while without talking, each thinking his own thoughts about the werewolf and invading a lovely girl's room in the dark of night.

Finally, he broke the quiet spell himself by yelling out, "'You on the end there, keep that fanny down!'" and his imitation made Lommy laugh. "Do you like the guy who's teaching us?" he asked Lommy.

Lommy nodded affirmatively. "Don't you?"

"Oh, yuh, I do," he stated emphatically. The guy was so clean and healthy-looking, so good-humored, how could you help but like him? At least, *he* felt that way, but you never knew how another person felt and that's why he had asked Lommy.

"There's one thing about him for sure," Lommy said. "He may know his onions about swimming, but he sure can't pronounce French names. You hear him during the roll call? 'Lum-do, Hector,' I thought he meant some other guy. But nobody said anything. 'Lum-do, Hector,' he says again. Cripes, I thought, he must mean me. There wouldn't be two guys here named Hector. 'Here!' I says. 'Fine,' he says, 'I thought maybe you had stepped out to tea,' and everybody laughs."

"I remember that," he said, laughing again.

"Everybody goofs my name up," Lommy continued. "Even my nickname. At my father's place—he owns a restaurant—a kid I know stuck his head in the door one day. 'Hi, Lommy,' he says. 'Hi,' I says. Well, the customers hear him, see, but they think he said Tommy. So from then on they call me Tommy. Watch, I'll go in there this afternoon, some guy'll say, 'Hello, Tommy.'"

They both laughed at Lommy's appellative misfortunes.

"Lommy, you think we can learn to swim in a week?" he asked.

Lommy was optimistic. "Oh, sure."

"I don't know," he said, shaking his head doubtfully. "You know when nobody was looking I tried to swim. I kicked just like he showed us. I moved my arms just perfect. And—I sank right down to the bottom."

"Aw, give yourself a chance. This was only the first day, remember that," Lommy said.

"I don't think I can learn in a week," he muttered pessimistically.

"Boy, Tony, your eyes are red," Lommy said. "You look like you been crying."

"It was the darn water," he complained. "I opened my eyes when I was going underwater across the pool."

"What did you do that for?"

"Oh, I like to look at the bottom. I shouldn't have kept doing it though. It stung like crazy and my eyes have been burning ever since."

"Fred warned me about the water," Lommy said. "It's the chlorine they put in it."

"What's that?"

"It's a chemical and it kills the germs. That's what makes the water green, the chlorine. Fred told me the pool's real nice when they change the water, you can open your eyes in it all you want then. But they don't change the water very often; they keep adding more and more chlorine to it instead."

"Why don't they change the water?"

"Costs money, I guess."

Lommy played soccer with a stone as he walked along, keeping it going on the sidewalk with short kicks. But after about half a block, the independent stone veered off into the street.

"Do you know how the Y got started?" Lommy said.

"No."

"It got started by a bunch of ministers."

"I thought so."

"Why?"

"I don't know. I just had that feeling."

"Fred was telling me the whole history of the Y. You wanna hear it?"

"Yuh, sure," he said enthusiastically.

"Well, in the old days when a young fellow traveled around, he'd be green, see, and he wouldn't know anything, and so he'd register in a hotel and he wouldn't know it, but this hotel would really be a whorehouse, see, and he'd go to his room and pretty soon he'd wake up and there'd be a whore in bed with him, they all had keys, you see, and well—a lot of young fellows got led into bad habits that way. So these ministers got together and they started these hotels in big cities just for young fellows, they didn't allow no women in there at all, and the idea spread. Then some guy thought up the idea—why not have sports in the building, too? That way you could keep these young guys healthy. So they built a gym in there and had games and stuff like that. So most of the Y's today, they're like the Gaw one, they don't have beds any more, they're just like a gym and a clubhouse."

A streetcar shook and rattled by. Across the street they could see the green lawns of the Common. They were about halfway home.

They were passing the window of the Olde Colony Bakery Shop and there was a big wedding cake in the window, with the small figures of a man and woman, the bridegroom and the bride, on top of the cake. The man was in black, the woman in white. He wondered if it was a real cake.

"Say, I just remembered!" Lommy said, grabbing his arm. "I got some dough. C'mon!"

Lommy made to go in the bakery, but his companion held back. "C'mon, Tony."

51

"No," he said, blushing. "I'll wait for you out here." He didn't want to go in and watch Lommy pick something out and then start eating it. That would be embarrassing. In a store he couldn't help watching. But if he didn't go in, afterwards he could walk along with Lommy but not look at him, look at the traffic instead, and just sort of pretend that Lommy wasn't eating anything and in a few minutes the thing would be eaten up and the moment forgotten.

"Aw, c'mon, Tony," Lommy coaxed.

"Okay," he relented, smiling. What the heck, why not? As a matter of fact, he really wanted to go in. This was because of curiosity. He had never been inside a bakery shop before, but of course he would never have told Lommy that. And now that he had consented and was actually going to go in, he felt excited.

"You pick it out," Lommy said.

"Oh, no." He was all blushes and confusion again. "I wouldn't know what you liked."

"I like anything," Lommy said emphatically.

Lommy opened the door and a bell tinkled. Lommy held the door for him to go in first. There was no one out front in the shop. But they heard feet coming from the backroom.

"Just one thing," Lommy murmured to him, "I only got a nickel, so maybe you better pick something out two for five cents." Lommy made this suggestion in a very nice way, not as if it were an order. "It'd be kind of messy splitting a five-cent one, you know," Lommy added. This was the first intimation he had that Lommy intended to share it with him.

The feet they heard belonged to a plump, cheery woman in her middle years. She had rosy cheeks and he got the irrational thought that she looked like one of her own nicely-rounded, pink-dabbed cookies. Her white uniform was so very clean and starchy that she could have been a nurse, parceling out pills instead of pies.

She greeted them warmly.

"Well, boys, what'll it be?"

"Well, let's see what you got"—he was stalling for time while he studied the displays behind glass.

She laughed at his aplomb.

Lommy did not push himself forward. He hung off to the side a bit and back. By this Lommy made it clear that he was going to let him do all the choosing himself. That Lommy could resist making suggestions with the endless choices there before their eyes indicated that he was in possession of a somewhat fantastic will power. And the woman did not try to hurry him in the least. She was as you should always be with a boy who has five cents to spend—patient. This was not so surprising. By her very friendliness she had already given evidence that she was a most unusual shopkeeper. Most Gaw shopkeepers were rather thin, nervous individuals and the sight of two boys in their shop usually sent them into erethismic spasms.

Everybody was looking at him expectantly, and he could not speak. His eyes raced frantically from shelf to shelf, much the same as trying to read the last few pages of a chapter after Ma had called to him to do something. There was so much. Even after he had set aside the section of bread, the section of cakes, the section of pies, and the section of cookies, even then there was too much.

53

All was quiet. The decision was his, and he was in a frenzy of indecision. Lommy had given him an impossible task. He was in a magic, delicious world of sight and smell. Before him were delicate, flaky shells, opulent with fillers of cream, raspberry, and lemon.

Before him were—cream puffs, magnificent cream puffs, the detachable tops pushed up by a swirly, careless abundance of whipped cream.

He pointed. "What's that?"

"Those are cream puffs."

"How much are they?"

"Five cents each."

Before him were—chocolate éclairs, magnificent chocolate éclairs, long and fat, swollen with custard.

He pointed. "What are these?"

"Those are chocolate éclairs."

"How much are they?"

"They're five cents, same as the cream puffs."

"What have you got that's two for five cents?" he croaked.

"Well, these jelly doughnuts—here—are very nice," she said. "They're two for five cents."

He did not commit himself.

"What are those?" He pointed. They had the delicate powdered flakiness of the cream puff but not its girth.

"Those are turnovers."

"Are they two for five cents?"

"Oh, yes."

"Good! I'll take two of those."

"Well, we have raspberry and lemon. Which do you want?"

"Can I have one of each?"

"Certainly," she said with a smile.

"Okay!" he said. "One of each!" and he began to hum a little. While she was putting the two turnovers in a little white bag, with the aid of a paper wrapper so that her hand never touched the turnovers—boy, what a clean place—while she was doing that, Lommy unobtrusively stepped forward and put the nickel on the counter and stepped back again.

If she had noticed that he was buying the turnovers with somebody else's money, she did not embarrass him by any word or sign and handed him the bag just as if it was his money.

"Call again, boys," she said merrily.

"Yes, we will—" he responded, equally merry "—if we ever get any more money."

Once outside, he shyly extended the bag to Lommy, but Lommy shook his head.

"Just give me one," Lommy said.

"Well, okay," he said, blushing. "What kind do you want, the raspberry or the lemon?"

"You pick first," Lommy said.

"Well, it's your nickel," he pointed out. "You should get the first pick."

"No, you pick," Lommy insisted. "They all taste good to me."

"All right then," he said. He very much wanted the lemon. He knew the flavor of raspberry from having eaten raspberry jam, but the lemon he had no idea what it was like. "I'll take the lemon," he said. So saying, and with great care so as not to lose a single crumb he took out the raspberry for Lommy and the lemon one for himself. The bag he stuck in his pocket.

They didn't talk. They concentrated on eating. His lemon turnover was so lovely and fragile that he felt crude and brutish in biting into it. But bite into it he did. He took a small bite, deliberately restraining himself. And this morsel was heavenly. He rolled it around in his mouth, lingering over it, savoring it to the full. But it was too good. The taste was too good. He took a bigger bite and lingered less long. He crushed the delicious flakes with regretful joy. And in a moment—all was gone. He smacked his lips. He licked his fingers. Then he took out the bag and carefully poured the crumbs into his hand and ate them.

Wow! It was the most delicious thing he had ever had in his whole life. What a generous guy Lommy was!

"Thanks a lot, Lommy," he said with feeling. "That was a real treat."

"That's okay," Lommy said. "You're my friend," he added simply, as if that were explanation enough for generosity.

Shamefully he thought of what he would do if he had a nickel and was going to spend it on delicacies. He would have kept his mouth shut about having the nickel and he would have waited till he was alone, quite alone, and then he would have bought the two turnovers. If he had a nickel, right now, even after this treat, would he share it with Lommy? He was afraid he could not answer that question the way a decent guy would answer it. He felt a slinking, secret shame that even though Lommy didn't know about it, was none the less real. Pig! he said to himself.

55

***

Tony Alfama and Hector L'Hommedieu walked home together. It was a nice walk, leisurely, talkative, and friendly. They discovered that though they had not met before, they lived only three streets apart. Probably the big reason they hadn't met was that they went to different schools. They were both in the sixth grade but the boundary line cut right between them. Tony walked southwest to get to his school, and Lommy walked northwest to get to his, and they both walked a long way. But next year for the seventh grade they would be together, for all the kids in the North End went to the same junior high, Cupp Junior High.

Before parting, they made arrangements to meet on the corner of Tony's street early the next morning. That way they could walk downtown together, and Lommy was going to show him around the Y.

Tony liked Lommy. He was so lively, so chipper, so full of life. He didn't seem to have any meanness in him, like the guys in the gang did.

Ma was waiting for Tony when he got home. "Well," she laughed, "can you navigate in the water yet?"

"Yes," he said, "I swim like a rock."

"How's that?" She didn't understand the expression.

"I go straight to the bottom," he said.

"Well, takes time, boy, takes time," she encouraged him.

That afternoon Tony went out on the corner. The guys had seen him coming home with the towel under his arm and they knew something was up. They asked him about it. If it wasn't for the darn towel, he wouldn't have told them. But with that towel as damning evidence what could he tell them but the truth?

They thought that was the funniest thing they had heard yet. They laughed uproariously.

Rudy Lenkowski bent his hand at the wrist in a quick girlish motion, the way queers are supposed to do. "Oh, Percy!" he called in a falsetto voice. "Would you like to borrow my water wings?"

"Wouldn't you know it that a pansy like Pneeku would be taking lessons?" Ray Archambault asked no one in particular.

"Pneeku won't have any trouble learning how to swim, Rudy," Jimmy Hedgeley said. "Shit floats, you know."

"You wanna learn how to swim, Pneeku," Ray Archambault said angrily, "you really wanna learn, huh? I'll teach you how to swim. I'll throw you in over your head, like my uncle did me. You'll learn then, just like I did." Tony could see Ray seriously thought that was a good method.

"I didn't know they let Portagees in the Y," Rudy Lenkowski said. "I think I'll cancel my membership."

"Aw, you guys are just jealous," Tony retorted, but it was a weak comeback.

And every time they saw somebody they knew passing by, they yelled, "Did you hear the latest? Pneeku's taking swimming lessons at the Y with all the other pansies!" and the announcement always set in motion another wave of laughter.

All afternoon long Tony kept thinking—Why don't I go home?

But he stayed there till five o'clock, and then he went home. The nice feeling he had gotten from the morning was gone. He wondered if he had met Lommy or if he had just dreamt it up. It seemed like a long time ago.

He was having supper with Ma when he heard someone calling him from outside. It startled him.

"To-nee! To-neee!"

He went to the window. It was Lommy. He opened the window.

"Can you come out?" Lommy called up.

"Sure. I'll be out in about five minutes."

"Okay."

"Who's that?" Ma asked curiously. She had been surprised, too. It was unusual for guys to come calling him. He wasn't important enough in the gang for that.

"Oh, he's a friend of mine," Tony answered her. "I met him at the pool today."

"Is he Portuguese?" Ma asked in her sweet, innocent way.

He couldn't help grinning. He knew what was coming. "No, he's French."

Ma nodded, frowning. "The French are a fine people, but tell me one thing—why is it you never go with Portuguese boys?"

"There were none at the pool," he said straight-faced.

"And what about school?" she countered. "Whenever you mention to me one of your school friends, he is never Portuguese. How is that?"

"There are none in my class," he fibbed.

"Aaah, liar!" she exclaimed. "The city full of Portuguese and you expect me to believe that? The more numerous people of any in this city, but what is there magic about you—wherever you go, the Portuguese disappear, where you are, there there are none!"

He could only laugh at her excitement.

"There are Portuguese everywhere," she continued, "if you only look for them. But you don't look for them. You close your eyes to them. You don't want to see them," she finished mournfully.

"Aw, Ma," he said.

"I know you," she said sadly. "You will forget your heritage as a Portuguese. You will hide your blood."

"Aw, Ma," he said, shaking his head hopelessly. "I'm not going to hide anything."

She warmed to the subject, and the picture got blacker with each stroke.

"I know you!" she cried. "You will be one of those who will marry a Frenchie girl or a Polander girl, any kind of a girl as long as she's not Portuguese! I know you!" she cried accusingly.

"Aw, Ma, take it easy, will you?" he soothed her. "Look, I just met this guy today. Is it my fault he comes looking for me? You don't want me to give my address when somebody asks me for it? All right, I won't.

The next guy who asks me where I live, I'll say—'Sorry, I can't tell you. My mother only wants guys named Souza or Medeiros coming around to my house.'"

She didn't say anything to that so he complimented himself on his forensic skill.

"And another thing," he continued, "while we're on this subject of marriage. I'm in the sixth grade. This year I'm not planning on marrying anybody. Next year I'll be in the seventh, then maybe I'll think about it, but this year, no."

She had to laugh at that, but she didn't completely surrender. "I know your tricks," she said musingly. "You make a joke to turn people's minds away from the things. I'm wise to you, boy," she said in English, springing the expression on him gleefully.

"'I'm wise to you?'" he repeated in mock astonishment. "Where did you learn that?"

"I keep my ears open," she said proudly. "And my eyes, too. I'm not dumb, you know. I know what's going on."

"I know you're not dumb, Ma," he said fondly. "You just like to have fights, that's all."

They parted on good terms.

"Don't stay out late!" she called to him as he went down the stairs.

"No, I won't!" he called back.

Lommy was waiting for him on the steps of the front piazza.

"I was having supper," he explained to Lommy.

"I figured you were," Lommy said.

They started walking down the street.

"Well, what do you wanna do?" Lommy asked him.

"I don't care," he said agreeably. "What do you want to do?"

"I don't care. Whatever you wanna do is all right with me," Lommy said.

"Why don't we just take a walk down the Avenue?" Tony suggested.

"Okay."

They walked a few feet and then Lommy said brightly, "I tell you one thing we could do!"

"What's that?"

"You wanna go downtown?"

"Jesus," Tony said doubtfully, "that's a long way. And I've been there once today, that's enough. Why?"

"My mother read in the paper they're opening a new wing at Grant's tonight and they're gonna have this big opening and they're gonna give away free balloons."

"Balloons?"

"Yuh, balloons."

"Anything else?"

"Like what?"

"Well, you know. . . like candy or something."

"No."

"Shit, I'm not going to walk two miles there and two miles back for a lousy balloon," Tony said.

"I was gonna get some for my kid sister," Lommy said.

Tony reddened. Lommy was making him feel like a heel again.

"You can get more than one, you know," Lommy went on. "You can keep getting in line. And a lot of people don't want them, you hang around and they say, 'Here, kid,' and they give you theirs."

"Okay, let's go," Tony said.

"No—no—you don't wanna go," Lommy protested.

"Yes, I do. I changed my mind, no kidding. I never been to an opening—I'd like to see what they're like."

"No, you're just saying that," Lommy said. "Besides I don't wanna go myself, to tell you the truth."

"What'd you bring it up for then?"

"Oh, I don't know," Lommy said, laughing.

By this time they were on Beel Boulevard.

"Say, I've got an idea," Tony said. "How about getting cigar boxes?"

"Swell," Lommy said.

The Blue Gable Grocery Store was on Beel Boulevard, but it was an exception. Most of the grocery stores were on the Avenue, the main drag which ran the length of the North End. But there were quite a few variety stores on the Boulevard. Every two or three blocks, there'd be a variety store. These were tiny places, usually run by an old man, and they sold cigarettes, candy, milk, bread, ice cream, cans of soup, and things like that. The grocery stores on the Avenue closed at six o'clock. So the variety stores got the nighttime business. Also, during the day, if a housewife in the neighborhood wanted a single item like a quart of milk or a can of Campbell's Vegetable Soup, she would go to the variety store

59

rather than walk the extra steps to the Avenue, one block away.

The variety stores had neither meat nor vegetables, but they had cigars. The cigars were attractively displayed under glass, the open boxes nicely lined up in two or three rows. It was these boxes that Tony proposed they go after. Cigar boxes were his favorite kind of box. He collected them. He had six of them home. Once, at the store on the corner of Lagoda Street, this nice man, he never forgot him, had given him two boxes. But soon after this the store changed hands, and the new guy was different. Often when walking along, if he had nothing better to do, Tony would peek in a store and if there were no customers in there, he would go in and ask. In this manner he had learned the personality of every variety-store owner on the Boulevard—which were genial, and which were crabby. Unfortunately, the latter class predominated.

Tony and Lommy made their agreement. They would go right down the Boulevard, canvassing every variety store along the way. Only one fellow would go in, the other would wait nearby. They believed that would increase their chances, for the sight of one boy was less likely to irritate a storeowner than the sight of two boys. They would take turns going in. And when they were through, they would split fifty-fifty, regardless of who had actually gotten the boxes.

"Suppose we just get one box?" Tony said.

"Then you get it, because you thought up the idea."

"Okay," Tony agreed. That was fair enough. "Suppose we get an odd number, say three, or five? Same thing?"

"No," Lommy said. "Anything we get over two, if it's an odd number, we'll flip for the extra one."

"You got a coin?"

"No. We can draw straws."

"Okay."

Tony volunteered for the first store.

He went in. It was a very quiet store. The guy was sitting alongside the refrigerator rocking in a rocking chair and smoking a pipe. All you heard was the sound of his rocking and a clock ticking.

"Do you have any empty cigar boxes?" Tony asked.

Without breaking the rhythm of his rocking and without taking the pipe out of his mouth, the man shook his head—just once.

"All right. Thank you," Tony said politely, and left.

Lommy went in the next one and had similar luck. The third and fourth places were no better. So they came to the fifth store. It was Tony's turn.

"Let's skip this one," he said to Lommy. "I'll go in the next one instead."

"Why?"

"Well, I've been here before. The guy's kinda nuts."

"I'm not ascared," Lommy said. "I'll go in."

"Well, I'm not scared either," Tony maintained, "but I know he won't give us anything."

"I'll go in anyway," Lommy said.

"Be ready to run," Tony said.

That sobered Lommy a little. "You come in with me."

"Okay."

The man was a cripple. He stood behind his glass counters, leaning on a crutch, his powerful barrel chest puffed out, his face fierce and unrelenting. He had much hair, much black hair. It lay thick and overgrown on his head, spilling out over his ears, like the mop of some wild young kid. And yet, the tufts of dry gray hair that bristled out of these same ears were the untidy sproutlings not of youth but of age. But he was not old, not old-old that is, like most of the variety-store owners. He looked in his forties.

"You got any cigar boxes?" Lommy asked. Tony stayed by the door.

"Cigars? Cigars? I got plenty cigars," the man said impatiently. He spoke with an accent.

"No. Cigar boxes," Lommy said. "Boxes," he repeated.

The man understood now. A look of annoyance and vexation crossed his face. "What do you want to bother me with that for?" he cried.

"Well, I was only asking," Lommy said defensively.

"Sure, I got plenty cigar boxes," he rasped harshly, "and they all got cigars in them. If I give you the box, what do you want me to do with the cigars? Huh?" he demanded angrily.

"Well," said Lommy, moving towards the door, "you could smoke them."

"You kids get out of here!" the man cried furiously.

"Let's go," Lommy murmured to Tony, as if the latter needed a reminder, and the two boys left in some haste. Once outside, by common instinct they ran for about a block and a half. Then they stopped, leaned against a fence, laughing, laughing, and gradually they sank to the ground with the helplessness of their jag.

"Jee-zus," Tony groaned weakly, "when you told him he could smoke them, I thought he was going to jump over the counter."

And they giggled some more.

But when at last they quieted down, Lommy said soberly, "I'd hate to have that guy get ahold of me. Did you see the hands on him? Those cripples are strong. They get that way from lifting their bodies around. There's one guy who comes in my father's place, he's strong like an ox. Nobody sasses him, believe me."

They went to two more variety stores, but after the excitement with the cripple their hearts weren't in it. They had received so far not a single box. So Lommy said, "Do you save stamps?"

"Yes, I do," Tony said. As a matter of fact he saved everything. With his stamps he didn't have them in any book or album, but had them loose in a cigar box. He had, he estimated, somewhere around one hundred different, mostly from two countries, the United States and Portugal.

"I know this place where we can get some," Lommy said.

"Swell, let's go," Tony said.

They cut down from the Boulevard to the Avenue, and Lommy led the way past the Lafayette Pharmacy, a cut-rate drugstore with an excellent business. Its window was about two feet deep with razor-blade packages, and the sign said: *From Manufacturer To You—Pk. of 5 Blades—1¢.* The packages had a checkerboard design, blue squares contrasting with white, and the name on the packages was *Bluebird Blades.* The Lafayette Pharmacy specialized in brands not widely known.

Tony followed Lommy around to the back, where there was a narrow alley. Lommy went straight to the treasure chest, which in this case happened to be five large trash cans. The trash cans were piled high with boxes and papers. Close by was a door with a depressing message from the Lafayette Pharmacy:

> *We Feature Acro Trusses*
> *Come In For An Expert Fitting*

"Sort through this stuff," Lommy directed. "You usually find a big bunch of envelopes all together."

Lommy went to work on one can, Tony on another. Tony didn't mind it at all. It was all clean stuff.

Tony went rapidly through the top layer, and then began working his way down into the can. But the lower you got, the more awkward it was, trying to sort through the papers, what with all that weight pressing on your arms from above. Tony noticed that Lommy, afflicted with the same trouble, had taken care of it by depositing a whole mess of stuff on the ground. So he copied Lommy, setting down whole armfuls of paper beside the can. He tried to make a neat pile, but of course some of the darn stuff spilled out sideways.

Tony didn't find any big bunch of envelopes all together, but he did find a few envelopes scattered here and there. He was in the process of tearing off the corner of an envelope that had a 2¢ red Washington when the door suddenly swung open.

"Hey, you kids get the hell out of here!" a voice called threateningly.

Tony did not stop to argue or even see who it was. He just ran. It was obvious to him the Lafayette Pharmacy had small regard for philatelists. And Lommy ran with him.

They pulled up a couple of blocks away.

"That's the first time anybody's ever bothered me there, no kidding," Lommy apologized.

"We sure are having lousy luck," Tony said, laughing.

They walked on the Avenue a ways. Then Tony had an idea. "Let's go up on the tracks," he suggested.

"Okay."

They immediately cut back to the Boulevard and kept going west until they came to the lonely and deserted Old County Road. There were no houses here. The railroad tracks ran right along by Old County Road, but no car would ever bump a train. The tracks were on a raised level, quite a bit higher than the road. To get on the tracks a car would have to jump the curbing of the sidewalk and climb a concrete wall seven feet high. So far no Gaw automobile had done it, although two or three had tried.

Lommy ran and jumped at the wall, but he didn't even come close to getting up it. He tried several more times. Once he got both his hands on the top, but there was nothing there for his fingers to grasp and so he just hung there until he tired and his hands slipped off.

"Whew," Lommy puffed.

Tony was watching him with amusement. He knew from experience that it was impossible for one guy alone to climb this wall.

Lommy stood close to the wall. He interlocked his fingers into a stirrup. "Here, I'll hoist you up," he said to Tony. "Then you can pull me up."

Lommy had showed him where to get the stamps, now it was his turn to show Lommy something. "You don't have to get up that way," he said. "There's an easier way."

"How?" Lommy demanded, mystified.

"Just keep walking—it's a little bit further."

Tony knew every foot of the way along here; he knew every crack in that concrete wall. He should. He had been walking home from school along this road for the past three years. It was quite a shortcut, as compared to going home by the Boulevard.

In a moment they were at his secret spot. It was a tree. It grew innocently not by the wall but by the curb. Without a word Tony bearhugged the trunk and started shinnying up. He thrust one leg over the low branch and pulled and squirmed himself up into a sitting position on the branch. Then he stood and climbed higher into the tree, moving from branch to branch. There was one branch, a good strong branch, and it grew straight out towards the wall. Tony tightroped this branch, running his hands along a skinny branch overhead to keep his balance. He was crossing the sidewalk in the air, so to speak. Whenever he did this, he always imagined himself unseen in this tree waiting for the Sheriff of Nottingham to ride by underneath and he would jump on him, as he had seen Robin Hood do in a movie. This strong branch was higher than the wall by about three feet. He went past the top of the wall, still tightroping along. When it was safe, he bid the tree good-bye and dropped down on the cinders. He stepped back to the edge of the wall to wait for Lommy.

Tony looked down at the sidewalk and at the road. He liked being up here. It gave him a safe feeling. Nobody could get at him. All his enemies were down there, running after him or trying to run him over in their car, and he was up here.

Lommy took a mighty leap off the branch, though there was no need for it and he could have as easily just hopped down, and he lost his balance and fell forward, scraping his hand on the cinders.

"Goddamn son-of-a-bitching cinders!" he swore with feeling, rubbing his hand. "Why don't they put sand on these tracks instead of cinders?"

They started walking across the tracks.

"What do you think of my tree, Lommy?" Tony asked. "Pretty good, huh?"

"Yuh, darn good," Lommy answered. "A thing like that is good to know."

"That's right," Tony agreed. "You never know when a cop or somebody might be chasing you."

"I'm gonna remember where it is," Lommy vowed. "How come you know about it?"

"Oh, heck, me and a guy named Eddie Cormier come by here every day from school. I could climb that tree with my eyes closed."

"Gee, you're lucky." Lommy said. "There's nothing like this near my school."

There were four separate tracks, each with its own raised roadbed of gravel. Tony and Lommy crossed these tracks like rollie coasters, going up and over, up and over. But when they got on top of the last one, the track that Tony in his own mind always called Track Four, they made themselves at home. They walked along this track, Tony trying to step on every tie, and Lommy trying to tightrope one of the rails but always falling off.

Tony liked this track best of all. It was the safest. If something was coming up ahead, all you had to do was dive off the track onto the adjoining grassy embankment and you were safe. But when you were out on one of the middle tracks, it was a long way to the side. In your hurry you could easily slip and fall in the loose gravel. You didn't have much time, and especially if it was a passenger train. Man, those passenger trains really shot through here. Sure, they whistled, but how much good did that do? The tracks curved, so you couldn't see the train and consequently couldn't tell which of the four tracks it was coming on. You could maybe jump from Track Three onto Two, but it might be coming on Two. And that train moved fast, it was right behind that whistle. The whistle—and then, quicker than you could move— *wssshhh*—the train!

Once he got caught out there in the middle. He heard that old whistle and he panicked. He didn't think he had time enough to make it to the side. He was on Track Three and the whistle sounded like it was com-

65

ing from either Three or Four, so he jumped toward Two. He landed on the neutral ground between Two and Three, in that black valley of cinders that ran between the two roadbeds. And in that moment he looked up and the train was bearing down on him. It was coming on Track Two. He wasn't on the track, he knew that, and yet his heart went *boom—boom* like it was going to explode. This is the end, he thought. Tons of metal hurtled at him in a frenzied roar, and even the mighty earth shuddered. A powerful blast of air tugged at him and tried to suck him under the fearsome wheels, but he dug his feet into the cinders and leaned backwards. And the passengers, so close, close to him, passed in a blur.

That was it for him. No more middle tracks. On that day he became strictly a Track Four man and had so remained. Also, another thing about this track. The cops would give you holy hell if they caught you on the tracks, and Track Four was far enough over so that you were not visible to anyone on Old County Road, whether it was a lone cop swinging his billy club or a police car cruising around looking for somebody to give hell to. On Track Four you could walk in peace and security.

"I wish a train'd come by," Tony said to Lommy. "I'd show you something."

"What?" Lommy asked.

"I'd show you how to hear a train even after it's far away. You know how?"

"No. How?"

"Easy. After it goes by you put your head down on one of the rails and you can hear the wheels clicking for a long time."

"I'll have to try that," Lommy said. "To tell you the truth, I've never been up here much."

The embankment beside the track gave way to flat ground where a spur provided backdoor service to a group of ramshackle warehouses and two yellow-brick buildings. The warehouses with their wide sagging roofs were no longer in use and were gradually falling apart, board by board. The two brick buildings stood close together and they both were very grimy, receiving as they did the promiscuous belching of any passing train. One of these two brick buildings, in addition, had broken glass, rusty tin cans, and old tires scattered all over its back area. This building had been empty ever since Tony could remember. But the other building was still in business and, in fact, was going strong.

There were people working in there even now, and five o'clock, the hour when most working places close, had long since come and gone. This building was Danby's Brewery.

A most peculiar smell, not exactly distasteful and yet not pleasant either, came out to them from the brewery. Tony sniffed it and wrinkled his nose. Danby's Brewery always had this smell. Ma made a certain dish with *favas*, the Portuguese beans, and when that dish was cooking on the stove the whole house smelled something like this brewery smell, sort of a strong and bitter smell. Except that Ma's smelled worse.

Along with the smell there came from the brewery a fine spray. It was a delicate spray, it didn't penetrate and soak your clothes like rain did. Yet it was definitely there, not visible but felt against the cheek— wet, cool, and mysterious. Tony opened his mouth wide and lapped at the air with his tongue and tried to drink it in. "Do you think if I did this long enough I'd get drunk?" he asked Lommy.

67

Lommy, instinctive connoisseur that he was, rolled some around on his tongue. He smacked his lips thoughtfully. Then he took a couple of swallows. "Tastes like just plain water to me," he pronounced.

"Every time I come by this brewery that spray hits me in the face," Tony said. "What do you think it comes from, Lommy?" He had often thought about this but he had never been able to figure it out.

"I don't know," Lommy said. "Maybe Old Man Danby is pissing into a fan."

There were two freight cars standing still on the spur. They were uncoupled but were not far apart. They were the kind of freight car that you looked down into. So Tony went to the first car and Lommy to the second and they climbed the iron ladder that was at the end of each car.

Tony's car was half-filled with big jagged chunks of shiny black coal. "There's coal in mine," he called out to Lommy. "What's in yours?"

"Nothin'," Lommy answered.

Tony pretended the car was moving and he hung onto the top rung of the ladder with one hand and stuck a leg out in the open air and leaned away from the car and rode along, facing the front, ever watch- ful for what was ahead, as he had seen the freight men do.

Tony and Lommy came down from their perches and cut across back to Track Four. They walked along. They went over the Locke Street Bridge; Tony's street was just one block away. The bridge was high up off the ground and automobiles passed underneath. It was scary crossing the bridge because you did not have the feel of solid ground under your feet. Sure, the ties were there, and ties were solidly in place, being supported by huge black-coated iron girders that ran the length of the bridge. But there was no gravel, no dirt, no ground between the ties. You looked down at your feet and you saw gaping space, and it was a long way down. What did it matter that the space between the ties was definitely not wide enough for a body to slip through? The space was there, you could see a long way down, and your imagination did the rest. Also, there was no safe embankment on the bridge, just tracks. You always kept thinking—Suppose a train comes now?

They went off the bridge and passed a green shed belonging to the Silk Mill. Nobody knew the real name of that mill. It had always been called just the Silk Mill in recognition of its unique place among all the cotton mills of Gaw. Beyond this shed Sharples Street ended. A high board fence barred passage from Sharples Street onto the tracks. But two adjoining boards of the fence had been worked loose from the bottom and all the kids slipped in and out easily. Going through this fence and across the tracks was a shortcut when you were going up to the Bostwick to play ball. Otherwise you had to go around, you had to go under the Locke Street Bridge and that took longer.

Tony stopped on the track.

"You know Olivio Costa from Lagoda Street?" he asked Lommy.

"Is that the guy who got his leg cut off?" Lommy said.

"Yuh, that's the guy."

"Well, I've heard of him but I can't really say that I know him."

"Well, I don't know him either—to talk to," Tony admitted. "But I know who he is, that's what I mean."

"To tell you the truth, I never even seen him," Lommy said.

"Oh, you must have seen him," Tony insisted. "He comes walking down the Avenue every Saturday night. You can't miss him because he limps. He kind of drags one leg, you know."

Lommy shook his head.

"He's kind of a fat guy," Tony added helpfully. "He always looks like he needs a shave."

Lommy snapped his fingers. "Say, does he wear one of those funny leather hats the airplane guys wear—it's got flappers for the ears?"

"Yuh, that's right!" Tony exclaimed. "That's the kind of hat he wears!"

"Oh, I've seen him then," Lommy said. "Jeez, he's an old guy. I thought he was younger."

"He's not so old—he's about fifteen."

"He looks at least twenty," Lommy said.

"That's because he shaves," Tony said. "He's only in the eighth grade at Cupp. He should really be in the ninth, see, but he stayed back a year on account of his leg."

Tony climbed the embankment which sloped rather precipitously down to the track. He was by the Sharples Street board fence. "I'll show you something," he called down to Lommy. He looked carefully at the two loose boards of the fence and tried to judge a certain distance from them. He moved sideways a little bit. Then he tapped the ground with his foot. "This is the exact spot he was standing. Right here, Lommy."

Lommy climbed up.

"No kidding?"

"Yuh."

"How do you know?"

"Oh, a guy he was with showed a guy on my street."

Tony looked thoughtfully at the track they had just vacated. "He was standing right here," he said. "He had his ice skates over his shoulder. He was going to go to King's Road Pond, see. And this freight train was going by, slow, see, and he was just standing here, waiting for it to pass, but this ground is hilly and it was all iced over, and all of a sudden his feet slip and he can't stop, he goes sliding down the hill—right under the wheels."

"Jesus," Lommy breathed in horror.

"Yuh," Tony agreed.

Tony had seen those freight wheels. He shuddered at the scene his mind was painting for him, the severed limb, the screaming boy. "I'll bet there was a lot of blood," he said.

Lommy looked sick, really sick. "Don't tell me no more about it. Please, Tony, I'm not kidding," he said.

"Sure, okay, Lommy," Tony said with sympathy. He was surprised and regretted his callousness to Lommy.

They climbed back down on the track and continued walking. Two blocks away from Sharples Street—just to show how illogical the City was—Dunmore Street ended and there was no board fence blocking

69

passage onto the tracks. Here anybody could get on the tracks.

And here the embankment was of a more gradual slope than it had been. At the top of the embankment sat an old man, the grandfather, and close beside him, a small boy of about six, his grandson. A few feet away was a goat tethered on a short rope that did not reach the tracks. When Tony and Lommy got close, the goat stopped eating the grass and, alert and poised, followed their every step with twitching ears. Gee, it acts just like a watchdog, Tony thought. The small boy looked at them solemnly, his eyes wide. But the old man, he had a scraggly gray beard, smiled and nodded politely. Lommy gave him a half bow and Tony said with friendliness—"How do you do?"

When had he ever come by here, Tony thought, when that goat wasn't around someplace? And usually with the old man. The old man was the mere wisp of a man, meatless, looking as if the first breeze would float him off. Yet his eyes contradicted his frailty. His eyes were strong, serene, and enduring. His was an old-world face, a face that had watched the plants turn brown under the sun in the season of drought. "In my village," Ma said once, "there is much time between feasts."

Here at the very limits of Dunmore Street, close to the tracks, all by itself in an otherwise vacant field, was a cottage. Its clapboards had once been youthful and gay in a coat of bright yellow paint, but the years had faded and discolored this paint and the sun had blistered and peeled it. The paint underneath the yellow, gray, showed through in many places. In the front yard of the cottage rested a tricycle with the front wheel missing. The window in the back bedroom had a pane of glass replaced by a piece of cardboard, a common-enough sight in Gaw. Indeed, certain tenement dwellers could in complete modesty undress with the shades up.

In this small house lived, it seemed to Tony, about two dozen people. He had at different times seen babies crawling around on the ground, boys his age, fellows of twenty with shoes shined, middle-aged people, and the old. There were brothers and sisters of assorted ages and he wondered, Was it possible that only one mother was in there producing babies? But the strangest thing about these people was this—whether they were young or old, whether they were male or female—they all looked alike. It was like twenty-four twins. They all were dark-skinned. They had coal-black hair, which the girls wore long. And they had as their trademark, young or old of either sex, a nose of such magnificence that it dwarfed the rest of their face into insignificance. Dark and with this scimitared prow of a nose, they were surely a strange-looking race. He had never seen anybody like them before and so he had asked Ma what nationality they were. She knew of them, for they had lived in that cottage for many, many years.

"They are Assyrians," Ma said. "It is a people something like Arabs. But they are a people with much brains. They milk that goat and they don't have to buy milk from the stores."

"I wonder if it tastes like cow's milk," he said.

"What's the difference?" Ma snorted. "It's just as good for you. Milk is milk."

The old grandfather with the goat was of this family. Yet, oddly, he was the only one who didn't look like they did. He could have passed for a Greek. His children must have completely taken after his wife, Tony reasoned.

So here they were, the only Assyrians in the whole city of Gaw. Tony had to marvel at it. Think of crossing the ocean for thousands of miles and coming to live by some railroad tracks all by yourself with no one else from your own country to talk to. It must be like being exiled to a desert island. And he foresaw many difficulties here in their lonely migration. Who would the boys marry when they got old? They did look different, so would the girls of other nationalities be willing to marry them? And for the Assyrian girls, it would be still worse. They would grow up to be old maids.

They were a dark and strange people, these Assyrians, but he liked them. They minded their own business. They didn't cause anybody any trouble. They did not drink. And Ma was right, they were smart. One of their boys had graduated from high school, and Kenny Farnsworth's big brother said he was the smartest guy they ever had at high school. This boy was now studying at M.I.T., which was supposed to be the toughest school in the whole United States. Kenny Farnsworth's big brother said only geniuses could go there; he said the students were given so much studying to do they could only sleep four hours a night. And this Assyrian boy was there now at M.I.T., making good, and this fact pleased Tony very much. Whenever he heard of anyone from the North End making good, especially someone he sort of knew, it always made him feel proud. It was as if the success were his own.

Tony and Lommy left the Assyrians behind and came to the Merriwell Bros. Feed Company. On the spur by this company was a

71

single freight car, the kind with sliding doors in the middle. The doors happened to be wide open, so the two boys hopped aboard.

Tony immediately stretched out on the wooden floor and groaned with delight. "I feel like I've walked far enough for one night, don't you?" he said.

"Yuh, we'll go home after we leave here," Lommy said.

The freight car was empty, but Tony found beside him on the floor a clue as to what the load or part of the load had been. He picked it up and showed it to Lommy. It was a kernel of corn, bright and yellow and hard.

"That's for pigeons," Lommy stated authoritatively. "I know a guy who has pigeons. He feeds them whole corn like that one day and cracked corn the next. He alternates their diet, see."

"Boy, I'd like to have a couple of pigeons," Tony said, sitting up.

"Yuh," Lommy agreed. "Say, you know where I was this afternoon?"

"No, where?"

"I was washing dishes for my pop. And guess who comes in. The inspector. This guy is so sneaky he won't come in the front way; he's afraid we have a buzzer system to the kitchen, I guess. I'm in the back there, in the kitchen, and all of a sudden the back door opens and there he is. 'You sneaky old bastard,' I felt like saying, 'I'll bet you expected to catch me pissing on the dishes or something, huh?' Well, let me tell you about this guy. He carries a thermometer around with him, see, and whenever he sees some water, he whips this thermometer out and he takes its temperature. So there I was, washing dishes in the sink, and he sticks this thermometer in there for about two seconds, and he says to me, 'Too cold. Put some more hot in there.' I was ringing wet from the steam from that water. The sweat was rolling down my face, no kidding, and he tells me the water's too cold. So after he left I told my pop, I says, 'The next time that guy tells me the water's too cold, I'm gonna say, "Let's see you put your hand in it."'

"'Holy Jumping Jesus!' my pop says. 'That's all I need around here, a comedian for a son. Don't you know,' he says, 'that guy don't like jokes? Never talk back to him,' he says. 'Whatever he says, that's it. If he says it needs more hot, give it more hot.'

"'Who's gonna buy the new skin for my hands?' I says.

"'Well,' my pop says, 'you don't have to stick your hands in it. Run some hot in there, and then go do something else. Come up front and get some more dishes. Stall around, use your head. In a few minutes he'll be gone. What the hell, use your head,' he says. 'He's inspecting, he's gotta say something, but it don't mean anything. That thermometer of his probably got stuck. But just don't get him mad, that's all.'"

"What happens if he gets mad?" Tony asked.

"What happens?" Lommy said with feeling. "He closes you down, that's what happens. That's why my father is afraid of him. He can close us down any time. All he has to do is put a little sign in the window— *Closed. By Order of the Board of Health*—and that's it, brother. After two weeks you open up again and by then all your customers have got into the habit of going someplace else to eat."

"Boy, he has a lot of power over you then, doesn't he?" Tony said.

Lommy nodded. "That's why my father gets nervous when he's around."

"What's the name of your father's place?" Tony asked.

"Ducky's Lunch," Lommy said with quiet pride.

"Ducky's Lunch! No kidding! Gee, I've gone by there plenty of times. It's right by Channing Street, isn't it?"

"That's right."

"Sure, I know that place. How come I never saw you there?"

"I don't know. I'm around there plenty, I know that."

"It must be close to where you live, because you told me you lived on Channing."

"I didn't say I lived on Channing. I said *near* Channing. We live right on the Avenue, over the restaurant. There's two tenements over it, and we got the bottom one."

"That makes it handy for your father, huh?"

"Yuh, it does. It takes him thirty seconds to get from his house to work. That's the way to save time. Not like these guys, they live in the North End and they go to work in the South End. And the people who live in the South End, they work in the North End."

"So you kinda help your father around the place, huh?"

"Yuh, I wash dishes. Sometimes I sweep the floor. Stuff like that."

"How about drying the dishes?"

"Naw. You don't dry dishes in the restaurant business," Lommy informed him. "You just put them on a rack and they dry themselves.

The air dries them. The air is cleaner than any rag could be, right?"

"Yes, I suppose so. I never thought of it that way. I should tell my mother. She dries them with a dishrag."

"All the housewives do," Lommy said, "even my own mother. You can't tell a woman anything about the kitchen."

Tony laughed, sensing in Lommy's pessimistic statement the admitted defeat of the L'Hommedieu men in their attempt to make changes in the dish-wiping habits of their womenfolk.

"Where does your father work?" Lommy asked.

"He died when I was just a kid," Tony said.

"Gee, that's too bad, Tony," Lommy said with genuine sympathy.

74

"He used to work right there," Tony said, and he pointed out the open door. "That was the last place he ever worked at."

Tony was pointing across the tracks. Across the tracks and across the road was the Bostwick Mill. It was an immense structure, not tall, only three stories high, but stretching indefinitely. It dominated the entire area, Bostwick Field where the kids played ball, Bostwick Hill where they slid in the wintertime, and Bostwick Woods where they went blueberrying. It had even usurped the name of the road; this part of Old County Road had become known as Bostwick Road. But kids generally did not bother with particularization. "Let's go up the Bostwick," they said simply, and that covered the whole area.

In the growing darkness the mill was enshrouded in shadows. Once hundreds of people had worked there and at night the windows had been ablaze with light. But now, the windows were dark. There were no people there. There was no machinery there; it had been moved to a Southern plant. The mill was empty. A quiet, empty mill is a melancholy sight, and when there is added to this the silence of a lost father, then the stillness twists inside you in unanswered pain. Tony stared at the mill with an unuttered cry of loss and desolation.

Neither boy said anything for a while, and then Lommy spoke.

"I'd like to ask your advice about something," he said.

"Sure, go ahead. Shoot," Tony said.

"Well, it's kinda personal," Lommy said.

Tony didn't say anything.

"You won't tell anybody?" Lommy seemed a little bit nervous.

"No, I won't tell anybody," Tony said, trying to reassure him.

"Well, I love this girl in my room—" Lommy said and paused.

Tony waited.

Lommy breathed out heavily. "Whew, if anybody from my room ever found out, I'd sure be in a fix," he said.

"Well, they won't find out from me," Tony maintained. "I tell you what, don't tell me her name. That way I can't possibly tell on you, right?"

Lommy was stung by Tony's proposal.

"No, I'm gonna tell you her name. I trust you, Tony. You're my friend," he said. "Her name is Yvonne Garnier."

"That's a pretty name," Tony said loyally.

"It's a beautiful name," Lommy said quietly, not even aware he had corrected Tony. "And she's a beautiful girl. When I look at her, Tony, I—gee—" In place of words he shook his head in wonder. "Boy, I got it bad," he concluded.

75

"Yes, I can see that," Tony said.

"Tony," Lommy said briskly, thinking of something, "you know this guy on the radio, he comes on every Sunday afternoon, he sings songs—darn it, I forgot his name," and Lommy screwed up his brow trying to remember. "Oh, you know who I mean," he said impatiently, "he comes on right after *The Shadow*."

"Oh yuh, I think I do," Tony said guardedly. He didn't want Lommy to find out he didn't have a radio.

But apparently his identification had not been positive enough to suit Lommy.

"Oh, you know the guy," Lommy insisted. "He starts his program off this way—" and Lommy sang, with feeling even if not in the right key—

I come to you
on wings of song,
tra-la-la-la.
And then he hums.

"Oh, that guy!" Tony stated positively. "Yuh, I know him."

"Well, two Sundays ago I was listening to him," Lommy continued, "and it was really something. He starts singing a song about her, can you imagine? Honest. The name of the song was 'Yvonne' and I'm telling you the truth, that song was written about Yvonne Garnier.

Every line fit. I got paralyzed, because I had been sitting there thinking about her, and all of a sudden he says, 'Yvonne,' and I didn't know there was any such song out. Oooh," Lommy groaned, "it's a beautiful song." He started singing again.

> *Yvonne,*
> *with your lovely face*
> *and your French grace,*
> *Yvonne—*

He broke off. "Shit, I can't sing," he said despairingly. "The teacher always puts me with the frogs. But I been dreaming ever since I heard it that I could sing like he can and I'd sing it to her. Jeez, it's a beautiful song though. I wish I had all the words to it. Do you think if I sent in they would send me the words?"

"They might."

"You don't know the song, huh?"

"No, I don't . . . I must have missed that program."

"Boy, I love that girl. You know how it is when you dream about a girl. You dream about kissing her and feeling her up, right?"

"Right."

"Well, when I dream about Yvonne, I never feel her up. I don't even kiss her. Oh, I might get one kiss from her, you know, like a goodnight kiss, but that's all. In fact, if a girl came up to me and said, 'Lommy, come on with me. I'll give you all the kisses and all the feels you want,' and Yvonne was there and she said, 'Come on with me. I won't give you a single kiss or anything. I'll just let you walk with me'—I'd go with Yvonne. That's how much I love her."

Tony nodded understandingly.

"Now this is the part I wanna ask your advice about," Lommy said. "I wanna ask her for a date."

"Yuh—" Tony waited, encouraging him to go on.

"Well, that's it. I never asked a girl for a date in my life. I don't know how to go about it."

"Well, I never asked one either," Tony admitted.

"Yuh, but you're smart. You'd know how."

Tony relaxed in the melting warmth. He knew the sudden, joyous wisdom that comes from someone else's confidence in you.

"How would you go about it if you was me?" Lommy asked.

"Well, if it was me—I'd wait for her after school."

"That's no good," Lommy said. "Everybody'd see me."

"No, not the way I'd do it," Tony said. "I'd let her get ahead of me, see. I'd follow her for about two or three blocks, till I got away from school—and then I'd catch up."

"That's good, that's good"—Lommy nodded, complimenting Tony on his cleverness. "So what do you say then after you catch up—'How about a date, Yvonne?'"

"No, no," Tony said quickly, his sense of timing outraged by Lommy's haste. "You don't ask her right off the bat like that. First you want to make a good impression, see. So when you first go up to her, say something like this—'May I walk with you?'" Tony reflected and shook his head. "No, that sounds too polite. She might think you're a sissy. Say—'Do you mind if I walk with you?'"

"That's really good!" Lommy said happily. "'Do you mind if I walk with you?'"

"That's right." Tony nodded encouragement like a dramatics coach.

And now the spotlight was on Lommy at stage center and he spoke with the throbbing sincerity ordinarily reserved for bewigged actors playing the Valley Forge scene.

"'Yvonne, do you mind if I walk with you?' 'Do you mind if I walk with you, Yvonne?'"

"I like the one with Yvonne first," Tony said. "'Yvonne, do you mind. . . ?'"

"Me, too," Lommy said. "Now what do I say after that?"

"Well, maybe she'll say, 'Yes, I do mind," and you won't have to say anything," Tony said puckishly.

But this was no joking matter to Lommy. "She won't say that," he said seriously.

His certainty intrigued Tony. "How do you know?"

"I know," Lommy said, as if he had some information that Tony didn't have.

"Well, just talk about anything," Tony said, getting back to the point. "Your teacher or something that happened in school that day, anything like that. Then after a while you say, 'You know, Yvonne, I like you a lot. Would you care to have a date with me?'"

Lommy put his hand to his head. "Shit, it won't work!" he cried despairingly.

"Why not?" Tony countered defensively, taken aback by such pessimism. His knowledge of how to go about these matters was based on imagination, not experience, and nothing wilts imagination faster than disbelief.

"I ain't got the nerve to talk to her!" Lommy confessed.

They were both silent for a moment, and then Tony said, "You could write her a note. That way you wouldn't have to talk to her."

"Jesus, that's it! That's it!" Lommy said. "Tony, I knew you were smart and you didn't disappoint me. I'll write her a note and I'll hang around the room after school like those kiss-asses do and I'll just walk by her desk, and accidentally bump it, you know, and I'll slip the note in. Tony, you're a genius, no shit."

Tony smiled happily.

"What would you say on the note?" Lommy continued.

Tony deliberated. "Well, I wouldn't just ask her for a date because if she said yes, you still wouldn't have it all fixed up. I'd name some definite place and ask her if she can meet you there."

"How would you word it?"

"Well, first of all, what do you plan on doing on this date?"

"Oh, just take a walk," Lommy said. "I tell you, this walk with you gave me a real good idea. I didn't know where to take her, but now I'd like to bring her up here on these tracks. We could walk along and then we could stop and rest in a freight car like this. We could sit here talking, just her and me. Boy! But you know, if I had her here in this freight car, just the two of us, all alone, she might get the idea I brought her here just to try some funny stuff. But honest to God, all I wanna do is talk to her and be with her, so help me. Do you think she'd be scared? Do you think she'd think I was one of those kind of guys?"

"No, I don't think so," Tony reassured him. "If she didn't trust you, she probably wouldn't come in the first place."

Lommy nodded. "I could tell her in the note—*Meet me under the Locke Street Bridge.* What time do you think?"

"Well, it gets dark pretty quick, so you wouldn't want to make it too late. How about six-thirty?"

"Yuh, six-thirty would be good. She must eat about five. Finish at five-thirty. That would give her an hour to get there. I'll be there at three-thirty," Lommy half-joked, and then he turned his attention to the language of love. "How would you word it in the note?" he said. "Make it sound real nice."

"Well, you could say it something like this—" Tony cleared his throat and Lommy listened attentively—

> Dear Yvonne,
> I have been dreaming about you
> for a long time. Can you meet me
> under the Locke Street Bridge
> tonight at six-thirty?
> (Signed) Lommy L'Hommedieu

79

"No, I don't wanna sign it with my name," Lommy said. "Somebody else might open her desk and grab it."

"Well, okay, how about signing it this way—*Someone Who Loves You*?"

"That's good. How about—*Someone Who Has Loved You Since The First Day Of School*?"

"Yuh, that's fine," Tony said. "I just thought of something though. If you don't sign it with your name, how is she going to know it's you?"

"She'll know it's me," Lommy said confidently.

"How?"

"She'll know," Lommy said mysteriously.

"Do you think she likes you?" Tony asked

This was a most important and delicate question, but Lommy did not hesitate. "I know she does!" he cried triumphantly. "Look—I'll tell you something that happened last week and you decide for yourself. Miss Blundy picked me to pass out the paper and every dame in that class was saying to me, 'C'mon, Fatso,'" or C'mon, slowpoke,' or 'Gimme two sheets,' and stuff like that. But when I came to Yvonne's desk, and boy, was I nervous, I looked at her but she wouldn't look up. She wouldn't take her eyes off her desk, and boy, was she blushing! Now tell me—what would she blush for if she didn't like me?!"

It was irrefutable logic.

"There's only one thing that could stop me from getting this date," Lommy stated darkly.

"What's that?"

"Her old lady. Her old lady might not let her go out nights. I kinda have that feeling, that she's strict, you know. I seen her once. She talks fast."

"Maybe Yvonne can skip out anyway," Tony put in optimistically.

"Yuh," Lommy said halfheartedly.

"Do they call you Fatso at school?"

"No. A couple of dames do, just for a joke. I'm not fat."

"No, you're not. That's why I wondered." He was just plump.

"You know, Tony, I like talking to you about Yvonne," Lommy said in compliment. "Do you know you're the first person I ever told I love her? I like telling somebody about her. Before, it was all bottled up inside me, you know what I mean?"

"Yes," Tony said.

They were both sitting with their backs up against the side of the boxcar.

"Say, would you like a cigarette, Tony?" Lommy asked.

"Yuh, I sure would!" Tony said enthusiastically. A real cigarette was a treat. All he ever got to smoke was corn hair in the summertime.

Lommy unzipped his handsome navy-blue jacket and reached inside his shirt pocket. He brought forth a pack of cigarettes. He tapped the pack on the side of his hand with a studied casualness. The heads of two or three cigarettes popped out invitingly. He extended the pack to Tony.

"Thanks!" Tony said, as he extracted one. "What kind are they?"

"Wings," Lommy said.

"That's a good kind," Tony said.

"My favorite kind are Old Golds and Wings," Lommy stated matter-of-factly.

Tony waited for Lommy to put the cigarettes away and to bring out the matches. It turned out that Lommy didn't have a book of matches. He had instead the long wooden single kind. Lommy scraped one across the floor of the boxcar and held the blaze of sudden light for Tony. Tony, and then Lommy, lit their cigarettes from this same match. Then Lommy blew the match out.

Tony sat back and inhaled with much pleasure. Of course, he didn't really inhale, that is, make the smoke go in his lungs. He didn't know how. He just inhaled the smoke into his mouth, held it there a moment, and then blew it out. There was one guy at school, a Greek, who could inhale into his lungs, talk unconcernedly for several sentences, and then blow out the smoke in a sharp stream. But very few guys could do that.

"Where'd you get them?" Tony asked.

"I got them this afternoon. I was sweeping up in the front by the counter and I found them on the floor. They musta dropped out of some guy's pocket. So I just kept them."

This posed an interesting question in ethics to Tony.

"Suppose you had found some money, would you have kept that, too?"

"Oh, no!" Lommy said, shocked. "I'd give that to my father. See, with cigarettes, it's different. My father don't smoke, he'd only give them free to some guy who walked in. So what the heck, why shouldn't I enjoy them, instead of some perfect stranger to my family?"

"That's right," Tony said. He agreed with Lommy.

Gee, he liked Lommy. You could relax with Lommy, something you could never do with the gang. You had to be permanently on your guard with them. They were always pushing or punching, or thinking up something mean to do to somebody. And he trusted Lommy. He felt he could tell him personal things, just like Lommy had told him. But there wasn't a single guy in the gang he could trust. He had tried them all out, told them things, secrets, how he felt about this or that. And every time there was a quick and vicious betrayal. The boy he confided in would wait until all the gang was there and then taunt him with his secrets while the whole gang howled with enjoyment. That evening a full measure of scorn and ridicule would be lavished upon him. The awful truth was, he thought sadly, that despite years of knowing the guys in the gang, he didn't have a single real friend among them. This boy here, sitting with him, was more of a friend to him after one day than any of them had ever been. When he was with them, he felt separate. But when he was with Lommy, he felt he was with Lommy— they were together.

Tony leaned back in contentment and peace. He took a big puff on the cigarette and blew the smoke out with quiet satisfaction. This was nice.

CHAPTER 3

CHOOMS

The date with Yvonne did not materialize. Lommy lost his nerve, even for a note. And during that week at the Y, Tony failed to learn how to swim. However, it should be added in fairness that this was not the fault of the instructor, who was a most competent teacher.

It might seem, therefore, with so much lack of success that the week was a failure and a total loss for both boys. Actually it was not, for they both ended the week richer than they had begun it. They each had a friend now. They were pals. And who knows? Perhaps having a friend is as valuable as learning how to swim—although such a sentiment might not be accepted by the safety-minded.

In reference to a gang, Lommy was in somewhat the same position as Tony. Lommy did not live on a street. He lived on the Avenue and there were no gangs on the Avenue. But he had gone around the corner and joined the Channing Street gang. Channing Street was a pretty rough neighborhood, much worse than Tony's street. The Channing Street gang was mostly Greeks and Polocks. They stole things and they were always fighting—in earnest, not make-believe—among themselves and with guys from other gangs. These latter fights were challenges; they did not involve whole gangs, but pitted just one guy against one guy. The rest of the guys would watch. Lommy did not care much for the Channing Street bunch. He was ready to spend his time elsewhere. And three blocks away, Tony was in a similar state. The two boys held the same denominator in common—separateness. So they came together.

But this was not a conscious choice on their part. It was spontaneous and unplanned. At first Tony saw Lommy only occasionally. Then, progressively, he saw Lommy more and more—and the gang less and less. Now when he was in his house and grew lonely, it was not to the corner that he strolled to sit by the billboard or on the curbstone. Instead he walked into the narrow alley behind Ducky's Lunch and called, "Lommy! Lommy!"

It was on one of these trips into the alley that Tony realized what had happened—he was no longer dependent on the gang. He could exist without them and was in fact doing that very thing. This knowledge did not, strangely, fill him with exultation. He had always had high hopes of friendship and fun with the fellows in the gang. Even after a bad night he always came back the next night optimistic and hopeful. He had dreamt of happy games and a street team in sports and things like that. And now he had given up. He had deserted the gang. And he sensed what his desertion meant—the end of hope and the acceptance of defeat. This was a hard truth to face; it didn't make you feel happy.

So Tony and Lommy were pals. And people noticed. Mrs. Miffin, the old white-haired English lady who lived all by herself on the first floor of Tony's house, noticed. She seemed to enjoy the sight of the two boys always venturing off to unspoken destinations. At least, she always smiled in a special way when she saw them together. It was as if she understood what they were up to. They went and they came back. And when they came back, Mrs. Miffin and Ma were sitting in chairs on the front piazza. "Aye"—Mrs. Miffin turned to Ma with a laugh. That was her word for yes. "Aye, 'ere cooms thee chooms." Here comes the chums.

Chooms. It was a strange word on his ears. Not just the pronunciation, but the word itself. Nobody used that word around here. It was a word from another time and place. Mrs. Miffin had an old and tired face but when she said, "Chooms," for a brief moment her face had life and sparkle. When she said it, he got a prickly feeling that Mrs. Miffin was not an old lady in Gaw in 1936 but was a pretty young girl in England in 1880 and she was remembering the boys. Could she once have been as young as he? It was a thought to shake up any young lad. And then the corollary, even worse—Would he someday be as old as she?

So they were chooms. And they were always going to one another's house to call the occupant out. In the back of Ducky's Lunch Tony called. And Lommy would open the window upstairs and stick his head out and say, "I'll be right out." Generally he was available right then for an immediate excursion. But should he happen to be working downstairs in his father's kitchen, then generally he could come out only for a couple of minutes. He would open the kitchen door and walk down the half-dozen wooden steps and there on the bottom step, sitting and stretching out, coated with grease and smelling of old French fries, he would make some hasty arrangements for the future with Tony

Ducky's Lunch was located on the Avenue, five stores over from the corner of Channing. It was a crummy district, although Tony of course would never have told Lommy he thought that. Yet even though it was a crummy district, Tony liked it. It was more interesting than his street by far. It was an active, moving world, ever-happening, ever-charged, ever-fascinating. He always walked by the stores here with a feeling of restrained excitement. He looked in every window, watching, watching, alert. You never knew when there would be an explosion.

One time he was walking behind this man. The man was Portuguese, small, about thirty, with thinning hair, and a rather meek and apologetic manner. He kept looking down at the sidewalk. He would take a quick look at a person's face and then drop his eyes. He walked with short, nervous steps, and every now and then he'd glance back over his shoulder. When he came to Kaznicki's Tavern on the corner, the man went in. But in about two seconds he shot out, his face contorted in terror, and soft little moans escaping his lips in his frantic haste to dodge around Tony, who was in his way. And there sprang out of Kaznicki's a hairy beast, also Portuguese, in a checkered lumberjack shirt, barrel-chested, and his face was contorted with rage. He made as if to give chase but then thought better of it. The meek man was halfway up the block and moving fast. The beast shook his hammer fist after him. "You foot-kisser!" he roared. He was a frightening picture of morality aroused. He stood there for a baleful moment and when the small Portuguese looked back, he shook his fist at him again. Then he went back into the tavern. The last Tony saw of the small Portuguese he was still moving fast. Gee, Tony thought, no wonder the guy had been so nervous before and had kept looking back over his shoulder—the whereabouts of that hairy bruiser had been on his mind. And the possibilities in this unresolved drama were so intriguing that a person could spend days thinking about the incident. Tony took the foot-kissing accusation literally, for it was too original an epithet to be taken lightly. He wondered: Did it involve the wife of the hairy man? Did it involve the brother of the hairy man? What exactly had happened?

85

Another time coming around the corner onto the Avenue he almost collided with a bum. The bum was wearing white tennis sneakers with his toes sticking out the sides, a pair of yellow corduroy pants held up by a belt of twine, an olive-drab CCC shirt too small for him, and a brown suitcoat with a tear along the shoulder seam and a side pocket half-ripped off. His eyes were blue dots in a blood-red ocean. But though he was a bum, he was still trying to keep up appearances. He was clean-shaven, his hair was combed, and he was wearing a sparkling green tie. Thus, he was not the common variety of doorway bum who more or less lets himself go.

The bum was in a hurry. But he was out of condition, he could not run. Instead he took long steps and sort of glided along. Ordinarily you probably would not have looked at this bum twice. But to see him moving rapidly—or any other bum for that matter—was such a startling sight that a person stared. And Tony saw the probable cause of his hurry. He was holding a plucked chicken under his coat, trying to keep it out of sight, but his coat kept flapping open.

Sure enough, by the time Tony got on the Avenue who was it that came puffing along, a little rotund figure in white, with bloodstains down his front, but Omer the butcher? It seemed that as a means of catching the eye of passers-by, Omer had gone and stretched a wire outside along the entrance to his store and had hung chickens from the wire. The display had worked with the bum. It had caught his eye. He snatched one of the birds and hurried off. But though Omer's back had been turned, those chickens were tied to his pocketbook by an invisible string and the fleeing bird pulled him right out onto the sidewalk. Some people said he saw the wire bouncing after the snatch, and it was then that he put down the hamburger he was doctoring and dashed out. But those who knew Omer best said he didn't even look at the wire, he just turned around and ran out.

So it was that Omer hurried past Kaznicki's Tavern in hot pursuit. But Omer was such a picture of well-fed plumpness, so pink-cheeked, so round-bellied, so much like one of his own prize fat capons, that it seemed indecorous that he should be chasing some collapsing derelict of a human being for a paltry skinny two-pound fryer. One longed to yell at him, "For chrissakes, let him keep it and next time keep your chickens in the back where they belong."

Those were the kind of things that happened on the Avenue near Ducky's Lunch. It was a crummy but interesting district. The district, according to Tony's arbitrary calculations, started on the corner with Kaznicki's Tavern. This was the corner of Channing and the Avenue. There was nothing unusual about Kaznicki's. It was a typical working-man's tavern, a dark and dismal place. It was so dark in there you couldn't see who was inside without a flashlight. Not only from the street, but even after you were inside. It took a while for your eyes to get adjusted. Tony knew that, because he had gone in there once to deliver a message to Kaznicki, a powerfully-built Pole, from Lommy's father. And Tony had been disappointed. He had expected to see something wonderful in there and all he saw was two or three sullen men drinking beer in the gloom.

87

Next to Kaznicki's was a place with a fancy name, Poolarium, but it was just a poolroom. Up front was a glass display counter where a man sold cigarettes, cigars, candy, and soda pop. This rather small area was cut off from the back by a wooden wall that went the width of the store. In the center of this wall was a doorway, a doorless doorway. Instead of a door they had a curtain hanging down. This curtain was quite a gay ladylike thing, mad with flowers, bright with flowers, swirling with flowers, lusting drunkenly with flowers, a floral confrontation, a cheap negligee in a cheap hotel.

If you happened to be passing by when a fellow went in the back and pushed aside the curtain, you got a tantalizing glimpse into the world of indolence and pleasure. You saw the player standing there, raptly studying the position of the balls while he absent-mindedly rubbed chalk on the end of his stick, like a batter standing aside and rubbing dirt on his hands and watching the pitcher and thinking. And in the summertime when the front door was left open you heard the clicking of the balls behind the curtain. You heard the muffled dissiliency of the break on a far-off table. And nearer, the challenge, "I'm putting the number 12 ball in the side pocket," and the tapping on the pocket with the stick. The 12 ball lay behind a fence of balls. The pause. And then the shot. The cue ball sent against the side of the table, flicking off, spinning, catching the 8 ball by surprise, and the John Alden 8 ball making the contact, a gentle kiss, nudging the target ball into a sweet and sudden plop.

And along with the clicking you heard the cursing. There were curses of friendly encouragement, directed at the ball of course, and curses of triumph and curses of dismay. The lyrics were pretty much the same in all moods, though rhythm and accent might vary, much like our popular songs. The swearing of these unknown voices marked them as buffoons, clowns, average fellows, playing only to see who would pay for the game. The pool sharks never swore, not at the play. They played in silence and concentration. A play on the table did not provoke them, neither to Hallelujahs nor Damnations. Only if they should catch an opponent in an error as the latter marked up the balls, then they might venture an oath—quick, all-encompassing, joyless, and vicious. They were not playing pool for the fun of it. They had the day's earnings riding on this game.

So the sharks played without superfluous noise. You heard only ball meeting ball. But the touch was the sharks' own. They broke with crackling authority; they shattered the triangle into a spinning chaos of balls. And their subsequent shots were clean and crisp. They sent the cue ball crisscrossing along a precise path to crash the stated ball sharply into the pocket. There were no flubs or bouncies. No, they did not swear, not at the play. They did not inveigh against a spin. They did not proclaim and strut. They let the clowns do that. After all, is not the shark deadly enough without speeches? And when he bares his teeth in a grimace of friendship, he is at his most dangerous. When he leaves his fellows and approaches a meal, when he shows his teeth and sidles up to a meal, then it is dinnertime. He softly hums a lovesick melody while he sets the table. He masks his ferocious skill with a bad shot, and another. He permits his playmate latitude. He permits the balloon fish to swell up and then he rends him with one slash. In silence he feeds his merciless voracity.

How did Tony know this? He had never witnessed a shark feeding. He had never been inside the Poolarium. He did not need to. He knew it because three fellows had been leaning up against the window of Ducky's Lunch and as he and Lommy approached, Lommy had murmured sideways to him, "Take a look at the guy with the red bandanna. He's a shark." And in the fellow's confident slouch and narrow eyes Tony read the story of a thousand feedings on the green table.

Next to the Poolarium was a strange place. It was practically an empty store. There was one man in there, one chair, one desk, and that was all. The man sat at the desk with a telephone and a notebook. You'd think he'd get lonesome in there and have the desk swung around so that he'd be facing the street and could watch who was going by. But he had the desk sideways. You got a side view of him—except when he turned and looked at you. This man was all alone in there, morning, noon, and night, summer and winter. In the summer he opened the door for the fresh air. In the winter he didn't have any heating system. All he had was a little portable kerosene stove that he kept close by, almost touching his chair. He would twist around and warm his hands over the stove. This heat, plus the fact that he kept his overcoat on, made him able to stand the winter, but for sure it was cold in there because he breathed out steam.

89

This man dressed in black. You looked at him and right away you thought of a funeral. He had black shoes, black pants, black suitcoat, and a black hat. He never took this hat off his head. He sat there at the desk all day with it on. But the main thing about this man was his face. With his high cheekbones and the deep gouges that cut across his cheeks, he could have been Abraham Lincoln. But his fixed look of glazed impassivity, his bug eyes staring out without blinking, his lips carved and wordless, these marked him as a creature from another world.

One night Tony and Lommy were walking along the Avenue. They were looking down at the sidewalk as they walked, but just by accident they happened to look up when they passed this man's store. The only light in the place was a desk lamp, a bulb with a cupped metal shield over it. The light was pressed down so close to the surface of the desk that much of the store was in shadow. But above the light in gloomy repose they could see his spectacular head and they could feel his presence. A figure in black, sitting rigidly in his chair, staring at the wall. Just as a joke Tony turned to Lommy and said in a low voice, "There's Frankenstein's double."

The door was closed and the man could not possibly have heard him through that window, but Tony would have sworn he had. At his words the man immediately swung around in the chair and fixed him in a hypnotic stare, his eyes popping out of his head and lit up like a fiend's. Tony was glad Lommy was with him. If he had been alone, he probably would have run. And if he had been alone and the man had got up, he certainly would have run. That's how scary the guy looked.

But it was Lommy who finally gave the guy a name. Lommy had seen him get up from the desk once and walk, and he never ceased to delight in imitating that walk. According to Lommy, he walked like a mechanical man, stiffly, and going from side to side. So Lommy named him after a guy he had seen walk like that in the movies—the Zombie. And that's what they called him—between themselves.

He Answered the Call. That's what an ad writer would have said about him, for the Zombie was the dispatcher for Lefty's Cab Service. He was the link between passenger and cab. While others were sleeping he was at his post, watching over the silent city, alert, ever ready to speed a cab along darkened streets on its errand of mercy. He was helping keep

America strong and free through an improved communications system.

But even in the daytime there were calls.

A driver stuck his head in the door.

"Whatcha gut fawme, Lester?"

The Zombie pulled his heavy lips apart and in the bare store his words were hollow and echoing, as if spoken in a cave.

"202 Loring, third floor," the Zombie said. "They're taking an old man to Good Sam."

The full blessings of American civilization had not yet been conferred upon Gaw. In Gaw very few tenements had phones, a telegram meant bad news, and a taxi was used only for emergencies, like taking an old man to the hospital. In the America outside a busy mother puts her son in a cab and sends him off to his dancing lesson. But in Gaw, if you had someplace to go, you walked. Or, if you wanted to spend money to get there, you took a streetcar. That cost seven cents and that was enough.

Very few people in the North End owned a car. This was obvious when you walked down a street, for you would see a car parked at the curb only occasionally. Since the tenements had no garages and there were three families in the average tenement house, the curbing would have been jammed with parked vehicles if a car had been an article of common ownership.

Now this lack of automobile ownership acted to the advantage of Lefty's Cab Service. For there are certain times in a man's life when he needs an automobile—times when a streetcar just won't do. And that Lefty was well aware of this was made clear by a cardboard sign he had in the window:

Cars available for
Funerals Weddings Parties

Lefty got just about all of the North End funeral and wedding business. Well, it was easy to figure out why. His only competitor in the North End was Downtown Taxi, a snobbish concern that was trying to disguise its place of residence by a tricky name. And look at the Downtown cabs. Cheap Chevys, painted a bright green, with a huge yellow *25¢* covering the front door, and an advertisement for Danby's Beer on the trunk. There were a lot of vulgar fellows in the North End and if they ever saw the bride being driven through the streets in a car with a big *25¢* painted on the door, they would make all kinds of cracks about a two-bit this-and-that. No, for a wedding or a funeral, you wanted a car that reflected your good taste and judgment and for that you went to Lefty's. His whole fleet of cabs had dignity. They were Packards, old but running smoothly, big, roomy, comfortable cars, and painted a serene black. And they had no *25¢* on the door and no winking man with a sudsy glass of beer on the trunk. All they had was a small card stuck in a side window—simple black letters on a white background—*TAXI*. Take that card out and take the black peaked cap off the driver's head and you had a noncommercial vehicle.

And Lefty also had the advantage in the drivers. Both of his drivers, Prado and Gus, were men in their forties, family men, mature, portly, they weren't young kids who would race the motor. And the drivers for Downtown looked like something that had been left behind by the carnival, rawboned, small-eyed, and with sores on the mouth; they had the same face as in a magazine picture Lommy had of a mattoidal Texan grinning and pouring gasoline on a Negro's body. There was just no comparison between Prado and Gus and them.

Here they come! They have just left the church! Listen to those horns! All heads turn. Here comes the first car, the colored streamers playful in the breeze, the cans clacking on the street, the bridal couple baptized with rice and grinning out with happiness and embarrassment. The bride turns and chatters at the maid of honor, not knowing what she is saying, seeking only relief from the excitement. And there in the second car, it's Prado! And he is grinning happily, too. His car has all the parents, resplendent in unaccustomed dress, new clothes, new

91

shoes, yes, the parents anchored snugly in the vise of their new shoes and the fathers choking in their tight starched collars and the mothers encased in their corsets like mummies, their flesh doubled back upon itself, and everyone sitting stiffly on the edge of the seat in this strange mechanical beast, *o automóvel*, with both feet on the floor lest they lose their balance and fall off. But they are beaming happily all the same.

And now here's another procession. And Prado is here, too. And the children and the parents, too. Only they have changed places. Now the children ride in the second car, in Prado's car, and one of the parents rides up ahead in a long black car. The children are grieving, weeping, and they are bent over, holding white handkerchiefs to their faces, and Prado is somber. The long black car is like one of those hideous beetles that lie poised in the dark under the piazza, and a shudder passes through the twelve-year-old boy as he follows the car with his eyes. Though he is young a small voice says within him—Walk, brother, laugh, brother, eat, brother, but you too shall someday be the guest of honor, and all the king's horses and all the king's men shall not keep you from it.

In death the poor occupy the same interred volume as the rich and achieve the same silence. Thus, the poor at last find that common equality as declared by Our Forefathers—all men are destroyed equal. But it takes several cups of coffee at Ducky's to cheer Prado up. Do you think he is putting on an act when he drives so somberly? "I have to stay by the cab when we get to the cemetery. If I go in there and watch, I'll start bawling like a baby. It brings back memories for me." Prado is a true son of the Portuguese.

There was one word on that sign in Lefty's window that puzzled Tony—*Parties*. If you were having a party over at somebody's house, wouldn't everybody just walk there? Why would you need a taxi? He asked Lommy about it.

"Oh, these kind of parties are different," Lommy said. "These are drinking parties. You know on Saturday night all the bars close at twelve midnight, that's the State law, see. But just outside town, in North Bournemouth, there's a place called Snooky's and they stay open till two in the morning. So say these guys are drinking at the Square Deal Cafe on Saturday night and it gets to be a quarter to twelve. Okay, they know that in fifteen minutes they're gonna get kicked out on the street. So they phone up—'Send us a cab right away. There's eight of us here—we wanna go to Snooky's.' And just think of the dough—that's out of town so it's thirty-five cents. Eight guys, that's eight times thirty-five cents . . . well, you figure it out, it must be around five bucks."

"Well, no," Tony said, a little shocked at Lommy's arithmetic. "It's . . . uh . . . about two-eighty."

"Well, okay, two-eighty for one trip. And don't forget they're stranded out there. They don't have any way of getting home. So at two a.m. he goes out there and he brings them back—that's another two-eighty. Gus told my father they make more money between eleven and three Saturday night than they do all week, and it's all hauling guys out to Snooky's."

"Yuh, but there's just one thing," Tony said. "You said the State law says every place has to close at twelve o'clock. So how come this Snooky's stays open?"

93

Lommy smiled. "Well, you know the guy who's supposed to close them down—?"

"Yuh."

"Well, they just pay him some money."

"Oh!" Now he got it. So that's how they did it. There was an explanation for everything apparently. This was Tony's first lesson in practical politics, taught to him by a village police chief with a two-man force. Children can hardly be expected to know that the payoff is endemic in American history, as much a part of our inheritance as the Pioneer Spirit. The payoff, in fact, has been a freedom so freely indulged in by uncounted editors, ministers, judges, and legislators that one wonders why the Founding Fathers with their customary foresight did not include it in the Bill of Rights.

There was one other thing about Lefty's that set Tony to wondering. He had watched the Zombie speak into the phone and write down an address in his notebook. The Zombie held the pencil in his right hand. He had watched Prado and Gus drinking coffee at Ducky's each with his black peaked cap pushed back on his head. They carried the cup to their lips in their right hand. So the question suggested itself—Who was Lefty?

He asked Lommy. "Maybe Lefty was the guy who put up the money for the business," Lommy said. Maybe so. Tony never found out for sure. He spent much time waiting for Lefty, but he never did see him.

Lefty's Cab Service was the third store from the corner. Except for the Zombie, his desk, his chair, and his little stove, it was an empty store. But the store next to Lefty's, the fourth store from the corner, was really empty. There wasn't even a cigarette butt on the floor. This store had been vacant for years. The window on the right-hand side of the door had been broken and was now completely boarded up. But the window on the left-hand side was intact and up high on it were the trailing remains of small gold letters in their gravestone memento— *Szczych's Cleaners.* Despite knowing the cleaning business from A to Z, and despite encouragement from Washington because he was small business, Mr. Szczych had failed. When the mills closed down in Gaw, the people stopped keeping themselves so cleanly pressed. The people had no further need for Mr. Szczych's services because they had already been taken to the cleaners by an industrial system that victimized them at every turn.

The next store was home for Lommy—Ducky's Lunch. And on the window: *Complete Dinners—25¢.* There was a booth by each of the two front windows, but nobody ever sat in them. The customers sat at the counter, which was a horseshoe counter with its open end facing the kitchen. Lommy's father both cooked and served. He cooked things to order, like hamburgers, but most of his food he prepared beforehand when he wasn't busy, like soups and stews, and he left them on the stove in pots and then later when people started to come in for supper, all he had to do was warm up the pots and dip out a dipperful of whatever was chosen.

Lommy's father could generally be seen on a quiet afternoon sitting on a high stool inside the counter's circle, hunched over, his chin cupped in his hand, his elbow on the counter, chatting with his lone customer, reaching over and sliding the ketchup bottle to him.

Lommy's father had been a snappy dresser in his younger days, which was when he got his nickname. In the summertime he used to wear a dark blue coat, white flannel pants, and white shoes, and he kept the pants and shoes in absolute snow-white immaculateness. He became known as "the guy in the white ducks," a reference to his pants. This somehow shortened to Ducky, and the name stuck. But all that was gone now. He still wore white, yes, a white shirt and a white apron, but the shirt had lost its starched freshness the day before yesterday and too many pieces of stew had brushed up against the apron. When you added to that a two-day-old stubble of beard, he just did not look much like a sport any more.

He was of medium height, thin in contrast to his son's plumpness, and pale. He was quiet and thoughtful. He had the face of a man who accepts his lot in life but is not going to sing about it.

Excluding the noneating cup-of-coffee drinkers like Prado and Gus, Mr. L'Hommedieu's business was almost exclusively with single men. Married men ate at home with their wives and children. And as for whole families occasionally eating out, that was a custom that found no practitioners in the North End of Gaw. It was a question of money. If a father had been seen entering a restaurant with his wife and children, it would have been looked upon as an act of spectacular lunacy. Ma had the prevailing attitude on this matter. Ma had never been inside a restaurant in her life but she had looked through windows. She knew plenty about it. "The girl goes and gets you a spoon," Ma said, "but for her trip you pay. She gives you a napkin, nice, high-class, but for that napkin you pay. And the man cooks your food—do you think he does that free? And what about his rent, huh?" she demanded fiercely, as if the silent Tony were a cunning adversary. "Who pays for that, huh?" And if the expense factor were not enough, there was an added consideration for the fastidious. "Besides, who knows what they put in those dishes," she muttered darkly. "Rotten meat it could be and with much pepper you would not know."

So Mr. L'Hommedieu's business was with the old, with the young, but always with the men who lived alone. Many young men ate their evening meal regularly with him. These were often young men who had had trouble with their families, perhaps with the father, or the mother, or an older brother, or all three, and had been kicked out or had left, and were now living in a room someplace. Some of these fellows later made a complete break with their families and left town for good. Others could not or would not will that final severance; they lived six blocks away from their families in a state of suspended and stretched affection, mutually smoldering and spying.

But one group that ate at Ducky's Lunch was a world to itself. These individuals showed no symptoms of the disturbed and restless ego. They were not seeking a home. They were neither young nor old. They lounged about a good deal but they were not bums. Neither were they unemployed. Their work schedule might be haphazard and flexible, but

95

the work itself was intense and demanding. They were Greek gamblers.

Around suppertime, say a quarter after five, these Greeks began to gather in front of Ducky's. They greeted one another. "What's new, Leon?" "What's shaking, kid?" "What's the deal, Christo?" But in their mouths these harmless greetings became secret communications, charged with meaning. And they measured each stranger with hard, distrusting eyes. And then they swung Ducky's screen door open and passed inside.

By six o'clock they were through eating and they came back out, belching heartily and sucking on toothpicks, to line the front window. The more successful of them flashed diamond rings in the waning sunlight, the first time Tony had ever seen a fancy ring on a man. All of them, the jeweled and the jewelless, joined in sporting the gambler's pride—truly distinguished headwear. They wore enormous felt hats, dimpled on the sides, clean, well-blocked, soft-gray, expensive—hats with such towering crowns that in their short stature these Greeks appeared to be one-half body and one-half head. But at six o'clock they came out of Ducky's and they put one of their pointed shoes on the wooden shelf at the base of the window and they spat particles of food into the air and they looked on with amused contempt at the saps rushing by—going home to kids screaming and women's voices. It was a disgusting vision, and they turned to one of their confreres. "You wanna buy a camel-hair coat cheap, Constantine?"

The Greeks shot dice. At cards they were like Italians singing Wagner, an unfortunate combination. At pool they were barely tolerable. But at dice—ah, they were like Italians singing Puccini; it belonged to them. They didn't learn the game; they invented it. They were uncanny. They had skill, artistry, genius. They didn't need luck. Real winners don't need luck. Lommy's father said, "You know, when a Jewish baby is born they slip a violin in the cradle with him. But when a Greek baby is born—they give him a pair of dice."

Yes, they were dice men. "A guy who will get down on his knees and roll with a Greek is the type of guy who sticks his fingers in sockets to see if the electricity is on. I'd just as soon go to Boston and let an Irish alderman hold my money as shoot dice with them." That's what Lommy's father said.

But every now and then two or three of these Greeks would get their names in the paper, for though poverty was not against the law in Gaw, gambling was. Once about twenty fellows were arrested for "violation of the gaming law." These fellows were arrested, of all places, in the Powoc Arena, where they had been shooting dice, of all places, in the ring. With so large a group in so small an area, some of them had surely been on the ropes. But think of making your point in front of several thousand unoccupied seats. With a little imagination you could hear the clapping. And then they were dragged off. *Marko Kantharides, how do you plead? Not guilty, Your Honor. It was like this. I was standing in front of Ducky's Lunch when along comes this guy, an acquaintance of mine, and he says, Let's go downtown, Jean Harlow is playing at the Venice. So I says, Okay, and we're walking along and when we comes to the Arena, it was all dark, he says, I gotta go inside and give the house key to my brother Constantine. I'll wait on the corner for you, I says. No, you come with me, it won't take a minute, he says. So I goes with him and I'm no sooner in there than all the lights go on and everybody is running every which way and some cop is shoving me in a wagon. I was there about two minutes before I was arrested, and that's the truth, Your Honor.*

This was Lommy's world down here on the Avenue near Channing Street. There was a certain atmosphere down here. The bums staggering along, the quiet darkness in Kaznicki's, the clicking of the pool balls, the Zombie sitting there like a rock statue, Prado humming as he polished the windows of his Packard, the gold letters left behind by Szczych, the Greek gamblers leaning up against the window of Ducky's Lunch at six o'clock, the whirring of the big ceiling fan in Ducky's on a lazy summer afternoon. Certain faces, certain sounds, certain sights, they were all part of Lommy's everyday existence. And because Tony came down here so often to see Lommy, they became part of his existence, too.

Tony came down here and he called Lommy and he said, "Let's go," and they went. Where did they go? They went many places. What did they do? They did many things.

For one thing, they went camping. This actually was not Tony's idea of a real good time, but Lommy like to go, so Tony was agreeable. They did it this way. They started early in the afternoon because they had a long way to go. They always went to King's Woods, which was a considerable distance past Bostwick Woods. They went to King's Woods because they knew every foot in Bostwick Woods. King's Woods was bigger and stranger, you could get lost in there, and it was therefore more fun.

In a clearing in King's Woods they built a campfire and while they waited for it to get going good, they sat around and watched it and had a smoke. Tony provided the cigarettes. He opened a small yellow tin of Dill's Best Tobacco. Inside, compact, neatly rolled in newspaper, were corn-hair cigarettes. He got this corn hair by more or less poking around in garbage cans on the street, and people like *Senhor* Fragoza knew he smoked it and saved it for him. Ma knew he smoked it but she didn't mind. Every cigarette in that tin was choice. He used nothing but the dried brown and black hair. The yellow silky hair he threw away—it didn't burn good.

After their smoke, they got down to business. They searched among the bushes for a branch with a good fork on it and when they found such a branch they cut it off and trimmed it to a decent size. They cut two such branches. They had each brought from home one potato and now they secured the potato in the fork of their own branch and extended the branch over the fire. This was the part Tony didn't like. For he had to crouch close to the fire and the concentrated heat of the fire added to the general heat of a hot day made him sweat like a horse. And the smoke which kept blowing in his face irritated his eyes and throat. And his potato always fell off the fork into the fire and retrieving it presented all kinds of problems.

Afterwards, when they decided the potatoes were done, his potato didn't taste half as good as when Ma cooked it, to tell the truth. But of course Lommy kept saying, "Mine's perfect. How's yours?" and he had to say. "It's good. It's really good." Then they put the fire out—threw dirt on it, stamped on it, pissed on it—and then they went home. He didn't think much of it, but Lommy sure like to go camping.

What he like to do and what they did a lot of that summer was Pitching. He owned a baseball glove. To get it he had made just about the biggest trade of his life with a guy at school. He gave up for it 32 aggies, which he had won pooning—42 Indian cards, 28 different, which he had gotten by trading—153 match covers, all different, which he had collected by walking all over the North End and picking them up out of gutters—and 2 Big Little Books, which he had gotten by trading. But now he had this glove. It was an old glove and kind of small for his hand but he could still catch with it. And Lommy had a glove and a black taped-up baseball.

They went on Tony's street, up the far end by the Gaw Mill, where it was quiet, and they squared off. They got on opposite sides of the street, each on the sidewalk. They had a nice flat stone which they used as home plate and hid after each game.

"I'm Carl Hubbell. You be Dizzy Dean," Lommy called from across the street.

"No, I don't want to be Dizzy Dean," Tony said, shaking his head. "I'll be Ben Cantwell."

"Ben Cantwell!" Lommy cried. "What do you want to be him for? He stinks. He won 4—lost 25 last year."

"Yuh, playing for the Braves," Tony countered loyally. "If Hubbell had pitched for the Braves, he would've won 4 and lost 25, too." He liked Ben Cantwell for two reasons. First, he played for Boston. But more important, he had a real hero's name, an American name, like in a sports story. Ed Brandt, who also pitched for Boston, was a better pitcher, but he could never be a guy with a German name like that.

99

And Tony peered into the sun to catch the catcher's signal and rubbed his pitching hand dry along the side of his pants, and then wound up slowly, kicked, and gave the batter an overhand curve. That is, he held the ball like you were supposed to hold it for a curve, two fingers along the stitching where the stitching would be if the ball had a cover, but the ball acted just like it did for his screwball, which he threw with his knuckles, and for his drop, which he threw with a loose five-fingered grip. It went straight. "Strike one!" Lommy the Catcher and Umpire called. And their pitching duel was on. Three strikes and a man was out. Four balls and he was on base with a walk. Four walks and a run came in. Each time that the pitcher struck out three men, he trudged across the street and became the catcher, and the catcher went out to the mound. And every game lasted a full nine innings.

The game of Pitching required cool nerve. Think of having the bases loaded, three balls and no strikes on the batter, and being able to fire three consecutive pitches right over the middle of the plate. Tony had done it. That took control and pitching heart, yes. But you had to have an honest opponent for this game, an honest umpire, not a guy who would call strikes balls like that louse Jimmy Hedgeley. Lommy was square. The game was fun with him.

When they first began playing Pitching, their control was only so-so. They had games of 8-5 and 6-3. But after they had pitched a few games, their control got better and better. The scores dropped to 3-2 and 2-1. Once they even had a game go 0-0 for twelve innings and then in the thirteenth Lommy tired and Tony won out 2-0. They played intense, exciting games through many a summer afternoon. They pitched till they were dizzy and staggering in the sun.

But their Sundays were reserved for the Textile League. The game was scheduled to start at two o'clock, so they left for Bellehaven Park at about a quarter to one. They cut through the wooded area of the park. It was cool and shady in the woods. It was easy walking, because all the under-brush had been cleared out. The pine needles were slippery and fragrant under their feet. They watched the squirrels run up and down the big trees. Birds kept going, "Kaa-kaa-kaa." It was real nice in there, peaceful.

100

They came out by the high wire fence that enclosed the tennis courts. Every court was taken, and the players, in shorts, ran first to the right, then to the left, then forward, then backward, smacking the ball, *zing, zing, zing,* and when they missed it, they yelled, "Good shot!" Tony noticed that these people who played tennis all had good manners. They lived in the better homes that were down here just beyond the park, big houses with lawns, each house all by itself and just for one family.

A few feet past the tennis courts and brushing up against some shade trees was another enclosure. The four arms of this wire fence defined an area modest in size but sparkling in attractiveness. The fence preserved from casual feet a beautifully kept lawn. It was the bright green grass that you see in a magazine picture when they're advertising house paint and they show the house and front lawn. This lawn behind the fence was like a rectangular table and at each corner of the table was a group of Englishmen. They were in their Sunday clothes, their black shoes shined, but most of them had taken off their suit coats. You could see the wide suspenders, the pin-striped shirts, the colorful elastic bands that went around their arms like garters and held the sleeves back out of the way. They'd chat with one another and then they'd bend over and pick up a ball and roll it diagonally across the lawn to their oppo-site corner. The balls were black and were good-sized. And then they'd chat some more and pick up another ball and roll it. This game was called Bowling on the Green, and it was a very hard game to under-stand, because there were no pins to knock down. Tony had watched this game plenty of times and he couldn't make heads or tails of it. As far as he could make out, the object seemed to be to hit one another's balls. The balls were not picked up immediately after they had been rolled. They were allowed to remain on the grass in their natural cluster, and then one of the guys from across the way would send another ball right into the midst of these balls, hitting first this one and then that one. It was a crazy game and it sure took a lot of players, but the Englishmen liked it. This was their game; the players were almost exclusively English. They were mostly middle-aged and old guys. And with the balls rolling back and forth from corner to corner, crisscrossing, almost bumping in the middle, one man called, "Oh, Arthur, hang on it!" Now what did he mean by that?—Tony wondered.

Next the two boys came to an open grassy field with ropes down the sidelines to keep back the spectators. A game had already started and there was a good crowd present. There was no grandstand or bleachers, so everybody had to stand. It was soccer. The players had those heavy shoes, thick stockings that came up to just below the knees, shorts, and the colored jersey of their team. Boy, this was a rough one today. The players went crashing into one another like it was football, and then they turned and exchanged words. "Slug him, Teddy!" a spectator called. "He can't fight any better than he can play soccer!" and everybody laughed. Tony picked up the team names from the jerseys; the Athenians were playing the Pulaski Club. This wasn't the kind of soccer he liked to see. He didn't like to see that rough stuff, that didn't prove anything. Any big oaf could knock a man down. What he liked to see was skill, finesse. He like to see a tricky ballhandler go down the field, dribbling with his right foot and then, coming upon an opponent, deftly changing the ball to his left foot on the run, and flash right by the man. And he loved to see a player move the ball forward with a high bouncing pass off the top of his head—that was beautiful. But from the looks of these players you wouldn't see any of that today. They should take lessons from the Portuguese, he thought smugly. For this was one sport at which the Portuguese excelled. In this league, which was a very active league and had fourteen teams—all social and athletic clubs—a Portuguese team was always on top. Right now the Luso-American Civic Club was leading the league. And what about in the twenties when the champs of Gaw, the Ponta Delgadas, went out and played in the State Tournament, and won that, and then went out and played in the New England Playoffs, and won that, and came back to Gaw—champions of all of New England. Even now, almost ten years later, people still talked about the Ponta Delgadas. And it always made Tony feel proud to hear them, for the Ponta Delgadas were all Portuguese from the waterboy on up. Still though, it was funny, for even though the Portuguese did well at soccer and it therefore should have been his favorite sport, he did not much care for the game. It didn't get him like baseball. He felt no tension, no excitement watching soccer. But baseball—wow!

They walked on, past the wading pool filled with happily shrieking children while the mothers sat on the grass, watching, watching—"No, no, *no*, Johnny!" They walked on, past a crummy field, with holes in the infield, where the Intermediates were having a game. These were guys around sixteen, seventeen, and they had a regular league, but they didn't have any uniforms, just two or three bats, and they used old balls. Nobody was watching them.

They came in sight of the big grandstand. They were behind it. When Tony saw how many people were gathered by the ice-cream counter built into the back of the grandstand, he felt the need to hasten. He wanted to get a good spot. "Come on!" he urged Lommy. "Before it fills up."

They took giant steps and marched around to the front of the grandstand. They were not interested in the grandstand. That was for old people who tired quickly and had to sit. They wanted to get close to the action. A thick rope was stretched along the third-base side and another along the first-base side. The ropes were a few feet off the playing area and ran parallel with the base and foul lines, going all the way out into left and right field. The first-base side was no good. Later on in the afternoon the sun would be in their eyes on that side. So they made directly for the third-base rope. The front rank was filling up fast, but they just did manage to squeeze in. Tony gripped the rope with pleased anticipation. It was perfect. They had a clear, unobstructed view of the play. But they had come just in the nick of time, for in a few minutes there were people standing behind them.

They were alongside the third baseman.

"I wouldn't stand here if Roger Lajeunesse was pitching today," Lommy said.

"Why not?"

"Did you ever see him try to pick a guy off third? He'd bounce it right off our heads."

Tony laughed.

"I'm not kidding. You know, he tried to pick a guy off first once and he knocked out the shortstop in the Intermediate game. So that whole team came over here, waving handkerchiefs. That meant they surrendered, see."

It was a preposterous story because of the distance involved, but that made it all the funnier. Tony laughed some more.

The infield was having a little pepper with the manager batting ground balls to each player in turn. "Get two!" he commanded, and the ball went around the horn, and the first baseman burned it in to the catcher. The manager laid down a surprise bunt and the first baseman tore in for it, picked it up barehanded, wheeled, and fired to the second baseman, who was covering first. "Attaboy, Harry!" The manager smacked one hard over the second-base bag. The second baseman raced over, gloved it backhanded, and threw the man out. It was beautiful. "Jesus," Tony said, shaking his head admiringly. "Yaw-yaw-yaw-yaw-yaw-yaw-yaw!" the manager cried. And as in a good pepper game, the members of the infield intoxicated one another with their play. They whirled like dancers. They jumped high and came down with the ball. They dove low and came up with the ball. They never missed.

Off to the side behind third base another batter clipped balls with a long skinny fungo bat and sent long high flies into the outfield. Five or six outfielders were out there. They moved one step, two steps, put the glove up, and they had it.

Other ball players were standing here and there, lobbing the ball back and forth, taking it easy. Some players were just arriving. A car pulled up behind the spot where Tony and Lommy were, although it was illegal to drive a car in that area. Three ballplayers got out and the car drove on to turn around behind the grandstand. The three players elbowed good-naturedly through the crowd, went under the rope, and tossed their gloves on ahead. They had walked from the car in their stocking feet, and now they sat down on the grass in a cozy semicircle and began putting on their spiked shoes. They were sitting close to Tony, and he watched their every move.

"I tell my wife to make a bow with these laces so she puts a knot in them," Wingy Tavares said, laughing.

Poker-faced Henry Suchniak smiled slightly.

"Gee, what a neat guy," Andy Buda said, laughing. "He puts bows in his laces."

Poker-faced Henry Suchniak smiled slightly again.

Tony knew all three players very well. They were three of the best players on the Chace team. Wingy Tavares was the right fielder. He was dark, short, only five feet four, but just about as broad as he was tall. He had tremendously strong arms and shoulders. He was the Chace home-run hitter. But he didn't hit long fly-ball home runs. He hit line-drive home runs. He could put the ball over the outfielder's head on a line, and nobody else in the league could do that.

Cool-eyed, square-jawed Henry Suchniak was the grand old man of Textile League baseball. He was forty-two years old, and he had been playing ball in this league for over twenty years. He had broken in with the old Takalonka team in 1915, in the days of the World War, and here it was 1936, and he was still playing. This seemed absolutely incredible to Tony. Think of the players Henry must have seen come and go in that time! Henry was the Chace left fielder. And if his endurance was remarkable, his batting average was even more remarkable. As old as he was, he was the leading hitter on the team, in terms of percentage, not power. He hit only singles, but he hit a lot of them. And he was a very hard man to strike out. He choked up on the bat and he could hit foul balls all day long. He would spoil all the strike-zone pitches until he got the pitch that he wanted and where he wanted it, and then he would promptly single. His patience was unbreakable, and he had unnerved more than one pitcher into anger and a quick downfall.

Wingy Tavares's weak point was his throwing arm, which was inaccurate. Henry Suchniak's weak point was his legs, which slowed him up in the field and on the bases. The third player, Andy Buda, had a rifle arm that was always on target and he moved around in the field with the light-footed grace of a gloved Nijinsky. Also, he was a consistent .300 hitter. In other words, he was one sweet ballplayer. Andy was the shortstop for the Chace team. He was just a kid compared to Henry, twenty years old. He was a good-looking, good-natured boy. He had regular features, clear skin, blue eyes, and blond hair cut to a length of half an inch. Earlier in the year Andy had been signed by a minor-league team someplace in Pennsylvania, but he had been released and had come back home. At the time of his signing, back in May, everyone had had high hopes that Andy was getting a start on a professional career that would eventually see him become Gaw's first player to get in the Majors, but now it didn't look like he was going to be the one to make it. Tony painfully scratched Andy's name from his list of dreams.

It was Sunday at the ball park! It was lazy, relaxed, unhurried, enjoyable Sunday. What a contrast to the weekdays, Tony thought, when the games started at 6:15 and the ballplayers dashed home from work, got a quick bite to eat, and barely made it to the park in time to hear the umpire's "Batter up!" command. The weekday games lasted six innings, and the big problem was light. Everything was hurried, for speed was essential if they were to get in the six innings before darkness. And if a team delayed the close timing by banging out four or five runs in an early inning, it meant that for the spectators the last inning would feature shadowy players chasing an invisible ball.

But on Sunday they played a full nine innings under the warm sun and there was no anxiety about the game being called because of darkness. And with the whole afternoon stretching before them, the fans and ballplayers both could relax and savor every dramatic moment to the full. The pitcher could step off the mound with the bases loaded and tie his shoe. The manager could rush off the bench and rail at an umpire turned sphinx while the fans mocked his trip and forensic performance with the raspberry. On Sunday there was time for things like that.

Two great rivals were going to play today, Chace Mill vs. Greelock Mill. It was going to be a great game. Chace was the champ from last year and they were leading the league again this year. Greelock was in second place; they could tie for the lead by winning today.

The Chace team played every Sunday. Sometimes they played a league game, like today. Other times they played a visiting team from out of town. The schedule called for the Chace team to play on Sunday instead of some lousy team because the league officials knew that Chace always drew a big crowd. They were the best and everybody came to see them get beat. Unless they were playing an out-of town team, of course; then everybody cheered them.

The players on the Chace team did not all work at the Chace Mill. In the old days you had to work at the mill you played for, and a good ballplayer was always sure of a job. But with the upheaval in the mills, with so many of them closed down and with the greatly shrunken work force in the ones that were still running, such a rule was no longer practicable. So now a ballplayer could sign up with any team he wished. It was freedom, but it was freedom divorced from employment. The ballplayers would have preferred the old rule and the old days.

But now it was Sunday at the ball park and Greelock was challenging Chace. It promised to be the game of the year. And now one of Tony's dearest heroes came out on the grass between the foul line and the rope, just a few feet from Tony and Lommy. This eloquently silent figure was the ace of the Greelock pitching staff—Bill Casavan. He was a lefthander but for some reason they did not call him Lefty. They called him just plain Bill. And he was out here on the grass to warm up. He had his catcher in front of him, towards the grandstand, and he began throwing to him.

Tony liked the Chace team better than the Greelock team. He liked the individual players on the Chace team. The players on the Greelock team were kind of a dull, drab lot. They were competent players all right, but they didn't have the spark to do things that made you remember them. There wasn't anybody on the team with the comfortingly familiar face of Henry Suchniak and his thick durable legs, no one with the gleaming white teeth of Wingy Tavares and the crack of his bat, nobody with the flashing pink-cheeked smoothness of Andy Buda taking three steps toward second and rising in the air as if on springs to pull down a line drive. Somehow when you looked at a Greelock player, you didn't see his face, you just saw the uniform.

Yet Tony was rooting for the Greelock team today, in spite of his preference for the Chace players. In a way, it was precisely because of the Chace superiority that he was rooting for Greelock. For it meant that the odds before Bill Casavan were staggering and therefore appealing. Tony had much reason to root for Chace. Not only did he like the Chace team better, but the Chace pitcher, Lennie Salgado, was Portuguese. Nevertheless, he swept all this off the board. He was sticking with Bill Casavan. He had always liked Bill Casavan, and today more than ever before, Bill Casavan needed a boy's faith to sustain him, a faith that could be sent out to him on the mound in invisible but palpable rays.

Yes, Bill Casavan carried the game on his shoulders for the Greelock team. If the Chace sluggers were going to be stopped, it was he who would have to stop them. No one else. And now Tony watched him warm up, nobody near him, the starting pitcher in all his solitary glory, throwing to a real catcher with a real catcher's mitt and not just to any old guy with a fielder's glove. Many other people knew Bill's importance and watched him, too. The Chace players, however, affected not to see him. They looked right past him.

Bill Casavan was slim. Also, he was good-looking. Tony had read several Frank Merriwell soft-cover books, and it seemed to him that Bill Casavan looked just like Frank Merriwell and acted like him. Bill didn't glare at the umpire when he was pitching and he didn't sling his glove down in disgust when he came in to the bench. He did not swagger; he did not shout. He was a gentleman at all times.

Bill Casavan wore his baseball cap beautifully. There was no one on the field who looked as good in a baseball cap as Bill did. He didn't wear it jammed down on his head like a winter hat. He didn't wear it tipped back on his head with the visor sticking way up in the air in an overly jaunty style. He wore it tipped a bit forward on his head, giving his eyes the maximum protection from the sun. It was a becoming, casual style.

And Bill caught the ball on the return throw from the catcher in a casual style, too. He stuck his glove out there and always made a one-hand catch. His glove was a thin thing, with hardly any padding in it. When he finished an inning on the mound, it was thin enough for him to stick in his hip pocket.

Tony concentrated on watching Bill's stuff. He kicked and that arm whipped around. The ball smacked into the catcher's mitt, a real hand-stinger. Bill had a lot of zip on it. His next pitch was a change of pace. Delivered with the same motion as his fastball, the baseball came off floating through the air, the stitches immobile in the sun. Then he threw a curve. The ball broke so sharply that Tony wondered, How could a guy possibly hit that?

"What stuff, huh, Lommy?" Tony commented in admiration.

"Yuh," Lommy said. "I'm glad I'm not hitting against him."

"Casavan looks good today." They heard an old man's quavering voice behind them.

"He's not strong," a gruff voice answered the old man authoritatively. "He's not built for nine innings."

"We'll see, we'll see," the old man said with chuckle.

That's the way, Pop, stick up for him.

But the gruff voice wanted to get the last word in. "Now if this game was going to go six innings, I'd say he had a chance. But nine—never."

"We'll see, we'll see," the old man said cheerfully, politely, but not retreating an inch.

That's the way, Pop.

The Greelock manager came over and talked quietly to Bill. Tony strained his ears but couldn't hear him. Bill nodded agreement to the manager's words. The manager stood there a while and watched Bill throw, like a father watching his little boy. Then he walked off.

He had no sooner gone than the ball slipped off Bill's fingers and bounced in front of the catcher. The catcher tried to smother the ball but it hopped on by him. The catcher turned and gave chase. Suddenly Tony was worried. This wild pitch was unlike Bill. His control was always good. But suppose today he had the stuff to beat Chace, but by being overcareful and missing the corners, he walked Chace to victory? But Bill didn't seem worried. He waited calmly for the catcher to return with the ball, hands on his hips. His handsome face was expressionless. He was chewing gum in a slow, reflective rhythm.

Over by the first-base side, warming up on the grass between the foul line and the rope, was Lennie Salgado, the Chace pitcher. Lennie was strong-armed. He didn't have the variety of pitches Bill Casavan had. But he had more speed. He didn't try to fool the batters. He just threw the ball by them.

Lennie Salgado was the best pitcher in Gaw. This was not opinion. There was disagreement about who was second best—Tony picked Bill Casavan—but as to who was the best there was no discussion. Tony had watched Lennie pitch many times and he had never seen him get knocked out of the box. He left one game in the third inning, but that was because of a leg cramp and he was ahead 3-1 at the time.

Lennie had been with a minor-league team last year and had been a successful pitcher but suddenly he grew tired of it. He simply walked off, left the team. Asked about it, he explained, "I didn't like all those training rules." To him that was reason enough.

He was not a hustler. When he hit a ground ball he took about three steps down the line and then turned for the bench, usually even before the ball had got to first. But with *his* fastball, maybe he didn't have to hustle. He threw that fastball effortlessly, without strain. But it smoked.

He was twenty-six years old. He was big for a Portuguese, five feet ten. He was burly. And as if to show that he was unimpressed by today's or any other day's game, he was the only ballplayer on the field who was not clean-shaven. Visible underneath the short sleeves of his baseball shirt and coming down to his wrists was the bright red of a close-fitting undershirt. Actually, the red wasn't so bright any more; the sun had faded it. This red undershirt was Lennie's trademark and good-luck charm. He never pitched without it. There was some question as to when it had been washed last.

Lennie was a clown. Even now warming up, when he should have been serious, he kept turning to yell wisecracks to his teammates. Suddenly, instead of making a proper pitch, he threw the ball high in the air. "Let's see how you are on foul balls!" he called out to the catcher. Yes, he was always laughing and joking. Except one place—on the mound.

And finally there was the umpire dusting off the plate. The field was cleared of players. There was that moment of quiet expectancy that preceded every game. There surged through Tony the wild hope that something would be resolved by this game, some sought completion achieved, some certainty assured. He could not reach for what he wanted; it existed on an untouched plateau of being. Before every game he felt the promise, the wild happiness, but as the innings passed, the elation flowed away, the promise dissipated into nothingness, and he was left with a bleak depression. It did not matter who was playing, or whether the game was dull or exciting. It always ended the same for him—emptiness.

But in the blunt call of the umpire, "Play ball!" all psychic cravings were chased away. The drama was about to begin. The duel between the two best pitchers in the city was about to start. The game between the two best teams in the city was ready to go. The pitcher fidgeted, kicked dirt, fixed the mound just so, went to the rubber and turned into a statue, staring ahead like a stone Columbus, and then he moved. The first pitch. Up went the fat finger in blue, a vigorous gesture. "Str-r-r-rike one!" The game was on. Tony turned and looked at the grandstand. It was filled. They sure had a big crowd here today.

On the second ball pitched, the batter lofted a high foul ball in Tony and Lommy's direction. The Greelock third baseman broke fast and rushed over, his head thrown back, his glove held poised. He came right up to the rope, right by Tony. But the ball bounced with a resounding crash on the roof of a car that was illegally parked there, beyond the rope and the spectators. The third baseman jogged back into position.

Tony turned to Lommy. "Did you see his glove?" Tony had had a good chance to admire it at close range. It was a big glove of rich mahogany-brown leather with a deep oiled pocket.

"Yuh," Lommy answered. "I wish I had a glove like that."

"That's the kind of glove they use in the Big Leagues," Tony said.

"I saw one like that in the window at Moe's for $13.50," Lommy informed him.

"Whew." That was a lot of money. In fact, for plenty of people in Gaw that was two weeks' wages. Well, as far as his getting one was concerned, the price might as well have been $113.50.

The first inning went scoreless, but in the second Greelock got something going. The first man hit a low liner straight at the third-base bag. It skimmed the top of the bag and slithered along the grass into left field. It went for two bases. The Chace catcher called for a pitchout and tried to pick the runner off second. He threw the ball into center field, and the runner made it to third. A man on third, nobody out, and Herve Prevasseur up. It looked good for Greelock, and Tony rubbed the palms of his hands together in happy anticipation.

Big Herve Prevasseur was the first baseman for Greelock and the most dangerous hitter on the team. He was lean and sinewy. He was an unusual-looking Frenchman. He was tall, swarthy, and grave. He had high cheekbones, piercing black eyes, and coarse black hair. It was probable that some earlier Prevasseur had engaged in the fur trade with the Indians up there by Quebec.

Salgado delivered.

"Ball two!"

Salgado scowled at the call.

Salgado stretched and delivered again. A foul tip. Strike one.

Two balls and one strike.

Salgado stood on the hill, the ball in his fist, staring contemptuously at the batter. He reared back and gave him the fastball straight down the middle. What speed he had on it! Prevasseur swung from the heels, but he was much too late with his wing. To be funny, the catcher zipped the ball back immediately upon receiving it, and there was Salgado with the ball in his glove and there was Prevasseur just finishing up his swing.

Despite the man on third, Salgado turned his back on the plate and gazed unconcernedly out to center field.

"Start swinging before he throws it, Herve!" some guy yelled out and everybody laughed. Prevasseur didn't want to be left at the station with the next pitch. He had two strikes and he couldn't take chances. So he mentally prepared himself to swing and to swing early. In a sense, he was following the fan's advice. But it was a fatal commitment. The ball was way, way outside, but Prevasseur swung viciously, missed it by a couple of feet, and from the momentum of his swing went sprawling on his back into the dirt. He could not have made himself look more foolish if Salgado had paid him.

What happened to Prevasseur was a forewarner of gloomy things ahead for Greelock. The batter who followed Prevasseur popped to second, and the next man up bounced a one-hopper to the pitcher. The inning was over. Salgado had done what Tommy Bridges had done last year in the World Series after Stan Hack had led off in the ninth with a triple. Bridges had got the next three men out, and the sure run had been left stranded on third. Salgado had duplicated the feat. It was great pitching—for Bridges and for Salgado.

"There's the best ballplayer we've had in this burg for ten years," the gruff-voice man said behind Tony and Lommy. "You know what his record was at Carmel?—8 and 2. He was a winning pitcher. Did you read what Flaherty said in the *Observer*? He talked with the Carmel manager and the manager told him if Salgado had stayed, Rochester in the International League would have bought him. Rochester was definitely interested in him. And that's Double A ball, one step away from the Majors. And that stupid bum walks off. All because he's lazy."

The next three innings were scoreless. Neither side threatened. It was excellent pitching and a fine game, 0-0, going into the sixth. But in the top of the sixth things began to happen. And—wouldn't you know it?—just then old white-haired Mr. Bilsboro, the Secretary-Treasurer of the Textile League, had to stand in front of Tony and Lommy, blocking their view, shaking the can with the slot in it, jingling the coins into an insistent dance. "Help the boys out. Every little bit helps. Thank you! Thank you." Tony always felt embarrassed and guilty when Mr.

111

Bilsboro came up to him and jiggled the can right in front of his face and extended it by his cheek and over his head. He felt mortified, like Mr. Bilsboro and the crowd were thinking, "C'mon, you cheapskate, put something in it." He really wished he had a nickel or a dime to drop through the slot. Once he had seen a kid do that, and Mr. Bilsboro gave the kid a great big smile and said, "Thank you, son." Still, he reflected, it must feel even worse to be a grownup and not put anything in it.

The sixth inning disturbance by Chace was not the least bit complicated. Henry Suchniak worked Casavan for a walk. And then Wingy Tavares came up. Wingy, always an ominous figure in the box, coiled and set, with the bat well off his shoulder, not moving, not smiling, waiting. . . . Wingy liked the very first ball pitched. It was an outside pitch. Wingy caught it on the fat of the bat and gave it a screaming ride down the right-field line, the ball staying about three feet inside the line. Wingy was a left-hand batter and so the Greelock outfield had shifted to the right for him, but the ball shot out there so fast the right fielder had no chance to make a play. There was no fence behind the outfielders. The field went and went and went and then there was a street and across the street there was one of those big houses with a lawn. The right fielder was sprinting further and further away from the game, crossing the street now, headed for the lawn. "How's he gonna get back, Rabbit? Did you give him streetcar money?" somebody yelled at the Greelock manager. Meantime Wingy was jogging around third. Shaking the outstretched hands of his clustered teammates, his white teeth flashing the big smile that would stay on his face until the next time he got up, Wingy crossed the plate. It was apparent he was bursting with good feeling. And why not? Be you man or boy, what is there to compare with the feel of solid wood on horsehide?

Although no one knew it then, that was the game right there. That home run took something out of Bill Casavan, some secret spring of belief went dry in him. He did not quit, but it was clear he had lost something. Suddenly he seemed a slight figure on the mound, thin and tired. Fatigue washed over him like a sudden rain. He got out of the sixth without further damage, though two singles by Chace came after Wingy's homer. But in the seventh—real trouble. Yes, he was tired. His face contorted with every pitch. You could almost hear him grunt with the effort. His control was less sure. What used to catch the corners,

112

now missed. And he was losing his stuff. The ball didn't come in as fast or break as sharply as it had in the early innings, even Tony could see that. What used to be cleanly missed by the batter, now was fouled off. What used to be fouled off, now was being met, hard. Tony watched grimly while the Chace men powdered the ball. They were clearly enjoying themselves as they whistled base hits to all fields. They marked up three runs in the seventh, making the score 5-0. In the eighth the parade of Chace base runners continued. With only one man out, and two more runs in, the Greelock manager slowly trudged out to the mound and sadly conferred with Bill Casavan. Bill came in to the bench, while the crowd, remembering his pitching of the first five innings, gave him a fine hand.

Ahh, Tony sighed, 7-0. And the pitcher to replace Bill was a new guy on the Greelock team. Tony had never seen him before. The guy was a real giraffe, tall and skinny, with a big Adam's apple. He looked awkward throwing, like he might fall over. And the foreboding that Tony felt watching the guy take his warm-up throws was reinforced by a closer look at the guy's legs. He wasn't even wearing the right kind of stockings. The Greelock team stockings were red with two white bands running around the top and this guys's stockings were solid black.

As Tony feared, the guy was a joke. It was more like batting practice than a game. By the time the weary Greelock fielders had thrown the last man out in this top of the eighth, the score was 13-0.

In the last of the eighth the Greelock batters continued their puny hitting, striking out and popping up. Their hitting had been exasperating in the earlier innings but by now everyone was quietly resigned to it. In the top of the ninth the giraffe surprised by putting the side down in order, one-two-three. Or was it that the Chace players were getting humane and cooperated?

Into the bottom of the ninth they went, and Lennie Salgado eased up a bit. A couple of hits went sailing into the outfield. A runner tried to score from second on a single. There was a long slide at the plate, and straddling the cloud of dust the umpire jerked his thumb up—Out! To Tony the man looked to be out on a close play, but for the Greelock manager it was a heaven-sent opportunity. What else can any self-respecting manager do when the game has fallen about his ears in total and irretrievable ruin except pick a fight with the umpire? The

Greelock manager stormed off the bench like it was a 2-1 game and engaged the umpire in heated discourse. The fans laughed and laughed for all through the discussion some fellow with acceptable talent howled to the moon like a dog out on the moor. And then when the Greelock manager started his walk back to the bench, he was accompanied every step of the way by the same dog, this time yelping, in the exact cry a dog makes when he has been hurt.

Greelock did score later in the inning though, twice, and there the game ended. Some game, 13-2.

Tony and Lommy walked out of the park slowly.

"You want to come next week?" Tony asked Lommy.

"Sure," Lommy said.

The announcement had been made in the seventh inning that the Plymouth Cordage team, a very strong club, was coming to town next Sunday to play Chace.

Well, next Sunday he'd be here cheering for Salgado, and maybe then he'd have something to cheer about, not like today.

CHAPTER 4

Cozy's Cafe

Sunday afternoons were reserved for baseball at Bellehaven Park.
Saturday nights were equally reserved—for nightclubbing. The two
boys caught the floor show at Cozy's Cafe every Saturday night. Cozy's
was a bar on the Avenue and, of course, there were many bars on the
Avenue. But Cozy's was unique; there was no other place like it in the
whole of the North End.

The Avenue was a street with a split personality. On one side of the
street were the nice food markets, the big clothing stores employing five
or six people, and the appliance stores with gleaming white refrigerators
lined up along the wall for inspection. The famous stores were all here:
The A & P, Thom McAn Shoes, Woolworth's 5 & 10. . . . There was a
dress shop that called itself a *shoppe*, and the kids without intended
humor pronounced it as *shop-pee*. There was a shop with a shameless
window of headless mannequins laced into corsets, heavy-duty corsets
that looked like they weighed twenty pounds each and were bullet-
proof. Tony always averted his eyes self-consciously when he passed by
this shop. There was a *Gentlemen's Furnishings* store, an assertion that
bothered Tony as improper and misleading, not because of the
Gentlemen, but because of the *Furnishings*, a word he had come to asso-
ciate with tables and lamps and not with ties and shirts. There was a
ladies' hat shop with the floor completely covered by a thick rug. There
was a jewelry store, by which young couples always stood; clocks aquama-
rine and cameo pink, circular, square, and hexagonal, their hands stilled at
unlikely hours, looked down from the top shelf on trays heaped with ear-
rings, necklaces, bracelets, rings, a young girl's fairyland of junk, and all
this treasure held under a light so powerful, so blazingly incandescent that

for one quick alchemistic moment brass reflected the quiet assurance of gold, while back among the Bulovas there flowed through tubed glass the blue letters *Credit*, blinking on and off, and under it, steady, not blinking, *Gladly Given.* "Every ring certified." Yuh, but by whom?

In short, on this side of the street were all the fancy stores, all the ostentatiously clean stores, the brightly lighted stores, the modern stores with huge windows. This was the side of the street where remodeling took place. This was the respectable side of the street. This was the side of the street that got the big crowds on Saturday night.

On the other side of the street, no remodeling took place. This side was the home of Ducky's Lunch, the unpainted, small-windowed side, the shabby side of the street. All the bars were here, bars, poolrooms, vacant stores. There was a small barbershop with one barber and two barber-chairs, a wasteful arrangement. There was a pawnshop with all the goods of this world in its window—guitars, shoes, fishing tackle, hammers, micrometers, coats, typewriters, radios, roofing compound, compasses, silverware, spark plugs, poker chips, binoculars, a lawn mower, and enough guns to stage a Teamsters' membership drive.

There was a store run by a Portuguese for the Portuguese, a live-chicken place, the roosters cock-a-doodling to old friends from inside cages of wire mesh, the hens squawking back complaints, and both waiting to be picked out for the Sunday dinner. The Portuguese liked their meat fresh.

There was a potato wholesaler, a cool and dusty store, unadorned with slogans to catch the public's eye, displaying no bright merchandise, presenting only sacks of potatoes piled on top of one another along the walls. This store was run by a tiny white-haired man, Pop, and his lifter, a torn-shirted, hard-muscled youth of nineteen, always happy and whistling, ever cheerful his cry, "Where do you want these, Pop?"

There was a tire shop with racks of hundreds of used tires. Some of the tires were worn down to a visible network of thread; the mileage guarantee on these would naturally have to be modest . . . say, five blocks. *We Fix Flats—50¢* was painted in big red letters on the window.

There was the Warsaw Social Club, a vacant store for three years before the club rented it. The club sponsored the well-known Warsaw Warriors of the Greater Gaw Basketball League. And they also sponsored a Drum and Bugle Corps, seen in all the parades, the girls pretty in purple satin shorts. The Corps was composed mostly of boys and girls in the fifteen through eighteen age bracket, all Polish, of course. Every Wednesday night this Drum and Bugle Corps met at the club for a spirited practice, and what a helluva racket they made with all that tooting and banging away, but fortunately there was no bar next door with a business to be hurt.

There was a cobbler shop, a very small shop. The window display area was covered over with rusty nails and leather shavings and ripped-off soles and broken laces, all lying where they had happened to fall from the adjoining work counter. The cobbler was Portuguese and he was stitching a sole on, guiding the shoe along the path of the needle with one hand and turning the wheel with his other hand. Nearby on the wall was tacked the thin cardboard bottom of a shoe box. Printed neatly on this cardboard were two lines of slender penciled letters, almost unreadable, partly from the fading of age and partly from being covered over with dirt. The letters said:

Not Responsable For Shoes
Left Over 30 Days

His son, in grammar school, had drawn up the sign for him, at his request. Actually he kept the shoes a lot longer than 30 Days—about two years, in fact. But he felt a need for the protection of legal language. He was learning how to be an American, how to be a citizen in the country that invented fine print. One cannot be too careful in a whereas culture shaped by lawyers and other sharp-witted persons.

There was a secondhand furniture store. One foot inside the door and the customer was face to face with a blunt admonition nailed to a post—*Positively No Spitting!* The proprietor was a hygienic Hebrew ahead of his times like Pasteur. But across the street, on the nice side, they would have been more tactful; they would have said *Please, No Spitting.* To the right of the warning post was a special area, a section of floor space reserved for model displays, roped off on three sides to produce the maximum effect that can come from unity and isolation. This area, featuring a Hollywood-style bedroom suite for the up-to-date tenement, was of special interest to that numerous class which is always in evidence during any economic upheaval, the *nouveau pauvre*, the social descenders who are trying to keep down with the Souzas. It was an authentic Hollywood-style bedroom all right, but it looked like the room where William Randolph Hearst had bedded down that mule who dragged logs to his fireplace. The pieces were pretty well scarred. And there close by the green spread on the bed was another blunt message to the public, *Keep Your Feet Off This Bed!* and again no *Please.* And if that wasn't enough, just outside the roped bedroom, by a pile of six mattresses, a cold announcement chilled the air—*Don't Ask For Credit.* No doubt of it, this proprietor was a churlish fellow. He was on the right side of the street. But other storemen spoke of him admiringly, "He's the only guy in Gaw that never got stuck."

No, this was not the nice side of the street. The evidence was quite clear on that point. The plaster walls of the barbershop were cracked, the chairs featured in the furniture store's *Close-Out on Spring Items— Everything Must Go!* sale had loose legs, nervous-looking thieves walked into the pawnshop followed by criminal-looking detectives, all day long the uproarious Portuguese chickens alternated their dimwitted cries with greenish-black droppings, the tire shop man stacked tires so smooth it looked like he had received this shipment from the Dump, cackling laughter came from behind the drawn curtains of the Warsaw Social Club, the cobbler opened his mouth and spat a clam on the floor, and a black rat ran out into the street from the potato shop.

And then of course all those bars, never two together, but spread out at regular intervals, like relay stations at which the weary traveler could rest and change horses. These bars attracted a clientele that would not have added much to the social tone of any side of any street. First, there were the unemployed. Surveys have shown that while workers with money drink, workers without money also drink. The only difference is they drink slower. The unemployed worker sat at the bar, apart from his fellow man, in isolated and mute desperation. There was no conviviality, no buying of rounds. That belonged to another era—the Roaring Twenties. Now it was every man's beer for himself.

These unemployed worker-drinkers were mostly middle-aged. Young men did not come to these bars. In some of the larger, metropolitan cities the cocktail lounge has replaced Sunday Mass as a meeting place for young fellows and girls, but that had not happened yet in Gaw.

The unemployed were, frankly, happy that there was a shabby side to the street. On this side of the street, if you weren't well-dressed, you could still walk along feeling comfortable. On this side of the street, if you had big holes—potatoes they were called—in the heels of your stockings, you could walk along and not feel that people were staring at you.

The unemployed were like the rats in the maze. The rats learn that at the end of one passageway in the maze is an electric shock grid. They also learn that at the end of another passageway is a food basket. Now when the rats are not looking, the scientist switches the grid with the food basket. The rats go to eat and are electrified instead. Thus, the grinning scientist punishes learned behavior which previously has been rewarded. Almost immediately the rats begin to exhibit neurotic behavior patterns. They run around in circles, trying to catch their tails. Why? Because, says the scientist, their customary routines and expectations have been scrambled. The rats are now in a state of unresolved tension with the environment. They are confused. They are liable to become withdrawn and not eat properly.

119

The unemployed were like that. Their routines, their sense of balance with the environment had been scrambled. Their problem-solving techniques had previously been successful. They used to go to work, come home tired, go to bed, get up the next morning, and go to work again. Now that was all changed. Somebody had slipped the food basket out of the maze and had put an electric grid at the end of every passageway. Now all they had was leisure time, and they had not been trained to make constructive use of that leisure time. They didn't have any satisfying hobbies. So they were confused. They were withdrawn. They were not at peace with the environment. And they did not eat properly.

The unemployed were not the only people to frequent the bars along the crummy half of the Avenue. A second large group was in attendance. This group was not unemployed. Neither was it confused or withdrawn. It was at peace with its environment. It might not—well, speaking of the devil!—a representative member of this group has just now stepped out of Kaznicki's Tavern. He stands undecided whether to go north or south. "C'mon, Popeye," he tells his companion. He heads north. He slides his left foot along. He is not injured. It is only that his left shoe lacks a lace and if he took his foot up in the air the shoe would fall off. He walks over to the gutter and puts an arm around a lamppost. He needs the support only because he is bending over the gutter. He brings his thumb up and closes off one of his nostrils and blows his nose forcefully into the gutter. And then he does the same with the other nostril. Then he straightens up.

"I'll tell you one goddamn thing, Popeye," he says to his companion. "The smartest goddamn general they ever had in that goddamn Army was General Leonard Wood."

Who is this man with such an interest in military affairs? A former Army officer? Perhaps. But one thing is certain. He is a member of an ever-growing group of Gaw citizens known to the public at large as—bums.

The bums were an economic mystery. How did they live? They had no income and, unlike the unemployed, they had not even the memory of income. How was life sustained? Well, they sold screwdrivers and silver spoons to the pawnshop for fifteen cents apiece. But after all, how many screwdrivers and silver spoons does a man have?

The bums were like the wild cats on Tony's street who belonged to no one and were fed by no one. These cats made themselves scarce during the daytime because they were attacked on sight. Kids threw rocks at them and old ladies quietly opened their windows and leaned out with pans of hot water. *Swoosh!* But at night when the moon illuminated the earth, at night when all was quiet, at night at three in the morning, these cats, not one or two, but twelve or fifteen of them, gathered in Tony's yard by his swill barn and danced around their leader, a cat with an uncompromising voice who screamed disaster and scorn at his sleeping enemies and worked his followers into a frenzy until they serenaded the street in full chorus, pouring out their cat hatred of human beings, and in their beds the people heard this with helpless rage and cursed nature's world steadily until the dawn came to their windows, and then they sighed for they knew the cats were slinking away, and they rolled over to sleep, but too soon, for then they heard a lone cat calling to them in a prologue to man's day, a crazy cat without heat, a clown cat laughing cat-style, a cuckoo cat mocking all human life and effort. No wonder old ladies ran for some water whenever they saw one of these cats.

The cats were not intimidated by civilization. Neither were the bums. Unkempt, ragged, with eyes of startling reds, the bums walked the Avenue without apology. Their steps might falter, but the path was always open before them. People hastened to give them room. Even on bustling Saturday night, as if by Moses-magic, the waves of the crowd parted upon their unsteady approach.

And in the contrasting worlds of the Avenue the bums did not need orientation lectures to tell them which side they stood for. They knew. In fact, some of them had not crossed over to the respectable side for years. Why should they? What need had they for grocery and clothing stores? What could they do with all the junk from the 5 & 10—ribbons, small jars of paste, and imitation leather cases to hold combs? On this side of the street were the real necessities of life, bars to drink beer at, lunch counters to drink coffee at, alleys to go wee-wee in, doorways to sleep in. The bums were visionaries exploring new frontiers of living, searching for the ultimate freedom—freedom from bread.

The bums were middle-aged men. They were not transients. They did not flit about the country like gypsies. Gaw was their home. They flourished under the warm sun, but winter was hard on them. In freezing January you would see one of them coming down the street in a light summer jacket, a scarecrow equipped for June. And so they lived.

121

Since the bars serviced a substantial number of unemployed workers and bums, they could not therefore be gay places. An air of penury hung over all the stools, like every nickel counted, and gaiety cannot exist when one is forced to measure each swallow. And then too there were no women. Drinking without women is like Beethoven played on a harp. Something is missing. The hop that women give to beer can never be overestimated. Soldiers spending a long evening in the PX with just their buddies will attest to that.

Yet in the interests of perfect accuracy it cannot be stated that female voices had never been heard inside an Avenue tavern. Tony had heard a few. These were no ordinary females. It took nerve to enter a working-man's tavern in broad daylight. Respectable people put only one judgment on women who swung open those swinging doors. Well, actually the doors were all of one piece, solid wood with just a little peeping glass, but the judgment was the same. But there were women who dared. They were few in number, but mighty in deed. In an increasingly organized world, they remained one of the last bastions of individual enterprise. They were completely unorganized. And they were free to their very bones. They would have resisted organization. If some rabble carouser had jumped up on one of the round tables at the Square Deal Cafe and cried, "Whores of the world, unite! You have nothing to lose but your chancres!" they would have thrown empty beer bottles at him.

But entering a workingman's tavern in broad daylight was no easy thing to do—even for a whore. Women know that their most valued possession is their good name, and after all, whores are women. In fact, whores are unusually careful about their reputation and guard it for the jewel it is. They are the quickest of all women to take affront. They are most sensitive to aspersions. Then how was it that they lapsed and permitted themselves to be seen in Kaznicki's Tavern? It has to do with age. The young whore always tells you she is only temporarily in this line of work and is saving money to start an interior decorating business. A psychiatrist would put it this way—she does not accept her identity. But the old whore has lost that shyness and embarrassed shamefacedness of the young whore. After the age of forty-five there seems to be a slackening of the moral fiber. After forty-five they do not seem to give much of a damn any more. There seems to be a kind of "to hell with it, let the chips fall where they may" spirit.

Thus, the taverns got women. But none under the age of forty-five. And they had had a hard life. They looked their age.

And one afternoon, just as the radios were asking—Can a girl from a little mining town in the West find happiness with the richest lord in England? Can a woman find love and romance after thirty-five?—why, just then the queen mother of whoredom came down the Avenue and she was asking—Can a fun-loving girl from a medium-sized mill town in the East have a friendly beer with a no-good bum after forty-five?

She came down the Avenue in the grand manner. She swept down the middle of the sidewalk, regal in her bearing, and overbearing in her regalness, looking to neither right nor left, letting the peasants get out of her way as best they could. Obviously this was a woman who knew her worth. In fact, she often said in advice, "Never sell yourself short."

Her skirt hung askew and was badly wrinkled, but this was overlooked in a brilliant touch—a yellow scarf of gossamer silk that was draped around her neck and trailed off the shoulder. It made the ensemble.

With simple joy she sang as she walked. The song was "Isle of Capri," and she sang in a throbbing voice full of remembered love. *"It was on the Isle of Capri that I met him, 'neath the shade of an old apple tree. . . ."* The words didn't seem quite right, but the melody was there.

Hers was a face that had launched a thousand ships and waved good-bye to the sailors. Hers was a face that Tony had seen in a history book at school, the battered face of one of Hannibal's veterans leading an elephant down out of the Alps by the trunk.

She was a whore, yes, but not a common prostitute. She did not solicit, neither on the street nor in bars. Rather her role in the everlasting frolic of fornication was more that of a friend, a companion. She stated her code thusly: "I like a good time. If a fellow wants to show me a good time, if he's good company—okay. But if he's not good company, I don't care how much money he has, let him find somebody else. I'm not a gold digger."

She strode along with unfeminine vigor, and yet the rhythm of her flesh proclaimed her woman. On the breast of her blouse, in fine red cloth, surrounded with an elaborate embroidery and fantastic flourishes of gold thread, appeared the letter *W*. It stood for her name—Winona.

123

About five steps behind the wide-hipped Winona walked her shyly smiling escort. He had asked her to have a drink with him. As he walked along, he made a curious sound. It was one of his shoes. The sole had worked itself loose. It was now hinged across the shank and kept flapping up and down as he walked. So with a last pulsating note from Winona and a final *slap-slap-slap* from his shoe, the two of them disappeared inside Kaznicki's Tavern.

Tony and Lommy happened to be lounging around on the corner, trying to make up their minds where to go, when Winona and her friend passed close to them and entered Kaznicki's Tavern They heard Winona greet Kaznicki with an exuberant shout. Kaznicki acknowledge the greeting but with restraint. He knew Winona.

Through the screen door Tony and Lommy heard her raucous laughter. She was having a good time. But it was not destined to last.

Winona was the only woman in the bar and she was taking advantage of it. She was playing the coquette, passing off innuendoes with everyone, even bringing the guy way down on the end into it. She could be most arch when she wanted to. But her escort did not like it. He felt he was being ignored. So he began to get a little hot under the collar. Halfway through their second beer he remonstrated with her in edged undertones.

Winona shook the walls. The fellow was not being good company.

"Nobody owns me!" she exploded. "Not after one lousy beer!" she snarled in contempt.

"Awright, awright," her escort pacified her sullenly. He was aware of the audience.

Kaznicki was polishing glasses at the far end. "Keep your voices down over there!" he called out. This was a common dilemma for him, caught between wanting to throw them out and wanting their trade.

"Aw, mind your own business, you dumb Polock!" Winona let him have it, half in fun, and half serious.

This was too much.

Kaznicki rushed over, the vein throbbing in his great bull neck.

"Listen, this is my own bar. Nobody's going to tell me to mind my own business in my own bar."

"Kaz, you take things to heart too much," she said.

"That's all right," he said. "But you shouldn't talk that way."

"It was a personal matter, Kaz," she said with dignity.

"It sounded like a public matter to me."

Kaznicki went back to his glasses. He leaned over to a customer. "Do you know how to spell dames?" he asked in a low voice. "*Trouble*, with a capital *T*."

But as far as Winona was concerned, the trouble was over. With a laugh she had gone down the line a bit and bummed a cigarette. When she came back she made a couple of more jokes and then drained off the last of her beer.

"Let's have another one, Freddie," she said jovially to her escort.

That worthy silently initiated an act of disengagement. He took his glass, which still had some beer in it, and moved to a stool about six stools away.

"Buy your own beer!" Freddie jeered.

There she was in an impossible situation, alone with an empty glass, humiliated and thirsty. There was only one thing left for her to say.

"Kiss my ass!" she bellowed in a bullfrog roar.

Lommy jumped, and the blast almost knocked Tony off the car fender he was leaning up against. It sounded like she had yelled it in their ears. Her invitation was uttered with such passionate sincerity and open honesty that there was little disgusting or dirty about it. It was less vicious than reflective, a philosophic statement rather than an indecency. It was a kind of summing up for her, the accumulated wisdom of fifty years of living crystallized into one simple concretion—a cry of defiance. Confronting the unending indignities of life upon the anvil, she dramatized the perilous human experience. Against the shaded absolutes of a grim universe, she spoke the curtain line for the evanescent human being.

Winona had to leave then. Kaznicki requested it. She sang as she left, "Pennies from Heaven." *"Every time it rains, it rains pennies from heaven. . . ."* Farewell, fair Winona. Your spirit shall always be there, wherever there are men and beer, wherever there is a darkened tavern and a good time to be had by all. You were never a gold digger.

It would seem that you had to write off the crummy side of the Avenue. Low-caliber stores, dismal bars, shabby people, there seemed little here that could attract two wide-awake and discriminating boys. Yet it was to this crummy side that Tony and Lommy came every Saturday night. One place drew them. This place was a magic land, a place of entertainers and acts, a place where "gaiety reigns supreme," as the M. C. used to put it—and correctly. Be it Broadway or the North End of Gaw, there is no business like show business, and show biz in all its glamour and excitement and fascination was here. The place was Cozy's Cafe.

Cozy's was divided into two parts. The first part was a regular bar, with stools and a bartender and so on, just like any other bar except that it was better lighted. Cut into the wall that the customers had their backs to was an archway and this archway opened into a big room. This room had an alternate entrance, a door that opened out on the sidewalk. This big room was where the fun was.

Oh, to be here on a Saturday night! The noise, the shouting, the singing, the smoking, the drinking, the clapping, the laughing. Saturday night was the drinking night in Gaw. A lot of people didn't drink at all during the week, but something about the chemistry of Saturday night set their blood to stirring and drove them from their homes into the bars. But though other bars might have a crowd, none had a crowd as big as Cozy's and none had as nice a crowd. Nobody was in here drinking in their working clothes. The men were shaven and in clean clothes. Bums stayed completely away. And in contrast to the other bars, lots of women came here, always with fellows, of course. It is true that some of these women were as old as Winona and a few, in fact, were older. But there were others in their thirties and some in their twenties. This last group, Tony noted with pleasure, included some girls who were not at all bad-looking.

The most astonishing thing about the Cozy crowd was its unbelievable

125

good nature. Despite their being packed in together, which should have made for irritations and short tempers, and despite the presence of the women, which should have made for incidents, Tony in all his Saturday nights here never saw a fight and never heard people snarl at one another. Good cheer and good fellowship were everywhere. It was a happy place.

Yes, Tony had never seen a place where everybody seemed to be having such a full-throated good time, and Saturday night they were really jammed in here. Booths went all around the walls of the room, and every booth was filled to overflowing. There was none of this two-or-three-people-in-a-booth stuff. A couple would walk in from the street and wander around looking for seats that did not exist. And somebody from a booth, a filled booth, would recognize them and call them over. This kind friend would then direct his party to make room. They would squeeze and squeeze and the two fellows on the aisle would sit with their rumps half off the bench. And if that didn't work, a girl would sit on her fellow's lap.

In the center of the room were small square tables and chairs. These would, of course, be filled, too. An aisle went around the room, between the booths and the tables. The waitresses, neat in their black dresses, moved with much speed in this aisle, rushing back and forth, from the customers to the bar and from the bar to the customers. They carried trays loaded with bottles of beer, the bottles looking wet and cold, looking delicious, and upside down over each bottle tinkled a clean glass. The waitresses needed muscles and track shoes to keep up with the calls of the thirsty. "Nine Danbys here!" And when the floor show was on, the aisle near the archway would fill up with spectators, drinkers, who had stepped over from the bar to watch. These people would stand there, glass in hand, watching the stage, and the waitresses, sweating and out of breath, would try to slip through the mass of bodies, puffing hopefully, "Coming through! Coming through!"

Tony and Lommy made it a point to arrive at Cozy's Cafe early. The floor show started at 8:15. They always got there about a half hour before. They did so to be first in line by the screen door. After the floor show started, three or four other kids would come and stand behind them in the entranceway. So Tony and Lommy had the best view. They didn't plant themselves solidly in front of the screen door. They stood there, but alertly, ready to jump aside when someone wanted to get in or out.

Fortunately, the stage was not at the far end of the room. It was about halfway down the room, over to the right of the door, up against the wall. They could see it good. It was not a big stage. There was room on it for the piano, the microphone, the performer, and not much else. It was not a high stage either. It was about a foot up off the floor.

While Tony and Lommy waited, there was much of interest here. They watched the hundred different little scenes going on. This man whispering, this man telling a joke, this man kissing his girl, this man proposing a toast, this man putting his arm around the waitress, this man filling his mouth with pretzels—there was an infinite variety of activities and they watched them all.

There was only seeming bedlam here. There was actually a closeness of spirit here. And the crowd proved it right then. One booth started singing a song, and the whole room took it up, everybody in that whole place singing it. It was "That Old Gang of Mine." It was the only kind of song they ever sang together, old-time sentimental songs, and how sad the voices and the words.

127

> *Good-bye forever, old fellows an' gals,*
> *Good-bye forever, old sweethearts an' pals,*
> *God bless them!*
> *Gee, but I'd give the world to see*
> *That old gang of mine!*

Yes, there was only seeming bedlam, for when the entertainment was on, the crowd was quiet. They were a fine audience. They loved to watch the acts. Good or bad, they were with the performer all the way. They were always warm and appreciative.

And then the floor show started.

First, an accordion player, a young guy, started things off. He was darn good. He played several numbers, first a waltz, then a march, and finally a popular song, "Moon over Miami." "I'll betcha that cost at least fifty bucks," Lommy said, nodding at the sparkling accordion. "Probably," Tony agreed. It was a huge accordion. You'd think a guy'd get awfully tired holding it up.

The accordionist got a good hand and he made believe he was going off the stage, the way they always do, just pretending, and then he played his encore. It was a patriotic medley, and he very skillfully blended the themes of "Over There," "Anchors Aweigh," and "The Caissons Go Rolling Along," going from one song back to the other. They really clapped for that, and he went off, looking pretty happy.

"And now," the M. C. said, "presenting Gaw's own Sophie Tucker—Martha Foley!"

This woman came out. She was spectacular in an evening-gown type of dress, with bare arms and little pieces of something glittering all over the dress. She was old though. Her hair was sort of thinned out. Her hair was red, but it didn't look like a natural red; it looked like maybe she had dyed it. Her face was ghost-white, thick with powder. And when she started twisting the height-adjustment thingamajig on the microphone, you could see the flabby underside of her arms sort of jiggling back and forth. If I had arms like that I'd wear long sleeves, Tony thought cattily.

"Thank you, thank you, for all that applause. It was wonderful, really wonderful," Gaw's own Sophie Tucker rumbled into the microphone. She had a deep bass voice. "For all you lovely people I'm going to sing one of my favorites—and one of your favorites, too, I'm sure."

The piano started up behind her and she stepped back a bit from the microphone.

> *Just Molly and meeeee*
> *And Baby makes threeeee,*
> *We're happy in my blooooo heav-vun. . . .*

She raised both her fists as she sang, like she was going to hammer down on the man's head at the closest table, which might not have been a bad idea because he was a powerful exhaler of cigarette smoke and it was like she was standing in an old car's exhaust.

She had a good strong voice and Tony doubted that she really needed the microphone. After "My Blue Heaven," she sang "Bill Bailey, Won't You Please Come Home," and the crowd really loved it. They wouldn't stop clapping and one guy paid her the ultimate compliment; he brought a shot of whiskey up to her on the stage, just like they bring roses to opera singers, and she downed it without batting an eye. They kept clapping so she put the finger tips of both hands to her lips and blew them all a kiss.

She went off the stage then but five guys went and got her and brought her back. So she sang one more number, "Darktown Strutters Ball."

The next act was a comedian. He came out wearing funny clothes. His coat was too big, his shoes were too big, and his pants dragged.

"I'd like to recite a little poem I learned on my mother's knee," he said. *"A lady bug was walking along the grass/When she slipped and fell right on her aa—"* the word froze in midair while he looked around as if shocked at what the audience was thinking *"—antennae."*

The crowd laughed uproariously.

He took his hat off to a pretty girl seated at a nearby table, and it was a trick hat. It must have been attached to his head by an elastic band, Tony figured, even though he couldn't see the elastic, for the guy let go of the hat when it was in the air and it snapped back and hit him on the side of the head. He staggered from the impact. He made a complete circle looking for his adversary. "Where is he? That bum!" He assumed the boxing stance and did a real fancy two-step. He rubbed his thumb across his nostrils the way boxers do. "Come out here and fight like a man!" Everybody laughed and laughed.

"It's your hat!" somebody yelled.

"My hat?" He looked puzzled. He took it off and held it before him. It was a derby hat. He examined it. He held his fist threateningly to it and made believe spitting in its eye. Then he snapped his wrist and sent the hat spinning over the heads of the audience, and it sailed out, made the turn, and came back to him. Everybody applauded.

"Boy, I wonder how he does that?" Tony said to Lommy. "I'd like to be able to do that."

He started singing a comic song about a street peddler selling bananas in Havana, although he really talked the lines more than he sang them. His Cuban accent was very good. After each stanza, he did a cute little dance step.

"Excuse me, boys."

Somebody behind them wanted to get in. They jumped aside. Holy smokes! It was Cozy LeBeau!

Cozy LeBeau was a man of impressive appearance. Short, of enormous girth, always with a big cigar in his mouth, Cozy looked like one of the well-fed types seen lounging about the corridors of the City Hall in Boston, a member of the Mayor's entourage, a contractor perhaps, or, more likely, a judge. But while it was true that Cozy was serving the people, he was neither Irish nor in politics. He owned and ran Cozy's Cafe.

Boy, what a gentleman! Tony marveled. His own doorway, and he says, "Excuse me, boys." He was the only storeowner in Gaw who would have said that. The rest of them would have said, "Hey, you kids get the hell out of here!"

Cozy walked in, waved to a few people, and walked on through into the bar side. Tony watched him all the way. Gee, what a nice guy, he thought. He felt warm gratitude toward this genial man with the two sparkling gold teeth in the front of his mouth clamped down on an unlit cigar. Cozy did not smoke his cigars; he chewed them. This habit did not particularly strike Tony one way or the other, although a trained Freudian observer would have smiled at this compulsive Oedipean gnawing, this monstrously obvious exercise in father hatred.

Tony turned his attention back to the acts. The comedian went off and it took five puffing men to carry out the equipment for the next act. It was a dumbbell. It was a good-sized dumbbell; the two round balls on the ends were each the size of a basketball. The whole thing, bar and balls, was black.

Then the strong man came out. In contrast to the first three acts he was not conscious of the crowd. He did not look at anyone. He might as well have been by himself. He had a cape around his shoulders, like the Count of Monte Cristo. When he got up on the stage, with a dramatic flip of the wrist he whipped the cape off his shoulders and sent it undulating through the air like a grand ocean wave. And Tony saw right then and there that when you're in show business, you don't just take something off quietly like an ordinary person does. You do everything with style, because, after all, everybody is watching you and it wouldn't do to be ordinary, because then who would want to watch you?

The strong man was not a young man. He was in his forties, with thinning hair. He was nice and cool in a black one-piece gym suit; it looked like a bathing suit. On the front of it was a red-and-white Olympic shield. And on his feet he had the soft-leather high shoes of the boxer. But despite the gym suit, despite the boxing shoes, and despite the tape on his wrists, he did not look like a strong man is supposed to look. His arms were big enough around but shapeless, not with sharply defined muscles. And his legs were white and hairless. If you had seen him on the beach, you wouldn't have looked at him twice. He looked like he might have been a strong man at one time but not any more. He looked out of condition.

The strong man took a chunk of white chalk and rubbed it thoughtfully back and forth across the palm of first one hand, and then the other. The he laid the chalk on top of the piano and turned dramatically to the audience. But he did not look at them; he looked over their heads. He flexed his arms. He took a deep breath and his chest ballooned mightily. He let the air out. He took another deep breath. He deflated. He looked down at the dumbbell. He set himself.

"I don't think much of this for an act," Tony commented to Lommy. "Suppose he lifts it—all right, then what? What else can he do? What can he do for an encore?"

"He could lift it again."

"No, you can't repeat the same thing twice," Tony wisely said. "That would be monotonous. In other words, all he can do is this one thing—lift a dumbbell. That's not much of an act."

Lommy did not think much of the act either, for when the fat-padded strong man suddenly seized the bar of the dumbbell and staggered backwards, grimacing and groaning, Lommy said, "Aaaa, it's a fake. I'll betcha those balls are hollow." He no sooner said it than the strong man gave up and half-carried and half-dropped the dumbbell to the floor. *Boom!* It was no fake. The dumbbell weighed plenty all right.

The strong man stood alone, apparently beaten. But his failure had bound the crowd to him. Before they had looked on with interest but without involvement. But now they really wanted him to lift that dumbbell. He was man, their representative up there on the stage. And they waited quietly, with him, for a renewal of the struggle.

The strong man stared at the dumbbell. He was concentrating his power. He breathed deeply. He grabbed the bar. Up it went in two decisive moves—to his chest—and from his chest high up over his head. He held it aloft and walked about the stage in triumph. There was great applause.

The strong man put the dumbbell down and looked directly at the audience for the first time. There was something tired about his eyes. A slight smile came to his lips and he acknowledged the applause with an almost imperceptible nod.

Tony thought the act was over, but no, the strong man turned to the

131

piano and took up something nobody had noticed before. It was an iron bar. It was a foot long. He held it high in the air and showed it to everybody. He brought it down to his waist and purposely dropped it on the stage, so they could hear what it sounded like. It sounded like solid iron. Then he handed it to a man at a nearby table and invited him to test it for strength. The man did so and was satisfied.

The strong man held the bar before him, a hand on each end. Slowly he applied pressure. He gasped, his face contorted, his eyeballs bulged. The bar's rigidity held, but then almost imperceptibly, slowly, slowly, ever so slowly, like a stalk in a soft breeze, the bar began to bend. The people were with him all the way. Everybody was clapping, and the clapping got louder and louder. It was very exciting. He made a horseshoe out of it and waved it on high, this time with a big smile.

"Jesus, that guy is strong!" Tony said admiringly. "Did you see him?" he asked Lommy, whose eyes were riveted to the stage. Tony felt like clapping himself, but he didn't dare because it might draw attention to their presence by the door and some guy trying to act like a big shot might come over and tell them to beat it.

The strong man went off and a young guy came on. He was dressed in a shiny satin outfit, bright blue pants and an orange shirt with pleated sleeves. He brought with him a low metal table. It was painted silver. He hopped up on this metal table and with the piano behind picking off an introductory measure or two for "The Sidewalks of New York," he began tap dancing. He really got the rhythm of that *East Side, West Side, all around the town.* He was good all right, and then suddenly—his pants lit up! They lit up like a neon sign. And then his pants went off and his shirt lit up and then his shirt went off and then his shirt and pants lit up together, all the while he kept dancing.

"How in the heck does he do that?" Tony asked, mystified.

"Oh, that's easy," Lommy said. "He's wired up. He's got little bulbs in his clothes and he's got a battery somewheres, probably in that table—you notice how thick the top to it is?—and when his foot hits a certain spot on it he connects up to the battery and the lights go on."

Then the tap dancer, still dancing, turned around on the table and his back lit up with the letters *HI.*

But this fellow was not only a tap dancer, he was also a comedian. After his dance was over, his helper rushed forward and took away the table, first handing him a black case with a handle, the kind that type-writers come in. But the case held a phonograph player, as everybody saw after he set it on the piano and opened it. His comedian's act went this way. He put a record on the phonograph and then he came forward and when the man on the record started singing, he made believe he was doing the singing. He opened and closed his mouth at exactly the right moment every time. You had to give him credit; it must have taken an awful lot of rehearsing to get it that perfect. The record was an opera record and he tried to make it funny. When the guy on the record held a note for a long time—like those opera singers do—he made funny faces and staggered and sank to his knees and grabbed his throat and when the note finally ended, he let his tongue hang out. On the next note he grabbed his stomach and pretended he was getting sick. The people laughed a lot but Tony didn't think it was too funny, not as funny as the first comedian anyway.

The next act was also a young guy but he was dressed in a regular suit, a dark blue suit, with a white shirt and tie. He was a singer. The act didn't look like it was going to be much. He didn't bounce around full of confidence, like the tap dancer. His manner was very quiet. But he fooled you. He was a wonderful performer all the same. He could really sing! He set the mood with "Dinner for One Please, James," and every-one relaxed in melancholy. *"Dinner for one please, James/Madam will not be dining/Yes, you may bring the wine in/Love plays such funny games."*

Then he went into "A Beautiful Lady in Blue." *"A beautiful lady in blue/She thought I was someone she knew/Her lips so divine/Were not meant for mine."* He sang this song with such a sense of belief, with such longing, that he transformed the lyrics into a dream of love that was real and true. The song and this singing of it struck a responsive chord deep within Tony and it seemed to him that this song was the saddest and the most beautiful song he had ever heard.

This is the best act of the night!—that's what Tony wanted to tell Lommy, but he didn't, because the song might not strike Lommy the same way and Lommy would think he was nuts.

The young guy was singing it again *". . . She thought I was someone she knew . . ."* and Tony was in an enrapt, dreamy state—

"What the hell are youse kids doin' here?"

Tony jumped. It was like being shaken from a sound sleep.

The words had come to the kids in the doorway not from Cozy's Cafe but from behind them, from the world outside. They turned around.

It was a behemoth in blue, a weed from the Old Sod, a wearer of the green, a drinker of free cups of coffee at Ducky's Lunch, an eater of free pieces of pie at the same establishment, a taker of free rides on the streetcars, a disperser of kids on the corners, an ender of games in the streets, a confiscator of baseballs, footballs, tennis balls, golf balls, rubber balls, a stopper of any fun anyplace by any kid—in short, a cop. Yes, their hour had come. The hostile and implacable forces of law and order filled the doorway in the huge form of one of Gaw's Finest. He carried great weight in the community; his coat seemed less a coat than a tent draped around a body that had stuffed itself over the years not wisely but too well. He was red-faced and there was a thick growth of hair bristling out of his nose. He had small blue eyes, small cold eyes, and he was not smiling. In the magazine ads smiling cops are always taking little kids by the hand and leading them across the street, but in Gaw the cops did not help little kids across the street. When they passed a kid on the sidewalk, they stared at him hard like he had done something wrong, so that even if he hadn't done anything wrong, he reddened guiltily and felt like he had.

"Whatchas doin' here anyway, huh?" he demanded.

Tony stupidly thought he wanted an answer. "We were watching the acts," he said.

"Oh, youse was watching the yacks," he said, addressing himself to Tony, nodding his head slowly with mock understanding. His face darkened in anger. "I'll give youse a nack—right where it hurts! Now come on, get the hell ouda here!"

They squeezed past him silently. But he could not resist a parting shot of revolting piety, a spoonful of sickening Irish morality. "Youse kids should be ashamed of yuhselfs. Suppose yuh muddas knew youse was here? Don't youse respeck yuh muddas, huh?"

Victims of decency, Tony and Lommy wandered off down the Avenue. They were disconsolate. It didn't seem right that when they were having such a good time and not hurting anybody and when the owner himself didn't mind, it didn't seem right that a cop could kick them out.

"Well, at least we saw most of the acts," Tony said.

"Yuh," Lommy agreed.

"Let's cross over," Tony said.

They crossed over to the busy side of the Avenue. They joined the crowds walking along doing their Saturday-night shopping. The stores stayed open late on Saturday night.

The store that got the most business was the 5 & 10. Tony and Lommy stared at the window of the 5 & 10. The window was about a foot deep with peanut brittle—the pieces, big and little, sticking every which way, like somebody had shoveled it in there. The 5 & 10 had two doorways. On the right side of the window a steady stream of people kept pushing in through the swinging doors, while on the left side of the window another flow of people kept pushing out through those swinging doors.

Again and again Tony noticed that standing by the entranceway windows of furniture stores and clothing stores and appliance stores were young married couples. You could tell they were married and not engaged because the fellow didn't have his hands all over her. Sometimes the fellow would have a tiny infant in his arms. They would stand there and the girls would point at something in the window and talk a blue streak, *blah-blah-blah-blah*. The fellow would just listen, no particular enthusiasm or even interest on his face.

This sight, continually seen, sent shivers down Tony's spine. He saw it as a warning on the wind. There was something frightening about marriage, something terrible and joyless and emasculating about it. To spend the Saturday nights of your life endlessly looking into windows at beds and dresses, to be led around by the nose to look at refrigerators—what an ignominious and depressing future.

"Let's go to the Beano place," Tony said.

"Okay," Lommy agreed.

They crossed back over to the other side. They passed Ducky's Lunch. Lommy waved at his father.

The Beano place was in a regular store, a fairly large store. All they did here was play Beano and they were open every day. In the afternoons there would only be four or five players sitting around but they'd still have games. At night more players would show up. Like the bars, the Beano place was open every night. Tonight, Saturday, there was a good-sized crowd present.

The place was run by two guys. One guy, a skinny guy, sat by himself at a small table in the window. The floor under him had been built up so that he was up high. Close by his side was a microphone and a rotating drum with all the numbers in it. He was the caller. He'd spin the drum, *clack-clack-clack-clack-clack-clack*, then he'd stop the drum, pick out a number, and read the number into the microphone. You could hear him outside easy.

The other guy was the floor man. He walked up and down by the long wooden tables where the people sat playing. He sold cards, gave out beans, and checked the winning card, calling the numbers back to the skinny guy for verification. This floor man was a young guy. He was plump and pasty-faced, with a pale straw-colored mustache on his upper lip. He didn't seem to be too happy with the job, for he picked up the nickels of the customers with a slightly sour expression, like a waiter picking up a small tip. And if a customer had the effrontery to make small talk, he met it with a blank stare and walked away, leaving the customer with his words half-hanging in the air.

"You know that usher at the Bughouse, they call him the Prince of Wales, he walks with his nose sticking up in the air like this?" and Lommy threw his head back like he had a bleeding nose.

"Yuh, I know who you mean," Tony said, nodding. "He thinks he's hot stuff. He always has a couple of girls in the back row that he sits with."

"Yuh, that's him. Well, you see that guy there?—" Lommy said, indicating the floor man "—that's his brother."

"No kidding."

"Yuh."

"I liked Peanuts," Tony reminisced. "He was a good guy. Remember him—he had those scabs on his neck?"

"Remember him? He lives right around the corner from me! Yuh, he's a swell guy. He gave me half a candy bar once. An Old Nick."

"What happened to him? Did he quit?"

"No, he got fired. He was stealing popcorn and selling it on his street. That's when they hired the Prince of Wales, right after that."

Tony and Lommy settled down to watch the Beano players. They stood in the store's entranceway, right by the screen door, just as they had at Cozy's Cafe. The Beano players were mostly women, and mostly older women, from middle-aged right on up to white-haired.

The white-haired women were the most serious players of all. They played with patience, with excitement, and with determination. If they talked when they played, it was always a private mutter. They were trying to win a prize, but not any of the prizes that ringed the room on a high shelf. What need had they for some damn alarm clock? They had no place to go to be waked up early for. What need had they for some damn wooden salad bowl? They couldn't eat salads—not with *their* teeth. No, they were after something more elusive than an alarm clock or a salad bowl. They were after a victory. Defeated all their lives, scorned, they played here to win, to seize life by the throat, to force life to murmur in surrender, "Yes, you have won. You have beaten me. You have conquered. You are important. You matter." Here in this room, within these four walls, with this little card, they were Napoleon. They moved the beans around on the card and muttered and waited to become the only one, the rare one, the best one, the one who cried, "I won!"

137

Tony and Lommy watched several games. They participated in the excitement, for towards the end of a game, after many numbers had been called, the tension built up to the point where even they could feel it. By then there would be quite a few people who were right there, right at the edge of the winner's circle, poised and ready to drop in, just waiting for that maddening last number, and Tony and Lommy watched them, hunched over their cards, rigid with expectation.

All of a sudden Tony noticed that he and Lommy were not alone any more. Three other boys had come to the screen door. These boys were bigger and older, about fourteen years old.

"Beano!"

Everybody looked up, startled. This game had just started, only two numbers had been called—how could there be a Beano already?

"Beano!"

This time they located the cry. It was coming from the screen door. Everybody in the place looked at the door. The boy who had startled them laughed and stepped aside.

The second boy put his head to the door. "Do not remove your beans," he said in the weary nasal monotone of the caller. "There may be an error."

The caller tried to get the game going again. "Under the O—72," he said into the microphone.

"Under the B—6!" the third boy called out.

"Under the C—three little fishes!" the first boy joined in.

This was too much. All eyes were on the door again. There were quick intakes of outraged breath and indignant "Oh!"s by the younger ladies. There were shakings of the head and disapproving tongues going *"Tst, tst, tst"* by the older ladies.

The floor man started for the door. But the boys weren't quite through. They grabbed the screen door and banged it shut several times. Then, laughing wildly, they ran away down the street.

The floor man came to the door where Tony and Lommy were.

"Hey, you kids get the hell out of here!" he said to them.

They had been here for a good thirty minutes before those wise guys came. The floor man had seen them during those thirty minutes. He knew they weren't the guys who had done the yelling. So they figured the floor man was just going through the motions. He had to say something to them, because everybody was looking at him and expecting him to say something. So, secure in their analysis, Tony and Lommy didn't get the hell out. But they did move back about three steps. It was a gesture of acquiescence. They were sure that this discreet acknowledgment of his authority was enough to satisfy the floor man. And in a few minutes they would slip back to their old place by the door and no one would say anything. All would be forgotten.

But the floor man fooled them.

"Goddamn it, I mean it!" he snarled, and he opened the door and jumped out at them. *Wsshhh!* Jesse Owens never got off those starting blocks faster than they got out of there. They dodged people on the sidewalk like a halfback running for a touchdown. They looked back. The Prince of Wales's brother was out on the sidewalk, looking in their direction, but not running. They stopped running.

They had those three wise guys to thank for this. That's how it always was. Some guy always spoiled it for you.

They wandered disconsolately down the Avenue. There was no other place to go now.

Across the street was the Grand Theatre. They crossed over. The girl in the box office was figuring the night's receipts. The manager was in the box office with her, standing close behind her, looking over her shoulder, his eyes never leaving her hands as she deftly stacked the dimes in piles of ten. The manager's big belly was propped up on the back of her chair, and his big rump was pressing rearwards against the door. Things sure looked mighty crowded in that little box office.

Tony and Lommy looked at the big posters facing the sidewalk and then they went around behind the box office. Here on the side walls was a feast of scenes from the different pictures. They studied these scenes, which were behind glass, with much interest. They looked at the *Now Playing* pictures, the *Our Next Attraction* pictures, and the *Coming Soon* pictures—all in all six pictures. The Grand had double features and changed its bill three times a week.

Tony looked at Bob Steele crouching behind a boulder with his six-shooter out. This was under *Now Playing*. On Fridays and Saturdays one of the pictures was always a cowboy picture.

"I don't care much for Bob Steele," Tony said

"Why not?"

"Oh, he's too small. It doesn't look right when he knocks out a big guy. It looks like a fake."

"Yuh," Lommy agreed.

"Same thing with Buzz Barton. He's too small. He looks like a kid."

"The guy I don't like is Hoot Gibson," Lommy said. "He was supposed to be good when he was younger. But now—he's too old. He looks like my grandfather, you know, and the girl is supposed to fall in love with him—shit."

"I saw Jack Hoxie once," Tony said. "He's no good either. He's too fat."

"You know, when you come to think about it, there's hardly any more good cowboys left," Lommy said. "Buck Jones, he's about the best."

"I don't like him too much," Tony said.

"Why not?' Lommy asked, taken aback.

"Oh, he's too husky. I saw him once when he jumped on his horse from a second-story window and you should have seen that poor horse—it practically broke his back. His belly went right down to the ground, no kidding. And then Buck Jones digs in his spurs to make this horse go, the crooks were running out the front door, you know, and the horse barely moves. You could see it was too much weight for him."

His favorite was Tom Tyler. Tom Tyler looked like a cowboy was supposed to look—tall, dark, lean, whip-hard, silent, something almost sinister about him. But the trouble was he had seen Tom Tyler only that once. He would have liked to see him lots of times. He noticed that every so often Tom Tyler was at the Grand but he never had the dough.

"I wish I had seen Tom Mix," Tony said. "They say he was good."

"Yuh, well, he's from the old days, like Hoot Gibson."

139

Lommy was lucky. He got to go to the movies almost every week. A man from the Grand Theatre came by Ducky's Lunch every Monday and put a cardboard placard in the window. This placard listed the week's pictures at the Grand, and for allowing his window to be used for advertising, Lommy's father was then given two free passes by the man. Each pass was good for one free show at the Grand. Lommy's mother used one of the passes and Lommy and his sisters took turns with the other pass. In the expected schedule of rotation Lommy should have gone to the Grand about once a month, but by making deals with his sisters, by doing dishes for them and shining their shoes, he went a lot more often.

140

Tony and Lommy walked away from the theatre. In that same block, between two stores, there was a glass door. This door had no name on it, just the street number in big numerals—868. To open, it had a bar to pull instead of a knob to turn. You could see through the glass a flight of stairs going on up. Tony had often wondered what was up those stairs. There were many tenements above stores, but that door was too nice and the stairs too wide for there to be tenements in this building.

And now to Tony's open-mouthed surprise, Lommy went up to the glass door and as nonchalantly as if he lived there, he opened it.

"C'mon," he said to Tony.

"Where you going?" Tony said, mystified.

"C'mon. You'll see."

Tony followed obediently.

They were at the bottom of a long flight of stairs. They started going up. Everything was terribly quiet. All they could hear was the sound of their own footsteps. The stairs were in semidarkness, just enough light to see where you were going.

They at last came to the top of the stairs. They looked down a long open hallway. Everything was in shadows. Tony was apprehensive. He could just see a man suddenly jumping out at them from the shadows and shouting, "What the hell are you kids doing here?" Maybe a cop. And what could they say? He might think they were trying to rob the place. It looked suspicious, two guys in a building at night.

"C'mon," Lommy said.

Without a word Tony followed.

They started walking down the hall. It was an office building. Each office was a room that opened out on the hallway. Each office had a wooden door with the upper part made of glass, frosted glass so that you couldn't see inside. Tony read the names printed on the frosted glass. *Harry Kaplan, Attorney At Law. William Phelps, Insurance.* Then two vacant offices. Then *Dentosol, Sales.* What was Dentosol? he wondered.

As they went along, Tony noticed that lawyers occupied the most offices, with insurance agents second. But a good fifty per cent of the offices were vacant.

The building oppressed them with an eerie silence. They did not talk, reluctant to disturb that silence. Tony was glad when they came to the stairs at the end of the hall. He was anxious to get out of here. They went down the stairs fast.

"You're gonna see something," Lommy promised him as they pounded down the steps.

"You been here before, huh?"

"Sure, plenty of times," Lommy said.

They pushed open the door and stepped outside. It was remarkable. They were not on the Avenue. They were on a side street that cut into the Avenue.

"That's my secret place," Lommy said. "I go in there when I wanna give somebody the slip. Nobody knows that place has a backway. That's why I showed it to you. It might come in handy for you someday."

"Yuh," Tony breathed, grateful.

"Some guy might be chasing you someday."

"Yuh," Tony agreed.

It *was* a secret passageway. And Tony was walking along the Avenue one night when he got a funny feeling and looked back over his shoulder and saw two men in black trailing him. Their hats were pulled down low, their collars were up, and their hands were in their coat pockets. They were spies, following him, sent to kill him, and they were catching up to him, getting closer and closer, when he came to *868.* He dashed up the stairs. The two spies decided to wait out front for him. But he kept right on going, right out the backway, and when they got suspicious and entered the building and discovered their mistake, it was too late, he was far away and safe.

They went back up on the Avenue.

It was getting late.

"Well, we might as well go home," Lommy said. "There's nothing more doing tonight."

"Right," Tony said.

**

The next Saturday night they went to Cozy's Cafe. And the Saturday night after that. Tony thought he would always go—that the floor show would always be there. He was looking forward to the day when, grown-up, he would walk in Cozy's on a hot summer night and order a cold wet beer and watch the acts from the inside and sitting down.

Things got even better. Cozy installed a four-man band on the stage to play for dancing before and after the acts. A dance floor was created by clearing away maybe two tables at the far end, and if there was not room enough for fancy dancing, the couple at least got the chance to stand close together and talk. The band featured a saxophone—a sax that cut the smoke with the sweetest notes ever blown, a golden sax, its song floating above the noise, passing out into the night air, haunting, heard once, heard forever. Tony admired all the musicians. It seemed to him a wonderful thing to be able to make music.

But if summer comes, can winter be far behind? Disaster follows happiness like the seasons. Cozy's came a cropper. It seemed that in their desire to please, Cozy's waitresses were carrying things just a bit too far.

Lommy had found out that Tony didn't take the paper so a couple of days after it happened, Lommy brought Tony his family's copy of the *Observer*. It was a front-page story, with headlines and pictures.

Tony and Lommy had watched the acts Saturday night, and a good-looking young man had also been in attendance. But this young man had been on the inside. He and his waitress seemed to hit it off quite well. So, at midnight when the bar closed, instead of going out into the street, he went upstairs with the waitress. There were rooms over the cafe. And each room had a bed in it. The waitress closed the door and took her clothes off and slipped into bed. "Come on, get under the covers, you great big bull," she said. Did she suspect that he was an under-cover man for the police department? At any rate he then went to the window, opened it, stuck his head out, and blew his whistle.

In seconds the street was filled with police officers running faster than at any time since the first day of free lunches. They had been lurking in doorways, if pachyderms can be said to lurk, and now they raced into Cozy's, past the bar, past the phone booth, past the painting of the Seine's gray mists, and now the stairs shook under the impact of the thundering herd.

They burst into the room before the waitress had time to hook up her bra. "You're a no-good son of a bitch," she said to the good-looking young man, and rightly so, Tony thought. It seemed like a sneaky thing to do. To ingratiate himself into her good graces, to make believe he was her friend, and then to trap her like that. It seemed treacherous. Children are not sophisticated enough to know the complexities of right and wrong. They see everything in simple colors.

For some reason, perhaps not wishing to be accused of the law's delay, the police did not give the waitress time to dress but wrapped a sheet around her and hustled her off downstairs into a waiting car. They likewise hustled off two other hustlers, plus Cozy LeBeau, plus a man known simply as Frenchy, whose duties were never made clear. The customers were let go relieved, but unrelieved.

143

A photographer was there to take a picture of the poor waitress, wrapped Gandhi-like in her sheet, and Chief O'Leary was there. "We have had Cozy's Cafe under surveillance for a long time," he said, "My men moved in smoothly according to plan." A difficult word like *surveillance* in Chief O'Leary's mouth rather astounded those people who knew him, but the Chief was an avid listener to a radio program called *Gangbusters* and he kept picking up words from it.

The good-looking young man, however, knew even more words. But then again he was no cop. He had been borrowed from the district attorney's office.

"Did you converse with the woman called Mabel in the cafe?"

"Yes, I did."

"What was the tenor of her remarks?"

"She invited me to a room upstairs for purposes of engaging in a lewd and immoral act."

"Was there remuneration mentioned at this time—in the cafe."

"Yes, she said that there would be a consideration involved."

"Could you tell us how much that was?"

"The sum mentioned was two dollars."

"Did you pay her?"

"Yes, I did."

"Did you pay her in the cafe or upstairs?"

"I paid her in her room."

"What took place after that?"

"She disrobed."

Wow! She disrobed. What a lovely word, full of promise, delight, and pleasure. Tony's eyes focused on it, and the print immediately faded into a series of graceful movements and striking poses. Every detail, every ripple, every tantalizing whisper of revelation was caught by his imagination, and he lingered, for to him a woman undressing was not a simple act but a whole play. The only word he had known for the same thing was *stripped,* and how crude that word sounded to him now. Disrobed. That was a word he would not soon forget.

Cozy LeBeau, that keeper of a disorderly house, was sent to jail for six months and put on probation for two years. Mabel was treated kindlier by the judge. She was given a suspended sentence. Perhaps the judge was thinking that to be lit up by a flash bulb on a dark night, bug-eyed, clutching at a sheet like a modest Yankee bride in her shift, with the men in blue on both sides of you, and to have that photograph appear first on the front page of the *Observer* and then later in the Sunday supplement of a Boston paper—perhaps that was punishment enough

Tony and Lommy were solidly behind Cozy LeBeau in his time of trouble, because he had been such a gentleman to them. Then he came back, released from jail. He was not the same man. He was more subdued. He had lost his ambition. He had lost his interest in making the place jump. The dance band disappeared. The floor show disappeared. Without these two attractions, the crowd dwindled off. The waitresses, most of whom allegedly had a second trade, were let go. The bartenders were let go. Cozy donned an apron and got behind the bar himself.

Now on a Saturday night the room where there had been so much revelry was all darkened and still. There were no more singing voices rising in pleasing harmony. On the other side, at the bar, there would be a few men sitting quietly. The clientele was changing. The same kind of people who went to workingman bars now came to Cozy's. The place, Tony realized sadly, was getting more and more like Kaznicki's every day.

Thus, the one man who had dared light up the gloom of Gaw with a happy bar gave up. The single match of gaiety in the North End went out, blown dark by the unrelenting winds of morality.

Tony had thought there would always be a floor show at Cozy's. He thought this because as far back as he could remember, there always had been. Now he knew better. And so did Lommy.

They went there no more.

145

CHAPTER 5

GROWING UP

Tony and Lommy entered the seventh grade at Cupp Junior High. At *147* that very same time the director of a small private school in a well-to-do suburb of Boston had decided on a bold move. It was a highly regarded, progressive school and the director was determined to shine a light on a subject too long in the darkness of superstition and misinformation—sex. He gathered together in a classroom all the seventh and eighth graders, set up the white screen, pulled the drapes, turned off the lights, and set the film projector to whirring.

The movie was in the form of a lecture with the lecturer standing up in the front and looking directly at his audience, which was the class. The lecturer was a kindly old white-haired doctor. The kids knew he was a doctor because he was wearing a white coat. He picked up a long wooden pointer, the same kind teachers use, and said, "Let's find out, shall we?" There flashed on the screen the drawn figures of a man and woman, without clothes, and there was much stirring in the room as the kids sat up straight and craned their necks, trying to get a better view. But they needn't have bothered. What they were looking for wasn't there. A certain appendage, the very essence of man's masculinity, was missing. In fact, the only way you could tell the man and woman apart was in the hair on their heads. The man's hair was straight and parted on the side, the woman's curled down to her shoulders. The insides of both figures were drawn in, guts and organs all jammed in together, horrible-looking, and the girls shuddered and uttered a soft "Ugh."

The kindly old doctor began explaining things, pointing here and there on the figures as he went along. Then the man and the woman suddenly went off and a big diagram of a woman, mostly her bottom part, filled the whole screen. You couldn't see the doctor any more although you could still hear his voice and you could see his pointer reaching across occasionally.

"The uterus is about the size and shape of a Bartlett pear," the doctor said, reaching across. "It is hollow and has powerful muscles."

His pointer moved again.

"The ovaries resemble almonds in size and shape. Each ovary contains some fifty thousand undeveloped eggs."

Then a little bug began bouncing inside this diagram of the woman, like in a cartoon picture, and the doctor said, "The spermatozoon in appearance resembles a tadpole, although of course it is much smaller in size. It has an oval head and a long whip-like tail with which it propels itself. It moves about an inch in seven minutes, quite a lively pace considering its microscopic size." On the diagram the bug landed on the egg, and the doctor said, "This is the supreme event—the creation of a new human being."

And with that stirring culmination, the movie ended.

The producers of the film had written, "The film has been specially prepared to satisfy the sexual curiosity of young people. It will answer most if not all of their questions."

If this film had been made available to Tony and Lommy and all the other boys in the seventh grade at Cupp, things might have been different. But as it was, they were left to satisfy their sexual curiosity on their own. Like good students, they looked in their school books for knowledge. Now the school books were watched over closely by the School Board. The Board was ever vigilant in preventing the use of any impure or improper teaching materials but one book slipped by undetected. How this could have happened is not known. Perhaps a careless reading . . . perhaps collusion with certain interests . . . no one knows. But whatever the reason the book did slip by and was placed in the hands of every student at Cupp. This was most regrettable, for the book became a chief source of pornography for the boys. A filthy book can do irreparable damage to impressionable young minds, and when this filthy book is bought with taxpayers' money and then issued to every pupil by the school authorities, so that in effect parents are subsidizing the moral tainting of their own children—then this is not only deplorable, but shocking.

Tony and his friends read in this book at every opportunity. They were looking for dirty words. The book was the dictionary. And words that were not in their desk-sized dictionary could be found in the dictionary in the library. This library dictionary was the dictionary to end all dictionaries. It looked like it weighed fifty pounds. It was so big and heavy that it required a special stand to hold it up. It was the fattest book Tony had ever seen.

When a boy found something interesting, he passed it on. He put the back of his hand to his mouth and whispered, "Page 672." The free exchange of information existed among the boys, as it should among all research workers.

Tony was the acknowledged scholar of the group. The other boys could find words like *nipple* and *breast*, but he could go into the jungle of a dictionary and come out with words that nobody had ever seen or heard of before. He brought out *anus, rectum, intercourse, coition, penis, testicles.*

They looked at him with awe and amazement.

"How do you find them?"

"I just look," he said modestly.

"Yuh, but where?" they demanded.

"Oh, I just go through the pages," he said. After all, could Charlie Gehringer explain how he always threw to the right base? It was instinct, that's all. He had an instinct for it.

Once Tony had found a word, he turned to it over and over again, day after day. He stared at the definition until the words seemed not words but an architecture, each word a building, in fixed and immovable relationship. If someone had whispered *penis* in his ear, without thought, like one of Pavlov's dogs, there would have flashed across his mind *the male organ of copulation.*

It was the first time in his life that Tony had ever looked up words in a dictionary, although teachers had been urging him to do so for a long time. As he worked, he became aware of the lexicographer's quirks. First there was this matter of defining A with B, and defining B with A. He looked up *intercourse* and found that it meant *coition.* With feverish fingers he flipped the pages, sure that he was on the trail of a description, but when he got to *coition* all it said was: *intercourse.* He never did find a description. Then there was the matter of what seemed to Tony an incomplete or one-sided definition. For example, *penis.* It was true that a great many men used it for copulation, but was it not equally true that these same men probably used it just as often for urination? Why was this not mentioned? Did the lexicographer have a sex-ridden mind? Then there was the matter of flouted logic. For example, *masturbation* was defined as *self-pollution*. Now if the act of masturbation in its glandular sense was similar to the act of intercourse, then why was *intercourse* not listed as *pollution of a woman*? These were questions that Tony never sent to Webster's; they remained unanswered in his mind.

The existence of certain words surprised Tony. He had never dreamed that there were polite words for certain things. He had thought that if you went to a doctor's office, you could just point and that was all. But apparently there was a word for everything. He felt like winking at the venerable lexicographer, as if he had caught him in a rendezvous with a dissolute woman. The lexicographer said *anus* with a straight face and the boys in the street and the men in the factories said something else, but everyone meant the same thing, didn't they?

The boys found their dictionary work an exciting adventure. They were alert for other stimulating things. In Art class, with Miss Draper, a most energetic teacher, they were supposed to draw imaginary flowers. As was customary, most of the class looked at her dully and in a frenzy of frustration the good woman seized a piece of chalk and jumped to the board, crying, "Oh, my goodness, there are so many you could draw! Take the handcuffs off your imagination!" Giving herself over with artistic abandon to her task, she attacked the board with great sweeping strokes and in a few moments several flowers arched over in the sun's rays.

But the moment she was done and stepped aside, the class, the boys specifically, behaved in the queerest of fashions. Some coughed, some had to blow their nose, some looked down at their shoes, some examined their hands, but all were fighting for self-control. If one boy had laughed, the class would have broken up. They would have fallen from their seats and they probably would still be there today, thrashing on the floor, laughing, holding their sides in. It was all due to the imaginary flowers on the board. Miss Draper had inadvertently drawn a flower, the one second from the left, that bore an unmistakable resemblance to what the boys had come to know as the male organ of copulation.

It was particularly hard on Tony for he had a tendency to laugh even quicker than most. Tony, red in the face, stared straight ahead, his fingernails biting into his hands. From behind him came the insidious whisper, "Tony, Tony." It was Alfonso Fonseca. He did not dare turn around. If he did, Alfonso would purse his lips and pantomime an obscene sucking and he would have to laugh and then there would be hell to pay. The class would break up and Miss Draper would hold him personally responsible. She would demand to know why he had laughed and perhaps even send him to the office.

He did not turn around. He held it in—the whole period. For it was there inside him the whole period, even after the board had been erased, and it was inside the other boys, too. Not until the bell rang and they were safely in the corridor did they unbend. Then they leaned on the green lockers and laughed and laughed and laughed. The Traffic Patrol was looking at them. You could get a citation for making noise in the corridors. So they went into the Boys' Room and there by the urinals and sinks they laughed and laughed. Then they went to their next class, climbing the stairs, laughing all the way.

Their next class was Hygiene with Miss Harrington. Miss Harrington was a good teacher for Hygiene; she looked and acted the part. She had rosy-red cheeks, no make-up, and her hair was in a boyish bob. She wore flat white shoes and walked down the corridor like she had told them to walk, with shoulders thrown back and knees pumping high, like a fullback going into the line. And she was as healthy as all hell. In icy December and January the first thing she did when they came in the room was say, "You people look draggy to me! Open those windows! Wide! Everybody up! On your feet! Now follow me! Up-down-up-down-up-down-one-two-one two-one-two-bend-bend-bend-one-two-that's-it-one-two-one two-stretch-stretch-stretch-those-mus-cles-one-two-one-two-breathe-deep-ly-breathe-deep-ly-one-two-one-two," and for fifteen minutes they stretched, twisted, bent, and shivered, with her doing every single exercise and not even puffing at the end. She was in great condition and with her broad shoulders and husky build, someone should have wired her name to Coach Elmer Layden for next season.

Today when they went into Hygiene, Miss Harrington was waiting for them at the front of the room. She waited until they were settled in their seats and the bell rang and all was quiet.

They looked at her.

Miss Harrington took her hand and placed it right smack between her breasts. "Who remembers what this is called?" she said. Her fingers were pressing into what had to be soft flesh.

Immediately the boys jerked into life like someone had just turned the cold water on in the showers. Throats were cleared, feet were scraped, handkerchiefs were brought out, and no boy dared look at another boy.

"No one knows what this is called?" Miss Harrington said, playfully running a finger up and down the valley of the moons, the long valley, where the red pony would like to play. She shook her head in soft remonstrance. "Now think. I know someone knows."

"I know, teacher—"Tony heard Alfonso Fonseca whispering behind him "—they're called tits," and Tony strangled.

Linda Oliveira raised her hand. "The stertum?"

"The sternum, Linda," Miss Harrington said, nodding.

They were studying bones and it was awfully hard to remember all those scientific names. They had Hygiene just on Mondays, so that made it a whole week between classes. That was too long a time; you forgot everything.

Miss Harrington raised her hand in the air and wiggled all the fingers. "Who remembers what these are?" she said, smiling.

Several faces frowned, trying to remember.

"Oh, come on," Miss Harrington coaxed. "It starts with a *p*."

"Pelvic!" Linda Oliveira cried out.

"Noooo," Miss Harrington said, shaking her head. She gave up. "Phalanges. Remember?"

"Oh, yes," Linda Oliveira said, mad at herself. "I always get those two mixed up."

Alfonso Fonseca leaned close to Tony. "How'd you like to get your phalanges on Elsie Cunha's sternums?" he murmured.

Elsie Cunha was a girl in their room who never said a word to attract the boys. She didn't have to. She just smiled and that was enough. She was built along the lines of a youthful Clara Bow and she knew it. She wore tight skirts and wiggled from class to class and all the boys followed her behind in the corridors.

They had Hygiene and they had Art and they had many other classes. They had Penmanship, they had Gym, they had Music, they had Electric Shop, they had Social Studies, they had English, they had Mathematics, they had a full day.

Each class had a different teacher, and of all these teachers one in particular exhilarated the boys. That one was Miss Draper. They always entered her room with a feeling of repressed excitement that was absent from all other doorways.

Most of the teachers at Cupp were older women with lumpy bodies. You couldn't tell where one part of them left off and the next began. But not so with Miss Draper. She had clear and distinct lines. Her legs were one thing, her hips were another, her belly was a third, her breasts were still a fourth. Her breasts were still a fourth, but by any sensible mathematical computation that fraction should have been raised to at least seven-eighths, for Miss Draper's breasts were a vision of golden harvests. Inside her blouse they arched in full pride, straining at the cloth. They cleared the mind of trivia, they regressed the beholder to an infant hunger, they introduced carnality to the innocent.

Miss Draper was in the very blaze of summer ripeness. This was evident in the rise and swell of her bosom. It was evident in the full-flowing lines of her figure, in the rich pulsations of her being, in the poised affirmation of her flesh, soft and yet taut, expectant. This was no young fig, green and hard. This was a mature woman. Tony guessed she was about thirty-five years old, and it was a wonderful age for a woman to be, he emphatically believed.

It seemed incredible to Tony that all the skinny shrunken women walking the streets of Gaw should be married and Miss Draper not be. What was wrong with the men of Gaw? That this silken plum should go unplucked, it sweet meat untasted, it seemed unbelievable.

Yet in his romantic soul he was content that she was unmarried and, in fact, he desired her to remain forever so—or at least until he grew up. In the dreams that he put himself to sleep with every night, Miss Draper played a prominent part. He walked with her hand in hand along the shady path in Bellehaven Park and kissed her under a tree. He grasped her drowning figure in the water when their ship went down and towed her to a desert island where he built her a rude shelter out of boughs and leaves—they were, unfortunately, the only survivors. She awaited electrocution in thirty minutes and he entered the prison disguised as a reporter, but when he got to her side, he took out the sub-

153

machine gun concealed under his shirt and blasted their way out; they hid out in a deserted tenement half a block away from the Heap Square police station. He entered her African hut when she had leprosy and all others had fled in terror. He announced his presence, "I'm here, Miss Draper," and he nursed her back to health—fortunately, the disease did not leave behind so much as a pimple. In the exigencies of his soaring deeds, Miss Draper's clothes always got torn, particularly her blouse. She was of course unfailingly grateful to him—one might even say, warmly grateful—perhaps even, throbbingly grateful. For no matter where the Fates placed her, whether in the ocean or Death Row, her opulent curves always became his to be enjoyed in privacy and leisure. In some secret spot, far from the madding crowd, there they made love in the moonlight.

Actually Tony had a real-life rival and he was jealous of him. It was Mr. Hopwood, who taught Electric Shop. Mr. Hopwood had curly brown hair and spoke in a lazy drawl. He was Miss Draper's age, single, and kept smiling to himself like some particular bit of good fortune had fallen into his lap and he was enjoying thinking about it. It was a wholly suspicious smile as far as Tony was concerned, the kind of smile a man would have if he were looking forward to a date with Miss Draper that night. Tony would look up from his bench and there would be Mr. Hopwood at his desk, all by himself, smiling, and somebody would go up, and the smile would instantly metamorphose into a scowl.

They were wiring houses for doorbells. They started out with a one-story house, went to a two-story house, and topped it off with a three-story house, Front and Rear Door. Tony was glad to learn how. Maybe someday he'd put a doorbell in his own house; now you had to knock on the door.

On their wooden board the boys stapled the wire, following the blueprint, and when they thought they had it, they brought the board up to Mr. Hopwood's desk for an O.K. Mr. Hopwood was scornful of them. He could tolerate only the one or two geniuses who never made a mistake. To them he spoke in intimate undertones. But for the befuddled who kept splicing the wrong wires together, he made a dog noise in his throat, not a growl, more like a groan, and with a bright maniac smile pulled out every wire on the board and said, "Start over."

On the other hand, Mr. Hopwood could be serious and helpful. He might fix up a wire or two on your board, tie in to the current, and say,

"Try it now." You pressed the buzzer—*yowie!* An electric shock. Mr. Hopwood would throw his head back in his swivel chair that tilted backwards and look up at the ceiling and go, "Haw—haw—haw!" And all the way back to your bench he kept time with your steps, "Haw—haw—haw—haw!"

This was the man that the whole school believed was in love with Miss Draper. Was he? Tony had not once seen them together. Yet—. It was hard not to believe in the romance, because everyone else believed in it, and it seemed like a logical, natural, inevitable pairing-off.

It was a romance built up on dribs and drabs of anonymous reports, all of them unverifiable. Someone had seen Miss Draper and Mr. Hopwood talking in her car before school that morning. Someone had seen them riding down the Avenue the night before. Someone had seen them riding across the Ossawona Bridge last Saturday. Always they were riding in Miss Draper's car, a little green coupe, which was undoubtedly the most sighted car in all of Gaw. And on foot they had been seen entering the Venice Theatre downtown. They had been seen sitting on a bench in Bellehaven Park—kissing. Fragments, fragments, but their total weight was staggering. And then the climax, one in a long series. It passed through the school like an electrical impulse. *Mr. Hopwood proposed to Miss Draper last night.* Kids swore to it. Everybody believed it. And Tony believed and doubted. . . .

Was there a romance? Tony wanted proof, proof, proof with his own eyes. He took to studying Miss Draper in class. When she was short-tempered, irritable, and had shadows under her eyes, then Tony became suspicious. He saw her fatigue and unhappiness. He looked at her accusingly, driven to condemnation by a sense of her own guilt. And Alfonso Fonseca whispered Tony's own thoughts into his ear—"A hard night with Hopwood."

But he was most alert when notes were brought into the room. One day a sealed note came, brought by a boy. Miss Draper tore at the envelope and Tony watched her closely, as did, it might be mentioned, the whole class. She unfolded the message and began reading quickly. Tony studied her face for any sign of delight, disappointment, whatever, but there wasn't even a flicker. She had great self-control. Alfonso read along with her. *"Meet me tonight in Bellehaven Park, same time as usual. Don't forget to bring the rubbers. (Signed) Hopsie."* She took the note and went over to the wastebasket and tore it into many small pieces. Then she returned to the class.

"How about coming back here after school, Tony?" Alfonso proposed quietly. "We'll get that note and paste it together."

"She locks her door," Tony answered.

Evidence was hard to come by. But Tony still tried. He kept his eyes and his ears open. He kept his eyes opened on Miss Draper and her remarkable figure. It would have been a joy declined to look elsewhere. She always was sure of his rapt attention.

In the ordinary class Tony could hope to win the notice and the admiration of the teacher through the excellence of his work. In Art he did not bother to hope this hope. For as these things often work out, Art was the subject he wanted most to shine in and Art was the subject he was weakest in. He had an eye for art. He saw form and color. But his hands could not translate what he saw. His hands were dumb and when they tried to speak, the results were primordial and graceless. The average second grader could equal his work, and a talented first grader could surpass it. The first time Miss Draper saw his drawing she stared in shock and disbelief while he blushed with embarrassment, being quite aware of the level of his work. Obviously here was a pupil who was going to have to be graded on Effort alone. If she had thought of it, there was a possibility open. She could have made an Abstractionist out of him, for in that field even chimpanzees do respected work. But she did not and he struggled on. It was difficult, for he had pride and did not enjoy being the low man in the class. But everyone must eat a pound of it in their life, and it was a good experience. It offered him insight into the helpless terror of the moron. To do your best and not even come close to the mark, he knew what that felt like now.

He and Miss Draper worked out a humane, satisfactory relationship. She did not make him a subject of public conversation. She understood the reality of limitations. When she walked up and down the aisles, looking at everybody's work, she looked at the desk before his and the desk after his, but she did not look at his desk. She passed by him, carefully averting her eyes. He understood. He blushed with chagrin, but he understood and he did not at all blame her. He was sensitive to her feelings. That was why he never raised his hand for help or took his paper up to her. He had no wish to torture her.

He was not so fortunate with the class. They did not ignore his work as he would have wished. Oh, there was great activity and concentration on his part, laborious strivings and much erasings, but only beginnings. And then some smart aleck like Armand Langevin, who was inhumanly fast and casually skillful, would walk up front to deposit his finished drawing. On his way back Armand would look at Tony's efforts, suppress a laugh, and go back to his seat and spread the whispered word—"Look at Alfama's." Pretty soon Linda Oliveira, giggling, would say, "Hold it up, Tony. I won't laugh, honest." Embarrassed beyond all fury he would reply to her churlishly, "Aw, hold your own up!" If he finished on time, which was seldom, he took his paper up and slipped it in the middle of the pile, losing it there, he hoped. He never once placed it on top of the pile, where it would be visible.

157

But there were moments of solace. Ah, yes, moments of bread and wine with thou in the wilderness of Room 10, Art. The blood works under its own laws of chemistry and some days Miss Draper's spirit soared and the belief in life was in her and she dared the impossible. There were days when she could look the abyss in the eye and say, "Come on, Tony, let us lick this thing together."

April affected her like that.

She stood in front of the class at the start of the period.

"Everybody sit up straight! No talking! Hands on desk—clasped! Look at me now—everybody! That's it. Now close your eyes. That's right. Close them. And keep them closed until I tell you to open them.

"Spring—spring—spring is in the air! The robins are singing, the flowers are just peeping out, we are shedding our heavy coats. Alfonso Fonseca, keep your eyes closed! Now what's the first thing you think of when you think of spring? Is it a robin redbreast? Is it a pussy willow? Alfonso Fonseca, stop whispering! Whatever it is, we're going to draw it! Today we're going to have a Spring Festival, our own Spring Festival, right here in this room.

"Now how many already know what they're going to draw? Raise your hands. That's fine. All right, hands down. Now for the rest of us who still don't know—keep your eyes closed, class—say to yourself, 'Spring, spring, spring, spring, spring. . . .' Is something coming? Take the handcuffs off your imagination! What do you see, actually see, there before your eyes? That's what we're going to draw!"

Tony wouldn't have dared draw what was before his eyes. The last thing he had looked at before closing his eyes was Miss Draper's breasts, and with his eyes closed he still saw them. The spirit of spring was Miss Draper's breasts.

In a few minutes pencils and crayons were out and everyone was going at it. With her great energy Miss Draper walked almost feverishly up and down the aisles, encouraging, praising, suggesting. She came to Tony's desk and this time she looked. She frowned. "What is this?"

"A robin," he said, smiling shyly.

"Slide over," she said matter-of-factly.

Miss Draper never helped the kids who could do it. That was the penalty for being good in Art.

In Art the rows were double, and the two seats were close enough together so that when you moved over, you didn't slip down between them. Tony slid over, nudging the boy on his right to make room, and Miss Draper sat down. She had part of Tony's seat, and Tony, ahhh, Tony had the other part. How delightful to be squashed up against Miss Draper! What pleasure known to man or boy could compare with it?

"Now let's see . . . ," Miss Draper said.

The heat of her being burned all the starch out of him and left him weak and limp. Her arm was against his arm, her thigh pressed against his thigh, her perfume was in his nostrils. He breathed her in, unobtrusively, but deeply, inhaling the fragrance of her like a drunken naturalist in fields of clover.

"Let's take this out a bit more . . . ," Miss Draper murmured, her pencil flashing bold arcs on his paper.

Her hair glowed from brushing. She wore it in natural waves, loose, and as she bent over his paper in earnest, her hair parted in the back and swung forward. A strand brushed against his cheek. It stayed there on his face for a moment, tickling him, and he got the wild idea that this strand of hair was connected up to her mind, was under her control, and that she had sent it out in full knowledge to tease him.

"That's more like it . . . ," Miss Draper said, like she was talking to herself.

The movement of her hair had left the back of her neck uncovered. He turned slightly and glanced down innocently. The rich creaminess of her neck was exposed to him, like some secret place. The ivory skin was so close to his lips. Oh, Lord, he pleaded, take away these thirty-nine other kids and I'll kiss her on the neck! One last covetous feasting of the eyes and he turned away.

Miss Draper studied the drawing. "Well . . . ," she said.

Then it happened. His eraser was on the far corner of the desk. She raised her arm and reached across him to get it. Her breast in all its glory came smack up against the meat of his arm. It was so unexpected and yet so definitely, so solidly, so fully, so firmly there, that he knew he was not dreaming it, imagining it. He was hemmed in by the boy on his right; he could not move an inch out of the way as good manners seemed to call for in a case like this. Thus, his conscience was clear.

Then she began to erase. She erased with her elbow in the air. Her breast still lay against his arm. And as she erased with short vigorous strokes, her breast jiggled against him in orgasmic rhythm, her breast danced against him in bedded embrace. Her breast—oh, Lord!—he could feel its absolute full-firmedness. His arm was alive; it had been turned into a hand and was squeezing one of her glories; it became a hungry mouth alive to every nuance of sensation.

She stopped erasing, leaving him in a glazed condition, sodden with pleasure. "And now let's put some feathers on him, shall we?" she said.

His eyes were still fogged over. He could not see his paper. He could not tell what she was doing. But he wanted her to know he was conscious and was listening to her. "Yes," he said.

"There!" she said with satisfaction. "I think that's better." She got up.

"Yes, it is," he agreed, nodding, and pretending to appraise her work. "Thank you. Miss Draper." Good-bye, you lovely creature.

She was gone.

And suddenly someone had turned off the 220 voltage. For the first time he became conscious of the eyes on him, the other boys, who had enviously watched him all the while, the other boys, who observed every breath Miss Draper took, the other boys, who were like a circle of too-small mongrels with eyes intent on the big bitch traipsing around. Tony gave Armand Langevin a beatific smile.

"Tony! Tony!" came the insistent whisper behind him, but he did not turn around. Sitting with Miss Draper was too perfect a moment. It existed by itself. It didn't need Alfonso Fonseca. He didn't want to spoil it by any foul aftereffects.

Sitting with Miss Draper—a moment like that is what a boy lives for.

***

Tony, Lommy, Alfonso Fonseca, and the other boys passed into the eighth grade. Their preoccupation with sex intensified.

More than one boy around school had the reputation of being "a dirty guy," but Alfonso Fonseca was known as "a real dirty guy." But such is the magnetism of the devil that Alfonso's company was not avoided. Rather it was sought out.

Alfonso constituted a one-man library of dirty books, a one-man walking lending library of eye-popping treasures. He was the Pied Piper of Pornography, for as he walked the corridors between periods a long line of boys trailed behind him, charmed by his music, following him to the Boys' Room, where the doors closed after them forever. There in the Boys' Room Alfonso let them browse through the reading matter on his shelves. From his pockets, from his notebook, from underneath his shirt, from the bottom of the used-paper-towels basket, from every conceivable place, he pulled out his treasures. Alfonso loved his library, he loved books. He well knew the enjoyment of reading. As the poet says, *"A boy, a book, an unturned door. . . ."*

Alfonso let the material circulate overnight, and it had a wide reading. Library cards were not required. Overdue books were no problem, for a tardy return could mean being scratched off the borrowers' list. So successful was Alfonso that even the very dumbest guys, who could barely read, used his library—a vindication of the methods of modern education, which stress interest and motivation. Had Alfonso been a Curriculum Consultant from Columbia he could have written an article for the *NEA Journal,* "Making the Library Period a Meaningful Experience for the Nonreader: *We Look at Pictures!"*

Alfonso had any number of *Spicy Detective Stories* and *Film Fun* magazines, which were after all rather mild and could be found on the magazine rack of any smoke shop. But he had better things. In fact, he specialized in cartoon booklets which could not be found on any magazine rack of any store. These cartoon booklets were uniformly eight pages long, and a perfect size, small enough to fit in your back pocket. They featured magniorganed heroes and superbly proportioned heroines. Unlike *Spicy Detective Stories,* which always stopped when things

160

were getting interesting, these booklets left absolutely nothing to the imagination. They were riotous exercises in satyric lusts, and down to the final knotted tangle of arms and legs on page 8, the boys stared with shining eyes.

Alfonso had *Boots and Her Buddies* (with Rod), *Ella Cinders* (with Patches), *Joe Palooka* (with Ann Howe), *Maggie and Jiggs*, *Tillie the Toiler* (with Mac), *Blondie* (with Dagwood), *Major Hoople* (not with Martha), *Wash Tubbs*, *Moon Mullins*, *Hair-Breath Harry*, and many others. Only one question bothered the boys. Looking at a bare Boots, they asked, "Do you think the guy who drew this is the same guy who draws Boots in the *Observer*?" Alfonso snorted, "Of course it's the same guy. It looks just like her, don't it? You could tell if somebody else was faking it." The boys were somehow troubled by the double life the cartoonist and Boots were leading, and from then on when ever they looked at Boots in the *Observer*, their minds kept drifting off the asinine adventure she was embarked upon and they saw again a certain couch where she and Rod had whooped it up for eight pages.

Where did Alfonso get all these cartoon booklets? Nobody knew. Alfonso just smiled mysteriously when asked. But apparently his supply was inexhaustible, for he always had a couple of new ones to show them. Any large number of boys seen trooping into the Boys' Room meant that Alfonso was in there. And in Music class with all the girls up front singing away and the back row of boys not singing, everybody standing, and the girls looking in their music books and singing, *"I would be true/For there are those who trust me,"* in the back row the boys were looking in their music books at the open pages of *Hair-Breath Harry* and *Tillie the Toiler*.

Alfonso also had what he called "glossy photographs." These were contained in thin magazines, one photograph to a page. The photographs were of Hollywood starlets outfitted in a pair of patent-leather pumps and nothing else, beautiful girls, their lips artfully, invitingly, wantonly parted, their darkly nippled breasts casual in unconfinement, their lovely bellies willing before the camera. Wow! What pictures! Sometimes the girl was pouting most attractively and had a chain wrapped around her wrists as if to say, "I am your prisoner." Sometimes there was a long cigarette holder in the girl's mouth and, besides the skyscraper-heel pumps, she had on black net stockings and arm-length black gloves and nothing else. Wow!

Alfonso was very proud of his "glossy photographs." He pointed to a particularly succulent morsel and said, "The only way you can get pictures like these is to prove you're an artist. You notice here—it says *For Artists Only?*"

"How did *you* get them?" somebody asked.

"I'm an artist," Alfonso said.

Alfonso brought with him to school the artifacts of an advanced civilization, contraceptives, although where he got them in Catholic Massachusetts is any druggist's guess. Alfonso held up the tiny box. "These are Tiger Lilies," he said. He took one out of the box and unrolled it and let the boys feel its sheer texture. It was very exciting to see it and more exciting yet to touch it. "This is the best safe made," Alfonso pontificated, like a qualified pharmacist. "It feels like you got nothing on," he said in tribute to the American rubber-goods industry.

"How much do they cost?" the boys asked breathlessly. It was the first time they had ever seen one.

"Three for a quarter," Alfonso said.

"Where'd you get them?"

Alfonso shrugged his shoulders. "I got lots of them. These are just plain safes, but you should see the ones I got home. They're special. They got a big button on the end and they drive the dame crazy. They're called Merry Widows."

"Gee!" the boys breathed, eyes wide. They saw a girl going crazy before them or under them, going right out of her mind with excitement and begging them for mercy. It gave them a pleasant feeling of power and mastery. Tony made a mental note of that name—*Merry Widows*—for possible future use.

What was the significance of Alfonso Fonseca and his safes and glossy photographs and cartoon booklets? Did Alfonso affect anyone's morals or was he merely an agent, an aphrodisiac, a match among dry fagots? One thing was certain. With his distribution of excitingly illustrated materials, he was a stimulus toward self-pollution. He was responsible for orgies of onanism. Old Alfonso, always grinning, black hair cropped close, bushy black eyebrows, black eyes shining, white teeth flashing, Tony came to know his grin, his softly insinuating voice, his tempting words. "C'mere, Tony, I'll show you something." Tony felt the excitement and fear the nearness of the devil always brings, but he went.

Into the Boys' Room they marched, Tony flushed with excitement and anticipation. There Alfonso opened his notebook to the Social Studies section and Tony caught a glimpse of Alfonso's neatly written ink report on Pike's Peak with a penciled sketch of Lieutenant Zebulon Pike. Then Alfonso turned the page of Pike's Peak. There it was. Tony caught his breath.

"What do you think of that?" Alfonso asked with a grin.

"Not bad," Tony admitted, staring. "Not bad."

"You wanna borrow it?" Alfonso said generously. "Go ahead. Take it. Give it back to me Monday."

"Okay. Thanks, Alfonso."

And Tony walked out of the Boys' Room, his head light and his knees weak at the thought of what was in his notebook. He went directly to his locker and put his notebook behind his lunch and gym clothes. He closed the door, turned the combination to zero, and jiggled the door handle several times. It was locked. He took several steps and then came back and tried the door once again. It was locked. With a last nervous glance over his shoulder to see who might be watching him, he walked away. He knew how he was going to spend the weekend.

163

***

As with Tony, so with Lommy and the other boys. Sex in the eighth grade was not an apparition, a curiosity that could be dispelled by a lecture on eggs and seeds. Neither was it a drive. It was a conflagration, a blaze that roared through the trees of their forests and showered them with hot visions of naked women. It was a fever, scalding to the touch, that consumed all their mental energies. They were seething with it, burning up with it. And they could not resist its power any more than leaves in the wind can resist being blown about. How many times had Tony vowed never again to borrow a magazine from Alfonso and failed in his resolution the very next day? In his struggle to end the abuse of the self, how many times had Tony gone running through the streets to Bostwick Hill and back, trying to enervate himself and his impulses, and all to no avail?

The boys were often embarrassed by erections These erections came on suddenly, uncalled for, without reason, often when the mind was innocent of any dream. What could be lascivious about figuring the cost of a loan of $300, borrowed for 2½ years, at a rate of 3% interest, compounded semiannually? And yet there it was. And like as not, the period ended then and they had to stand up and go walking through the corridors in grotesque outline. Or, the teacher called upon them to recite and they had to stand up. So they recited with a hand in their pocket, trying to guide the monster into inconspicuous repose. It truly was a monster, an obstinate beast with a mind of its own.

Does one's youth have to be sex-ridden? Anthropologists have pondered this question. Different cultures, they say, produce different psychic patterns and different behaviors. For instance, young men in the South Seas start sleeping with girls at a relatively early age and their days are free from tension and they have practically no dream life at all.

Another culture, the English, is interesting in this regard. Mr. Oliver Cockermouth, a major English literary figure but a minor writer, has given us an account of his youth in his delightful *Passion for Poetry*. His fourteenth year, for example, was spent in Surrey. His parents had left for India where his father was an officer in the Salvation Army, in charge of tambourine repair for all units in Asia. Oliver was left behind in the care of his uncle, Sir Henry Fitzhugh-Darcy of Surrey. Picture, if you will, Oliver in Sir Henry's book-lined study, lying on the floor, devouring Shelley, Keats, Wordsworth, his faithful dog Fortinbras at his feet, a log crackling in the fireplace, the only interruption being his eccentric Aunt Allegra coming in with his tea and those delicious little seed cakes she alone knows how to make. The boy Oliver drinks the tea and eats the cakes and can contain himself no longer. He rushes out into the charming English countryside and shouts Shelley in a mad torrent to the four winds.

It should be born in mind that Oliver Cockermouth was fourteen years old at this time. The boys at Cupp in the eighth grade were also fourteen years old. But what a difference! There was no sex but much Shelley in Oliver's life, and with the boys at Cupp there was much sex and no Shelley. They had, in fact, never even heard of Shelley. They had a fixed opinion of poetry and if they had been told that this poet's first name was Percy, they would have smiled understandingly.

It is a sad fact that while the American school has shown zeal in attending to the needs of children, it has not recognized any need for poetry. Well, yes, the boys at Cupp knew the first few lines of *Paul Revere's Ride*,

TONY: A NEW ENGLAND BOYHOOD

they knew *Trees* by Joyce Kilmer, they knew *The Village Blacksmith*, but those are really rhymes rather than poems. They knew no host of golden daffodils, no skylarks, no Grecian urns. What Oliver Cockermouth termed "the poietic crystallines" was absent from their lives, the crystallines missing, the poietic gone, yes, their days gonepoietic.

Oliver Cockermouth was able to sublimate his sex into odes. He was helped in this by a culturally significant factor—the rich English heritage in poetry. Could his feat have been duplicated by an American in the context of our society and traditions? It is doubtful.

What are words worth? The American does not know. Brown in the face from playing tennis in the sun, he is healthy and active. Shall he give up athletics for poetry? No. He is a doer. He makes money. He travels to Hawaii on the *Lurline*. He roasts a pig at a great Hawaiian luau and puts an apple in its mouth, and should the swine burn, he cannot fashion a lament. He can only make guttural sounds in his throat, like a beast in the forest. Even when the American has money and leisure, his habits remain essentially vulgar. In his book Oliver Cockermouth tells of visiting a wealthy Southern gentleman and of his disgust at watching the man spit past valuable paintings, the brown juice running down his chin, and his servant coming up with a fresh plug, "Your chaw, sir."

165

***

These were flesh-driven days for Tony and Lommy. They wandered about the city sniffing the breeze like two tomcats. They were looking for girls, for excitement, and yet what would they have done had they found a girl or two? That was a question. Of course, Tony had imagined this meeting in a thousand settings. He always swept the girl masterfully into his arms. They kissed soulfully. "I'm awfully glad I met you," she whispered in his ear.

And while they waited for two girls to greet them and their wild adventure to begin, Tony and Lommy went about watching, watching. They went to Bellehaven Park, but they ignored the baseball diamond. They walked along the wire fence of the tennis courts and evaluated the players. What they were looking for was not a girl with the backhand of Helen Wills Moody but a girl with the backside of Jean Harlow. But a girl like that is hard to come by. Still they found one to their liking and sat on the nearest park bench and watched her play.

She was a very attractive girl, about eighteen, in shorts, beautifully tanned, long-legged, supple. They were entranced by her every movement and stroke. In the early soft-quiet summer evening, with little kids shouting far away, and the squirrels running up and down the trees, they sat on the green park bench and watched her small athletic breasts bounce up and down as she ran to and fro. Once her partner, a good-looking blond guy, made like Babe Ruth and powdered the ball over her head and over the fence and Tony ran, retrieved it, came up to the fence, threw it gently back in to her, and was rewarded with a smile that warmed him for the next thirty minutes.

And Tony thought, What a wonderful thing to be playing tennis with a girl like that on a perfect summer night, and then maybe afterwards to walk home slowly in the gathering darkness, hand in hand. Would that ever happen to him? Would he ever play tennis in the park with a beautiful girl?

"How much do you think a tennis racquet costs?" he asked Lommy.

"Oh, you can get 'em all prices," Lommy said. "You can get a cheap one for two bucks. But then you've got to buy those balls—three of them at a time. That's where your money goes."

On their way home that night, it was around nine o'clock, Tony and Lommy passed one of those nice yards with grass and the air was suddenly sweet with lilac, and they heard a girl giggling behind a screened porch and the boy laughing and the swing creaking under them, creaking back and forth, and Tony saw her flash before him again, with her slim but shapely legs, her smooth-as-honey legs, and he heard her calling out so aptly, "Love-fifteen," and then he remembered her smile, and he was overcome with longing for her and had he been Zeus he would have that moment flown to her side. But he was only human, only fourteen years old, with nothing to offer her, neither good looks nor tennis ability, so he kept walking, sad at his hopeless desire.

They went to Bellehaven Park and watched the girls play tennis. And sometimes they walked in the opposite direction, deep into the South End, to Lindamar Beach. This was some five miles away, or a ten-mile round trip, and it had always seemed like too far a distance to walk. But that was before they got interested in girls.

They walked along the cement sidewalk of Lindamar Beach. To the right, below them, was the sand and the sunbathers. They went over to the concrete wall that came up to about their waist and looked down on the people. This part of Lindamar was known as Little Kids Beach. It got its name because all the mothers seemed to congregate here with their kids.

It was bedlam. Little kids were running around like crazy and their mothers were chasing them, yelling at them, dragging them back from the water. A cute little girl had a brightly colored pail and shovel and she filled the pail with sand and dumped it over the head of her brother. He started screaming like he was being cut open and the mother turned around and smacked the girl and then there were two of them screaming.

"Let's get out of here," Tony said. His head was aching already.

They passed by the Kids Bathhouse. It was built along the beach, facing the sidewalk. The WPA built this bathhouse. Kids fourteen and under could undress in there and check in their clothes and after their swim take a shower to get the salt water off—and all free. In the days before they built it, you had to come to the beach with your bathing suit on, under your clothes. Walking along in a prickly wool bathing suit on a hot day, you sure got itchy.

On the other side of the bathhouse was Jews Beach. This again was like Little Kids Beach. Nobody told the Jews they had to come here. They were free to swim anyplace at Lindamar. But by long custom this particular stretch of sand was theirs. They always came here, and other people always stayed away. It was strange how things got started, Tony thought, and yet was it so strange? Weren't you more comfortable with people like yourself?

Tony and Lommy went over to the wall and looked down on Jews Beach. They never stayed here long. The Jews almost always came as a family. There would be a Jewish girl but she would be flanked by her fat momma and her fat poppa, and it just didn't seem right to be looking at a girl and having ideas about her when she was with her mother and father. Tony and Lommy drew the line at that.

So they went over to the wall and idly looked around.

"Did you ever see a skinny Jew after he hits forty?" Lommy asked. "What do you think makes them so fat?"

"I guess they eat too much." Tony said.

"Look at the gut on that guy over there," Lommy directed. "I'll bet he hasn't seen his pecker in twenty years."

Tony looked out to sea. The waves were coming in, coming in and then going out. They never stopped, he realized, day or night, whether anyone was watching or not. There was a sort of a screwy man on his street, Mr. Patnaude, who was trying to invent a perpetual motion machine, although to what purpose Tony had never been able to figure out, and it seemed to him that these waves here were that perpetual motion machine.

"Never marry a Polish girl," Lommy advised him suddenly. "They're pretty as hell when they're young but they lose their looks fast. Their face changes, you know. . . . By the time they're thirty. . . . And they lose their shape, they get heavy. I don't mean fat, just kind of heavy."

Tony accepted this as true as soon as Lommy said it, and he felt quick, secret guilt, as if he were a Polish girl.

"Let's go," Lommy said.

"Just a minute," Tony said. He had spotted a girl coming, a girl in a blue bathing suit.

She was Jewish and she was alone. She was sixteen, maybe seventeen, and fully matured. She came, trouncing through the sand, her buttocks rolling in melodious rhythm, sending sheathed waves across the ridges of sand. Oh, she was splendid! Her beauty was not that of model slenderness. Her beauty was one of girth, of amplitude, of abundance. Yet she was not fat, not in the slightest. No, no, no. It was simply that her body was not a niggardly meal, a jigger of carrot juice, a thin sandwich of creamed pimento cheese with one dull green olive; her body was a splendid feast, the tables laden with delicious meats and fruits bursting with sweetness, enough here to assuage even the most ravenous. And each breast was molded like the globe on the teacher's desk, each breast a world in itself. Oh, eurythmic Rebecca, oh, gravity-defying daughter of a tailor, oh, magnificent nonsagging Semite, oh, vision of naked proportions, oh, great-flowing woman!

"Man alive," Lommy breathed.

She stopped a few feet in front of them. She unfolded a towel—Tony had never seen one like it, so big—and she spread it carefully over the sand. She got down on all fours to smooth out the wrinkles, her buttocks facing the boys.

"Ride him, cowboy," Lommy murmured.

She was out, as a sports writer would put it, to partake of Old Sol. She was no sooner seated on the towel than she was digging in her woven-straw handbag and in a moment her fingers came forward dripping—not liquid myrrh—but oil, suntan oil.

She rubbed the oil on her calves, on her knees. Then she ascended to her thighs, to her great thighs. First the outside. Rubbing herself seemed to relax her. With Oriental half-lidded eyes, she did the inside of her thighs in slow deliberate insolent circles, inflaming the boys.

"Watch it, baby," Lommy warned her. "You're getting close to the house I live in."

The boys were now thoroughly hypnotized. They followed her hand, relieved of will.

She slipped out from under the shoulder straps of her bathing suit. The boys gaped unashamedly. They waited for a fantastic, heavenly exposure. But the cloth, the damn cloth, stayed up. She applied the lotion to her shoulders placidly.

Finally, she put the bottle away. And she stretched out, like a great glistening fish beached high and dry on the sand. Languid, somnolent, she must have felt their eyes burning into her flesh, more intense yet than the sun's rays, for suddenly she turned on the towel and fixed them with an unwavering eye, her lips curled in scorn and accusation. *I know exactly what you're thinking, you dirty bastards* was her clear message.

And they reddened and were indignant and self-righteous. They looked past her off into the ocean, they looked to the right and then to the left, and then they turned their backs on her and leaned against the wall and watched the people passing by on the sidewalk. No one likes to be called a bastard.

A little further down the beach was the Adults Bathhouse. This was just like the Kids Bathhouse, the people went in there and undressed, checked in their clothes, and after their swim took a shower—the only difference was they had to pay ten cents. The section of beach on the near side of the Adults Bathhouse was where the ordinary people gathered, the French, Polish, and Portuguese. But on the far side of the bathhouse was Tony and Lommy's favorite watching spot—Cape Verdeans Beach.

All the people here were colored. They came from the islands of Cape Verde off the coast of Africa. Ma had told him all about them. They were Portuguese Negroes, a mixture of Portuguese and Negro blood. They were not as dark as American Negroes; they were more like milk chocolate in color. And they were different from American

Negroes in other ways, too. Tony had heard about the Negroes in New York, who were surly and hostile and carried razors and cut up any white man found in Harlem after dark. The Cape Verdeans were not anything like that. They didn't carry razors and they were very friendly. Why, he and Lommy walked through the colored district in the South End every time they came to Lindamar and they were as safe there as they were on their own street, maybe even safer. Tony liked the Cape Verdean people and he was proud of them. They acted the way you were supposed to act and he attributed this to their Portuguese blood.

Tony and Lommy went over and leaned on the concrete wall and looked down at the Cape Verdeans. There was no other place like this on the whole beach. It was a madhouse, but a happy madhouse. Fellows, frolicsome and laughing, chased girls, vivacious and uninhibited, across the sand. There was shrieking and whooping and running down to the water's edge and there was shrieking and whooping and running back from the water's edge.

A well-formed girl called for help to her girlfriend as a handsome young fellow dragged her into the water, but the girlfriend, wanting to keep her friendship, did not come.

One guy was out in the water, about chest deep, smoking, and he made the cigarette go into his mouth without using his hands and he closed his mouth over it and he ducked underwater, his head completely under, and then he came up, opened his mouth, the cigarette popped out, and he continued smoking.

Another guy on the dead run dove headlong into the sea, in water about knee high. Hidden rocks were out there. "I saw a guy do that once and he cracked his head open," Lommy said. Well, with your girl watching, you had to do something.

There was activity, excitability, chattering. This was not like the whites' beach, small silent groups eyeing one another warily. This was like one family, one big happy family. The colored people were different from the whites, Tony thought. They were more natural and unselfconscious. They didn't keep looking around to see who was watching them. They weren't even aware of you. They just enjoyed themselves, and that was why he liked to watch them, because everybody seemed to be having such a good time.

Amidst the general air of happiness, some were happier than most.

Tony and Lommy looked at several couples stretched out on the sand, nuzzling, not kissing, just nuzzling. But one girl in particular held their attention. She was not lying down. She was standing on the beach by the concrete wall, the same wall they had their elbows on and were looking down from. She was over to their left. She had slinky hips, and when she moved, it was music. She had liquid hips, and when she took one step or just fidgeted, she flowed.

The fellow she was with got in front of her and cut her off from escape by putting his arms stiff against the wall—with her between. He looked into her eyes and talked intently. She laughed. She leaned against the wall and looked up at him with tilted belly. She laughed again. It was a teasing posture. Every now and then she flicked her belly against him, lightly, white-hot, scalding him, and she laughed. He looked deep into her eyes and he was in a bad way. He looked like he was going to explode or something.

"You know where I'd like to have her?" Lommy said. "See that tube over there?" he said, jerking his head at a boy who was playing with an inflated inner tube in low water. "I'd put her on that tube and I'd take her way out there in the ocean. Just me and her on that tube, see, and from here all you'd see would be a little speck bobbing up and down, going up and down, up and down, and everybody'd think it was because of the waves, but Tony—the waves wouldn't be doing it."

"Lommy," Tony said seriously, "let's say that you fell in love with a colored girl. Would you marry her?"

Lommy frowned and shook his head doubtfully.

"I don't know about that," he said. "I think you could fall in love with a colored girl, sure, but I don't know about marrying her. The colored people don't have it so good. Look at those houses they live in, falling apart. Why would you want to join them?"

"Yuh, I guess you're right," Tony said.

They watched Slinky Hips stroll off with her fellow, hand in hand. She had nice legs.

"I'd sure like to screw a colored girl," Lommy said.

"Yuh," Tony agreed.

"They're supposed to be hotter than white girls," Lommy said.

"Yuh," Tony agreed.

"You can tell they're hotter, too. Just the way they walk."

171

"Yuh," Tony agreed.

"You know what I'd like to do when I get big?" Lommy asked.

"No, what?"

"Join the Navy. You go around the world. You go to every foreign port there is. And you know what I'd do? I'd screw a girl in every port. I'd screw a girl from every country in the world, a German girl, a Russian girl, a Swedish girl, and so on, one girl from every country, and then I'd compare them. I'd find out which nationality in the whole world is the best lay."

It was an exciting idea. Tony saw himself conducting his own comparisons, but not as a sailor in waterfront dives. He was a rich man, traveling the world over, not leaving a country till he had sampled its entry in the contest. He saw a phlegmatic Eskimo girl spread-eagled on a pile of furs in a cozy igloo. He saw a Chinese girl, eminently scrutable, small-boned, delicate-featured, dainty, graceful in a silk gown slit on one side from her hip down. He saw a Negress, but not Slinky Hips, with her wavy hair, skin like coffee heavy-on-the-cream, and as thin a lip as you'd care to see. This was a Negress with kinky hair and fat lips, so black she was blue, that deep midnight blue, barebreasted as in the *National Geographic*, powerfully shanked, and there in the jungle clearing, the beat of tom-toms in the background, he knew her oiled embrace and musk-scented nipples. Oh, shades of Ole Marse!

***

Lindamar was a nudist colony. After all, a girl in a bathing suit, all her fine points so clearly displayed, it took but a moment for the imagination to strip her to the buff. The two boys left Lindamar with their heads spinning, their memories cataloguing all the breasts and legs and bellies they had seen that day.

But then autumn came and the wind began to blow and the leaves fell down and the girls went indoors. Then winter came and there was snow on the ground and the snow turned to slush and the slush to ice and the streets were deserted. But when your glands are growing up, the season is always summer and you're always on the beach. They followed their cold red noses through the streets until they came to the Roller Rink. They climbed the stairs. This used to be a theatre in the old days. Ma had told him of seeing Charlie Chaplin here when she was engaged, the place loaded with Portagees all laughing. Now it was a roller rink.

They could hear the skaters spinning by behind the door. They opened the door and walked in. They were in a little open room alongside the rink. Here a man took deposits on the skates and collected in advance for using the rink. But he didn't charge you anything for just watching.

The room was pretty bare. There was only one place to sit, a long wooden back-slotted bench where you sat to put on your skates. But this bench did not face the rink so Tony and Lommy never sat on it. Tony did not like the Roller Rink. It was drafty in here and dimly lighted and everything was old and dingy.

There were kids of all ages skating. They rolled back and forth, their skates making a helluva clatter on the wooden floor. Back and forth they went, back and forth, back and forth, it seemed kind of monotonous.

173

Tony and Lommy stood and watched the skaters. But they were not here for the night. They were headed someplace else. The only thing was, it was so bitterly cold outside they had come up here just to warm up. The Roller Rink was just about halfway to where they wanted to go and made an excellent resting and recovery place. As soon as their numbed ears and feet returned to normal, they would be on their way.

In a few moments they did leave, ran down the steps, and proceeded up the Avenue. They walked briskly in the cold weather. And presently they were at their destination, the land of lanes and frames and strikes and spares and slacks. They were at the Bowling Alleys, the only bowling spot in the North End. Oh, it was nice in here, and it didn't cost anything to get inside. It was a new place, with those long fluorescent lights, so that the place was brightly lit and yet with no glare. It was the perfect-size place, six lanes, big enough to have a variety of people and action, small enough for you to see everything that was going on. There were three rows of seats, real seats, not a bench, to sit in and watch and nobody came around and told you to beat it. In fact, the man who ran the place was very nice. Whenever he saw them coming in, he knew they weren't going to bowl, he knew they were just going to sit and watch, and he never once gave them a dirty look. The seats were comfortable and the air was warm and they no sooner had settled back than they felt relaxed and drowsy, but nicely so.

This was one night they never missed—Thursday night, Ladies' Night, when the girls got a reduction on the bowling price. Naturally there were more girls around on this night than on any other night of the week. Although Saturday was a good night, too, with a lot of dating.

The people didn't bowl here with those gigantic balls like you saw in magazine ads, where the guy bowls 300 and then he turns around and relaxes with a Camel. Those balls looked as big as basketballs and they had holes in them for your fingers. These balls here weren't that big. They were about the size of a softball, maybe a little bigger. They didn't have any holes in them either. You just palmed the ball and took a step and rolled it underhanded, almost like pitching in a softball game. Tony had never bowled with either size ball, big or small, but it seemed to him that it would be more fun with the small ball.

Tony and Lommy came here to look at the girls. Of course, there were probably other reasons, too. Where else could they have gone on a cold winter's night, where it would be both warm and free of charge? It was a lot cozier here than inside Tony's house, and it reminded him of what Ma had said about the mills—that everybody loved to work in the mills in the wintertime because it was a lot warmer there than in their own houses where they froze.

So Tony and Lommy looked at the girls. But they were gentlemen about it. They didn't stare openly, at least not when the girls were looking. And when either boy wanted to refer the other to some bowleress with outstanding form, he did not just blurt it out. He looked straight ahead and talked inconspicuously out of the corner of his mouth. Or he shielded his mouth with a hand and spoke behind it. Or he innocently reached across to scratch his shoulder and simultaneously turned sideways and murmured, "Jeez, lookit the tits on her! By the candy machine."

And now Lommy turned to Tony and directed him. "Jeez, lookit the ass on her! The dame in the red slacks, first alley."

Tony was already looking. He watched her move about. Ah, what sinuous grace, how truly feminine was her walk. She was charmingly pantsed, tightly slacked, beautifully filled, semicircled with mathematical precision, mooned and cleaved for happiness. It was a pleasure to watch her bowl.

A young fellow and his wife were bowling in the lane next to Red Slacks, and it was very interesting. The fellow had been having a good time, enjoying himself, acting like a kid, getting a big kick out of knocking down the pins, giggling when he missed. Then Red Slacks had walked in with three other girls and taken the lane next to his and he wasn't the same again. He wanted to look at her and yet he couldn't, what with his wife standing right there. The best he could do was sneak a glance her way every chance he got. But his behavior changed on the spot. He wanted to impress her. Suddenly his shoulders were thrown back and there were heroic posings and struttings. When he spoke now his comments, although seemingly addressed to his wife, were meant for Red Slack's ears. He no longer rattled off the carefree little nothings used with an intimate. He was like a man running for public office, every sentence a pronouncement, every word deliberate and premeditated. And he bowled in earnest now. When he knocked over ten with one roll, his wife squealed, but he had the unconcern of a champion.

But, alas, it was all in vain. Red Slacks was deaf, dumb, and blind to his loud witticisms and quick smiles. She looked right through him with indifference, like he was so much space. Obviously, she was not interested in somebody else's husband.

But the husband stayed in there punching. It was messy. His wife became aware of the change in the climate and in her husband's temperature. She saw Red Slacks walk and she saw the sparks flying off her husband as he raced his motor. She was humiliated and she reacted with gaiety, and as she got gayer and gayer, he faced her with a hostile coldness. Finally, he gave up the struggle for Red Slacks and, friend to no woman, retired behind an armor of sullen dignity.

How preposterous it all was! The terrible power, the tyranny of a woman's body! Willy-nilly we stare, willy-nilly we act the fool, and Tony, caught up just as much as anyone in hot desire for Red Slacks, felt the ridiculous anonymous helplessness of his position. How was he any different from a dog chasing a wet bitch through the streets? How was he any different from a puppet kicking and bending while some unseen hand yanked the strings? How was he any different from a chunk of metal dropped into a beaker of chemicals to react with the stultifying certainty of science? One well-filled pair of slacks and his mind went out of control and his dreams leaped like madmen one upon the other. Why should he snicker at the young husband? He knew that only his own youth and lack of money kept him from bowling in the lane next to hers and making a play for her just as the young husband had done. And yet it was a discouraging thing to see. He had thought that marriage settled and solved things of that nature, but here was this husband acting no different from an unmarried man. In fact, acting as if his wife handicapped him and that he wished she weren't around. His wife had obviously not solved the disturbing problem of desire for him. Was marriage a good thing? Could a man be constant to one woman? Tony wondered about it. And as he wondered he continued to watch Red Slacks with hypnotic fascination. He felt disrupted, shattered, dissatisfied, and frustrated.

***

Tony had a mental list of things that he was going to do when he got big and had some money, and bowling was high on the list. It looked like a lot of fun. And he was sure that he would be a terrific bowler. It took control, that was all, just like pitching. Just send the ball straight down the middle of the alley.

But winter passed and Tony and Lommy left the alleys. In the springtime they hearkened to train-whistles. They went up on the Locke Street Bridge on Saturday afternoons and looked over the edge at the cars passing underneath. The edge was built up with timbers so you wouldn't slip off. It was like leaning on your window sill at home and looking down.

Locke Street ended here. That is, it bumped squarely into Old County Road. The cars had to make either a right or left turn, a ninety-degree turn, onto Old County Road. The cars naturally had to slow down to make the turn. And this was perfect for the boys. For they found that at a certain angle, with a slow car, you could look right down through the windshield at the driver and whoever else was in the front seat.

To be spying on people without their knowledge, how very enjoyable it was! And each car was an exciting new prospect. Sometimes they saw a fellow driving and his girlfriend sitting so close to him that half of her was behind the wheel. One time they saw a fellow driving with his girlfriend close by and she had her hand someplace it shouldn't have been. "Ho-ly smoke!" Lommy cried. "No wonder there's so many accidents!"

But their favorite was women drivers. They like to see a woman driving alone. For when a woman was alone, she felt safe and did not keep pulling down her skirt as she would have with company. The skirt edged its way up her legs until you could see her knees and maybe a little more. And she was completely unaware that up on high two pairs of eyes were admiring her skill in braking—how fortunate for her modesty. One time they saw a girl driving alone and she had nice legs—they never did notice her face—and the seat must have been tilted, for her legs were at an inclined angle, and they got a bird's-eye view right down between them, right to the point of seeing her pink panties, and they almost fell off the bridge in surprise and appreciation. Wow!

They couldn't relax too much on the bridge. There wasn't room on it for both them and a train. So they listened and when they heard a train-whistle, they moved off the bridge fast. After the train passed, they went back. But on the bridge Tony kept having this bad dream, that he was trapped there and a train was coming. His only chance to save himself was to jump off the bridge to the street below. And he didn't know if he would have the guts to do that. Would he freeze up? But worse than that dream was the one where he didn't have to worry about jumping, when his foot was caught between the ties and he could only wait. When he dreamed that one, he went weak and faint all over.

There was something else to watch out for. They had to keep their eyes peeled for Cop Haggerty. His call box was on the corner by the bridge and he always came walking up Locke Street. If they saw him coming, they sneaked off the bridge, keeping their bodies low, and then ran far away down the tracks.

They kept a sharp eye out for him, because, if caught, it meant a long bony finger sticking in your face. "Don't you know you're in violation? Don't you know you were trespassing on Private Property?" It meant a thirty-minute lecture, blah-blah-blah-blah, on your mother, your school, your country, the World War and Chateau-Thierry, Charles Lindbergh's flight, and God-knows-what-all. And if you grinned, just once, that would be the end. You'd have to report to the police station and get a police record. So they used all their will power not to grin. They had to look serious and repentant.

"I'm going to let you go this time, boys, but—"

"Oh, thank you, sir."

"—but I'm warning you, if I ever catch you up there again, I'm going to run you in."

"You won't catch us again, sir, honest," they said fervently.

"All right. See that I don't."

"Thank you, sir," they said, and they walked off. They walked fast because they knew they were going to laugh soon and they wanted to get a safe distance away.

Poor Cop Haggerty, the Irish flatfoot. He was a misfit in his profession. Every profession has requirements. A newspaper editor must not bite the interests that feed him, a lawyer must be prepared to rob client and foe impartially, a politician must speak in public but be persuaded in private, and a policeman must be a threat and not a speech. Cop Haggerty talked to them when he should have seized his club and waved it under their noses and sworn at them with conviction. Instead, what was this business about Lindbergh's mother?

The whole trouble with Haggerty as a cop was that he couldn't scare you. Something fierce and implacable was lacking in him. Why was this? Was it because he was skinny, the only skinny cop in all of Gaw? Was it his lack of gut that made him go in for oratory? Was it his awareness that he did not look like a policeman the reason why he could not bring himself to act like one? With his watery pale-blue eyes, with his long skinny plucked-turkey neck, with his facial expression permanently set in mournful lines, Haggerty looked more like an undertaker or a minister than a cop.

***

Cop Haggerty came as far as the corner by the bridge. Here he called in and then he turned around and went back down Locke Street. Tony had passed by a few times when he was calling in. Tony was very curious as to what Cop Haggerty said into the opened box. Tony strained his ears every time, but though you could hear Cop Haggerty speaking you couldn't make out what he was saying. Tony imagined it went something like this: "Hello, Police Headquarters? This is Officer Haggerty, reporting in from Locke Street. All's well on my beat."

Around the bridge corner was Old County Road, on no policeman's beat because of its lack of houses and people. Once around the corner Tony and Lommy made jokes and felt strangely relaxed and happy. They didn't analyze it, but it was because they felt free. They knew they wouldn't be meeting Haggerty and have to endure valuable-time-consuming lectures. And as the weather warmed into summer, they went around the corner on their way to the Bostwick. They deserted the Locke Street Bridge for greener pastures.

Oh, to be on Bostwick Hill now that July was there! To stretch out full length in the grass, face down, with the grass tickling your ears. To smell the grass, the herbs, the dandelions, the buttercups, the sweet purple clover. . . . Growing, blossoming things everywhere. The frozen seeds of the winter's earth exploded in the July sun, overcoming the air with their sweet and melancholy passion, singing with fragrance the brief intangibility of existence. The fragrance was almost too strong in the daytime, baked to a crescendo by the hot sun. But at night, after supper when the boys came here, the sun had passed in the sky and the fragrance had quieted down—still there, but more subtle.

And what a view! Like you were on top of the world. You could see the railroad tracks and a freight train slowly chugging along. You could see the black tar of Bostwick Road and a lone car taking the curve. You could see the Bostwick Mill, stretching immense and quiet. You could see all these things and more, but Tony and Lommy did not come up here for the view. They came for the lovers.

The lovers were of two sorts. Those who wanted to kiss and hug and just generally have a fine but clean time stayed on the hill. But those lovers who really meant business walked up the hill and beyond it—to Bostwick Woods, a place where privacy was to be had.

The Bostwick Woods were behind Tony and Lommy, to their right a little bit. By sitting on top of the hill you could see both ways; you could see who was coming up the hill and after the couple passed, you could flip over and lie in the grass like an Indian scout, invisible, and watch the couple stroll innocently along the edge of the woods as if absolutely nothing was on their minds and then suddenly—*zing!*—into the woods they disappeared. Tony and Lommy stayed on the hill. It would have been too risky a deal to follow the couple into the woods, because you didn't know exactly where they might be. You might step on them.

A path had been worn through the grass of Bostwick Hill by the climbing and descending feet. Tony and Lommy sat a few feet off this path. That way when the couple went by, they could get a good look at the girl. They were finding out which girls in the North End were lays. This was valuable information. Of course, they realized that probably a lot of the girls were engaged to the fellows and soon would be doing it legally. Still, it was interesting information.

But it was also fun to watch the couples who stayed on the hill. One such couple arrived in the early evening, just minutes after Tony and

Lommy got there. Tony idly plucked blades of grass and watched this couple approach the hill.

The girl was pretty and slender. She had soft brown hair. She was wearing an attractive dress that had wide alternating light and dark blue stripes. She was about eighteen.

Her boyfriend was about the same age, maybe a little older. They were a quiet pair. The boy held her hand as they walked along but they didn't talk much. The quiet of understanding was between them. When they came to the hill, the boy helped her up and they climbed about two-thirds of the way to the top and sat down. The girl remained in a sitting position but after a minute or two the boy stretched out on the grass, put his head in her lap, and lay looking up at her.

Tony watched them. The girl was running her hand gently through the boy's hair and looking down on him with eyes of love. It was such a picture of the serenity and security of love that Tony was smitten with an overwhelming yearning. When would he lie in a girl's lap and have her run her hand through his hair and look at him like that? When, when, when? He envied this fellow lying placidly there more than all the guys he had ever seen hugging and kissing, because this fellow was not just getting an excitement out of a girl's body. You could do that with any girl, no matter what she thought of you. But this fellow had a girl who loved him.

"See that guy and girl over there?" Lommy asked.

"Yes," Tony said. His eyes had not left them since they'd come.

"That's gonna be me and Yvonne," Lommy said. "In four years."

"You're going to wait four years, huh?"

"Yup. When I'm eighteen I'm going to start going with her."

"How do you know she won't be going with somebody else by then?"

"Not her! She's waiting for me."

"How do you know?"

"All right. What is she always asking my sister about me for? 'Does he like any one girl in particular?' Ha!" Lommy laughed happily.

Tony sniffed. A certain peculiar smell, sharp and familiar, was in the air. He looked around. He rolled over three or four times, moving sideways. He stopped at a pale-green herb. He tore off a piece of it and rolled back to Lommy.

"Smell this," he commanded Lommy.

Lommy sniffed. "Whew! It stinks."

"Oh, it's not so bad," Tony said. "You know what this is good for?"

"No," Lommy said, interested.

"Poison ivy. When I had poison ivy, my mother came up here and picked a big bunch of this for me." He sniffed the herb, remembering the nice neat compact bundle tied with string and the smell it brought into the house.

"What do you do with it?"

"Well, you get a pan of water and you put the plants in the water; you let them soak for a long time, see, so that after a while you have sort of a solution. Then you throw those plants away, they're all used up, see, and you wash your skin, wherever you got poison ivy, with the pan of water, with the solution. No soap though, you just use that water."

"Does it work?"

"Wellll, I don't know. . . . I don't think it helped me much, to tell the truth. But my mother says I would have been worse without it. I know one thing—I always itched like crazy right after using it."

"You know what I heard is the best way to treat poison ivy?" Lommy asked.

"No, what?"

"Well, I heard that if you get some hot towels—"

A short whistle sounded behind them.

Lommy glanced over his shoulder. "Don't turn around!" he warned Tony in a low voice. "It's the Queer with the Dog. If he catches your eye, he'll come over and we'll never get rid of him."

The Queer with the Dog was an older man in his fifties. Once he had sat down on the grass beside them and given them this sad story— his wife had died, he got terribly lonely, he didn't have any children and lived all alone in a rented room, wait till you're old, and it doesn't do anybody any harm, so how about it? But they said no.

"Here, Skippy, here!"

The queer was calling his dog. Ha, that was smart of him to have a dog. Sure a dog was company, but it also gave him a good excuse to come up to the Bostwick often. People who'd see him would think— Oh, there goes an innocent old man out taking his dog for a walk, how nice—and they wouldn't think any more about it. But he was actually on the prowl looking for kids. That dog was just a blind.

"Come on, Skippy! Come on, boy!" He whistled at the dog again.

He was right behind them now. Tony was busy with one of his shoes, not looking up, and Lommy was looking off to the right. The path was on their left. The queer went by.

Tony had his shoe off. He was pulling on his stocking, which had bunched up on the sole of his foot.

"Don't look up!" Lommy warned him out of the corner of his mouth. "He's looking back."

Tony put his shoe on carefully. By then he felt it was safe and looked. The old man was down to the bottom of the hill. He turned on the narrow dirt road and who should be coming along the dirt road toward him but Gil, another queer, but much younger. Gil was in his twenties.

"Oh, boy, let's watch them!" Tony said. "Let's see what they do!"

"What do you want them to do?" Lommy asked.

Tony was interested to see if they spoke to one another. Would they be like fishermen, commiserating on their lack of luck and comparing notes on places to go looking?

The two queers passed each other, the old man looking straight ahead and Gil looking up at the sky. They didn't see the other fellow— it was so deliberate, so obvious. It could not possibly have been accidental. Well, it takes one to know one, Tony thought. Then he got a bright idea.

"There's two queers there, right? Now why don't they fool around with one another instead of going around looking for young kids?" he asked Lommy.

"I don't know," Lommy said. "I guess they like young kids better."

"If they went together, that would solve all their problems," Tony said.

"Well, the next time one of them talks to you, why don't you ask him about it?"

"That's an idea, maybe I will."

"I got better things to do than worry about queers," Lommy said. "Here comes Gil. Let's make believe we don't see him."

Tony unlaced his other shoe and concentrated on getting the wrinkles out of his stocking. Gil had propositioned them once. It was so strange. Tony couldn't figure it out. He could understand the old man being a queer. An old man like that with half of his hair and teeth gone, what girl would want to have anything to do with him? But Gil was different. He was young and good-looking. He could probably have his pick of the girls. On these beautiful nights when he could be with a girl, instead, two or three times a week, he was in the woods playing with himself. It didn't make sense.

Gil came up the hill whistling loudly.

"Hi, fellas!" he called cheerily.

"Oh, hi," Tony said lukewarmly, giving him a little wave.

"Nice night!"

"Eat it," Lommy muttered under his breath.

"Sure is," Tony said.

Gil went on, towards the woods.

"The queers are taking this place over," Lommy complained. "It used to be you'd see maybe one queer a night. But lookit that, we've seen two of them already and the night's not half over."

"Maybe the queers are having a convention tonight," Tony said. "They're gonna elect a president."

"Well, I know who I'd vote for," Lommy said.

"Who?"

"Two Minutes."

Tony giggled. Two Minutes was another queer. The first time they met him they were walking through Bostwick Woods along the path. They went around a bend, not thinking of anything, and suddenly there he was, as big as life, a little off the path, alongside a bush. His pants were down and his dingey was out and he was going to town on himself.

"Hello, boys," he said.

They were too flabbergasted to return his greeting.

"How about it, boys? You wanna make a little money?"

"No, thanks," they said, and kept walking.

"Wait a minute, boys," he implored.

"We're in a hurry," Tony called back, as they kept walking.

"Come back, boys!" he cried out desperately. "Fifty cents for two minutes!"

So that's how he got the name of Two Minutes. They passed him one night soon afterwards near the Locke Street Bridge and he kept jingling the change in his pocket and jerking his head meaningfully in the general direction of Bostwick Woods. Those guys never gave up.

But the queers around here weren't so bad really. They talked to

183

you, they tried to persuade you, but if you said no, they didn't grab you or anything like that. The only thing was, after Two Minutes and a couple of similar incidents, you were a little nervous when you walked through the Bostwick Woods because you never knew but around the next bend there might be one of them with his pants down.

It was growing dark on the hill now. A squat, tough-looking girl came up the hill with a French guy. She was laughing raucously, like he was telling her dirty jokes. He had a pencil-thin mustache.

"That guy looks like a muff diver," Lommy said.

They didn't hold hands or show any affection. And they headed straight for the woods.

A sure screw, Tony thought. But wasn't that the way it went? If you wanted to have a sweet and pretty girl, like the girl in blue, the most you could get was some kisses. To get a screw you had to go with one of these repulsive types.

Tony looked over to the right. The girl in blue and her fellow were gone. What the—? How could they have gone without him seeing them leave? To go home, to get back onto Bostwick Road, they would have had to cross in front of him and he would have been sure to see them.

"Where'd that girl in the blue dress go?" he asked Lommy. "The one that was over there"—he pointed.

"She went in the woods."

He was shocked. "Aw, you're kidding."

"No, I'm not."

"When?"

"Oh, a long time ago."

"How come I didn't see her go?"

"I don't know. Maybe 'cause they didn't make any noise. All I know is I happened to look over there and I saw her and her boyfriend going into the woods."

"Jesus!"

"What's the matter?"

"Aw, I'm just surprised. I didn't think she was that kind of a girl, to tell you the truth."

"Listen, Tony, I'm gonna tell you something. They're all that kind of a girl—with the right fella."

"Well, you know, you saw her. Sitting there with him, not even kissing. What would you think?"

"They were just waiting for it to get dark, that's all."

"Well, I sure had her figured wrong," Tony said, crestfallen.

"Don't let it get you down," Lommy said comfortingly.

Tony nodded.

"Now here's one for you, Tony. Did you ever stop to think of this—dogs do it in the daylight, but humans do it in the dark. Why?"

"Less chance for an audience I guess."

"Yuh. That's probably it," Lommy said. "It'd sure be nice though to be a dog, wouldn't it? See a girl you like, you hop aboard, no matter where you are. That'd be the life."

"I'd feel funny doing it in front of people," Tony scrupled.

"No, you wouldn't!" Lommy the social scientist contradicted. "Not if that was the custom. Not if everybody else was doing it."

"You know though with that girl," Tony said hopefully, "maybe they just wanted to go through the woods . . . you know, explore around."

"Are you kidding?" Lommy snorted. "That guy is exploring around all right, he's looking for home plate. I'll bet he's giving her six inches right this minute."

Now that the darkness had started, it came fast. And suddenly everything seemed very quiet. Except for the crickets, who were making their strange noise all around them. The two boys stared at the lights in the distance without saying anything.

Then Lommy spoke. "Listen!" he said.

Tony listened.

"Hear it?" Lommy asked.

"No, what?"

"Listen!"

Then Tony heard it. It was a car, coming along the narrow dirt road that ran by the bottom of the hill. Then the car lights bounced into view. The car went right by the hill, slowly, at the most ten, fifteen miles an hour, for there were bad holes and ruts in the road.

"Come on! Let's follow that car!" Lommy cried excitedly.

It was just like in the movies when the hero jumps in a cab and says, "Follow that car!" They ran down the hill and took up the pursuit, staying about twenty-five yards behind the car, trotting to keep up.

185

The guy's left taillight wasn't working. They followed his single tail-light along the curving road, hurting their ankles in sudden holes. Then Lommy grabbed Tony's arm. "Hold it!"

The taillight wasn't moving. Then all the lights, headlights and tail-light, went out, and the motor shuddered and died. Everything was quiet and dark again.

"Did you see where he stopped?" Lommy said.

"Yuh," Tony said. The car was parked behind the Bostwick Woods, at the far end of the woods, so close to the bushes there it was practi-cally touching them.

"If we went back, we could cut through the woods and sneak up on them," Lommy said. "You game?"

"Sure!"

They turned around and started trotting back, going along the dirt road, then back up the hill, and from there along the edge of the woods until they came to an exact spot. "It'd be right about here," Tony announced. On the other side of the woods in a direct line was the car.

They entered the woods, Tony leading the way. He was more famil-iar with these woods than Lommy and his experience took precedence.

It was an exciting thing to do, sneaking up on a car, and dangerous too, thought Tony. The guy might not be in any mood to appreciate guests. Then Tony thought of something else, something real alarming.

"How do you know they'll stay in the car?" he asked Lommy. "How do you know they won't come out into the woods?"

"If it was you, would you take a girl and stretch her out on some dirt where she's gonna get her clothes all dirty and where the mosqui-toes are gonna bite you in the ass, or would you keep her in a car where you can both keep clean and there won't be so many mosquitoes?"

"H'mmm," Tony said noncommittally. Who could tell the prefer-ences of lovers?

When they got about halfway in, Tony turned to Lommy. "From here on, no noise," he said.

Tony moved low, his hands before him like feelers, quick and ghostly, sensitive to every twig and leaf that hung in the air. He imag-ined that he was an Indian perfectly at home in the woods. He was an Iroquois sneaking up on a pioneer girl washing clothes in the river. His moccasined feet crept noiselessly through the forest.

But Lommy behind him was no Indian. He walked straight up and he swished the branches freely.

Alarmed, Tony stopped and gave him hell. "Ssshh! For chrissakes, Lommy, you're like an elephant. Get low!"

As they got closer, Tony slowed and moved even more carefully. Lommy got the idea and he was much quieter.

"I think we're just about there," Tony whispered in Lommy's ear. "We better crawl the rest of the way."

"Suppose the guy chases us?" Lommy whispered back.

This is a helluva time to start thinking about that, Tony thought, but he said, "Then it's every man for himself." The living creature did not exist who could catch Tony Alfama when Tony Alfama was scared, that he knew, and Tony Alfama was scared right now.

Tony went down on his hands and knees and crawled forward. A really low branch was before him and he flattened out and pressed his belly into the ground and wiggled under it. He went on a little ways, then he stopped to rest and to listen. He wasn't absolutely positive but it seemed to him they were mighty close to that car. He stared ahead in the darkness, his whole body tense and ready for anything. He strained his ears for the slightest sound. He heard nothing.

He started up again.

Then exploding the quiet—the first sound of *them*! A man clearing his throat mightily and spitting.

They froze, their hearts pounding.

But nothing else came.

"Jesus, he sounds tough," Lommy whispered.

"Ssshh," Tony admonished.

They were a little bit off line. Tony veered to his left. Now they moved very slowly indeed. And then—there it was. In the gloom they could just make out the shadowed outline of the still car.

They stopped. They were too excited to talk. They just lay there, staring and listening.

From the inside of the car came a man's voice—an undertone. And then the woman's answering voice—a lazy drawl.

Then they heard it, unmistakable, the high-pitched activity of old seat springs, discreet but audible, *creak—creak—creak—creak*. . . .

187

In that dark sedan a man and a woman were at work. In that black box a man and a woman were melting the night air with their labors. In that four-wheeled bedroom a man and a woman were making the beast with two backs. In that pistoned pride of the clever hedonist who put America on wheels, a woman was vibrating. In that vehicled essence of American civilization, one more thread was being unraveled from the American moral fabric.

By God! thought Tony. This is the closest I have ever been to it in my whole life.

The man mumbled something to her. Then apparently they shifted their position, for there was a big noise of springs, and then afterwards, the same steady beat, *creak—creak—creak—creak. . . .*

"Ride him, cowboy," Lommy whispered.

I wonder who she is, Tony was thinking. Maybe she lives on my street. Maybe she lives three houses away from me, a piece of ass for the asking, and all this time I have been missing out on it. Damn it for not being the daytime! If it was the daytime, I could go out on Bostwick Road and see who she is when they drive by.

"Listen, I got an idea," Lommy whispered. There were dried clods of dirt all over the ground. Lommy picked one up and showed it to Tony. "Let's start hollerin' and throw these at them and then run like hell. He can't chase us—he's got his pants off."

The dirt clods would crumble on contact, and Tony could just see one of these clods sailing through the open window of the car and hitting the guy right in the crack of his ass—boy, would he be mad! Mad enough to chase them even without his pants? H'mmm.

"Aw, let the poor guy have his fun," Tony whispered back, vetoing the idea. Why not leave well enough alone? He didn't feel like running full steam through some dark woods unless it was absolutely necessary. But he had to admit, too, it wasn't only that he was trying to save himself some trouble. It was too lousy a trick for him. He had feelings of fellowship and sympathy for the guy. This was no time to be bothering him. And who knows, maybe someday he'd be in a car himself with a girl like that, and then how would he like it if some kids did that to him?

They waited, listening, but they heard nothing special, just the same old springs. After a bit, they gave up and retreated silently through the woods.

They went back on Bostwick Hill. It was a beautiful night. The sky was dark blue and all the stars were out.

They started for home, in no hurry, just sort of shuffling along.

They got out on Bostwick Road, on the sidewalk, that is. Although they would have been just as safe in the middle of the road, for there was no traffic.

The only light on Bostwick Road came from the street lights hung on telephone poles. The only thing was, these lights were spaced far apart so that most of the time you were walking in the darkness.

They were going along, not saying anything much, the only sound coming from the stick that Tony held lightly against the Anchor wire fence of the Bostwick Mill. It made a lulling, comforting noise, or so it seemed to Tony, for he had rattled against the Bostwick fence for years now. So they were walking along, Tony in a reverie, when all of a sudden they heard a girl laugh. Tony immediately flipped the stick into the gutter, for fence-rattling was an activity befitting a younger boy.

They were in the dark, a good distance from the next light, and the laugh had sounded in the darkness beyond the light.

Was she coming or going?

"Come on, let's walk fast," Tony said. If she was going, they could catch up to her. If she was coming, they could time it to pass her under the light so they could see what she looked like.

She laughed again. She was coming.

It was a light, bubbling laugh, youthful and pleasant, innocent and gay, and yet somehow oddly out of place on dark Bostwick Road.

"Lommy, suppose it's two girls?" Tony was breathless with the idea.

"Well, I'm ready. You?"

"You bet!"

They timed it perfectly. They came into the circle of light under the telephone pole at the same time the girl did.

Good Lord! Was that—? Tony almost fell over.

"Well, I'll be goddamned . . . ," Lommy murmured.

There could be no mistake. The same long-lashed eyes, the same soft brown hair, the same blue-striped dress. It was the girl they had seen earlier on the hill, petting a young fellow's hair and looking down at him with eyes of love. But gone now her quiet, dreamy mood and in its place a gay, animated, carefree spirit, talking a mile a minute. Gone

189

the young fellow and in his place a man old enough to be the young fellow's father. And gone her shy hand-holding and in its place a shameless hanging on like a new bride, her right arm hooked around his left arm, and her left hand hanging onto the same arm, clinging to his biceps. And now she was headed back to Bostwick Woods, once more to be pressed like a sweet flower between the pages of earth and man.

And in the moment of passing, Tony a mere foot away from her, she looked into Tony's face and Tony looked ardently into her eyes, concealing his shock, wanting her to know that his lips were sealed, that her secret was safe with him. But her eyes did not betray her. No spark, no glint of recognition answered Tony. She looked back at him as blankly and as guiltlessly as someone who had never seen him before. And in her impassive stare he glimpsed the false, loving heart of a woman, saw written in that stolidity the categorical imperative of woman, which is to deny all and admit nothing.

Lommy could hardly contain himself until it was safe to talk. He grabbed Tony's arm in his excitement. "Tony, she's a whore!" he cried. "Do you realize what that means? That means we got a chance with her!"

That an eighteen-year-old girl, clean and slim and pretty, could be a whore—it didn't seem possible. "Maybe she's in love with the two guys," Tony suggested. It would not be easy on her; she would have to juggle her time between the two boyfriends with great skill, never letting them meet.

"You mean you think she could be in love with an old man like that? Hah!" Lommy snorted.

It was true. He was an old man, at least forty, half bald and with a pointed nose. What in hell could she want with an ugly old man like that? Tony shook his head. He couldn't understand it. It didn't seem possible that she was a whore, and yet how to account for so strange a choice of lover?

"We've gotta find out where she lives," Lommy said. "Let's go back to Bostwick Hill and wait for her there. Then we can follow her home."

"I don't know," Tony reflected aloud. "It'd be easy to miss her in the dark." He looked at the mill fence, which was considerably higher than his head. "Follow me," he said, and so saying he put his toes in the wire netting of the fence and climbed to the top, swung his legs over, and then climbed down inside the same way. Lommy followed.

There were no lights inside the millyard. There was nothing left to steal. Tony walked toward the mill. It was really dark in here. He stopped at a wooden loading platform that stuck out from the mill. It was the perfect spot. They were lined up with the street light they had just passed. They could see anyone who passed underneath it. But they themselves were in darkness, secret and safe. Tony sat down on the ground and leaned his back against the platform. Lommy followed suit, sitting beside him. They were comfortable and cozy, and all they had to do now was wait for her to come back.

Lommy sang a happy song.

> *Doo-doo-dee,*
> *Dee-doo-doo,*
> *Boo-boo-boo,*
> *Boo-barr-bee-bee. . . .*

It was fantastic, Tony thought, the change in her. Which girl was the real girl? The first, the quiet one? Or the second, the lively one? He couldn't make her out at all.

> *Baa-baa-bee-ray. . . .*

But what was she doing with that old man? Could she be in love with him? Maybe she wasn't in love with him exactly. Maybe she was just fond of him and mistook that for love. Maybe the old man had a lot of money and took her places, to movies, and dances, and bought her presents, and she found all that hard to resist. She thought it was love, but a love based on gratitude is not a real love. Did she spend nights dreaming about the old man? No. But soon now she would meet Tony Alfama, and she would fall for him like a ton of bricks. She would fall for him so hard that she wouldn't want to have anything more to do with either the old man or the young guy. Those two guys would be pushed right out of the picture. There would only be him left, him and her, the two of them together, going up to the Bostwick every night, hand in hand, lying in the grass and looking at the sky, and then afterwards, in the dark—love.

"Jeez, two guys in one night! Talk about hot stuff—she's it!" Lommy rhapsodized. "We won't have no trouble. How about that? She goes out with that young guy and gets fucked and then she goes home and she's so hot she wants some more. So she picks up this old man and comes back for another fuck. Man! Wow! Whew!"

Was she a whore? Was she so hot that she had to have it and didn't care who she did it with? Would she go behind his back and make dates with other guys?

"How do you think we oughta work it?" Tony asked.

"Well, we'll follow her home, see where she lives," Lommy said easily, "and then tomorrow night we'll go there, wait till she comes out, and then we'll proposition her."

"Who's gonna do the talking? Will you?" Tony wanted him to.

"Sure!"

"What will you say?"

"Oh, I'll just go up to her and I'll say, 'Hi, beautiful. How's tricks?' So she'll look at me and she'll see that I'm younger than her, see, and she'll say, "Scram, willya?' And I'll say, "Look, sweetheart, I'm gonna level with you. I was on the Bostwick last night and I saw you play Cherry, Cherry, Who's Got the Cherry? with two different guys, so I know you love it, and I got what you want, baby. Me and my friend Tony here will fix you up just fine.'"

"Don't use real names," Tony cautioned.

"Okay. I'll call you Manny, okay?"

"Okay. And what will you be? We oughta get this straight first."

"I'll be Roger. Roger the Lodger. 'It wasn't the Almighty that lifted her nightie, it was Roger the Lodger, by God!'"

"Roger. Okay. Roger and Manny. Let's both remember that."

"We're gonna get laid, Manny, we're gonna get laid," Lommy chanted. "We're gonna feel her fanny, Manny."

But Tony was thinking over Lommy's technique and it didn't strike him quite right. "Say, do you think you oughta just go up to her and ask her point-blank like that? Suppose it's the wrong girl? She could get the cops after us."

"How can it be the wrong girl? We're gonna watch her go in this house. Then we're gonna watch her come out of the exact same house. Okay. And you got a good look at her, didn't you, same as I did? Okay then, tell me how we can make a mistake."

"Well, another thing, I don't think girls like to be asked point-blank like that. I think it'd be better if you said to her, 'How about taking a walk with my friend and me up the Bostwick?' That way she'd understand what you meant all right, see, but you wouldn't actually come right out and say it."

"Tony, I'm gonna tell you one thing—with a girl like this it's better not to beat around the bush. And I'll tell you why. She's experienced, right? And if we start hemming and hawing around, what is she gonna think? She's gonna think we're green, right? And if there's one thing an experienced girl don't like—that's a green guy. Anybody will tell you that, Tony—girls, it don't matter if they're experienced or not, they don't like guys that are green. Okay, so what the hell, why beat around the bush with her? She screws, right? She knows it—we know it. So why not come right to the point? She'll respect us more for it, believe me. She'll say to herself—'These two guys look all right to me. They know the score.'"

In the darkness they waited and they didn't have too long a wait. Soon they heard feet. They froze and strained their eyes at the telephone post. It was them. They gave them a good headstart, then as quietly as they could, they went over the fence and followed behind.

At the Locke Street Bridge the couple turned. They went down Locke Street, past the Boulevard, toward the Avenue. And Tony noticed the way they were walking. They were walking together, and yet they were apart and alone. She was not hanging on him. No talking. The happiness, the expectation, the excitement—gone. And he had seen two dogs do it once, the male following the female all over the place, at last getting what he wanted, and afterwards the two of them pulling free and going off in separate directions. And he wondered— Were humans like dogs?

The couple turned on the Avenue, heading north. Tony and Lommy closed the distance a bit, because people were getting between them and the couple, and they didn't want to let that precious girl get out of their sight.

"Lommy, do you really think she'll go with us?" Tony asked very seriously.

"If she goes with an old man like that, she'll go with us," Lommy stated emphatically. "Right?"

"I suppose," Tony said. It seemed logical, and yet—who could tell about these things? But it was almost too exciting to think about. His first time—and with a beautiful girl.

"This is our lucky night, Lommy."

"You can say that again."

There she was—up ahead—she screwed—and he knew it. There she was—in the palm of his hand—if only he worked it right. This was his big chance.

Finally the couple turned off the Avenue, at Lagoda Street. They went down Lagoda Street and the old man dropped off, going into a lit-up three-tenement house, with people yelling and swearing inside, as Tony and Lommy noted when they passed by.

"His wife," Lommy said. "'Where you been?' 'Oh, I stopped off for a cup of coffee and a piece of ass—I mean, pie, dear.'"

Alone, the girl continued down Lagoda Street. One block. Two blocks.

Gee, much further and they'd be in the slime of the Ossawona River. But she stopped short of that. She went in the third house from the river. It was a block tenement, one of those big ones, like a hotel, with four floors and two families to every floor.

There were empty garbage cans tipped over on the sidewalk. Tony and Lommy had to go single file by them. They belonged to her house, but obviously nobody had bothered yet to take them into the yard.

Light from the unshaded windows of the first floor beamed out on the front piazza, and Tony stared at the metal number of the house. It was a dismal gray 19, a flimsy, shriveled 19, but for him it was a magic number, encrusted with jewels and shining in the night. This number represented the opportunity to achieve that which he had been dreaming about for a long time. And as Tony stared at the number, it burned into his soul forever, so that at the age of one hundred they could have stood him on his head like a yogi and put him in a centrifuge and when he came out if someone had said, "Lagoda Street," he would have answered like his own name—"19."

"Let's make a deal," Lommy said. "We found her together, right?"

"Right."

"Okay. So nobody can come here alone, okay? We have to be together, or nobody comes, okay?"

"Okay," Tony agreed.

"Let's shake on it," Lommy said.

They shook on it.

They went home then, but the next night right after supper they walked to Lagoda Street, down to the river. The river stank and there was no place to sit because of the mud, but they pretended great interest in the rusted skeleton of a car that stood in low water. They contemplated the tin cans floating near the car. And they pointed to landmarks in the country town of Ossawona across the river. But all the while they kept a sharp eye on her house. No luck. She did not come out.

Every night they came to Lagoda Street, sometimes to the river, sometimes just walking around the block. They didn't want to hang around her house too openly for fear of attracting attention. But they couldn't seem to catch her. Sometimes they came right after supper, and then went someplace else, and then came back again later in the evening.

Then one night they had just turned the corner of the Avenue and were headed down the street, down Lagoda Street, when who should be coming up toward the Avenue, but her! She was all alone and there wasn't another soul on the street—absolutely perfect conditions for propositioning her.

"It's her, Lommy!" Tony cried. This was their chance. Now or never.

She was about half a block away and coming straight at them.

"You're gonna do the talking, right?" Tony demanded. He wanted to get everything straight and ready.

"No, you do the talking," Lommy said desperately.

Tony was so excited he was shaking all over. So the responsibility was to be his. It was on his shoulders. How he handled the next minute would tell the story of success or failure.

It was her all right—she was certainly pretty! And what a neat figure.

She approached them, not looking at them, and Tony smiled brightly at her.

"Hello!" he said cheerily. "Remember us?"

But she did not acknowledge the acquaintanceship in a manner calculated to promote friendship and understanding. She gave him a look withering enough to scorch the paint off the nearest house and walked by without a word.

Whew! He felt faint. The strain had been too much.

Slowly he recovered. And then he realized that all was lost. She had

195

not been friendly.

The two boys were dispirited. They kept walking, down to the river.

"Looks like no dice, huh, Tony?" Lommy said.

Tony nodded sad agreement. He threw a stone into the river.

"I wish I could figure her out," Tony said.

CHAPTER 6

MARY ON THE SANDS

The carnival was in town.

Every summer it came to the North End of Gaw for One Week Only. Prizes Galore! Fun for All! Bring the Family!

Tony and Lommy brought themselves to the entrance of the carnival. Business was good. People were standing in line to buy tickets, and there were two carnival men collecting the tickets, one on each side of the entrance passageway. It cost ten cents to get in.

Tony and Lommy walked away from the entrance. They had their own way of getting in. At least it had worked for them last year.

They went around the corner. They strolled leisurely along the line of tents. The high backs of the tents were an effective barrier. They could hear the sandpaper voices of the barkers and the excited cries of the people on the other side, but they could not see anything.

Each tent had been set up so that its sides touched the sides of the tents next to it. It was impossible to slip in between tents. But—further on, towards the back—the tent setter-uppers had miscalculated and there would be two tents with a foot of space between them. At least that had been the case last year.

But meantime in the event that some unseen carnival eyes were watching, the two boys did not make a big production out of examining the amount of space, if any, between the tents. In fact, they walked along several feet away from the tents and looked off into the field. The carnival was in the open field next to the Hook Mill on Loring Street.

They turned the corner, at the back, and then veered abruptly into the field. This sudden move away from the tents might have seemed rather odd for here in the back there was that looked-for crack of space, where two boys could tuck in their gut and glide silently through a tight sandwich of canvas into the carnival. But the only trouble was that standing close by this opening was a husky gypsy with a club in his hand. He grinned at them like he could read their minds.

They swung around the back of the carnival and went down the other side, still keeping to the sanctuary of the field. On this side a carnival hand was walking up and down by the tents, patrolling. Like the gypsy he was armed with a club. They came closer, to look him over. It was a typical carnival face. A long thin jaw, speckled skin, and dead-looking straw hair. He did not look friendly. He stared at them with cold eyes.

"Hi," Tony called, waving and smiling.

He answered by spitting in their direction.

"Oh, you carnival bastard!" Lommy said angrily under his breath. "Let's throw a couple of rocks at him and go home."

"No, no," Tony said.

"We're never gonna get in anyway," Lommy said pessimistically.

"Just wait a minute," Tony said. "Maybe I can think of something."

"The only place I saw where we could get in is by the gypsy, and he's got a club," Lommy said

Tony nodded, and scratched his chin.

"I wish we could get twenty cents someplace," Lommy said. "All I've got on me is four cents."

"Well, that makes us sixteen cents short," Tony said.

They turned around and walked slowly toward the back.

Tony wasn't quite ready to give up. He had no idea of what he could do, and the situation seemed hopeless, but he believed in miracles. He kept thinking, thinking.

The lights of the carnival were getting brighter in the night. The noise was picking up. The excitement was picking up—he could feel it in the air. It was Friday night and the place would be jammed inside. And here he was in a quiet field with the grasshoppers, cut off from all the excitement and fun. Goddamn it! He felt the desire to be in that crowd rising in him hot and impatient.

Wasn't that the way it went though, when you least expected something—bang! Seeing that gypsy there had really shaken him. It was the last thing he had expected to see. The carnival had never had guards before. Why did they have to start now? Some smart guy was always changing things.

"We might as well go home," Lommy said despondently. "We're never gonna get in tonight."

"Take it easy, Lommy. We might find some money."

"Hah! Look—I'm laughing."

Tony had a feeling about that carnival hand and he had been right. He liked the gypsy better than the carnival hand. The carnival hand had an American face. He looked like he came from some really American state, like, say, Kentucky, or West Virginia. But the gypsy had sort of a Portuguese face. He was dark and had flashing white teeth. Yes, he liked the gypsy better. He felt more at home with him. But didn't they say you couldn't trust a gypsy?

They turned the corner at the back, walking along easy, but keeping a safe distance into the field. The gypsy smiled broadly, as if he had been expecting them. He had not budged from his station by the opening. This was disappointing. Tony had thought they might make a run for it, if the gypsy walked up and down like the other guy. But he obviously was staying put.

Tony put his hand up and gave the gypsy a friendly wave. The gypsy nodded back—still smiling broadly, which was a good sign. Or was it?

Well, nothing ventured is nothing gained.

Tony took a couple of steps toward the gypsy. He spoke over his shoulder to Lommy. "Come on," he said in a low voice.

Lommy was alarmed. "What are you gonna do?"

"You'll see. Follow me."

Tony approached the gypsy in an apparent casual, friendly, light-hearted, trusting way, but he stopped a little over a club's length away and stood on his toes, alert, wary, and ready to run. Lommy stood further back yet, behind him, and to the side.

Tony nodded at the gypsy.

The gypsy nodded back, his second nod of the night, and he was still smiling broadly.

"Nice night."

The gypsy nodded, the smile the same.

"You with the carnival?"

The gypsy nodded, the smile even broader now.

"It's a good job, huh?"

The gypsy nodded twice, all his teeth showing.

Why doesn't he say something? Oh, Lord, maybe he doesn't know any English, Tony suddenly thought. He had talked once to an old grandfather who nodded and smiled all through the conversation and then afterwards Ma told him, "Next time talk to him in Portuguese. He doesn't understand a word of English." And this gypsy was acting the same way that grandfather had.

"Boy, I sure would like to work in a carnival!" Tony lied. "It must be very interesting—you get to see all the different cities."

The gypsy stopped smiling and spoke for the first time. "I stay on the lot. I never see the cities," he said, shrugging his shoulders.

"I still say it must be a nice life though. You're independent, you know. You don't have any boss over you."

What was Tony doing? Tony was a born salesman, a sure candidate for a gold pin and letter of commendation from Regional Sales. He was buttering up the gypsy, softening him up for the kill. He had never read *The Selling Manual* but he knew its valuable money-making secrets by instinct. Did not the *Manual* make the following points in the summary at the end of Chapter Four? *Concentrate on the target. Establish a warm, human, personal relationship. Make suitable comment on wife and children, etc.* Tony would have gone up to the target with a squaloid grin and pumped his hand vigorously up and down and said, "How are the kiddies, gypsy?" But he was not properly equipped. He had left his cigar and double-breasted suit at home. Under the circumstances, he was doing the best he could.

"Where do you go after you leave here?"

"Chicopee."

Tony cleared his throat. "Say . . . uh . . . any chances of you letting me and my friend here go inside?"

"Ho, ho!" the gypsy laughed, as if that was a good joke. "You boys try to go in without paying—I know, I know!"

"How about it? Will you?"

"Ho, ho! I lose my job if I let you in."

"We won't tell on you, honest."

The gypsy shook his head, but kept smiling.

Then inspiration came.

"I'll pay you for it."

The gypsy's smile vanished. This was business. His eyes narrowed cunningly. "How much?"

"All I've got on me."

The gypsy smiled in compliment to his tactics. "How much is that?"

"Four cents."

Tony held his breath. The gypsy looked at him. Then he looked to the left and then to the right. "Let's see it," he said.

Tony looked at Lommy for the first time. "Okay?"

"Sure!" Lommy said. He quickly passed Tony the four cents.

Tony was apprehensive. He didn't trust the gypsy. The gypsy could easily take the money and tell them to beat it. But he had to take that chance. He came close and handed the gypsy the money.

"If anybody stops you, don't tell them I let you in," the gypsy said.

"No, don't worry, we won't."

The gypsy looked around again and then he said. "Go fast, boys."

They went fast—before anybody could change their mind or something else happen.

They popped out of the slot sideways and ran off into the noise and activity. In a moment they were safely hidden in the warm belly of a big crowd. One last look over their shoulders to see if they were being pursued, and they relaxed.

"I gotta hand it to you, Tony," Lommy said affectionately. "You're smart. I never would have thought of that."

"Well, I didn't know if he would go for it," Tony said modestly, but pleased. "I just took a chance, that's all. And thanks for the four cents."

"Oh, forget it. Your share was just two cents anyway."

Gee, but it sure felt good to be inside. And they knew exactly where to go, too.

They leaned against an empty wooden stage and waited. Overhead a big painted canvas told the tale: *15 Beautiful Girls 15*. This was the hula-hula show.

"I wonder if the girls will be good-looking this year," Lommy said. "Remember that redhead last year?"

"Yuh, I remember her!" Tony said enthusiastically. His groin twitched in honor of her memory.

"Here comes the cheapskates," Lommy said in an undertone so they wouldn't hear him.

Five or six fellows filed out of the hula-hula tent. They were young, around eighteen, nineteen, and they had that shamefaced, guilty look.

They averted their eyes from the people passing and walked away as fast as they could.

Tony and Lommy knew all about the hula-hula show, because a young guy that ate at Ducky's Lunch had seen it and told Lommy about it and Lommy told Tony. It cost a quarter to get in and after you were in there the girls danced around like maniacs and took off their tops and shook their tits right in front of your face, you were behind a rope, and then when they had you all hot and bothered, the barker stopped the show and if you wanted to stick around and see them take more off, you had to cough up another quarter. Otherwise you had to leave right then. In other words, if one of these girls was a favorite with you, it cost twenty-five cents to see her tits and fifty cents to see her snatch. And oh, redhead, if I had the money I'd pay that in a flash, Tony thought.

The young fellows who had just left were therefore not the main audience. They had just seen the first half of the show, and they aroused Lommy's ire.

"Boy, I think that's stupid," Lommy said bitingly. "To go in there and not see the whole show—what kind of guy is it that would do that?" he asked wonderingly. "Would you do that, Tony? Would you go in a show and walk out on the most interesting part?"

"No," Tony confessed.

"Jerks," Lommy said, shaking his head. "They shouldn't let them in. Either you don't go in, or if you go in you stay to see the whole thing."

"Maybe they didn't have the money," Tony suggested mildly.

"For something like that, you can get the money," Lommy said firmly. "Those guys have money. They waste it on cigarettes and stuff."

In a few minutes the main audience came out. They didn't slip out quietly. They made a big racket, laughing raucously and shouting back and forth. They wanted everyone to know where they had been. There were a lot of middle-aged guys with big bellies in the bunch.

"Well, it won't be long now," Lommy said. "Them girls are putting on their panties right now."

There was a loudspeaker horn over the stage and somebody inside put on a record. A girl was singing and the words of the song weren't dirty, but man, the way she sang them! She sounded like she was being jazzed right then.

Slide down my rain barrel,
Come up my cellar door,
And we'll be jolly friends
Forevermore.

There was another song after that one *". . . you play with my yo-yo*
and I'll play with yours . . ." and then somebody turned off the machine.

In a moment the barker appeared on the stage, alone. He had a
tom-tom with him and he began beating it and calling out.

"Hey, hey, hey! Gather round! Gather round! We got girls here! We
got dancing girls here! We got what you want right here! No need to
look further, yah!"

The barker was really something to see. He looked sick. He looked
like if he laid down he'd never get up again. He was a small man with
thin arms and legs and narrow shoulders and chest. He didn't look like
he weighed over eighty pounds. But perched on this ascetic completion
of a body was an enormous head, a fragile eggshell skull with the skin
stretched tight on it. Dead eyes looked out not seeing anybody. And the
skin of his face was the dark brown of tobacco juice but it was a strange
and unnatural shade that did not come from the sun. But the most
amazing thing was that this juiceless bird of a man, this tiny frailty of a
man, had a voice like Hercules. He was all vocal cords. From his tiny
frame there came a deep barrel resonance. His voice carried far away
and you could hear every word as plain as day.

"That's right, I'm talking to you! If you're between the ages of eighteen and sixty, this show is for you. If you're under eighteen you're too
young, and if you're over sixty it won't do you any good anyhow."

"Does that barker look quite right to you?" Lommy said. "There's
something funny about him. . . ."

Tony nodded. "I think he takes drugs," he whispered.

The girls ran out then, a-whoopin' and a-hollerin'. There were five
of them and they lined up on the stage, two on the left and three on the
right with the barker in the middle. The girls were each a few feet apart.
They sort of did a dance together, not sexy, just kicking their left legs,
then their right, then twirling around and clapping their hands over
their heads, and doing other stuff like that more or less.

The barker had been doing just so-so in his efforts to get a crowd but with the appearance of the girls men seemed to spring out of the ground, as from dragon's teeth. They came from all directions and quicker than it takes to say, "Shake it, honey," they were jammed together in front of the stage.

Tony and Lommy had gotten there early and so they had staked out for themselves a choice spot—the front row. They were standing to the left of the barker, that is, by the two girls. Tony looked the two over carefully. He had to choose between them because he always liked to pick one girl out and then concentrate on her. So he held a beauty contest right there. But it was no contest. The girl closest to the barker was old for a dancer, at least thirty, and she had sort of a mashed-in nose, and her face had lost its freshness and she tried to make up for it with a lot of paint, and he didn't like the way she was grinning at the crowd, like a whore. The girl on the end was better. She was a brunette and younger.

The barker kept up his spiel, and then he started down the line of girls, giving a little introductory talk by each one. The girls were just standing there, moving their legs slow and easy, but when he stopped by them and his little talk was over, they'd show their stuff in an individual hula. He'd bang away on his tom-tom while they were shaking it.

"You've heard about Cleopatra's charms—well, if old Cleo was here today, this little girl would give her a run for her money. Inside that tent this little girl is going to perform for you the authentic Egyptian belly dance. Now you'll notice I didn't say an imitation Egyptian belly dance, which is what you see in other dancing shows. I said the one and only, the authentic, the genuine, the bona fide Egyptian belly dance, as it has come down to us through the ages. This is the same Egyptian belly dance that Cleopatra performed for Mark Antony, only it cost him sapphires and rubies to get her to do it for him. We're not going to charge you that much."

Tony looked at the brunette. She was self-conscious. She wasn't sure of herself. In the dance that the girls had all done together when they first came out, he had noticed that she was always a second or two behind the other girls. This was because she watched and never started a step until she saw them start it. Even now, just standing there, she kept looking at the other girls to see what they were doing. She must be new to carnival life and this dancing-show routine, Tony decided.

"I won't insult your intelligence and tell you this girl has danced before the crowned heads of Europe. This girl has never been out of the United States. But I will tell you this—she has just concluded a successful engagement in Chicago, Illinois, where she danced before bankers, governors, mayors, and a lot of people I could be sued for mentioning their names."

The brunette was nice. She was embarrassed and ill at ease in front of all these men. She didn't seem to belong here. Maybe she was off a farm somewhere. She was a simple, unspoiled, unsophisticated girl. She was just a sweet-faced farm girl.

"What this little lady doesn't know about the art of dancing isn't worth knowing, believe me, boys. She's going to put on a dance inside—well, I won't say it's a hot dance, but if you're wearing anything inflammable, just don't stand too close."

Yes, and she was innocent. She didn't know what it was all about. When the barker stood by her and banged his tom-tom for her to do her hula, she weaved her hips in and out but she didn't know how to make it look sexy. She tried, but she was unconvincing. Not like that grinning old whore next to her who slung her ass around like she knew what it was for, and had known for many years. No, his girl's hula did not agitate your blood. Why, he could weave his hips in and out as good as she did. But that tame hula made him love her all the more, for it proved to him that what he had felt about her all along was right— that is, that she was a nice girl and didn't belong here in the carnival half-undressed with all these men staring at her.

"This girl has come to us from Hollywood, California, where she appeared in several motion pictures. But she likes to travel and that's why she has consented to join our show."

Oh, she smiled at him. A shy and fleeting smile, but at him definitely. Was she trying to communicate with him? Was she trying to tell him that she understood his feelings about her and that she loved him in return? He would come back here for the next show. He would slip her a note. *Meet me under the Locke Street Bridge tomorrow afternoon.* They didn't have hula-hula shows in the daytime and she would be free. But how could he pass her a note in front of all these people without being seen? He couldn't do it. He would have to do something else. He would have to contact her some other way.

"Let's give the folks a little free sample, dear. But not too much. I don't want anybody passing out on us out here. I left the smelling salts inside."

205

And early Saturday afternoon he met her on the Avenue, shopping. She was coming out of the 5 & 10.

"Say, aren't you in the dancing show at the carnival?"

"That's right," she said, smiling brightly.

"I caught your show last night. You were terrific."

"Oh, thank you," she said, blushing.

"Where are you headed right now?"

"Oh, I was going back to the trailer. I wanted to see the city but I don't know anyone who could take me around."

"Well, I'd be happy to show you around."

"Oh, I wouldn't want to trouble you."

"It wouldn't be any trouble—honest."

"All right then! Let's go!"

And they walked to the Bostwick, Tony Alfama and the beautiful carnival girl, and there in the grass of Bostwick Hill he kissed her soulfully.

Just then there was a wild shriek, a wild bloodcurdling shriek coming from inside the tent, and an apparition ran out on the stage. It was an Amazon, a giantess, a Goliath of a woman, suffering the slings and altitudes of an outrageous height, displaying her arms and legs to a sea of faces, and by a pose, entertaining them. She was sensationally dressed, brilliantly attired with two perfect circles on top, two jeweled knobs, but your eyes were drawn hypnotically to the form of a jeweled inverted isosceles triangle with the apex safely nestled between her legs.

"It's about time you got here," the barker said, but not angrily.

She ignored this comment and ran past him to the left side of the stage, where Tony was.

She was a mountain of a woman. She towered above the other girls, an Everest among the Himalayas. She was big all over. Many tall women are cut straight as a board, but not her. She had everything she was supposed to have and in ample amounts. She was broad-shouldered, great-breasted, and her nicely shaped thighs were as big around as Tony's trunk.

The Portuguese men in the audience had eyes only for her, for nothing fascinates a small man like a big woman. A big woman warms him to the appreciation for the marvelous diversity in nature. A big woman arouses in him a sense of wonder and admiration. A big woman stings him into a spirit of adventure, like an uncharted ocean did to Prince Henry.

But there was more to her than size. She could dance. Oh, how she could dance! She warmed up with a hula, but not the kind you some-times see, where a girl will give a very artistic dance and move her hands around, the way the Hawaiians do. She ignored the demands of art. She knew what they wanted, and she socked it to them, giving them both barrels full right in the eye. And then she did something Tony had never seen anyone do before. She held her hips absolutely still and she made her belly roll up and down, up and down in undulating waves. It was breathtaking, and better than any hula.

Then she slid her hands along her thighs, pressing her smooth flesh—her lascivious, greedy hands like snakes sliding along her belly, slithering past her deep-holed navel—her hands sliding under her breasts, each hand cupping a breast and offering it out to the crowed in unrefused palm. Wow! And then she started to shimmy and shake all over, getting wilder and wilder, shrieking and snarling, running a hand through her hair fiercely, she with head thrown back, facing the sky and yelling all the while.

"What is she saying? What is she saying?" Tony demanded excitedly of Lommy.

"I don't know, I think she's swearing!"

That did it. That was it. The barker could have sent the other five girls home and filled the tent with her alone.

And now she was finished and just stood there, idly swinging her legs, looking over their heads, beyond them, like they didn't exist, with a contemptuous look on her face. And Tony knew she was the best dancer here, and he reflected on art. What made her so good? What made that sudden quiet and electricity in the air when she performed? And he had noticed that when she came out she didn't look at anybody, neither the barker, nor the other girls, nor the crowd. Even now she didn't look at anybody. She was solitary. And she believed in her dance. She had conviction. His girl was apologetic, the girl in the violet pants on the far end was listless. They didn't have conviction. But she believed in her dance. She believed in herself. What made your dance good—that you believed in it? Or did your dance have to be good first—and then you believed in yourself?

"If you think it's warm out here, wait till you get inside!" And the barker shook a big roll of tickets at the crowd. "We got six girls here, six for twenty-five cents! You fellows that are good in arithmetic figure that one out and you'll find it comes out to four and a-sixth cents per girl.

207

Now I ask you, are these girls worth four and a-sixth cents apiece?"

There were several boys in the front row, by Tony and Lommy. One of them was a Portagee kid, about a year or two younger than Tony. He had very dark skin, and long black hair half over his ears and growing way down the back of his neck, and he was wearing a white shirt that was so dirty, especially the collar, that it looked like he had worn it for a couple of weeks. This Portagee kid started bothering the giant dancer. He leaned on the stage and called up to her.

"Hey, Shorty, I'll see you after the show, okay? How about it tonight? How about it, huh? How about it tonight for a nickel? Whattaya say, you old bag?"

She didn't pay any attention to him, but she heard him all right, and it was building up inside her, for all of a sudden she lashed out at him with a vicious kick, just missing his head, and he scrambled back.

"Get away from me, you dirty little bastard!" she screamed at him. He reared back and spit at her, but kept his distance.

She turned and yelled angrily to the barker. "Jack, I thought I told you to keep these kids away from here!"

The barker hurried over. He was very mad because he had just started selling the tickets, and this broke the mood.

"All right! You kids get the hell out of here!"

And he glared down at them from the stage and waited for them to leave.

There was nothing for it but to go. The Portagee kid who had caused all the trouble ran away laughing and all the other kids followed reluctantly, shuffling away from the lodestar of woman. And so Tony and Lommy had to slink past the gauntlet of hostile eyes, the barker and the girls on one side, the crowd of men on the other side.

And as they joined the mash of traffic they heard a familiar voice behind them. "You only live once!" The barker was back on the job.

"Well, the girls were gonna go in anyway," Lommy said philosophically. "We saw it all."

"Boy, she was big, wasn't she, Lommy?"

"I'll say she was. If you got on her, your head'd come up to about her belly button."

"How big do you think she was?"

"Oh, I'd say she was about . . . six feet four."

"You know, when she first came out she caught me by surprise. I thought she was seven feet tall."

"That's because you were down looking up at her," Lommy explained. "Anybody that's up high on a stage like that is gonna look taller to you. I'd look big myself if I went up there."

Six feet four or seven feet, it didn't matter which, you great big sweet giant. And then he got an absolutely horrendous thought, an idea that made dreams of romance difficult if not impossible.

"Lommy, do you think—" and he got closer and whispered "—do you think she'd have a big twot?"

"Man, I'll say she would! Figure it out for yourself. She has a big head, big arms, big tits, big ass, big legs—is she gonna have a small twot?"

Tony frowned and concentrated on the possibility and all its ugly implications.

"It'd be embarrassing," Lommy continued. "You know, you'd be on her and she'd say, 'Put it in, honey,' and you'd say, 'I already put it in,' and she'd say, 'I don't feel nothin'.'"

Lommy cackled at his own joke, and Tony was acutely aware of the girls and people around them. "Lommy, listen—don't talk so loud, huh?"

"Nobody can hear me. There's too much noise."

"Yuh, I know, but—you know," Tony said, looking around to see if anyone was listening. It looked pretty safe. People were busy with their own conversations.

And his mind wrestled with this newly arrived-at prospect of limitations, this arbitrary negative in a grim arena where male defeat is shocking and ludicrous. No, he would not acknowledge it. He was Apollo and all women were his. The irreconcilable measures of love might be for others but not for him. Yet it was worrisome.

"Do you think men are that way, too—say a big man would have a big one, and a small man would have a medium-sized one?"

"No," Lommy said emphatically. "Just to show you, I'll tell you what happened to me once. I was in the john at the Bughouse and this man walks in, he was drunk, and he stands by the door and he says, 'I'm gonna hit that bowl at ten paces,' and he takes out his dick and he pisses all over the floor. I got a good look at his dingey. It was this big—" and with his thumb and forefinger he measured off in space an inch. "And that guy was a six-footer."

209

Tony nodded, happy at the news.

"I'll tell you another guy, a Portagee guy by the name of Soares. You may have heard of him, they call him Champ. He's famous around Heap Square."

"No, I never heard of him."

"Well, this guy, Tony, is just a runt, a skinny little runt. He weighs about sixty pounds soaking wet. And I was invited to go swimming once in a car with him and some other guys. And when we got there we stripped down in the car, you know, and that guy Champ—I'm telling you the God's truth, Tony—it hung down to his knees. His was bigger on the soft than mine on the hard. And that's why they call him Champ, I found out later. And he's just a runt, Tony. You and me are big guys compared to him.

"That doesn't sound right though, Lommy," Tony said, shaking his head. "If a man's you-know-what doesn't have anything to do with how big he is, then why shouldn't women be the same way?"

"Men are different," Lommy stated authoritatively. "You take a woman, Tony, hers is part of her body. It's built into her, you know what I mean? But you take a man—his is not really a part of his body. It sticks out. It's separate. So it can be any size."

Lommy argued persuasively, but Tony wasn't satisfied. Lommy's ideas didn't sound logical to him. Men and women had to be the same, one way or the other. But how in the world could you find out the answer to something like that unless you actually went out and experimented on a few women yourself?

Past the motorcycle-daredevils show the crowd thinned out and up ahead a man and his son were walking toward Tony and Lommy. The man was American, clean and well-dressed, and his son was about six years old, say a first grader. They were both happy. The man was smiling broadly and he had his son by the hand. The son was chattering excitedly—between bites, for in his free hand he held a delicious-looking hot dog. He had just barely started on the hot dog—he was maybe two small bites into it.

And from behind Tony, a flash, a moving figure, with wild hair and a dirty white shirt, running along smoothly, the Portagee kid from the hula-hula show, running by the man and his son, passing close to the son, and a hand quick and sure, closing unerringly over the hot dog, snatching it away, and the hot dog and its new Lusitanian owner speed-ing off, dodging people, disappearing.

The man was dumbfounded. He didn't know what to do. And his son began to cry. And he tried to console him. "Don't worry, Ted, I'll buy you another one," Tony heard him say.

And as Tony passed him, the man glared at Tony, as if Tony had done it, or at least, as if the Portagee kid was a friend of his. Tony flushed, for it is written that the guilt of the few shall be borne by the many.

The roulette wheel was spinning nearby, and the two boys stopped to watch.

"Do you think that's fixed?" Tony asked.

"Sure," Lommy said unhesitatingly.

Next door they watched a man try to pound a nail all the way into a block of wood with one blow from his hammer. The carnival man demonstrated. With hardly any effort. *Smack!* "Easy, see?" The man tried it. *Smack!* The nail stopped a quarter of an inch out. "Oh, too bad," the carnival man said.

They crossed over to the Ferris wheel. They looked up into the sky and watched the girls scream when they got to the top.

There were a couple of guys running the Ferris wheel. One of them happened to walk close by Tony, and Tony got a good look at him. He was a young guy, maybe twenty, with a torn T-shirt. He had little round green eyes close together; his mouth was wide open like a fish out of water; and he walked around with a somnambulistic stare, like he was in a trance. Where in hell did these guys who worked for the carnival come from? Tony wondered. What a creepy-looking bunch. They just didn't seem like normal people. He had read a book once about a carni-val. This stupid-acting kid wanted to run away from home and join a carnival, and finally he did. And the way that book described the carni-val people—they were great people, just like your next-door neighbors, only better. But the carnival people around here—all you had to do was take one look at them and you knew they weren't like anybody's next-door neighbors anyplace. That book was like a lot of books he had read—full of shit. You couldn't believe them any more than you could believe the fairy tales he used to love to read when he was a little kid. Still he like to read books. He could believe anything while he was read-ing it. But afterwards he had to admit that real life wasn't like that.

Yuh, that book told how carnival people were like your next-door neighbors, kind and helpful to young boys. And they were happy people, always smiling, enjoying their work. But just look around here at these barkers and concessionaires. Find one smile, Mr. Author. Find one happy face. Find one guy who was friendly. Find one guy who looked like he was enjoying his work. Find one guy who looked like he didn't hate the people standing in front of him.

Well, anyway, here was one boy who had no desire whatsoever to run away with a carnival. It looked like a lousy life to him. The only job in the carnival that he would be interested in was barker of the hula-hula show. He would take that job providing certain conditions of his were met. First of all, all six girls had to live with him in a trailer. And he'd screw a different one every night of the week—Monday, the giant—Tuesday, his girl—Wednesday, the whore—Thursday, the listless one—and so on. And wasn't it ironical that the present hula-hula barker didn't look like he was interested in women and, even if he were, didn't look like he had the strength to undertake a jazz?

They went over and watched the Guess-your-weight man for a while. Tony wished he had a dime. He was sure he would win one of those canes with the furry monkey bouncing from the handle. Nobody every guessed his weight right. They always guessed more than he actually weighed.

Next they stopped and watched a fat guy in overalls try to knock over some milk bottles on a shelf. He got three throws for a dime, and the bottles were built up in the form of three on the bottom, two in the middle, and one on top. He had to knock the bottles not just over but off the shelf. They watched that fat guy spend eighty cents without winning a thing. Jeez, he was lousy. He would aim one way and the ball would go flying off in another direction. Tony sighed impotently. It was painful to have to watch such an inept performance. "I'd like to try that just once," he said to Lommy with feeling.

"Me too," Lommy said.

They walked on. They came to a section where the different concessions were all of food and drink. There was the blue sailor boy of Cracker Jack, the twin prongs of Popsicles, and inside the glass bin a mountain of popcorn tumbling about in buttered and salted play. There was the rich autumn brown of root beer, the bubbles rising in the opened bottle, fizzing to the ear. There was the bright red of candied apples. There was the strange and fluffy cotton candy, delicate pink strands floating in the air. There was the cool sight guaranteed to make your throat go dry—a cone of strawberry ice cream, double dip. There was the smell of peanuts roasting. There was the smell designed to bring any boy to his knees—the smell of a hot juicy frankfurter being inserted in a toasted bun, then covered over with mustard, piccalilli, and chopped onions, a wax paper wrapped around the bun, and the whole thing, warm and melting in your mouth, being handed over the counter to a waiting hand.

And everywhere that Tony looked he saw somebody eating. He saw something in every hand being brought to every mouth. And suddenly the noise of the crowd seemed to get louder and louder. He was pressed on all sides by people having a good time, giggling, laughing, waving, yelling. Everybody was having fun. Everybody was doing things, eating, playing games, and going into shows. Everybody but him, that is. He felt like a goddamn ghost walking around here, walking and looking, and looking and walking—eating nothing, trying no games, seeing no shows. Yes, that's what he was, a goddamn ghost at the feast of life.

Son of a bitch. By God, when he got big and had money he'd make up for this. He'd come here with a pocketful of money. He'd stand there and eat two or three hot dogs, or four, as many as he wanted, and he'd wash them down with soda, orange, lime, and strawberry. And he'd munch a bag of popcorn, and yes, he'd try that fluffy cotton candy that he had never even tasted once in his whole life when he was just dying to find out how it tasted. And the same way with those candied red apples, he had been seeing them since he was a little kid and he had never had one yet. Well, he'd have one this time. It'd be his hand that held one, his tongue that licked one, his teeth that chewed one, his stomach that received one, and somebody else could watch the whole process for a change.

And the games—he'd try every game in the carnival. He'd throw baseballs at milk bottles, shoot a gun at moving ducks, pound nails, bet on the black or red, he'd play every game until he won a prize. Canes, dolls, stuffed animals, he'd have somebody along just to carry the stuff. And then he'd go to the shows and he'd see every show on the lot, the sword swallower, the knife thrower, the woman with the snake, the motorcycle daredevils, all the shows. And he'd see some kid standing there with nothing to eat, and he'd say, "Here, kid," and he'd flip him a bag of peanuts. Or he'd hand it to him so that the peanuts wouldn't fall out of the bag. But he'd have a great time! He'd do everything. And he'd spend every nickel in his pocket. If he came with twenty bucks—to hell with it, he'd spend the whole twenty. He wouldn't take a cent home—he'd see to that. And then he could walk down the street and he could say—I've been to the carnival, but not like a goddamn ghost. Like a human being.

"Do you wanna go over to the wrestling show?" Lommy asked.

Memories of a muscular, tough-looking guy in blue trunks dancing on the stage like a champ at Madison Square Garden, swinging an ominous right in his shadowboxing, inhaling noisily up through his nose the way fighters do. The barker—"I'll pay fifty dollars to anybody who'll get into the ring with my boy and still be on his feet at the end of three rounds. The same for wrestling. Fifty dollars for ten minutes without being pinned. My boy doesn't care which, he loves to box, he loves to wrestle." A lot of talk, bragging about his boy, riling up the crowd, insulting Gaw and its fighters. Then a big commotion in the crowd. Someone was trying to get through. Some brave volunteer was pushing his way through. The honor of Gaw was to be defended. "Make way! Let him through!" They patted him on the back emotionally. All necks craned. Who was it? St. George? No, it was Flippy Rezendes, the Portagee rassler, who usually appeared in the prelims at the Powoc Arena but who had once rassled Mephisto in the main event. Flippy went into the tent to undress and a couple of minutes later he climbed up on the stage, brown and splendid in his red trunks. In a loud voice the barker gave him a chance to back out. "I know how it is, you get excited, and some of your friends push you up here. But I want you to know that hospital bills are expensive. . . ." Flippy smiled slightly and shook his head, and his trademark, a ringlet on his forehead, shook with him. He was staying and the crowd cheered. Then more gab, working up the crowd, playing on their fears, for it was a fact that Flippy, at one hundred and sixty pounds, didn't look like he was any match for the big bruiser. The latter, unconcerned and formidable, kept dancing and throwing punches, even though it was going to be a wrestling match. Every time the barker pointed to him the crowd booed. So then it was arranged. Wrestling and to hell with the ten-minute limit. This was to be a real match. "A fight to the finish! No holds barred!" A fat Portagee man, all excited, waved a roll of bills. "I'll bet this on Flippy!" Flippy and the sniffer with the paper-thin ears went inside, and the tickets went on sale and the crowd pushed forward to buy them. There was only one thing the matter. This show was a repeat of the night before, when this same Flippy Rezendes had volunteered, and repetitive bravery comes to smell like a job.

"Do you wanna go over?" Lommy asked again.

"No," Tony said. "It's just a fake. Remember last year when Flippy Rezendes came every night? They fooled me the first time, but never again."

They came to a show that had a pretty good-sized crowd standing in front of it. The crowd was made up of both men and women in contrast to the hula-hula crowd, which had been one-hundred-per-cent men. On the stage was a man and a woman.

"What's this?" Tony wondered aloud.

"I don't know," Lommy said. "I know one thing though. It ain't a Miss America contest."

They both laughed.

Lommy's joke was in reference to the woman. She was not much to look at. She had black frizzled hair, coarse features, a definite mustache, and her figure was without appeal. She was wearing sort of an evening gown, light blue in color and shiny like satin; it covered her up pretty good, going down to her feet. But her arms were bare.

"Let's go up closer," Tony said. "I can't hear good here."

They worked their way forward.

"You may wonder how I can make that statement," the man said. He was the barker. "Well, I'll tell you this—this show has taken out an insurance policy with a world-famous insurance company located in London, England, and by the terms of that policy any man, woman, or child who can come forward and disprove that statement will be paid *five thousand dollars* on the spot. And I'll tell you something else—I have made that same statement in forty out of the forty-eight states in this great country of ours, and that insurance company hasn't had to pay out yet.

"All right, you say—'Oh, he's running that show. That's why he said that.' All right, don't take my word for it. Take the word of a famous group of international doctors located in Switzerland, Europe. We took her over to Switzerland, Europe, to be examined by this group of famous international doctors, and they examined her from head to foot—I mean they examined her—and you know you can't fool a doctor—and these doctors in their report certified that she is *the only living her-MAW-phro-dite in the world!*

"Now you may have noticed that I said *she*. I said *she* because this her-MAW-phro-dite prefers to be known as *she*. I could just as correctly refer to this her-MAW-phro-dite as *he*." The crowd tittered. "Isn't that correct?" he asked her.

She looked straight ahead, expressionless, and spoke in dull flat tones. "I can have sexual satisfaction from either a man or a woman." Either way she didn't seem too excited about the idea.

"Inside that tent, ladies and gentlemen, this amazing her-MAW-phro-dite will tell you her life story. She will tell you what it feels like to be a her-MAW-phro-dite. She will tell you intimate details of her private life. Recently one of our leading magazines, a name familiar to every person here, made a substantial offer to this her-MAW-phro-dite for the publication rights to her life story. She refused. And she refused for this reason: she knew that this was a family magazine brought into the home where children could get at it, and that therefore certain things in her life story would have to be left out, and rather than do that, rather than leave the most important parts out, she refused to have her story published. But I will tell you this, ladies and gentlemen, inside that tent she is not going to leave anything out. This is strictly an adult show—we don't allow minors in there. With her own lips this amazing her-MAW-phro-dite will tell you what couldn't be printed, what they wouldn't *dare* print.

"But you're not just going to hear things, you're going to see things, too. Inside that tent, ladies and gentlemen, this amazing her-MAW-phro-dite is going to remove her clothing." The side remarks of the crowd ceased abruptly and the air was quiet with their attention. "She is going to stand before you, ladies and gentlemen, just as the good Lord made her, completely nude, naked, and unashamed, and you will be able to see with your own eyes her amazing sex organ—a sex organ that is neither male nor female but a combination of both. And I guarantee that it will be one of the most unforgettable sights you will ever see in your life.

"Now I'm going to be honest with you—if you're looking for sex thrills, save your money because you won't find them here. We're not here to tease you. This is not a girlie show. This is a scientific, educational show. In the interests of science we have appeared before the medical faculties of all the leading colleges in this country—and I might add that we astounded those medical doctors—and we are going to put on for you the same high-class type of show that we put on for those doctors. We don't change a word. You will see everything a doctor sees. Naturally we cannot permit you to examine this her-MAW-phro-dite's amazing sex organ—" somebody snickered "—as we permit doctors to do, but except for that, you will see exactly the same show a doctor sees.

"So you fellows out there can feel perfectly at ease in bringing in your wives, sweethearts, sisters, mothers, or grandmothers. There is nothing off-color or suggestive about this show. We don't tell dirty jokes in there. There won't be anything said or done that will embarrass you. But we know that the ladies are sometimes shy about these matters so we separate the sexes inside. When you enter that tent, you will find an eight-foot-high screen going smack down the middle of the tent right up to the stage. Men go to the left, women to the right—you'll see the signs. You won't be able to see the men, ladies, and they won't be able to see you. So you will see this fascinating show in perfect freedom with those individuals of your own sex.

"And now for a few words from this amazing her-MAW-phro-dite!"

She said nothing, but dramatically slipped one of the straps of her gown off her shoulder. She was not wearing a bra so there was exposed one half of her bosom. It was flat and hairy. "This side of me is a man's chest," she said without interest. Would she slip off the other strap and expose the other half, the more interesting half, of her bosom? Everyone waited expectantly, but alas, no. She took the palm of her hand and placed it underneath this clothed and properly round breast and pushed up. There was no mistake—it was a breast. Again she spoke in her dull monotone, "As you can see, I have a fully developed mammal gland in this breast."

"That's just a small sample of what you will see inside!" the barker cried. "Once inside that tent nothing, absolutely nothing, will be left to your imagination! Because, believe me, ladies and gentlemen, we're not here to tease, bother, and bewilder you in any way, shape, or fashion. We are here to put on a scientific demonstration for you. And I'll bet I know what you're asking yourselves right now—'Just how much does this show cost?' Am I right? Now I'm sure that every one of you is the type of person who can understand, realize, and appreciate that a high-class show of this kind ordinarily costs seventy-five cents or more. When this amazing her-MAW-phro-dite appeared at the World's Fair in Chicago, that's how much it cost to see her—seventy-five cents. But we're not going to charge you that much. We're not even going to charge you fifty cents. You've been good to us, you've been a good audience, and we're going to be good to you. We're going to charge you the unheard-of price, the low low price, of *twenty-five cents!* Just two thin dimes and a nickel will put you inside that tent to see *the only living her-MAW-phro-dite in the world!* This is a show that no mature person will want to miss! This is a show that will startle you, amaze you, and add to your knowledge of medical science!"

The barker started unrolling the tickets and judging from the ensuing brisk sale, the crowd tonight was composed mostly of mature persons. Tony and Lommy were as interested in medical science as the next fellow, but their lack of funds and underaged status prevented them from joining in the pursuit of knowledge. Men and women hurried inside, and little wonder. For what is as satisfying as a clean dirty-show? And the textbook treats sexual aberrations with professional detachment, but under the soft curve of the graph, covered over with spadefuls of footnotes, there lies a silent partner from the scientist's buried life—a nasty boy.

Tony and Lommy lingered and watched the people buy tickets.

"What do you think it looks like?" Tony asked Lommy.

"Beats me," Lommy said, shaking his head.

"Boy, I sure would like to be inside that tent," Tony said.

"Me too," Lommy said.

What did her sex organ look like? Tony was going crazy trying to visualize it. The barker had said it was a combination of a man's and a woman's. But how could that be? A man's extended into the air. It was a material object, real and visible. It was something. But from everything he had ever heard about a woman, he understood hers to be a hole, a cavity, a nothingness. So how could there be a combination between something and nothing, between matter and space? What in God's name would it look like?

"The grownups have all the fun," Lommy commented bitterly. "Any time you see anything that's any fun, you can count on it, they're gonna say, 'No minors allowed.' It never fails."

"Well, we don't have the money to get in anyway."

"Yuh, but I'm talking about if we did. If we had the money, it still wouldn't do us no good."

"Last chance to see the only medically proven her-MAW-phro-dite in the world!" the barker cried.

"You know who that barker reminds me of?" Lommy asked.

"No, who?"

"You remember that guy who was in the window at the Lafayette Pharmacy with a white coat and making believe he was a doctor? Remember, he had a microphone and he broadcasted out to the sidewalk and he held up those bottles with all that awful stuff showing what happens inside your guts?"

"Yuh, I remember him."

"Well, this guy reminds me of him."

"You mean you think they look alike?"

"Yuh."

"I don't think they look anything alike."

"Well, they both had mustaches."

"Yuh, but . . . that's the only thing. The guy in the drugstore was fat and this guy here is skinny."

"Yuh, but he still reminds me of him."

Then the barker went inside and the few remaining people strolled away.

"C'mon," Tony said. "Let's go back to the hula-hula show. That guy has forgotten us by now."

"Okay," Lommy said.

"Let's not get in the front row this time," Tony said, as they hurried off.

***

It was a Saturday night some two weeks after the boys had been to the carnival. They started out early after supper. They walked down the Avenue the way they did every Saturday night, to look at the girls. But it was too early, nobody was out shopping yet. Woolworth's and Grant's were empty. So they kept walking. They walked downtown. And without thinking much about it, they kept on walking. After a while they found themselves in the shopping district of the South End.

219

"Well, we've come this far," Tony said, "what do you say we go all the way, Lommy? Let's go to Lindamar and look at the water."

"Okay by me," Lommy said cheerily.

So they pushed on, past the stores, past the houses, until they came to the high wooden fence of the Bumpus Mill. The Bumpus Mill ran for several blocks along the water's edge.

They were walking along by this fence when they saw her. She was up ahead, alone, and walking like they were, toward the beach. She was in slacks. There was nobody else around.

And when they got just a little bit closer, where the trees started, Tony grabbed Lommy's arm.

"Lommy!" he cried excitedly. "That's Crazy Mary!"

"*Who?*"

"Crazy Mary! She's a whore from the South End."

"Yoo hoo, Mary!" Lommy immediately called out to her. "Is that you, honey?"

"Hey, Lommy, ssshh," Tony cautioned. "Don't yell at her. That's no way to do it."

But Lommy persisted.

"Hey, cuckoo in the clock!" he yelled. "Are you there, honey? I mean, are you all there, honey?"

"For chrissakes, Lommy, what do you want to do that for?" Tony cried in exasperation. "What do you want to get her mad at us for?"

There was a pause, as if she was waiting for Lommy to say something else, and then they heard her yell out—"You go to hell!" And almost simultaneously Tony heard something whizzing through the leaves of an overhead branch. "Duck!" he cried. *Whango!* It crashed against the boards of the mill fence. It was a rock.

"What an arm," Lommy murmured admiringly. "Sign her up."

Tony stepped behind the trunk of the tree and stood still. "Come over here by me, Lommy. I don't want her to see us."

Lommy came over and they huddled in the shadows.

"How come you know about her?" Lommy asked curiously.

"Well, you remember that Sunday you couldn't go swimming and I went alone? Well, I was walking back and I caught up with this gang of colored fellows. They were following this girl and yelling things at her. So I says to them, 'Who's that?' And they says to me, 'That's Crazy

Mary. She's the biggest whore in the South End. She screws everybody.'
And they told me she even got sent to a special school, like a reforma-
tory for girls, for screwing. And her own mother sent her there, how do
you like that?"

"Maybe the old lady was jealous, huh?"

"Okay, let's go now," Tony said crisply. "We'll make believe we're
two different guys. And for God's sake, Lommy, don't yell anything.
Do me that favor, huh?"

"No, okay, I won't," Lommy agreed, chastened.

"It was dark, maybe she didn't see us good," Tony said hopefully.

They took off after her at a good pace.

"Is she really crazy?" Lommy asked.

"How would I know?" Tony said. "I've never even talked to her. You
see her yet?" he asked worriedly.

"No."

"Let's walk faster—before somebody else sees her," Tony said.

They skimmed over the dirt sidewalk, practically flying.

When they got around the corner of the Bumpus Mill, they saw the
water and they saw Crazy Mary. She was walking towards Kids Beach.

"Start whistling," Tony commanded Lommy in a low voice,
although there was no need for a low voice. "Act nonchalant. Act like
you never saw her before."

They got closer to her and Tony cleared his throat.

"Hi, Mary!" he called like an old friend. "Wait up!"

She turned and waited on the cement sidewalk by Kids Beach,
under the electric light of a lamppost.

Crazy Mary was English. She was nineteen years old, older than
the boys by four years. She was short. She had red hair, but it was a
strange shade of red, really almost orange. This hair was long and
stringy and entwined and looked like she had just been in swimming, except that it was dry. She had freckles all over her face. Her
two front teeth, uppers, were missing, so when she talked she self-
consciously tried to cover over the gap with her upper lip. For the
same reason, she laughed in her throat, but not in her mouth, keeping her lips straight and slightly open. These pale lips were not
brightened by any lipstick; she wore no make-up of any kind. And as
for the chief point or points of interest on a girl—her breasts were

bountiful but shapeless. It was as if she had stuffed her shirt with a pillow, like the kids do on Halloween.

Crazy Mary looked up at Tony under the street light by Kids Beach, with her back against the concrete wall.

"Do I know you?" she asked suspiciously.

"Mary, don't you remember me?" Tony sighed in plaintive disappointment. "Don't you remember—at the beach?"

"When?" She was still suspicious.

"Oh, gosh. Maybe three or four weeks ago," he bluffed.

She tried to remember.

"Did you have elastic trunks? Red elastic trunks?"

"That's right?"

"You was with a guy named Eddie?"

"That's right!"

"You and Eddie tried to duck me," she laughed.

"That's right," he laughed with her. "We had a lot of fun that day, didn't we?"

"Yes," she said. But then she frowned. "But you don't look quite like the guy."

"Well, that was three weeks ago. I've aged some."

"Say," she said, suddenly remembering something else, "didn't you two fellows just call me some names back there?" She pointed at the Bumpus Mill.

"No, not us," Tony protested innocently. "Why?"

"Oh, there was a couple of wise guys back there calling me names. I don't like it," she said emphatically.

"I don't blame you a bit," Tony said soothingly. "I think that's terrible, to call people names."

"What's your name anyway?" she asked in a more friendly vein.

"Manny."

"What street do you live on?"

"Vill Street," he said, naming a long street in the South End.

"Oh, Vill Street! Do you know a guy named Leon, he lives on Vill Street?"

"Leon . . . let's see. . . ."

"He rides around on a motorcycle."

"Oh, yes! I know him."

"Well, look, the next time you see him, will you give him a message for me?"

"I sure will! What is it?"

"Tell him Mary wants to see him again," she said, blushing.

"Okay, I will," Tony promised, but to himself he said, Make your own goddamn dates. I'm not a go-between. Even if I knew him.

"He's awful cute," she giggled.

"I'm jealous, Mary."

"Oh, don't be. You're cute, too. But you're not as cute as him," she added forthrightly.

"You know ever since that day at the beach there's something I've been wanting to do, Mary."

223

"What?" she giggled.

"This." He put his arms around her and drew her to him. He kissed her full on the lips. She tasted like her supper. Like butter. He had closed his eyes but halfway through the kiss something made him open them, and he saw that her eyes were wide open and that she was looking over his shoulder to see if anyone was coming. This kind of disconcerted him, so he closed his eyes again.

He came up for air and then he kissed her again. This time he pressed his belly into hers hard to see what it would feel like. It felt good. She did not protest; neither did she respond. She was limp. She felt like she didn't have a single bone in her body. But he made up for her sag with an unavoidable salute to womanhood that threatened to lift her right up off the sidewalk.

"Ahem," said Lommy. Poor Lommy hadn't said a word yet.

Tony released her. "Mary, permit me to introduce to you a good friend of mine—Roger. Roger, this is Mary."

"Hello, Roger," she said.

"I'm with you all the way, baby!" Lommy said enthusiastically.

"Don't call me baby," she said sharply. "I'm not your baby."

"Well, I didn't mean nothin'. . . . " Lommy was all confusion and embarrassment.

"What do you want to be called?" Tony broke in smoothly, putting his hands on her hips and turning her toward him.

"Mary," she said, smiling.

"Okay, Mary." He brought his right hand up and placed it squarely, or roundly, on her breast. He squeezed the breast with a vigorous rhythm, like it was milking time down on the farm.

"Not in public," she said primly and gently removed his hand.

"This isn't public. There's nobody here."

"What about him?"

"He's my friend."

"Well, somebody else might come. You don't know how people are. All I have to be doing is talking to a fellow on a corner and they come by and see me and that's all it takes. Next day they make up a big bunch of lies and spread them around town. You should hear the stories they spread about me!" she laughed, looking at him a little apprehensively. "Did you ever hear any stories about me?"

"No."

"Well, don't believe them if you do. They're all lies."

"I won't, don't worry."

"I have a lot of enemies in this town," she said soberly. "They call me names. Those bloody hypocrites. Pardon my language."

"Well, I won't call you any names," he assured her.

"You're nice," she said.

"Thanks," he said.

"You're a gentleman, too," she said. "You take some fellows, if a girl says no, they force themselves. But you don't. You respect a girl." She was referring to his right hand, which she had banished to her hip.

"I never force myself."

"I know it, and that's what I like about you."

"Thanks, Mary," he said. He slid his right hand up till it rested on her pillowy breast. She did not take his hand off. She did not seem aware of it. Being there excited him marvelously. Tentatively he squeezed her breast, but not as before. He squeezed quietly and unobtrusively, like a master thief. She didn't seem to notice.

"I could go for you in a big way," she said dreamily.

"I like you too, Mary," he said. "But what about my friend here? We wouldn't want to leave him out."

"Oh, he's all right," she said agreeably. "But I like you better."

"Can he come along then?" Tony asked pointedly.

"Sure."

Out here by the ocean, far from home, with a girl who did not know him, Tony felt very reckless and bold and knowing.

"Mary, you know what?"

"What?"

"You won't get mad if I tell you something?"

"No," she said, smiling.

"I'd like to go all the way with you," he whispered in her ear.

She giggled and slapped his face lightly and tenderly. "Oh, you're awful! What must you think of me?"

"How about it?" he insisted. "Will you let me?"

"Oh, you! Don't ask me a question like that!" But she said it playfully, not angrily, which Tony interpreted as a good sign.

And suddenly she moved away from him and ran down the sidewalk.

"Hey, where you going?" Tony called in alarm.

There were some concrete steps leading down to the sand of Kids Beach. She ran down these steps. Then she came over to where Tony and Lommy were, except that she was on the beach and they were up on the sidewalk, leaning over the wall.

"I went swimming yesterday," she said, "and I left my towel here somewhere. I'm going to look for it."

The Kids Bathhouse was built right out over the beach. You could walk under it hunched way over, for it was built on concrete stilts about four feet high. By its being open that way the waves could wash in harmlessly at high tide. Mary went straight to the bathhouse and disappeared under it. It was pitch-black under there; you wouldn't be able to see your hand in front of your face. How could she find her towel? Then it hit Tony like a ton of bricks. And it must have hit Lommy at the same time.

"Come on," Lommy said hoarsely.

They walked rapidly to the concrete steps and Lommy ran down them onto the sand. But Tony—Tony stood on the top step—and his legs just stopped there. He stood alone on his height, surveying the sand and water, like in a game they used to play on piazzas when he was a kid, King of the Mountain.

He could feel his heart beating in excitement. Mary didn't want to fool around on a public sidewalk under a light. She wanted privacy. She wanted darkness. And he had investigated under there many times during daylight. He knew one spot where, due to the slope of the beach,

225

there was just about three feet of space between the sand and the floor beams. He and Mary could crawl in there and because it was to the back, out of reach of high tide, the sand would be nice and dry and they could lay there real cozy.

There was no one around. The beach was deserted. It was perfectly safe. Mary was waiting there. She was a sure lay, he felt it in his bones. This wasn't like the deal on Lagoda Street. This was no false alarm. This was the real thing. It was unbelievable! He could actually lay a girl! He had walked the streets with Lommy, and hung around places here and there, always waiting for the dream to happen, always looking, searching for that girl, and now she was here in the palm of his hand, his for the asking. It was unbelievable.

Lommy looked up at him puzzled. "Come on," he urged.

"Okay," Tony said. But he didn't move.

In this hour of glory and triumph when he would finally know woman, a curious disquiet gnawed at him. Did he really want to do it with Mary? Talking dirty with her was one thing—that was harmless. But actually doing it with her—that was something else again. He stood there uncertain. The steps were before him. If he went down those steps, he knew what would happen. One little thing would lead to another and he would jazz her. That he knew for sure. The question was—did he want to go down those steps?

"Come on," Lommy said impatiently.

His head swirled with the urgency of the situation. He could not stall forever. He had to make up his mind one way or the other.

"Come on! Help me find it!" Mary called from the dark.

"We're coming!" Lommy shouted back. "Come on, Tony," he pleaded in an insistent, low voice. "This is what we've been waiting for."

This was no place for a cunctator. What was needed here was a man of upright resolution. This was a moment orchestrated for action. Would he plunge his sword into her scabbard?

And then like an ancient mystic he saw—or rather, felt—a vision. It was a ghostly belly, an acolous mass on the sand, glinting yellow-white in the moonlight, a limp and passive belly, and black flies hovered over the seaweed container, and the smell of rotting fish was in the air.

"Lommy, I'm not going."

"Why not, Tony?" Lommy asked desperately. "This is the chance of a lifetime!"

"I know, but I'm not going. You go though. Go ahead. I'll wait for you."

"No, I'm not going without you."

"Well, I'm not going."

"Then I'm not going either."

Lommy climbed the steps and they walked away from the beach. They said a silent good-bye to the towelless Crazy Mary. Generous to a fault, everybody's friend but friendless, this girl with the Raggedy Ann hair, this siren of the sands—they left her crouched under the bathhouse.

Thus, Tony spurned what he had sought. Why? It is hard to say. Was it because he was frightened of Mary? Did he fear that he would be unable to perform his masculine function in a creditable manner? No, such a thought did not enter his young and virile head. Was he afraid of disease? No, for he was unaware of the gambler's luck involved in dipping into pots of common ingress. Was it because he had imagined his first time a couple of million times and always it was with someone like Jean Harlow, even though she was dead, someone who looked like a goddess, someone with every inch of her pure perfect woman? And when he stood Mary alongside Jean Harlow, the dream came crashing to earth, was that it? No, for he was a wretched essentialist and his common sense told him there was one part of Mary that was unmistakably one-hundred-per-cent woman and it is the part we all concentrate on eventually anyway. Was it because, even though she excited him when he stood close to her, he knew he had no real feeling for Mary and that therefore making love to her would be an obscene parody of love, like masturbation, just kidding yourself with pictures and a wild imagination? Perhaps. Or was it something in him which until that very moment he had not known was in him—a desire to retain innocence? Did he realize then that innocence lost can never be regained, that knowledge learned can never be unlearned? Perhaps. Was it a matter of aesthetics, or of morality, or of pride? Why had he hesitated? What had restrained him, paralyzed him? Who can say? The meaning of an action often eludes us.

The two boys walked along in silence. They were disheartened. They felt like two healthy soldiers leaving the field of battle. They had been disarmed by a single girl. Their bluff had been called.

They were almost downtown before Lommy revived enough to compliment Tony. "You handled her real good, Tony," he said. "I could

227

see she really liked you."

"Thanks."

"You got quite a line with girls," Lommy said admiringly. "When I'm with a girl, I can't think of anything to say. But you—how do you do it?"

"Oh, I just bullshit them. That's all you can do with a girl. Bullshit her. If you talk to a girl straight, you know, like you and me talking now, they don't like that. You have to bullshit them."

"Well, you got quite a line with girls," Lommy repeated. "I never realized it before, Tony."

Lommy's praise made Tony feel pretty good.

"I'm always gonna let you do the talking," Lommy vowed.

They walked a ways, each thinking his own thoughts—then Lommy said:

"You felt her tits, you lucky bastard."

"Yuh."

"What did they feel like?"

"It was like floating on a cloud."

The boys went straight home and that night in bed Tony pulled the covers up over his virginal body and thought about what had happened at the beach. He was glad he hadn't done anything. He still had his cherry. He would save it, like a good-luck piece, and carry it with him into the unknown future.

CHAPTER 7

Looking for Work

Ma thought a lot of Tony.   *229*

"I prize that boy," she said one afternoon to *Senhora* Caldeira, her next-door neighbor, who had come over for a little visit. They were having a cup of tea together. Tony was at school. "When people come here, they see him sitting so quiet, not saying anything, with certainty they think he's a banana. But no, he is not a banana. His mind is not empty. He is thinking, thinking. That boy is deep like the ocean!" she sang rapturously. "He thinks deep thoughts! I know!

"Oh, at home he is full of jokes, you know. He puts underwear on his head and pretends it's a lady's hat. And when I turn my head at the table my plate disappears—he hides it on his lap. But so quick is he that a person truly is taken aback. And he takes a handkerchief and shows how a lady of high position blows her nose and how a bum from the streets blows his—oh, he makes you laugh! But he doesn't fool me with his jokes. He is really melancholy. Ever since his father died he has been that way. A cloud passed over him that day—" and her hand passed slowly through the air like a cloud "—and his soul knew something had happened. He had no words, but his soul knew."

Ma brought the cup to her lips and blew on it and took a cautious sip. A beatific expression came over her face, signifying that a most pleasant remembrance had come to her.

"But listen to this," she said, "this is remarkable—one time we were walking down the Avenue, Tony and me, when he says, 'Oh-oh, here comes my teacher.' It was this tall skinny lady with her hair all white, I have forgotten her name now, but her face light up when she see Tony.

"'Is this your boy?' she says to me.

"'Yes, this is my boy,' I says.

"'Oh, this is a prize boy you got here, did you know that?' she says to me.

"'Yes, I know that,' I says.

"'This boy,' she says, 'he is good in the school work, he is always polite, he is a number-one A boy.'

"And she put her arm around his shoulders—like this—oh, poor boy, he was so embarrassed, he was blushing—and she says, 'I wish I had forty more like him.'

"How do you like that?" Ma said to *Senhora* Calderia. "What a favorite with the teachers, huh?"

"He is not a troublemaker in the school," *Senhora* Calderia said.

"Exactly. He is not a troublemaker there. The teachers like him because he is attentive. He listens. He learns. Then he does good work. Always—nice marks."

"Not like that Manny Serpa," *Senhora* Calderia said.

"That big lout! And he lives close to the church!"

"My sister saw him steal a bag of rags from a ragman," *Senhora* Calderia continued. "He waited till the ragman went inside a house and then he walked right up to the wagon of the ragman and took a bag of rags. He hid it in his cellar. Then he will sell it to the next ragman who comes by. That's how he gets money for cigarettes."

"Sixty lashes across the ass is what he needs but nobody will give it to him!"

Ma was a gentle soul who would never dream of giving anyone a single lash but moral outrage sometimes provoked her into bloodthirsty outbursts.

"He's too big now," *Senhora* Calderia observed.

"Yes, but how about when he was small? That was the time to do it. Done then, he wouldn't need it now."

"Once his mother was called to the school, to the Cupp School. 'Mrs. Serpa, we've got to do something about your boy,' the principal said to her."

"I don't even know where that Cupp School is! I would get lost if I tried to go there," Ma said proudly.

Ma took a sip of her tea and relaxed contentedly as the pleasant warmth flowed through her and noxious thoughts about Manny Serpa drifted away.

Senhora Caldeira was the only lady she could talk to about Tony. All of her other friends had sons and it was bad manners to praise your son in front of others who also had sons—especially since, chances were, their sons had done nothing worthy of praise. But *Senhora* Caldeira only had daughters so in her case it was all right to discuss Tony. There could be no comparisons.

"But it doesn't surprise me he does well in school," Ma went on. "He likes to read and people who like to read usually make good students. He goes to the library all the time. And he does not read just skinny little books like some do, skinny books and with many pictures. He reads books this fat—" she measured it in the air with her thumb and forefinger "—and with no pictures—or maybe just one or two. I know—I have looked at them. A book like that, it would take me five years to read. But he—he reads a book like that—" and her lips curled in sudden contempt for this fat book "—faugh!—he reads a book like that in two, three days.

"Sometimes he's in his room, and I don't hear any noise from there, not a sound, so I get worried. Is that boy dead? I wonder. Did some accident happen to him? So I go to the room and I peek in. There he sits by the window, reading a book, but so quiet, not moving, like a statue, and he stays like that for hours. Remarkable, isn't it?

"But I don't want you to think he stays home all the time like some sick person. He has this friend, this companion of his, a boy called Lombee, or Bombee, or something like that, and the two of them go off together, they go to this place and that."

Ma studied her tea for a moment.

"He is a quiet boy then," *Senhora* Caldeira said.

"Exactly! He is a quiet boy."

"Maybe he'd be good for priest."

"Exactly! Exactly! That's what I thought. I observed him. I saw that he was a boy of quiet habits. Maybe he would be good for priest, I thought. So I said to him, 'Tony, I am going to tell you about a school that maybe you don't know about. This is a school far away from here, just where I don't know, but it's a thing easy to find out. This school is run by the Church. And it is not needed to have money to go there. Naturally, if you have money, you pay. But for those without money, they take you free, they give you everything, the books, a bed, food, everything free you understand.'

231

"'Is this a school to be a priest?' he said to me. 'Ma, I'm no priest.'

"'Now wait,' I said to him 'This is not a priest school. This is a school *preparatory* for the priest school. This school gives you a chance to see if you like that kind of life, and too, it gives the people in charge a chance to see if they like you. If you go there and find you don't like it, you can quit, you can come home anytime, and nothing is lost.'

"'Ma, I'm no priest,' he said to me. 'I don't have to go there to find out.'

"Well, what can you do?" Ma asked *Senhora* Caldeira. "If he doesn't want that life—well, he doesn't want that life," she said with finality.

Senhora Caldeira nodded.

Ma took a last sip of her tea and spit out a bit of leaf.

***

Tony wanted to quit school at the end of the eighth grade and look for work. But Ma said no. "I want you to graduate. It's only one more year. And what chance would you have to find a job, a boy, without experience, when the streets are full of grown mans, with experience, and they cannot find a job? You would have no chance at all, Tony. So you stay in school. Finish. Graduate."

So Tony remained at Cupp Junior High for the ninth grade. Soon graduation time approached and Ma could tell it was coming, because Tony took to singing a particular song around the house. This song was the song the whole graduating class would sing at the ceremonies. It was "Old Dog Tray" by Stephen Foster.

Now, just as with drawing, Tony did not have a good head on his shoulders for singing. He sang off key and for the life of him he could not remember the words to songs. For three years at Cupp he had taken Music, one hour a week. And in all those hours of singing, only a few lines had stayed with him, no complete song. But this all changed when the teacher introduced them to "Old Dog Tray" and they began rehearsing for graduation. For some strange reason this song really appealed to him. Whether the charm was in the words, or in the melody, or in the mood of the song, or wherever it was—he really liked "Old Dog Tray" and without any effort he remembered all the lines.

Tony broke into song around Ma at all hours. He sang in full voice, savoring every last drop of sentiment, and the lights could have been on him at stage center. And always the words went like this:

Old dog Tray's ever faithful,
Grief cannot drive him away,
He's gentle, he is kind;
I'll never, never find
A better friend than old dog Tray.

Finally Ma was moved to say: "My God, son, I don't mind you singing, but don't you know any other song? I am sick of hearing about this dog."

Then came the mid-June afternoon and over three hundred voices were lifted in heartwarming tribute to that venerable canine, Tray, and Tony was now officially a graduate of Cupp Junior High School. He did not have a diploma to prove it. Cupp did not give diplomas. But still it was down there in the records and it gave him a nice feeling.

***

It was not a good time to look for work. It would be like picking blueberries in January. Tony knew that. Too many people were out of work on his own street for him to be bouncing with optimism.

"The mills are on the bum," everyone said. It was true. The Gaw mills were cast in the role of Apaches in a John Wayne cavalry picture. They bit the dust one by one, as sharpshooting Southern competitors picked them off. The story was simple: wages in Gaw were low, but wages in the South were lower still. The cheap foreign labor of Gaw appealed to the government for protection from the American workers—those underpaid natives of No'th Ca'lina, those teeming masses of hillbilly coolies who could subsist on a bowl of turnip greens a day. But the appeal was denied and the struggle went on. Now under the ground rules of the free enterprise system, lower wages mean lower costs, and lower costs mean lower selling price, and lower selling price means liquidation for the opposition.

At a banquet at the exclusive Bobbins and Bales Club, the worried Yankee mill owners of Gaw listened to the guest speaker, Professor Tekel from the Harvard faculty, a man well known for his ability to look into the economic future. "Gentlemen," he said, "the handwriting is on the wall: *Your profits have been weighed and found wanting in the balance.* Verily, I say unto you, what shall it profit a man if he gaineth the whole order but loseth his margin? Gentlemen, the time has come to liquidate. Sell your spindles. Sell your looms. Leave Gaw. There is no more money to be made here."

A few of the mills joined the competition and moved to the South, leaving behind what sociologists call "a stranded population." But most of the mills stood their ground and accepted their fate, which was a slow death. And there the empty mills stood, with broken windows, the cathedrals of an industrial society, without worshipers. It was the end of an era. The encyclopedias would have to revise their automatic coupling of Gaw and cotton.

But the wheel of the free enterprise system was about to take a turn in Gaw's favor. The garment industry in the city of New York was characterized by small units of operation and intense competition. Each garment manufacturer realized that if he could cut costs, that is, wages, he would be gaining a lovely advantage over his fellows. But he was faced by a strong union and at the very first mention of a wage cut he would have to deal with the whole sickening paraphernalia of unionism—pickets, protests, demands, negotiations, walkouts, strikes. In other words, it would be one big headache. But suppose he could find a city, not too far from the fashion center of New York, with factory space available at low rental, and with an abundance of cheap nonunionized labor? Why not move there? Why not indeed.

So these garment manufacturers began to move into the empty mills of Gaw. It would not be good manners to say they sneaked into the city, but it could be said they came unaccompanied by brass bands. They did not want to alert the union they had left behind in New York. And with their six dozen sewing machines lost in a corner of a gigantic mill, the garment operations might have seemed like small potatoes. But Gaw was hungry and every little bit helped. The *Evening Observer* welcomed these new establishments, referring to them as "the needle trades," but the people called them sweatshops. Soon the shops were turning out a fair amount of shirts, dresses, suits, boys' jackets, pajamas, overcoats, and yes, bedspreads, pocketbooks, and belts.

It was not a good time to look for work. It was a time when the unemployed walked aimlessly back and forth along the Avenue, just to get out of the house. It was a time when silent men prowled the Dump like wraiths, looking for bottles and rags. It was a time when the people squeezed the green heart of In God We Trust with long bony fingers.

But Tony was not dismayed, for he had known no other time. He was buoyant, as youth is buoyant. He whistled in the streets. But he was not optimistic. He expected nothing.

As Tony saw it, he had three choices. First, the mills. There were still a few of them running, although none with a full shift of workers, except maybe the Rayon Mill. Second, the sweatshops. And third, delivery boy in a grocery store. All the grocery stores offered free home delivery so they needed a boy to make the deliveries and to do odd jobs around the store. Later on maybe he could work up into full clerk.

The mills paid twelve dollars a week, the sweatshops six to eight dollars, the grocery stores four to five dollars. Tony decided to try for the big money—the mills. If he didn't make it, he'd try for the sweatshops. If he didn't make that, he'd try for delivery boy. And if he didn't make that—well. . . .

He went to the mills. He went to the cotton mills from one end of Gaw to the other, to the Bumpus way in the South End, to the Chout way in the North End. He went to the Silk Mill, to the Rayon Mill. The Rayon Mill, with its stink from the chemicals they used, was running the best of any mill in Gaw. But no luck, there or at the others.

Perseverance—that's what he'd have to try. He picked out a mill to lay siege to. He picked the Chout. He had two good reasons: not only was it running two shifts, though neither a full one, but its location offered hope. The Chout Mill was so far into the North End it was practically out of town. It was past Bellehaven Park, past Cupp Junior High, past all the houses, past everything. There was nothing around it but railroad tracks and woods. It was a two-hour walk there, and two hours back. It was such a formidable walk few people would care to take it, Tony reasoned. And the less people who came to the Chout looking for work, the better his chances would be.

He concentrated on the second shift at Chout, which went from two in the afternoon to ten at night. He got there at one-thirty, the time at which the first workers started arriving. They hung around the front and then at one forty-five they started going inside.

The first day that Tony came he had the boss pointed out and he followed him inside and asked if there was any chance for a job. The boss, a stocky man, didn't even say a word. He just shook his head curtly.

Tony only spoke to the boss the first day. He didn't want to make a nuisance of himself and irritate the man. But he made it a point to get there early and sit in a prominent place near the door. That way the boss couldn't help but notice him when he went in, and it would be like sending him a message—"Boss, I'm here if you want me."

Tony hung around outside the Chout all afternoon and into the early evening. About eight o'clock he'd give up and start down the railroad tracks, heading for home a long way away.

Why did he hang around the mill door for over six hours? Because he had a crazy idea. It was a dream. Some worker inside would get sick and have to leave. The boss, desperate, would suddenly remember him outside and give him a chance. He would surprise and delight the boss with his speed and aptitude for the work. Meantime, the poor sick worker, it was unfortunate, but his illness proved to be a serious heart condition, and he had to quit the mills for good. The boss now appointed Tony to the vacated place on a permanent basis. Tony had a steady job.

That was the dream.

But one night about seven o'clock, a worker came outside to steal a few hurried puffs on a cigarette. He was in his underjersey, and the skin of his arms and shoulders was white like the jersey. Lint had floated down upon his hair with delicate adhesiveness, like little pieces of cobweb. He was about thirty-five.

"What are you doing, kid, always hanging around here?" he asked in a curious but friendly way.

"I'm looking for a job," Tony said.

"What—out here?" he asked humorously.

"No—inside. I figure if somebody gets sick maybe the boss will let me try out."

The guy's mouth fell open at this. "Jeez, I don't mean to discourage you, kid—but what a goddamn waste of time," he said, shaking his head.

"Why?" Tony said stoutly.

"Kid," the man stated flatly, "nobody in there's gonna get sick. They've all got families. They'd have to be carried out feet first before they'd lose a day's work. I got the bleeding piles myself and the guy next to me has the sciatica, but we're here, ain't we?"

Tony said nothing.

"And another thing," the man said, "you ever work in a mill before?"

"No," Tony said.

The man nodded, as if that was the answer he had expected.

"Listen—if anybody gets sick or canned—Captain Bly in there, he's got the names of fifty guys in his pocket, and they're all experienced. Now you figure it out. If he was going to hire a guy, would he hire you and have to break you in and for the first few weeks he'd lose money on you, or would he hire an experienced guy? Which would he do, huh? And remember, he ain't no Santa Claus."

"Well, I guess he'd hire the experienced guy," Tony admitted.

The man nodded.

"Listen," he said, "this is a free country so you do what you want. Don't let me talk you out of anything. If you wanna hang around here, you hang around. But I'm just trying to give you my honest opinion. I hate to see you wasting your time this way. If I thought you had a chance, I'd tell you, so help me."

"Well, thanks, I appreciate your talking to me," Tony said, and he meant it. This guy was the only guy in the whole mill who had taken the time and trouble to speak to him. The other workers just ignored him; they didn't give a damn about him.

"Where would you look for work if you were me?" Tony asked, thinking maybe the guy could offer him a tip or two.

The man didn't answer right off. He was sucking the smoke into his lungs with a concentration of pleasure, like a last kiss. Then he blew the smoke out.

"I don't know," he said, shaking his head. "It's pretty rough everywhere."

He squeezed out the light of his cigarette with his fingers. Then he slid the cigarette back into his pack; he had only smoked it halfway down.

"I'll see you," he said, and ducked inside.

That night going home along the tracks in the gathering darkness, Tony felt discouraged. Was the guy right? Was he just wasting his time?

***

It was a beautiful day, sunny but not hot. It was just past noon and Tony sat at the table waiting for Ma to bring him his dinner.

Ma put the plate before him. There was a small boiled potato and three cylindrical segments of fried eel. They had been having a lot of eel lately. *Senhor* Calderia caught eels in the traps he set in the Ossawona

River and he always gave Ma a part of his catch.

"How are they?" Ma asked, meaning the pieces of eel.

"They're good. They're fine," Tony said.

"I won't give them to you that same way tonight," Ma said. "I'm going to cook them different."

"Okay, good," Tony said.

Ma sat down in her favorite chair by the window. The chair was not directly in front of the window but off to one side so that she could peek around the curtain and see what was going on outside but all the time remain unseen herself. She could see the house next door and part of the street.

"Aren't you going to eat?" Tony asked.

"No, I'll eat later," Ma said.

Tony was cutting the potato into small pieces. He had learned that if you cut food into small pieces, it makes it last longer.

"You going to the library this afternoon?" Ma asked.

"Yes," Tony said. Today was Saturday and Saturday was his day to go to the library.

"You read too much," Ma charged. "It's bad for your eyes. You're going to be blind before you're twenty-one."

"Well, it's free, Ma. What else can I do that's free?"

"On your way back I want you to stop at the fruit store. I'm going to give you three cents. Get me a pound of string beans, They're three cents a pound. We'll have some nice fresh beans for supper tonight. I'd rather have *favas* but they don't have them there. I think Portuguese beans are more tasty than the ones they have."

"Okay," Tony said.

Ma suddenly came to full alert, peering around the curtain.

"Here comes the Frenchie!" she said. "Let's see what she is up to. Ah, the Great Lady is dumping her garbage. I'm surprised she doesn't have her husband do it. After all, some of it might touch her hand."

It was Mrs. Bibeau, their next-door neighbor. Her husband was a carpenter. The Bibeaus lived on the first floor of the tenement next to theirs. The Bibeaus lived on one side of them; the Caldeiras lived on the other side. A lot of things about Mrs. Bibeau irked Ma. Even the way she walked. She had a young woman's body and although she did not exactly flaunt it, on the other hand she did not carry herself with the proper modesty. Or so Ma felt.

"Aw, Ma, why don't you lay off her?" Tony remonstrated. "She's all right."

"They all want to be movie stars in this country," Ma said bitterly. "They all strut their ass around. Even to walk ten feet to dump some garbage they do it."

Tony shook his head, laughing.

"She puts on airs," Ma said

"I think living in this country spoils all the girls," Tony said dispassionately. "Things are too easy here. The girls get lazy."

"No, not all," Ma objected. "There are many fine Portuguese girls, watched over by their parents, who would make responsible wives."

"But I still think you're taking a chance," Tony said. "If a girl has been in this country any length of time, you can't be absolutely sure. I've seen some Portuguese girls at school who were just like Americans."

"That's true," Ma admitted soberly. "You have to pick carefully."

"When I get married I'm going to send direct to St. Michael's for a girl," Tony said, "get one fresh off the boat. That way I know I'll be getting the best."

Ma looked closely at him and he broke up, laughing and laughing till he groaned.

"Fool that I am!" Ma cried. "To talk seriously with you when you are only having a little fun with me!"

"You know," Tony said, "not to change the subject, but you know what I was reading in a magazine the last time I went to the library? I was reading about this lady Margaret Mitchell. She wrote a book called *Gone with the Wind* and she sold it to the movies—you know, they want to make a picture out of it. So guess how much the movies paid her for the book."

"How much?"

"Fifty thousand dollars."

"How much?"

"Fifty thousand dollars."

"Whew! She must be some Shakespeare. But I think you made a mistake. I think you read that wrong. Nobody's going to pay that much money just for a story."

"Well, that's what it said—fifty thousand dollars."

"Let me ask you this—did the fifty thousand dollars have a dot in it for the cents?"

"No."

"Ah! There's the mistake right there. Somebody left that dot out when they printed the magazine. Tell me this—how much would fifty thousand dollars be if you put in the dot?"

"Well, let's see . . . knock off two zeros . . . that'd be five hundred dollars."

"There, you see! They left off the dot. It's a mistake. For five hundred dollars I would believe it. But even that is hard to believe—five hundred dollars just for a story."

"Well, I still say it was fifty thousand dollars," Tony said. "You see, Ma, out in Hollywood they throw money around like it was water. Fifty thousand dollars to them is nothing."

"Don't you believe it! Money does not grow on trees. Not in Gaw and not in Hollywood."

Tony finished the last mouthful of eel and wiped his mouth off with his sleeve.

"Well, is it a good book then?" Ma asked.

"I don't know, I didn't read it," Tony answered. "I had heard about this book before, you know, so one day I was at the desk and this lady says to the librarian, 'Will you put my name down on the waiting list for *Gone with the Wind*?' So, okay, the librarian puts her name down and I waited till after the lady left, then I says to the librarian, 'Could you put my name down on that waiting list for *Gone with the Wind*?' So she says to me, 'How old are you?' And I says, 'Fifteen.' So she says, 'You're too young. This is a book for grownups.'"

"What is it?" Ma asked, frowning. "A dirty book?"

"I don't know," Tony said cheerfully. "Maybe it is."

"A dirty book written by a woman—it's disgraceful!" Ma cried heatedly, while Tony broke into laughter. "Well, why not?" she said resignedly. "In this country the womans smoke cigarettes in the street, they wear man's pants, they go to the barrooms and drink whiskey with the men—why not write dirty books, too?"

Tony spit out a piece of food that had lodged between his teeth.

"But you know what I was thinking?" he said. "Let's take this Margaret Mitchell. She writes a book, right? And she sells it to the movies for fifty thousand dollars. And I'm not even going to count the money she made selling it in bookstores, probably another fifty thousand, but we'll just forget that. Now, how long did it take her to write this book? I'd say two or three months. I think that's plenty of time to write a book. I wrote a long story for school once and it just took me a couple of hours. But let's say that she writes slow. Let's give her six months. Okay. So then we can say she works six months and makes fifty thousand dollars. Okay. Now let's look at a guy in the mill. He makes twelve dollars a week. Let's take this guy and say that he starts working in the mill at the age of fifteen and stays there till he's sixty-five—that's fifty years of work."

Ma shook her head. "He wouldn't work that long."

"Why not?" Tony said, impatient at the interruption.

"Because the mill would kick him out before he got to sixty-five. You think they want old men around there?"

"Well, just for the sake of argument, let's make believe that he stays there till he's sixty-five."

"Make-believe, make-believe," she said scornfully, "what good is make-believe? Can you eat make-believe? Why don't you talk about the true things and not make-believe?"

"All right, Ma," he said. "Who's telling this story, you or me? Do you want to tell it, or do you want me to tell it?"

"Go ahead, tell it!" she said. But she muttered disgustedly, "Make-believe, aaa. . . . "

"Well, anyway, this guy works in a mill for fifty years at twelve dollars a week. Now let's see how much that comes out to for one year. Let's say there's fifty weeks to a year, that'll make it easier to figure. And it would be twelve times fifty, which is equal to . . . let's see . . . six hundred. He makes six hundred dollars a year. Okay. And he works for fifty years. So you set it up six hundred times fifty and that would be . . . let's see . . . three zeros, six times five . . . that would be thirty thousand dollars. He makes thirty thousand dollars in his lifetime."

"What about layoffs?" Ma said. "Nobody works all the time."

"Ma, sshhh," he said. "This guy makes thirty thousand dollars. But it takes him fifty years to do it. He has to sweat in a mill for fifty lousy years to do it. And Margaret Mitchell makes fifty thousand dollars for six months' work. How does that strike you?"

"Wellll . . . ," Ma said, shrugging her shoulders.

"It doesn't seem right to me," Tony said. "It's not fair. The people in the mill work a lot harder than she does and they get a lot less money. It's not right."

"There's always somebody better off than you and somebody worse," Ma said.

"Ma, I'm going to tell you something," Tony said, his face intense and rapt, like he had just seen a vision, and truth and understanding were suddenly his. "Ma, there's a lot of money in this country. You just have to know the way to make it, that's all. You have to know the way. It's a secret way. And if you know the way, you make a lot of money. And if you don't know the way, you work hard for low pay."

"Don't start thinking like that, Tony," Ma said. "You start thinking like that and you will end by robbing a bank. Be satisfied with the twelve dollars a week, if you are lucky enough to get it. It will put bread on your table—that's all you need in this life."

"You have to know the way," Tony said dreamily. And he spent the next several minutes trying hard to think of the way, the secret, the magic word, the combination to the safe, but he could not think of it.

"It's not just the money that counts anyway," Ma said. "Look at teacher. Everybody says, 'Oh, a teacher is a fine job! They get over twenty dollars a week.' Yes, sure. It's a good pay, a wonderful pay. But a teacher has to live in a nice home. They can't live in a tenement, where it would be cheaper, because it wouldn't look nice for a teacher to live in a tenement. They have to spend a lot of money on clothes, they have to dress nice. When they buy some fruit or vegetables, they can't go to cheap stores looking for bargains—it won't look nice; they have to go to the expensive stores where the high-class people go. So, in the end, even with their twenty dollars, they are no better off than a person in the mill. Because they have to live more high than an ordinary person, they end up with nothing. They can't save anything."

"I think teaching's a darn good job," Tony said. "Look at the summer vacation they get. And it's a steady job, you get your money every week."

"Oooh!" Ma breathed, looking out the window. "Look at that! Look at that! She has come out without any clothes! Somebody should call the police!"

"Let's see!" Tony jumped up from the table and peeked around the curtain.

Mrs. Bibeau was a handsome, raven-haired woman. She was in

her middle twenties and had four children, all under the age of six. Three of them were with her now, running and screaming and chasing one another around the yard. The fourth, the baby, was in the house, probably sleeping.

Mrs. Bibeau was in a two-piece swimsuit, delightfully brief. She carried an old blanket with her and stretched it out in the dirt yard. Then she stretched herself out on the blanket, face up. Tony noted with warm gratitude that childbearing had not harmed Mrs. Bibeau's figure in the slightest. Her baboosies were, if anything, more attractive—full, laden with milk and honey. Oh, Promised Land. Oh, you sweet-titted creature. Oh, evermore Mrs. Bibeau, with you I wouldst sing and flow.

Tony would have liked to keep on watching but, what with Ma right there, he could hardly do that. And he would have been afraid to, anyway. Mrs. Bibeau might see him and tell her husband and he was not a guy you would want to fool with. Tony went back to the table and sat down nonchalantly, as if he had seen nothing out of the ordinary in this grand woman lying there nippled and bellied for a ride into paradise.

"That's a bathing suit," he explained to Ma. "That's the kind the women wear these days."

"A grown woman with kids and she has no shame," Ma said. "What an example for her daughters. She should be arrested, that would teach her a lesson."

"That suit is perfectly all right to wear. Ma. Thousands of girls wear them on the beaches."

"On the beaches—yes!" Ma cried triumphantly. "And when you are with your husband! But come here—do you see any beach out there? Do you see any sand? Any water? No. It's just a yard. A yard in full view of any man with big eyes who passes. It's not proper!"

"Well, this is a free country," Tony said.

"I wonder if her husband knows that while he is working his wife is prancing around the yard with nothing but a little rag around her hips."

"Well, why don't you tell him?" Tony suggested.

"The Lady of the Manor has plenty of time to give free shows to anybody who passes, yes. But to do the things she's supposed to, she has no time for that. Get off your hind end!" Ma ordered her. "Get in the house where you belong. Go do some work. Who is she, a rich lady with servants to be taking sun-a-bats?"

"A tan is supposed to make you healthy," Tony said.

"Look at those kids. So filthy dirty. The dirt is caked on them from days. You'd have to pry it off them. You'd need a screwdriver with certainty, not soap. But I don't blame them. They are just kids. It's their mother I blame. There she is, sprawled out half-naked, more than half, when she should be tending her kids. Why doesn't she take them in the house and give them a bath? Water's cheap. If water was expensive, I'd say all right. But water's cheap."

"Look, Ma, you're going to give me indigestion," Tony said. "Why don't you move over here to this window and then you won't have to look at her?"

"No. Let her move. I was here first."

"But she has only one yard and you have two windows."

"I don't care, I'm staying," Ma said stubbornly. "Let her move. Let her take her sun-a-bats at the beach where she's supposed to."

"I wonder if they make houses without windows," Tony mused aloud.

"Look!" Ma cried. "Look at that boy! He has a piece of wood—he's chasing the little girl—he's going to break her head open—wake up, you rich lady there—your kids are killing themselves right under your nose!"

"Take it easy, Ma," Tony said. "I don't see any of them dead yet."

"She is trapped in the corner! He is going to break her head open! Oooh!" Ma threw her hands up before her eyes.

Tony jumped up from the table to take a look.

The boy, about five years old, stood over the smaller, cowering girl with a piece of two-by-four in his hand. He was about to let her have it. The girl was screaming.

Mrs. Bibeau was lying placidly on her blanket. Her eyes were closed. Then they opened. She raised herself on an elbow. "Lucien!" she called out.

The boy looked at his mother and dropped the two-by-four. The girl ran away. Mrs. Bibeau dropped back down. And in a moment the yard was back to normal, with all three kids running and yelling and chasing one another.

Tony left the window.

"You can't hurt a Frenchman anyway," he said. "They all got hard heads."

"You have to stop things before they happen," Ma said. "Afterwards it's too late."

"Well, I can see this is going to go on all day," Tony said. "I'm getting out of here."

Not that he would deprive Ma of that window—even if he could. That pane of glass meant a lot to her. It was her window on the world. From it she could see not only Mrs. Bibeau but all the people on the street passing by. She could tell from their comings and goings who was working and who was not. She could measure the vigor in a step and tell who felt good and who had just climbed out of a sickbed. She could measure the purpose in a step and tell who was going someplace and who had nowhere to go. She could look at the shabby coat and run-down heels of a lady and know that she was going down to the corner store for a quart of milk. She could look at the best coat and high heels and fixed hair of this same lady and know that she was going on a shopping expedition to a fancy store on the Avenue. And she watched for this lady's return, curious as to the purchase; she watched for the wide, flat box of a dress, or the deep, rectangular box of a pair of shoes, or the awkward hugeness of a lampshade, or the pleasing cylindricality of a roll of wallpaper, or the solid compactness of a small bag of nails, or whatever—Ma knew what had been bought and she filed the information in the back of her mind.

Ma gave Tony the money for the string beans and then he went to his room to get his two library books. He picked up *Scaramouche* and flipped through the pages for a moment, bringing the scenes to life again. Oh, this was a wonderful book! He had never enjoyed a book as much as he had this one. It was so exciting, so full of action. Every page had held him, every line. And how slow he had read the last few chapters to make them last longer. And how sad the moment when he reached the last page and Scaramouche's adventures were over. Rafael Sabatini was the greatest writer in the world—of that he felt certain. He was lucky; he had stumbled across *Scaramouche* by accident. But today he was going to look up Sabatini in the card catalogue and see if the library had any more books by him. He sure wished they did, because the guy was tremendous.

"Well, I'll see you later, Ma."

"Okay, boy."

245

Tony went out the door, down the stairs, down the piazza steps, out onto the sidewalk. He started walking.

"Hey, Tony!"

He turned around.

It was *Senhor* Caldeira, sitting on the steps of his front piazza.

"You found work yet, Tony?" *Senhor* Caldeira called out.

"No," Tony said, shaking his head.

He walked over to *Senhor* Caldeira.

"Say, *Senhor* Caldeira, thanks a lot for those eels. They were very nice."

"Aaa...," *Senhor* Caldeira said, waving his hand, dismissing the eels. "It was nothing."

"Well, they were good," Tony said.

Senhor Caldeira was in his undershirt, the white shoulder straps somewhat soiled. He had his shoes and stockings off and he was rubbing in between his toes with one of the stockings. *Senhor* Caldeira suffered from athlete's foot—or in his case, feet. He rubbed his poor cracked skin until it was a fiery red.

"And so, Tony, you have not found anything yet?"

"Nope."

"Ooooooo," *Senhor* Caldeira breathed in excruciating pleasure. He was rubbing a particularly sensitive spot by his next-to-the-smallest toe.

Senhor Caldeira was lucky. He had a job and he always had had one. Most of the mills had closed down, but his had kept going. Also, he was a weaver, which was a highly skilled job and paid well. And in credit to him, there were not many Portuguese weavers. Most of them were English.

"How times have changed," *Senhor* Caldeira said sadly, shaking his head. "Tony, you don't know what this city was like in years past with all the mills running. The city then at night was like daytime, all the mills lighted up. And the streetcars going by, one right after the other, filled from front to back with standing people going to work. It was something to see. Not like today. And everybody, everybody had work. Well, just imagine. I was arrive with my family here in this city on a Monday. I was just a kid, twelve years old, and I did not know a single word of English. But two days later—on Wednesday of that same week—I was working. I had a job in a mill, bobbin boy. That's how easy it was to get work then. Not like today, huh, Tony?"

"No," Tony said ruefully.

"Today it's hard like hell to get a job. A kid today has no chances. Well, a man the same thing. Here, Tony, sit down," *Senhor* Caldeira invited him. Tony sat down. "But it's a funny thing. If a person had told us fifteen years ago what was going to happen to the city of Gaw, nobody would have believed him. No one could imagine such a thing. The mills all running and then suddenly they stop. I wish somebody would explain to me what happened. I don't understand it.

"Everything changes," *Senhor* Caldeira continued. "Nothing stays the same. That is what we have to realize in this life. I used to walk by this big building every day going to work. It was a big strong building, built out of stone, and I got so used to seeing it there after so many years that I said to myself one day, 'This building is going to be here forever. This building is going to be here after all the people now passing by it are gone.' The next day I come by and this building was knock-ed to the ground. They had twenty men there with hammers. They put something else in its place, a parking lot."

Senhor Caldeira fell silent then and just to be polite, Tony said, "Well, *Senhor* Caldeira, you have worked many years in the mills if you started when you were twelve."

"Yes, I have," *Senhor* Caldeira said. "Many years, Tony. But you know something?—I wasn't supposed to be in the mill when I was twelve. They had laws against it. You were supposed to be fourteen." He laughed. "So I always hide when the Inspector come. When the workers near the front door saw the Inspector enter, she was a lady, they pass the word, 'The Inspector's here. The Inspector's here.' And the news that she was there passed faster than she could walk, and so all the kids under fourteen—*fsssshhhtt!* They disappear. The ground swallow them up," he said, laughing. "Everybody had a place to hide. My place was behind some oil barrels, in a dark corner where everything was very dirty. A lady in clean clothes, you know, she would never go there. And so I never got caught.

"In those days, that was before the war, I made four dollars and eighty-five cents a week. The war made the wages go up—that was one nice thing about that war. But I made four dollars and eighty-five cents a week and of that four dollars and eighty-five cents I had to give the house four dollars and seventy cents. Yes, my father took four dollars and seventy cents. That left me with fifteen cents, but of that fifteen cents my father

247

made me put ten cents in my bank. I had a big iron bank there in the house with a slot on top of it. So I was left with five cents to spend. I work all week, hard like a dog, over fifty hours, for a nickel! Pretty good, huh, Tony?" and *Senhor* Caldeira laughed uproariously.

"But times have changed—in many ways. Take my daughter Mary. My daughter Mary works in the sweetshop—" *Senhor* Caldeira pronounced sweatshop as sweetshop and it sounded sort of funny to Tony, because it reminded him of a candy store "—she makes holes in the belts. It's a good job, nice clean work, and no running, she just sits there. Now she makes ten dollars a week—"

"How much?" Tony broke in, surprised.

"Ten dollars a week."

"Why, she told me she made six twenty-five a week."

"Yes, she did! But that was before! Didn't you hear? The government pass a law. Everybody in the sweetshops has to get ten dollars a week now. They can't pay less."

"Wow, what a raise she got."

"Yes, that's true. It's a fine raise."

Ten bucks a week! Wow, that was a good pay! Sweetshops, here I come! Tony thought happily. This was a terrific piece of news.

"So she makes ten dollars a week. No, Tony, I'm going to ask you something. I want you to take a guess. How much of that ten dollars do you think she gives to the house?"

"Oh, I'd say . . . if she makes ten dollars . . . she'd give eight to the house."

"No! You are wrong. Now guess again."

"What? She gives more or less than that?"

"Less! Less!"

"All right then, I'd say that she gives six dollars to the house."

"No! No! Guess again."

"Less?"

"Yes, less."

"Five dollars."

"No, not five dollars."

"Boy, I give up," Tony said, shaking his head. "How much?"

"She gives four dollars to the house *and six dollars she keeps for herself!*" *Senhor* Caldeira waited a moment to let this information sink in.

"Four dollars to the house and the rest she might as well light a match to it. She throws it away on dresses, shoes, silk stockings, bracelets, permanent waves—all junk like that. She wants to be a Hollywood girl. She goes down the Avenue and any junk she sees in a window, she buys it. She even goes downtown. The stores in the North End are not good enough for her." *Senhor* Caldeira sighed. "You see how times have changed, Tony? Today the kids do what they want. What do they care what their fathers and mothers think? They are concerned with their own pastimes, with their own pleasures, just like the American kids, and they don't care for anything else."

Senhor Caldeira looked gloomily out at the street.

"Tony, do you want to have a drink of wine with me?"

"I don't mind," Tony said.

"All right then! We'll have a drink of wine together!" And *Senhor* Caldeira was already half-cheered up.

"Oh, Aldracina!" he shouted without getting up. "Aldracina!"

"What do you want?" his wife's muffled voice came from inside the house.

"Bring two glasses of wine! One for me and one for my friend Tony here! Get the cool bottle, Aldracina—from the cellar!"

Every Portuguese worth his salt made his own wine, and *Senhor* Caldeira was worth his salt. He was famous among the Portuguese for making an especially strong wine. "He calls it wine but it's more like *aguardente*," Ma said of it. *Aguardente* was something like whiskey, only stronger. Tony had had a shot of *aguardente* once and it was like drinking fire.

"Oh, but I better ask your mother first," *Senhor* Caldeira said. "Maybe she wouldn't like you to have wine."

"Oh, she wouldn't care," Tony tried to assure him.

"We better make sure," *Senhor* Caldeira said. "*Senhora* Alfama!" he shouted. "Oh, *Senhora* Alfama!"

Ma came to the window and opened it and stuck her head out. "Yes?"

"Is it all right if I give your son a glass of wine?" *Senhor* Caldeira called up to her.

"Well, if he's old enough to look for work, I guess he's old enough to have a glass of wine," Ma said. "But one thing, Tony—if it starts going to your head, don't finish the glass!"

"All right."

"Drink it slowly!"

"Okay, Ma."

"If you drink it fast, it will go to your head!"

"Okay, Ma."

Ma then closed the window and went inside and *Senhor* Caldeira winked at Tony. "Well, you don't live far," he said. "If it goes to your head, I'll carry you home," and he laughed uproariously.

Just about then *Senhora* Caldeira came out on the piazza with the two glasses of wine.

"Ah!" *Senhor* Caldeira said. "Two friends engaged in a nice conversation with a little glass of wine, what could be better than that?"

"Your good times always end up bad," his wife said grimly. "If it doesn't agree with you, Tony, don't drink it all," she said, as she handed Tony his glass.

Senhor Caldeira was indignant at having his wine insulted. "Why shouldn't it agree with him? It's good wine."

His wife gave him a look and departed, wordless but uncowed.

The wine was as beautiful as a jewel. It was deep red, rich, yet clear. Tony felt some slight trepidation as he looked at his glass. It was a regular-sized water glass. The wine came to within a half-inch of the top. There was a lot of wine in that glass. *Senhor* Caldeira had the same.

Senhor Caldeira raised his glass ceremonially. "We drink to your finding a job, Tony."

"Thank you," Tony said.

They clinked glasses.

Tony took a good mouthful and swallowed. At the first touch of the wine his stomach trembled, then began to shiver and shake violently. It was like the time he had got the flu and laid on his bed shaking so bad his teeth kept clicking together. Only this time the chill was inside him and not on the outside. He fought to keep it so. He fought to keep his face impassive and serene.

"How does it taste?" *Senhor* Caldeira asked.

"Good."

"Not too strong?"

"No, it's not too strong."

Tony eyed the glass. It was his enemy. He had to conquer it. He had to drink it down, every drop. He would have liked to quit, right there. One swallow was enough for him. But what could he say? What excuse could he make? *I don't like the taste of your wine, Senhor Caldeira.* That would only offend *Senhor* Caldeira; he would not understand. Besides it was not the truth. Could he tell the truth? *Senhor Caldeira, this wine is too strong for me.* Yes, he could say that. And tonight at the supper table *Senhor* Caldeira would tell his wife and all his daughters about Tony Alfama. "One swallow and he was knock-ed out!" And then they would all have a belly laugh at his expense. And forever after they would have that on him. No thanks. The only course open to him was to drink it down, to the last drop.

"My daughter Mary," *Senhor* Caldeira went on, "she takes her money and she burns it—like this." He held up an imaginary five-dollar bill in his hand and struck an imaginary match on the sole of his shoeless foot and applied the match to the bill and sadly watched the money turn to ashes. "Wasted, wasted, wasted. . . . When you see my daughter Mary, do you think you are looking at the daughter of a millworker, a girl brought up in a humble home? No, that is not the daughter of a millworker you are seeing there. What you are seeing is a daughter of J. B. Morgan, brought up in a house of wealth. If she goes to the store to buy something and they have the same thing for three prices—low-priced, medium-priced, and high-priced—like an arrow she goes straight to the high-priced thing. And the higher the price the better. She will value it all the more. Well, if she wants to waste all her money, let her," he concluded. "It's her business, it's her money."

"The wine's good, isn't it, Tony?"

"Yes."

"I buy good grapes. Those cheapskates, they buy the cheapest grapes and then they wonder what's the matter with their wine.

"She has shoes. . . . She has shoes enough to open a shoestore. Red shoes, green shoes, brown shoes, black shoes, white shoes, blue shoes— any color you want she's got it. What is she, a policeman or a mailman, that she needs so many shoes? Does she walk all day? No, she sits all day," he said, shaking his head disgustedly. "It used to be that a person needed two pairs of shoes, one for work and one for Sundays. But today they have shoes for every occasion. She goes to church—she buys a pair of shoes for that, special church shoes. She goes to a girl's wedding from

251

her sweetshop—she buys a pair of shoes for that, special wedding shoes. Easter comes—she buys a pair of shoes for that, special Easter shoes. One day she came home with a piece of cardboard and a leather strap sewed to it. 'What's this?' I say. 'This is a new kind of shoe,' she say to me. 'They are going to be cold in the snow,' I say. 'You wear these when you go to the beach,' she say. 'They are called *sandals.*' You see, Tony? A special pair of shoes now to go to the beach. And what did she pay for them? Twenty-five cents? No. Two dollars! With certainty when the Jew from the shoestore sees her coming down the Avenue he yells to his wife, 'Here comes Mary Caldeira, the Big Sucker! Bring out the most expensive crazy junk shoes we got in the store—we will sell them to her!'"

Was he going to make it? Tony looked at his glass. He had a real fight on his hands. He was drinking it down in small sips, desperately frequent sips, but pitifully small sips. He would have liked to swish it down in several long gulps, but he knew such a course of action would not be wise.

"She even has a pair of wooden shoes to take a bath in the house. 'What the hell are you doing, Mary?' I say to her. 'Are you crazy?' I say. I tried to tell her about Portugal. 'Do you know that in Portugal we had one pair of shoes—if we were lucky, that is? And we went barefoot most of the time to save those shoes for special days.' That's what I said to her. And do you know what she said to me? 'Oh,' she laughs, 'Portugal. Those hicks. Those country people. They're living in another century.'

"'Mary,' I said to her one day. 'Someday you are going to get married. You and your boy will want your own house. But it takes a lot of money to furnish a house. You need knifes, forks, spoons, pans, plates, a table, chairs, bureaus for your clothes, a bed, sheets, blankets—do you know how much one single blanket costs? Plentee! But suppose you save your money now. Then you and your boy can furnish and prepare your house in time before you marry, and then after you are married, you move into this house with everything in it. Now wouldn't that be nice?' That's what I said to her. And you know what she said to me? 'I'll worry about that when the time comes,' she say to me. That's what she say. 'I'll worry about that when the time comes.'" *Senhor* Caldeira looked out at the street thoughtfully. "Mary is already an American," he said sadly. "That's how the Americans live, spend all their money, everything for show, why prepare for anything?"

Tony wasn't feeling too good. Something kept telling him he should quit. How had he got into this anyway? He had been on his way to the library and suddenly he found himself with a glass of wine in his hand. Well, this was the first and last time *Senhor* Caldeira was going to sandbag him this way. The next time *Senhor* Caldeira offered him some wine he'd just say, "Sorry, not today, *Senhor* Caldeira. I don't feel too good today, and I don't want to upset my stomach."

"But we need more wine out here, Tony!" *Senhor* Caldeira cried, his mood jovial again, his mood changing again, like he was a Jekyll and Hyde.

"Aldracina! Oh, Aldracina! Get up off your fat behind and bring the bottle! We need wine here! Oh, do you hear me, Aldracina?"

"Yes, I hear you," she answered grimly from inside the house. "I could be a block away and I would still hear you, you call so nicely."

She came out with the bottle.

"I can see from your manner that you're already half-drunk," she said.

"Not half! Not even a quarter!" *Senhor* Caldeira retorted.

"It is you I notice who is on his behind and not me," she said. "Always you accuse others of your own sins."

But *Senhor* Caldeira did not want to discuss his character. "Why don't you have a glass with us, Aldracina?" he invited.

"I have too much to do," she replied.

"It'll cheer you up!"

"I don't need cheering up," she said dourly.

"All women need cheering up!" *Senhor* Caldeira roared, and he nudged Tony in the ribs. "Isn't that right, Tony?"

Tony blushed and grinned.

"Be careful with your foul jokes!" his wife cried. "There's a young boy listening to you!"

"What young boy? I don't see any young boys here. I see a young man. Am I right, Tony?"

Tony grinned.

But *Senhor* Caldeira was feeling frisky.

He grabbed his wife by the wrist and tried to pull her down. "Come on, Aldracina, you will have a drink. It will be good for you."

"Aaa . . . let go of me, you old goat," she said, but laughing in spite of herself. "One glass of wine and he forgets his years!"

"That's what wine is for!"

But *Senhora* Caldeira went in the house and left the bottle with them.

Senhor Caldeira took the bottle and pulled the cork out. "A little more for you, huh, Tony?" he said and reached out with the bottle to pour some into Tony's glass.

To hell with politeness. "No! Not for me!" Tony's hand shot out and covered the top of his glass. "I have to go to the library," he added lamely.

"All right," *Senhor* Caldeira laughed good-naturedly, "you don't want any, I'll drink for both of us." And so saying he filled his glass right to the top.

Tony still had some left and he steeled himself for the final push. A sip. Then another sip. Then another sip. Then another sip. There. It was done. He had made it.

"Well, I have to go now, *Senhor* Caldeira," he said.

"Okay, Tony."

"Muito obrigado pelo vinho."

"Aaa . . . ," *Senhor* Caldeira said, and waved his hand in his familiar gesture, signifying that it was nothing.

"Okay, bye."

"Bye, Tony."

Tony went.

He went straight home.

Ma was still sitting by the window overlooking Mrs. Bibeau.

"What? Back so soon?" she said, looking at him curiously.

"I don't feel so good, Ma," he said.

"What's the matter?" she asked, alarmed.

"I don't know. I just feel lousy."

"Ah ha! The wine!"

"I'm going to lie down for a while," he said.

He went to his room and stretched out on his bed, on his back. Ma came and stood looking at him.

"I feel dizzy," he said.

"Fool! Why did you drink it?"

"What's the difference now?" he asked wearily. "I drank it, didn't I? It's done."

"I told you he made strong wine."

He nodded agreement.

"I don't know what he puts in it but it has a kick to it like *aguardente*," Ma said.

He didn't bother nodding.

"Do you want me to put a cold rag on your head?"

"Yes."

Ma went and took a handkerchief and held it under the tap and let the water run over it. Then she wrung it out, folded it neatly, and placed it on his forehead.

"Oooooo," he groaned.

And everything began to move around crazily. The walls whirled by. His bed was a raft and he was in the middle of the ocean and the waves were pitching his raft up and down and he hung on with both hands and the waves were getting gigantic—

"Ma, quick! Bring me a pan!"

Ma dashed out to the sink, which was just outside his room, and grabbed the metal roasting pan that she used as a dishpan and dashed back and thrust it into his hands just as he was leaning over the side of the raft and he—

But nothing happened.

His stomach was balanced on a knife's edge in the turbulence. All those lovely eels would not come up and would not stay down. He gagged.

"Oooooo," he groaned.

"Stick your fingers down your throat if you want to throw up," Ma advised.

"Ssshh, Ma," he managed to gasp.

The last thing in the world he wanted to do was throw up. He was fighting his stomach, but he was afraid he was losing the fight. The miserable, choking sensation of throwing up, a remembered experience that he looked forward to with dread, was about to be his.

He gagged again.

Sweat was on his forehead.

Oh, Lord, he felt miserable.

"Well, there's one good thing anyway," Ma said, leaning on the door, and speaking in an objective, detached way. "With a stomach like that you'll never be a drunkard."

"Well, that's good news," he murmured. "I'm glad to hear that." He was still leaning over the side with the pan poised.

But nothing happened.

255

After a while he put the pan down and fell back on the bed. Ma came and took the handkerchief and rewet it and placed it on his forehead again.

He lay there with his eyes closed.

"Do you want anything, boy?"

He waved a hand weakly, signifying no.

Ma then left him and he just lay there. He lay there for more than an hour, not moving. After that time he felt much better. He still felt lousy, terrible in fact, but at least he had his stomach under control. He didn't feel like he was going to throw up, so as far as he was concerned the worst was over.

He got up and staggered out to where Ma was.

"Oooooo," he groaned, sinking heavily into a chair.

"I feel like I been poisoned," he said.

"What about the library then?" Ma chatted brightly. "You going to go there today?"

"To hell with the library," he said with conviction.

***

It was late afternoon and Tony's legs were tired. So it was that when he came to the nice lawn of Bellehaven Park, where the park bordered on the Avenue, he flopped down on the grass to rest. He stretched out on the grass in luxurious repose, on his back, looking up at the sky. He gave a long sigh of contentment. His legs really ached and it was wonderful to get off them.

This day had really started a couple of days before. He had been walking down the Avenue when he saw a small red truck parked alongside the curb. And as he passed by the truck, just out of idle curiosity, he read the lettering on the door. It said: *Arthur Mothershead.* Now he was ignorant of Yankee practice, which pronounced this name as *Mother-shead.* Instead he read it as *Mothers-head,* and the name struck him as deliciously funny. He burst into laughter right there on the sidewalk, and he was still laughing when he got more than a block away.

Now he should not have laughed. Good manners dictated that he not laugh. And even more to the point, a minimum awareness of his own interests dictated that he not laugh. For Mr. Mothershead was his prospective employer, and it is not wise to laugh at an employer at any stage of the relationship. Tony realized this later and it worried him.

Mr. Mothershead had not been in the truck so he was safe there. Most likely he had been in a store close by. And what if he had looked out the store window and *seen* Tony look at his name and then start laughing? That would be just great.

Yes, Mr. Mothershead was his prospective employer. Tony hadn't realized it immediately. But the next day, for some strange reason that red truck kept coming to mind and he began thinking about the lettering he had read on the door. There had been more than a name there. The whole thing had said:

Arthur Mothershead
Lumber—Building Supplies
Ossawona, Mass.

257

And Tony began thinking: Ossawona, Ossawona. Why not Oassawona? Why not Arthur Mothershead in Ossawona? He had never thought of Ossawona in terms of job-seeking before, but maybe nobody else had either! Ossawona was just a country town. There wasn't much over there. But Arthur Mothershead was over there! And the longer Tony thought about it, the more optimistic he became. He had a hunch about this lumber place. Seeing that red truck was the turning point for him. The irony was that after looking all over Gaw he would hit the jackpot on his very first attempt in Ossawona.

Without telling Ma about the red truck and his high hopes, Tony left the next day for Ossawona. He walked to the end of the North End and turned down the winding Horsfall Road and walked across the Horsfall Road Bridge, which wasn't much of a bridge, and so into Ossawona. He walked quite a piece more and then he came to Arthur Mothershead's lumberyard. It was a good-sized lumberyard, which Tony was glad to see, for Mr. Mothershead's prosperity was all to the good. Tony looked around at all the lumber stacked neatly and he thought: Somebody has had to stack all this lumber; maybe I'll be the one to do it in the future.

Tony found Mr. Mothershead between the steel rods and the drain tile. Tony announced his business and the response was swift and to the point.

"You're looking for a job?" Mr. Mothershead said, pronouncing job in a peculiarly insulting way, and looking Tony over in some amazement as if he hadn't heard right. "Can you pick up a hundred-pound sack of see-ment? You don't look like you weigh that much yourself!" he cackled in snappy rustic humor. His joke, sadly, was not far off the mark. "You go on home and put some weight on before you come around here looking for a job!" Mr. Mothershead turned away. "Hunh!" he snorted.

And that was that. He had walked for over two hours to get an answer that took two seconds. He left Arthur shaking his shitty mother's head at the strange specimens that wandered in from the city. Well, the bastard had small round eyes. He never knew a guy yet with small round eyes who was any good.

Walking along, still in Ossawona, he came to a long one-storied beat-up wooden building. It looked like a warehouse. He walked around to the front where there was an office. On the window glass it said:

Ossawona Feed Co.
Wholesale—Retail
John C. Grimsby, Prop.

Tony climbed the four wooden steps. And the minute he swung the door open he knew he was in an old-fashioned place. The furniture was great massive pieces of oak; it must have taken about ten strong guys to move that desk in here. They didn't make furniture like that any more. And the pictures on the wall were from another time. There was one of Teddy Roosevelt charging up San Juan Hill and waving his hat. This place was probably in business in 1890, Tony thought.

The ceiling light wasn't on, like maybe they were saving money. The only light came from a gooseneck lamp on the counter. This lamp was curved way over and its bulb was shielded in a metal cup to protect your eyes. It didn't give much light except right there on the counter and the windows up front were small, so the place was all in shadows, especially back behind the counter toward the corners of the office.

There was just one person in the office, a man. Tony walked over to him. The man was behind the counter. He had the light directed into an open ledger, a huge ledger. He was running his finger down the entries in the ledger, apparently looking for some particular name and order. He was standing with his head bent over the ledger and he had a green visor sticking out past his sandy hair. Because of the position of his head, this visor covered up most of his face and Tony was unable to catch his eye. So Tony just stood there and waited.

Tony looked around. Everything in the place seemed old and dark and dreary. He looked at the Purina calendar on the wall. It was a month behind.

The man turned the page and continued his search from the top of the new page, running his finger down the entries.

He doesn't know I'm here, Tony thought with alarm. When he sees me, he'll be startled and jump two feet in the air. I better let him know I'm here.

So Tony cleared his throat. But the man did not look up.

Well, heck, he must know I'm here, Tony thought. That door made a helluva racket when I closed it. He must have heard that. Unless— unless he's *deaf.* But heck, why would they leave a deaf guy alone with a telephone?

The office was very quiet. The only sound came from a grandfather's clock up against the wall, which was going *tick-tock-tick-tock.* The man turned another page. Tony felt strange because whole minutes were going by and still the man did not look up. Tony felt an urge to speak. But it would mean interrupting the man. That would be starting things off badly. But this waiting was getting him. It wasn't that he was in any hurry. He had no place to go. It was just the idea of standing here, waiting, waiting, waiting. . . .

And the longer Tony waited, the quieter the office became. The lack of sound became real, like a pressure on his head. And that clock—it got louder. Grandfather's pendulum swung more and more insistently, more and more ominously. *TICK-TOCK-TICK-TOCK.* It was like the Chinese water torture Lommy had told him about. The Chinese let water hit a stone floor drop by drop and their prisoner listens to it night and day until the sound drives him mad. Tony breathed deeply. It was insufferable. He couldn't stand it any longer.

"I'm looking for a job." Tony said, and his voice sounded like it came out of a cave, muffled and weird.

And for the first time the man looked up. It was a classic Yankee face, drawn along simple lines, a masterpiece begging to be painted. He was wearing gold-rimmed spectacles. The forehead was set back; it was a long and narrow face. Cold blue eyes close together, a thin bony nose, pale bloodless lips, a sharp pointed chin like on a witch, and all against a background of yellow parchment skin. It was a face that had never had a laugh or a good meal. It was a face . . . it was a face . . . was it young or old? . . . who could tell? A young Yankee lad with very strong genes had carved his initials in Plymouth Rock in 1620 and then scattered this face all over Maine, Vermont, and Massachusetts. And now for a brief moment Tony looked into this face and he was looking into the face of three hundred years of Massachusetts history. . . .

The man looked at Tony. He looked at Tony for the amount of time it takes a butterfly to flick its wings. It was not a look of wonder, of scorn, of disdain; it was a look of acute and unseeing indifference. Then the moving finger returned to the ledger. Tony might as well have been a speck on the wall.

The idiot pendulum swung back and forth, and Tony felt very strange, like he was in a dream. He didn't know what to do next. What was wrong with this guy? He hadn't said a word and it didn't look like he was about to. He hadn't even insulted him like that other guy. And then Tony suddenly realized that silence is itself the greatest insult, that a question ignored because not worthy of an answer is more insulting that a question answered scornfully. Tony reddened.

It was John C. Grimsby. It could be no one else. Tony waited grimly. He was determined to wait him out.

But his resolve wilted in the exercise of his intelligence. There was nothing to be gained by sticking around here, he knew that. There was nothing to do but retreat mute and inglorious. He did. But he got one satisfaction. As he walked down the steps outside belonging to John C. Grimsby, he muttered under his breath, "You son of a bitch."

So Tony walked out of Ossawona, back across the Horsfall Road Bridge where the river stank, back up the winding Horsfall Road, back into the North End of Gaw. And when he came to the green grass of Bellehaven Park, he flopped on it. He had walked a long way today. He was tired. He wondered which was more tiring—working or looking for work?

Tony plucked a blade of grass. He was reaching the end of the line. He had just about run out of places to ask at. He had asked everywhere. All the mills. All the sweatshops. All the stores. Not just grocery stores, but department stores, hardware stores, drugstores . . . bakeries, laundries, dry cleaning places, and nothing no place. For months now he had looked for work, and the truth was he was no closer to a job today than he was the day he started. He was beginning to get discouraged.

A hearse sped by, all by itself. Tony frowned and watched it move out of sight. Those goddamn cars—he hated them. The law shouldn't allow them on the streets unless they were in a funeral. It was like bad news running up and down the Avenue. And the driver was probably just running an errand, on his way to a store to pick up a pack of cigarettes for his boss. . . . Well, of course, he might have been on his way to pick up a body and get it ready for the funeral. Maybe he already had the body and was on his way back to the funeral parlor. There could have been a dead man in that hearse, and here he was on the grass young and alive. Life was strange. And someday would he drive by in one of those, stretched out in the back, and some young guy be on the grass here—living, breathing, thinking?

That was about the only kind of place he hadn't asked at—funeral parlors. He stayed clear of them. After all, he knew what he could do and he knew what he could not do. Manny Serpa knew a guy who worked for Pacheco's Funeral Home and this guy told Manny what they did there to the dead bodies. First they cut the veins to let all the blood run out. Then they cut into your belly and pulled out all the guts, because the guy told Manny that was what made dead people stink—their guts, all that food rotting there—so you had to take them out. Think of slitting a man's belly open and reaching in and pulling out his guts. Oh, brother. To hell with it. He wanted a job bad, but he didn't want one that bad.

Gee, Lommy was lucky. He had a job and he got it without lifting a finger. Lommy quit school at the same time he did, but he didn't have to ask anybody for work. All he had to do was move in as his father's helper. His father was glad to have him. His father was going to teach him how to be a cook in a restaurant. "Cooking is a trade," Lommy had bragged to him. "I'll be able to go all over this country and walk in any restaurant and get a job. Or I can cook on ships at sea. Or I can go in rich people's homes, cook for them. I'd live with them in their mansion."

So Lommy was working and learning a trade, and he wasn't working and he was learning nothing. It was funny, because in school he had been ahead of Lommy. He had been in the smartest class and Lommy had been in one of the dumbest. But now, in real life, Lommy was ahead of him. Lommy was learning something, and he wasn't.

This thing of inexperience. Ma had told him he would have a hard time because he had no experience. And he wasn't stupid. He knew that experience counted for a lot. But still, being young and inexperienced might be a point in his favor. They could pay him less. Take a man with four or five kids to support, you would have to pay him more. And a boss who was trying to save money he might think of that. But so far it hadn't worked out in his favor.

There was a cement walk circling behind Tony. It led into the park. There were benches along it and trash cans. The trash can nearest to him had a newspaper on top of all the junk. He could see it sticking up. He got to his feet and went over to the trash can and cautiously examined the paper for evidences of garbage, excrement, or who-knows-what? There are a lot of clowns in this world. And ever since what happened to Manny Serpa right here in this same park, he wasn't taking any chances. In a park trash can Manny saw the Sunday comics, brightly colored and inviting, Flash Gordon and the beauteous Dale floating through space on the front page, Dale dressed for hot climes, and Manny grabbed the paper, and some bastard had gone to the toilet on the inside page, and it was No. 2. But this stray and forlorn sheet of the *Evening Observer* was in fine condition. It had been treated with the respect all good Americans show venerable organs of the press that speak for the moneyed element of a community. Daily these organs perform their incontinent acts upon an unsuspecting people; it is called freedom of the press. But this sheet of the *Evening Observer* was merely crumpled a bit. No politically disgruntled person had commented on its editorials and syndicated columnists by soiling it in some vulgar and shameful fashion.

Tony came back to the grass with the newspaper and sat down, and he had to laugh at himself. Why was it that with all the grass here he had to come back to the exact same spot he had left? What difference did it make where he sat? Was this piece of ground softer than some other piece of ground? It was silly. Yet he had to admit he felt more comfortable here, more at home, more like the spot belonged to him.

The paper was a disappointment. He had hoped for the comics or the sports page, but no luck. It was the back page—*Want Ads*. He looked the page over. A lot of furniture was for sale. There was only one listing under

Situations Wanted—some guy was asking for odd jobs. With just one listing you might think that everybody in Gaw had a job. But actually there were a lot of guys in Gaw out of work. They didn't put an ad in the paper because that cost money. Besides, nobody would answer it.

There were three ads in the *Help Wanted* column. He looked them over carefully.

Make $20 a week in your spare time. Sell Xmas cards to your friends and neighbors. Gee, a fellow would have to have a helluva lot of friends and neighbors to make that kind of money. Besides the people in Gaw didn't go much for Xmas cards. He doubted if his whole street put together would buy two buck's worth. It was mostly American people who send Xmas cards. *Send for assortment now. Write Box 112, Caro, Michigan.* Now where the hell was Caro, Michigan? He wondered if that was the place where they made that Karo Corn Syrup he had seen advertised.

Sell hot product. What was it—counterfeit money? That was hot. Or maybe it was dirty books. *No canvassing.* No canvassing. There were only two ways to sell that he could think of. One was door-to-door and the other was in a store. Did this guy own a store? *Write Dept. O, Johnson Cutlery, Attleboro, Mass.* Cutlery. Wasn't that knives? Hot knives. They were put in an oven before you sold them.

Are you earning less than $15 a day? Jesus Christ, this guy sure had guts. The whole goddamn town of Gaw was earning less than $15 a week and he asks a question like that. *I need five men to assist me in an expanding promotional field. Must be young, alert, and aggressive.* Well, he was young and alert. How aggressive did you have to be? Did you have to tear the shirt off the customer's back? *See Mr. Reeves, Room 305, Gaw Hotel.* It was probably a job like the guy who came around his street selling potato peelers. Yes, he'd like a job, Mr. Reeves. But he'd like to do some decent work. Not go around knocking on doors of people who didn't have any money to spare and pester and bother them to buy some junk they didn't need and could easily get along without. So stick it up your ass, Mr. Reeves, you and your $15 a day.

Tony returned the newspaper to the trash can and came back to his spot on the grass and sat down once more.

People are funny. They never know when they're well off. Yesterday morning he had gone to the pocketbook sweatshop on Duff Street. He had gotten there early at seven-thirty just in case somebody didn't show up for work. They started at eight o'clock. And as he stood there and watched the people file in, he noticed this—everybody was glum. There wasn't one happy smiling face. And he felt like crying out to them: "You people got jobs! You're earning money! You should be happy! You should be smiling and laughing and telling jokes when you go in!" If it had been him going in there, actually going in to earn some money, he'd have been laughing and singing.

And then he remembered something about the pocketbook shop he didn't want to remember. He actually hadn't gone inside and seen the boss. He hadn't let the boss know he was there. He had simply stood on the sidewalk and watched the workers go in. He hadn't the heart to go in himself and talk to the boss. He had already asked him for work on two other occasions, and the guy was always busy, and irritable at being called away from whatever he was doing. It was stupid. To stand on the sidewalk like a statue. To talk to no one. But that's what he had done. Then some time after nine o'clock he walked away.

More and more he was getting reluctant to ask. He felt different now than when he had first started looking for work. Then he had been on an even keel. Nothing had bothered him. He had taken everything in his stride. But now things were starting to bother him. He had been refused so many times it was starting to get him down, really down.

All his optimism was fake. All his high hopes today for Arthur Mothershead had really been low hopes. He had just kidded himself into thinking that Mothershead had a job for him. If he hadn't done that, he would not have been willing to walk all the way to Ossawona on the 10,000 to 1 chance that the bastard might come through.

Oh, you stinking, sour, and scabby world! The truth was he had lost all hope. Before he always had that little voice in him which disregarded all the yesterdays and kept saying, "Maybe this place is it." Now when that voice spoke to him it spoke falsely, words without faith, words he didn't believe in.

Oh, Ma was good about it. "It's not your fault, boy," she said. "There's just no jobs. Nobody can expect you to do the impossible. You can't make a job out of thin air."

But he was coming to his rope's end. He was tired. He was tired of looking for work. "It's like trying to find a needle in a haystack, isn't it?"

a Jewish shoestore man had said sympathetically to him. No, mister, it's worse. Because that needle you at least know it's there. All you have to be is thorough and you will find it. But who could assure him that in this haystack of job-hunting there was a needle for him? He might look from now until doomsday and never find it.

A pessimism was growing within him, deep and irremediable, not a pessimism that disappears after a good night's sleep, but a pessimism that seeps into every cell in the body and mixes with the protoplasm. He had looked for work for months. He had been to every place at least once. How long was he supposed to keep on? *Was there a job in this city for him?*

He looked around. There was no one in the park. The November winds were starting to blow and something cold was blowing inside of him, too. It got dark early now and it was getting darker by the minute and the black night was descending upon his spirit, too—enveloping it, making it his own.

Winter was coming. You could feel it in the air. The trees were without leaves. The birds had gone. Everything was shriveling up and dying. Soon there would be storms. Snow. Ice. Freezing cold. It would be real great walking around looking for work then.

He hated winter. Nothing was nice in winter. His house was so cold all he and Ma could do was bundle up and shiver in a corner. And on the streets the girls wore heavy overshoes and big bulky coats, so you couldn't see what their figures looked like. Not until May would he see a nice pair of tits again.

A streetcar rattled by, shaking from side to side, and the conductor clanged the bell. *Clang, clang, clang.* Why did he clang it? There was no traffic. Maybe he was bored with the quiet.

A heavy lassitude was in his bones, weighing him down. He stretched out full length. Maybe he'd never get up from this grass. Maybe he'd just stay here, year after year, and look at the sky. Feel the snow and rain fall on you. That wouldn't be so bad. Because if you were part of the ground you wouldn't get cold.

A wave of laughter rolled across the open spaces to him. He raised up on an elbow to look. There was a street that bumped into the park from below the Avenue. A small army of shopgirls was sweeping up this street, high-spirited and gay like schoolgirls on a holiday. They were relaxing after a hard day's work. Their sallies flew back and forth amidst laughter open and unabashed. They were enjoying themselves. Protected by their numbers and emboldened by the absence of potential husbands, they ripped off the paper garment of female modesty and engaged in a spirited mockery of males and the male function. One raspy-throated maiden, with that unmistakable Portuguese *je ne sais quoi* about her, raised her glass and her voice in honor of Al. "'Al, don't tell me your troubles,' I says to him. 'I don't care if you take that thing of yours and wrap it around a telephone pole and—'" but good taste demurs at the repeating of such a crude jest. Suffice it to say that it was a choice bit of ribaldry and the street resounded with the thunderclap of their laughter.

But the breath of life passed. The girls went on down the Avenue. Their voices faded away. All was quiet again.

All those girls could get a job, but he couldn't. How do you like that? A couple of months back he met a girl he had known in the sixth grade—Hilda Pires. She had been so goddamn dumb in school it hurt. She could read only very slowly and just small words. Yet now she had a job. She was working in a place making pajamas. She had a job and he didn't. What was the use of going to school and trying to do good work there? It didn't get you a job.

For no reason at all he counted the empty park benches. There were twelve of them. Twelve empty benches. It was quiet down this end of the Avenue, no stores, just houses and the park. He looked at the park. The park was empty, deserted, desolate. He and the park were friends. Nobody had any use for the park and nobody had any use for him. He felt terribly alone. He felt like he was on a desert island, all by himself, with no one to talk to.

Those girls were going home. Tonight at the table they could say, "Well, I earned this much money today." They could feel good. Say . . . where had they come from anyway? He knew every mill in the North End and there was no mill down that street. And he didn't know of a single sweatshop that was not in a mill. But maybe this sweatshop was in some other kind of building.

Tony got up from the grass and left the park. He crossed the Avenue and went down that street. He looked around. All he could see was regular tenement houses. A man was passing by so he spoke to him.

"Say, mister, is there a mill down this street?"

"Yeah, the Takalonka," the man said, giving him a real disgusted look as if he was a dope for not knowing. Maybe I don't live around here, mister. Did you ever stop to think of that?

But the Takalonka! How could that be? He had been to the Takalonka. It was way over on Pennell Street.

He kept walking. He crossed an intersection and passed more houses. And then he saw it. Down at the bottom of the street. It was a mill. He saw the mill fence, high gray pickets. And he saw some concrete steps and a door. And then he realized why he had been confused. The Takalonka ended on this street. This was the back end of the Takalonka. He had been to the front entrance but he had never walked around the whole mill or he would have seen this door.

The Takalonka had ceased operations as a cotton mill some years back. It was a three-storied mill several blocks long. And now he was going to try and enter it the back way. There was no telling what was inside. But they employed quite a bunch of girls, he knew that much.

When he got close to the mill, he happened to look up and he saw a man standing by a window on the third floor. The man was just standing there, looking down at the street. Tony stared up at him and the man, seemingly in response, stepped back and Tony could not see him any more.

The outside door was not locked. He opened it and went in. There was a wide wooden staircase. He began climbing. He had decided to try the third floor first because on that floor at least he was sure there was somebody.

The mill was quiet. The only sound came from his own feet. There was a lot of space between a floor and a ceiling in a mill so there were a lot of stairs. They circled around. But in a bit he was at the top. Before him was a door, ajar. It was a huge door, like in a castle, very wide and several inches thick. He pulled back on the latch but had to try again. It was such a heavy door it took both his arms and a strong effort to swing it open. He slipped around it, intending to enter with some dignity. But if this door had been reluctant to open, it was most anxious to close and tried to smash him in the back. He leaped forward with only inches to spare as the mighty door swung shut with the solid jarring thump of an oak hitting the ground. Missed me, he smirked.

Tony found himself in sort of a big closet, long and narrow, maybe fifteen feet long and five feet across. The walls and the low ceiling were made out of plywood. The only light came from a side window. He guessed this was the outer office of the place. Very likely it had been built special for them, for he had been in enough cotton mills to know they didn't have outer offices on the third floor. But it gave you a funny feeling. You were completely cut off from whatever was on the other side of those walls. It was like being in a box, a big box, but a box nevertheless.

Access into the mill was provided by a door at the far end. It was a regular-sized door just big enough for one person at a time to pass through. He went over to it and knocked politely. He listened impassively for the approaching footsteps, but they did not come.

He knocked again, harder.

Nothing. No answer.

He grasped the doorknob and twisted it. The door was locked.

He knocked for the third time, rapping the door sharply. It was a knock signaling the presence of a landlord or some other peremptory soul. He did not like to knock on a door like that. Yet what was he supposed to do?

He waited.

Nothing but quiet, absolute quiet.

It was queer. Somebody was in there. That man had been by the window just a few feet on the other side of this wall. Why didn't he answer?

An uneasy feeling began to stir in him. It was too quiet around here. He had the feeling that people on the other side of the wall were listening to him. What was going on here anyway? He remembered that man by the window—how he had jumped back when he looked up from the street, as if he didn't want to be spotted. Maybe—maybe he had stumbled onto something. Maybe the sweatshop wasn't on this floor at all. Maybe the sweatshop was on the first floor, and he had by accident stumbled onto a gangster's hideout. Maybe they were making counterfeit money in there. Why not? It had happened before. He saw a picture once where these crooks took over an empty warehouse to make fake gold bars, which they later switched with a government truck of real gold bars. Why not use an empty mill for something like that?

He had the prickly sensation of being watched. A pair of unseen eyes were on him. He turned quickly. There was no one there. But who knows where they might be a spy hole in the wall? He looked up at the ceiling.

And he suddenly realized a fearful thing—nobody knew he had

come here. Ma didn't know. He would vanish without a trace. The police wouldn't have any idea where to start looking for him. That man—that he had asked if there was a mill on this street. That man was his one hope. He'd have to count on him seeing his face on the front page, then remembering the incident and telling the police. But maybe he didn't take the paper. Besides, he seemed like a stupid man. He'd hate to have his life depend on him.

They were moving silently into place by the door, getting ready to jump him. He listened for their approaching footsteps. He strained his ears but he could not hear a sound.

Well, he was ready for them. He faced the door, alert and tense. He was ready for anything—to fight or run, depending on the circumstances. He cleared his throat in a resounding, aggressive, manly, unapologetic way, just to let the bastards know he wasn't afraid of them. And then he really threw down the glove. He knocked on the door again—forcefully.

He waited. Grim.

Nothing.

Then he suddenly got very scared. The stillness was too oppressive; it was shattering his nerve. He was going to clear out of here. He would come back sometime during working hours and after he had told Ma exactly and precisely where he was going and given her instructions on what to do if he didn't show up at a specified time. It was too creepy around here. It was too dangerous. It was—

BANG!

Tony's body jerked in all directions. Had he been shot? No, he didn't think so. He turned around weakly.

Halfway along the expanse of the side wall a space had appeared. It was at eye level and was about a foot square. It was a sliding panel, and the noise he had heard was this sliding panel being slammed open.

A secret panel! And so cleverly built into the wall that he hadn't noticed it when he first came in. And in that instant there whirred through his mind the quick mythic frames of a movie he had seen once—the gangsters' gambling club, the beautiful women inside with their rich escorts, the head gangster Rick in his private office in the back, the good guy's best friend trying to bluff his way into the club to get evidence, the door with the little sliding panel and the gorilla, "Who sent you?" and the good guy's best friend, "I worked for Al

269

Morley in Chicago," and the kids in the show all groaning because he doesn't know that Al Morley has come in from Chicago by accident and is inside right now talking to Rick, and the door closes behind the good guy's best friend, and the next time you see him he's dead. But that was a movie. He had watched it from the safety and comfort of a nice seat in a theatre. Now he wasn't looking at a movie. He was acting in it. He was himself on the screen, only there was nobody watching it. No witnesses. This was real life.

Tony stepped forward in the shadowy room, along the dark wood, to the opening in the wall.

There was a face framed in that opening. The face was that of a man but the eyes were those of some swift and deadly reptile, lying in wait in the tropic jungle, the eyes glittering, fixed and unblinking. His hair was black like his eyes and was slicked back, smooth and shiny like a pair of patent-leather shoes. And to make the picture complete—his cheek was slashed with the deep arc of a scar, from eye to chin. A gangster, an eater of raw flesh, a drinker of warm blood—excuse me for knocking, I didn't mean it.

"What do you want?" the man asked harshly.

"I'm looking for a job," Tony said. *Tell Rick Johnny Malloy is here. Tell him I'm alone. And I've got the diamonds on me.*

"Who sent you?"

The question did not surprise Tony. It seemed logical and fitting. "Nobody sent me," he said. "I came by myself."

"How'd you know we were here?" the man asked, looking at him intently.

"Well, I saw some girls going up the street," Tony said, trying to make his voice sound frank and believable, "so I figured they must work here someplace."

"H'mmm," the man said, not committing himself. He ran his hand lightly over the top of his head, checking if his hair was in place. "What'd they do—kick you out of school?"

"They didn't kick me out," Tony replied with dignity. "I quit. I graduated from Cupp Junior High."

The man nodded. "You Greek?"

"No, I'm Portuguese," Tony said, shaking his head.

"You look Greek to me."

"No, I'm Portuguese," Tony said regretfully, feeling somehow that the man preferred Greeks. Maybe he should have lied. But it was too late now.

"Well, Greek, Portuguese, it's all the same thing," the man said, shrugging. "They're all Latins."

Tony nodded. He was grateful for the equality.

"What's your name?"

"Tony—Tony Alfama." And he felt vaguely, wildly hopeful. This was the first time anybody had ever asked him his name.

"How old are you?"

"Sixteen."

He rubbed his chin. "Did you ever work before?"

"Nope, I never have," Tony admitted.

"Well, I'm going to ask you something, Tony. Did you come here to collect a pay envelope every Friday, or did you come here to work?"

"I came here to work," Tony said quickly. Then he thought about it a moment. Well, to do both.

"I had to let a young fellow go the other day. He was no good. He was lazy. He was Portuguese," he finished pointedly.

"Some Portuguese are lazy," Tony said, bobbing his head affirmatively.

"He was always sitting on the toilet, smoking."

"I don't smoke," Tony said quickly.

"And when he wasn't smoking, he was flirting with the girls."

"I wouldn't flirt with the girls," Tony said with feeling.

"You don't like girls?" the man asked, incredulous.

"I like girls, but I wouldn't flirt with them during working hours." Oh, fast thinking, ever faithful.

The man nodded. He studied Tony thoughtfully for a moment, not saying anything. Tony stopped breathing. Then he spoke.

"Well, I'm going to take a chance on you, Tony. I'm going to try you out."

Mary, Eternal Mother of Hope! He could have kissed him right on the scar!

"Thank you. Thank you very much."

"You come in Monday morning. Eight o'clock."

"Yes, okay. Fine. Thank you."

The man nodded and slammed the panel shut.

"Good-bye," Tony called.

He was all alone in the little room again. But what a difference. He loved these walls. With one hand he sent that heavy castle door flying open, and he had to restrain himself from sailing down the stairway without touching the steps.

He opened the outside door and he felt mighty strong. He walked up the street carefully, for the man might be watching him from the window and he did not want to act like a nut. But he turned the first corner he came to and there, safely out of sight, he let out a whoop of triumph. All the tenement houses, the people, he didn't care what they thought.

"*Wahoo!*"

And he sprinted. He ran for four blocks at top speed, and then, the pressure of happiness somewhat relieved, he slowed down, trotting, and then walking. As soon as he had his breath back, he began singing loudly a song from school:

> *Oh, you take the high road*
> *And I'll take the low road,*
> *And I'll be in Scotland afore ye!*
> *But me and my true love will never*
> * meet again*
> *On the bonnie, bonnie banks of*
> * Loch Lomond.*

What the name of the company was he didn't know. What they made there he didn't know. What his pay was he didn't know. What his hours were he didn't know. And he didn't care. He had a job. That's all he cared about. He felt like a million bucks.

When he got to his own street he quieted down. He walked along at a good pace, smiling to himself, thinking ahead to Ma's surprise. He bounded up the stairs of his house. Ma, the steadfast sentinel, was sitting in her favorite chair near the window.

Tony pounced upon her and pulled her in front of the window.

"Hey, what are you doing?" she cried in alarm.

"Hey, Mrs. Bibeau!" Tony called, pretending that Mrs. Bibeau was in her yard. "Look up here, Mrs. Bibeau! Look at who I got! This is the Mysterious Lady Behind the Curtains!"

"Is she there?" Ma cried in panic, and she struggled mightily to get away from the window.

"Here's the big spy, Mrs. Bibeau! The one who watches you day and night!"

"Let go of me!" Ma cried, but she did not struggle so hard now because she had seen the yard was empty.

"Did she talk to the mailman today, Ma?" Tony asked very seriously, still hanging onto her. "How many times did she go to the bathroom?"

"Let go of me, you idiot," Ma said, laughing. "People will see."

"I want them to see. That's why I'm doing this. I want them to know who the biggest spy on the street is."

But he let her go.

"What's the matter with you anyway? Are you drunk or what?" Ma said, rearranging herself in the chair.

"That's right! I'm drunk! Come on, Ma, let's have a dance!" And he grabbed her and dragged her out of the chair.

But she did not dance properly. Instead, she tried to smell his breath, coming close and sniffing. So he let her go.

"All right, if you won't dance with me, I'll dance by myself!" he announced, and he whirled and kicked and wiggled and whirled some more. "*Wheeeeee!*"

"Maniac," Ma said, laughing. "They're going to come and get you. Put you in Taunton with the other *malucos*." Taunton was where they had the *casa dos malucos*, the crazy house.

And he fell into a chair, out of breath.

"Guess what happened to me today, Ma," he panted.

"What?"

"I got a job!"

"No!"

"Yes!"

"No!"

"Yes!"

"Where?"

"At the Takalonka."

"Isn't that something?" Ma asked in open-mouthed wonder.

***

All day Saturday and Sunday Tony was terribly excited, waiting for Monday morning. Sunday night he went to bed early and he told Ma to wake him at six o'clock in the morning. They didn't have an alarm clock, but Ma was better than any alarm clock. She could wake up at any time she wanted and she never ran down.

When Ma came to his room that morning and said, "Tony," he shot out of bed like he never had for school. He slipped into his shirt and pants, and because it was cold, zippered himself into his winter jacket. He stuck his feet in his shoes and, not bothering to tie the laces, shuffled out to the table.

Breakfast was oatmeal, but it was not ready. "You got up so quick I didn't have time to make it," Ma said. "Why don't you go wash up first?"

"Okay," he said.

274

He got up from the table and took off his jacket and shirt. He laid them on a chair.

"Do you want me to heat you up some water?" Ma offered. "It'll just take a minute."

"No, no, no. Cold water's all right."

In the bathroom he got Ma's scrubboard and laid it across the top of the bathtub. Then he took the basin and filled it halfway with water and put it on the scrubboard. He washed his hands and arms first. Then he scrubbed his face and neck vigorously. He rinsed in the basin, but the water was too soapy. So he leaned over the bathtub and finished rinsing with water directly from the tub tap. It was quite cold and really woke you up. After he had dried himself and emptied the basin and washed it out, he put a little water on his hair. Then he went to his room and combed his hair. His bureau had a big mirror attached to it. By the time he put on his shirt and jacket and a pair of socks and tied his shoes, the oatmeal was ready.

He began gulping it down while Ma watched.

"Eat slower!" she commanded, frowning. "You have lots of time."

"I want to get there early," he said. "The first day, you know, I want to make a good impression."

"You get there too early and you will make an impression on only the night watchman."

"Please, Ma, no jokes," he said. "This is a serious thing. If you knew how hard I looked for a job, you wouldn't make jokes."

"I know how hard you looked for a job, boy," Ma said, surrendering.

After he ate he went into the bathroom again. When he came out,

Ma was making his lunch on the table.

"One thing, boy," she said, pointing a finger at him.

"What?"

"I don't want you lifting up any heavy weights. I want you to tell the man right away so there won't be any misunderstandings later on—you can't lift up heavy things. You're too small."

"Ma, are you trying to get me fired even before I begin? You don't go up to a boss and tell him things like that. If he gives me something to lift, I'm going to lift it. Or at least I'm going to try my best to lift it."

"Yes, sure, lift it—and ruin yourself for life!" she cried fiercely. "Go ahead, ruin your back so you will be good for nothing the rest of your days."

"Ma, I can't walk in there and tell the boss what I want to do and what I don't want to do."

"And who will pay for the doctor bills?" she shot back angrily. "Answer me that! Will he pay?"

"Ma, for chrissakes—"

"He won't pay. And you will spend one day at work and the next six months in bed. Listen to me, Tony, I know what I'm talking about! The nephew of *Senhora* Batalha, he worked for a butcher, lifting up big legs of meat, halfs of cows, things like that, and it ruined his back! Now he's good for nothing. Today he can't lift a box of matches without going to bed for two weeks. Do you want to end up like that?"

"All right, Ma, you win," Tony said with a show of resignation. "I'll tell him. No heavy weights."

"Liar!" she cried. "You will tell him nothing! I know you."

"I'll tell him, Ma, honest," he said, laughing. "The first thing. I'll walk right in and tap him on the shoulder and I'll say, 'Listen, bub, don't ask me to lift anything heavy, because I'm too weak.' That's what I'll say to him. And I'll be back home by nine o'clock."

"Aah," Ma muttered disgustedly. "You deliberately twist the things."

"Ma, we're arguing over nothing. We don't even know there's anything heavy to lift. Maybe they make cardboard boxes there."

"You don't know what they make," she charged.

"That's right, I don't," he admitted.

"Why didn't you ask him?"

"Ma, when you're looking for a job, he asks the questions, not you."

It was time to go. Tony picked up his lunch bag.

"So long, Ma. I'll see you later."

"So long, boy," she said, somewhat subdued.

"I'll tell you all about it tonight."

"Okay," she said, nodding.

He closed the door behind him and ran down the stairs into the fresh air. It was a clear crisp day.

Ma opened the window and stuck her head out.

"Good luck, son!"

He waved at her.

He went down the street, his street where he had lived all his life. It was quiet. Nobody was up yet. He strode along, and he hummed softly. He felt real good.

This was the great week, this was the great day. He was on his way to his first job.

He was sixteen years old.

His boyhood was now over.